THE LOVE LIABILITY

a romance novel

DIANA ELLIOT GRAHAM

Cover design: Diana Elliot Graham

Editor: Harpy Editorial @isabella_reads_

Publisher: Arrobehu (aka Diana Elliot Graham)

ISBN: 979-8-234-08061-5

Because there is no place like the home we choose.
And everyone deserves a Happily Ever After.

Prologue

six months ago

LOUISA

The back of this U-Haul looks like what happens when you give a person one day to move due to a chaotic breakup, a complete psychological collapse somewhere around the fifth 'EVERY-THING' box, and absolutely no architectural vision (or even history playing Tetris.) There is no system here. No logic. No evidence that the woman who packed this truck (*me*) has ever encountered the concept of a right angle or, frankly, even the concept of consequences. (Ask my dad.) Instead, the rental is packed to the brim with every worldly possession I own, crammed together like passengers on a budget flight with no legroom. Even though I'm only moving the contents from one small apartment I shared with someone to another small apartment I don't, every single item from the last decade of my life is currently in a pile of poorly labeled brown cubes like a densely packed metal coffin filled with every decision I've ever made (and too many thrift shop sweaters*)* all stacked with zero plan for unloading. It's a Ship of

Theseus life that has been disassembled and reassembled too many times to still be recognizable, but still somehow is.

The city smells like exhaust and hope, possibly exhausted hope, it's hard to tell from the curb. The version of me who decided I can absolutely do this alone was a woman of grit and conviction. The version of me currently standing here staring into the abyss, she is damp with the sweat of moving boxes since 7 a.m., and regretting every decision she has ever made (specifically the twenty-three boxes labeled for vibes rather than a plan for actual contents.) She is a woman who has started to suspect that version of herself was a liar. It's not the first time I have found myself in a predicament of my own making. Where I make decisions with eyes much hungrier than my stomach can actually consume. (Every relationship I've ever been in.)

And no one has ever accused me of having a plan. (*Clearly.*)

I've been unloading the truck for an hour. The compromised boxes with their crushed corners and prayer-held bottoms. My microphone was carried with a tenderness people reserve for sleeping infants, and is now sitting in the middle of my empty new apartment looking like a very expensive deity I'm about to beg for something. (I am.) I carried it in first. I always carry it in first. It is, in every meaningful sense, my firstborn child. The child I have poured every single dollar into. (Dollars I didn't have at the time.) The child who let me make a career out of inhabiting other people's words, rather than living inside my own life.

This move was a big one. Not only because of the rush, which was more self-imposed because I knew my lease (and relationship) was ending and it was time for me to get out of there. I just didn't pack until the last possible minute, when Chandler and Toby came by to pull an all-nighter. Different than the kind Chan and I pulled in college, less adderall this time, but just as frantic. And just like college, she got me through it by the skin of my teeth. Though that was a lifetime ago.

This was a move from a walk-up to one of those buildings with a name that sounds like the British aristocracy. (I would know, given the number of Princess Diana plates my mom had in the china cabinet growing up.) You know the buildings: the Carlisle, the Asher, or in my case, the Richmond. The only reason this apartment even became known to me is because I happened to eavesdrop during one of my shifts at the Double Shot, where I half-barista, half-gossip with my friends. I'd watched as the realtor grew progressively more purple in the face, annoyed that the owner was less interested in leasing the place for what it was actually worth than he was in never having to use the internet or "Docusign" ever again. He just wanted a ghost with a checkbook and a physical pen. Which was good news for me because I am a professional ghost. Besides the days a week I steam milk for lattes. Majority of my time is spent hiding in whatever closet I've converted into my recording studio. So, it was a match made in Luddite heaven. Even said that if all goes well, he'll sell it to me. Which could be interesting, to have somewhere more permanent. (Not sure I could get a mortgage, but a girl can dream.)

So here I am, standing in the entry to my new life. At least for the next twelve months with the option to renew, possible eventual lease to own.

I grab another box, one of the many labeled 'EVERYTHING' because sometime around one in the morning we lost the ability to categorize and started just emptying drawers like it was going out of business, and hike it onto my hip. Then a second box on top of the first, because I've always had a complicated relationship with self-preservation and what I consider my own limits of strength. (Emotional, physical, or otherwise.) I tuck the spare microphone stand under one arm and, in a move that future me will have questions about, I pinch my cup of Throat Coat tea between my teeth. Because I've run out of hands and the universe has not yet run out of ways to test me.

This (like me) is a disaster waiting for its moment.

I shove through the inner door with a shoulder hit that my rugby-playing big brother Theo would applaud. This is exactly the kind of forward momentum he's always encouraged, and I take my first triumphant step into the lobby of my new home.

This, it turns out, is the universe's moment.

My foot catches the edge of a rug. The microphone stand jabs my ribs (traitor), the boxes lurch, and the laws of physics, those iron-fisted, completely humorless laws that I have never once been able to understand, take over.

It's a full-body, slow motion, dance of failure. The finale? The second 'EVERYTHING box' lands in a sound that is the onomatopoeia of my life strewn across the floor. A clatter, a bang, a thud, and then the long, never-ending, rattling silence of chaos and consequence. (Also the names of my left and right tits. *Joking.*) The AA batteries, the command strips, the Crest Whitestrips I've been meaning to try for eight months, two lightning cables for a phone I no longer use but still own (just in case), and a photo of Theo and me as children at a stone-shore beach somewhere in Yorkshire. Both of us squinting into the same grey sky, just months away from being relocated to the sunshine state. No, that's Florida. Whatever state California is. The Hollywood, tech-boom state. The GOLDEN STATE, that's it. Like the Golden Gate Bridge. (Duh, Lou.)

The paper cup pinned by my teeth is also released and all twelve ounces of the herbaceous, yellow-tinted (*erm*—strong and pungent) glory of Throat Coat tea, launches into the air in a beautiful (horrifying) arc. But it doesn't hit the floor. It doesn't shower *my* scattered life with the rain of poor decisions.

It hits a man. (More like a brick wall.) Specifically, it hits him in the center of his chest, a chest that I watch move up and down with each breath, communicating, even at our distance, that its owner does not skip the gym for anything frivolous. And something tells me, he would consider sleep, and every single thing I own, to be frivolous.

The tea blooms outward across the white of his shirt in a pattern that might, in another context, be considered art. (Chandler would think so.) It spiderwebs into the silk of his silvery-blue tie and darkens the lapel of a charcoal suit jacket that, I will learn in approximately forty-five seconds, *'is bespoke,'* which is a word meaning *'extremely expensive'* and also *'you are a careless little girl and I hate you.'* (At least that's how it sounds.)

He'd been reading something in a leather-bound folder. His chin is tilted down, or was, before the collision of my entire life with his routine morning. Now his eyes are up and locked on me. They are dark, framed by lashes that are unfair for a man to have, the kind of lashes that on anyone else would soften their whole face, but on him, they don't soften anything. They frame a jaw so sharp it looks carved from stone. (It might be.) With a mouth that has never done or said anything careless in its life. He just has that look, you know? Like a man whose every movement is premeditated, who makes sure every single step lands with purpose. He is the embodiment of a person who in no world (especially any one I'm in) has time for this.

I, on the other hand, am a collapsing tower of Jenga bricks. Which we both just experienced in live time.

In the novels I narrate, this would be a meet cute. The cutest of meet cutes. The tea would spill charmingly, there would be a beat of held eye contact, someone would laugh first and then the other person would laugh too, and the whole thing would become a story we would tell jumping into shared sentences at dinner parties when people would say we're the perfect couple.

'And that's how we met, can you believe it?' would be it for the rest of our lives.

But we don't live in those novels, and I don't think he wants me involved in the rest of his morning, let alone his life. His gaze is lingering but no one is laughing. The lobby smells like licorice and clove, okay, that's my fault, but also his expensive cologne and the stick of peppermint gum he's chewing. Either that or he's grinding his teeth to prevent him from biting my head off. I squeeze my eyes closed for a moment. Maybe this didn't just happen. But when the scent of my sweat, humiliation, and his bubbling rage doesn't dissipate from around me, I crack open one eye and see the situation is still very much real.

He doesn't move, doesn't speak, doesn't blink those (seriously unreasonable) lashes. He just stands here, radiating a quality that I can only describe as controlled fury. You know the kind, too much self-possession to yell, and is therefore somehow more frightening than someone who would.

"Oh god," I finally say. And my voice comes out breathy, and apologetic. "I'm so sorry. That was... the rug came out of nowhere...*bad rug!*" I look down and shake my finger at the ground as if I am scolding a pet that's made a mess of the floor. (Though I'm the one responsible for the mess.)

I drop to my knees before he can respond and start collecting things, gathering his papers before I gather my own, because that somehow feels polite. I hand up a sheet stamped 'CONFIDEN-TIAL' and he takes it without comment. The bits and bobs of my own life, the batteries, the childhood photograph, the underwear (oh my god, there is a pair of my actual underwear on the floor of this lobby) remains scattered around me like a jumble sale staged by someone having the worst day of their life, which is apparently me. But maybe whoever's bad day this is needed the day off. So I'll take it for now. I just need to burn some sage when I get upstairs. Sage, make a simmer pot, pay an Etsy-witch, become a witch. I don't know.

"This suit is bespoke," he says, finally. His voice is a low rumble that I feel before I understand the words it forms. A depth like it is single handedly responsible for the thickness in the air. (It might be.)

"Fancy," I say, scrambling upright. "These overalls are from high school." I gesture at myself. The denim, my hair that gave up on being a bun several U-haul trips (and one rug trip) ago, the general chaos of my personhood. "So we've both got a thing. Except mine has daisies, does *yours* have daisies?" I slip my thumbs under the straps of the overalls to showcase the hand embroidered daisies on the bib of the denim hoping he finds some humor in the ridiculousness of this situation, because obviously, his 'bespoke suit' does not have daisies. "I did it when I was bored in math one afternoon, like a decade ago, and then I passed a pop quiz I had no business passing, and they have been my good-luck overalls ever since."

"This is your good luck?" He does not have a sense of humor about this. I'm not sure he has a sense of humor at all.

"Well, no, but maybe someone else's. Because, you see, if *I* have a bad day, then I've given someone else my good-luck day, because they needed it more than I did. So the good-luck overalls still work."

"That's not how it works."

"How do you know?" I ask as I cock my head to the side.

His face makes a small movement, and his nostrils flare ever so slightly as the smell of his tea-stained shirt reaches them properly.

"What is that?" It is not a question, but a man identifying a crime through locked jaw and gritted teeth.

"New meaning for the term tea-shirt!" I say, but he remains stone faced, even though Oscar, the doorman I met a few hours ago, laughs under his breath. "Sorry," I correct. "It's Throat Coat!" I say, too fast, too loud, too much for this person who wants to rewind the last minutes just to avoid knowing I exist in the same zip code (or world) he does. "It's medicinal. Very good for the throat," I say, as I tilt up my chin and awkwardly stroke the elongated column of my neck. "I'm a voice actor, which *feels* like relevant context. Obviously less good for the, erm—bespoke *situation*, but the intent was…"

I spot a dish towel in the wreckage. Trailing off my sentence, and focus, instead seeing the opportunity to fix the problem, make the new brooding man *not* hate me. The 'EVERYTHING' box coming through for me exactly once. And I grab it, and hop back to my feet to begin dabbing at the center of his chest. He goes rigid.

His hands come up in a silent, absolutely unambiguous protest, and then he reaches out and snatches the towel from me in one swift motion. He takes over and does not even chance a look at me while he does it.

"I have court in thirty minutes," he says. "I am now stained and smell like a Victorian apothecary."

"Oooh, court for what?" I ask, fixing my hair into a new (equally unruly) top knot as the one it was in just ten seconds prior. But his eyes just narrow as his eyebrows pull together in such a clear unspoken comment of *'you've got to be kidding me.'*

"I can make it up to you," I say, desperate, pivoting into the only currency I have. "Like I said, I'm a voice actor, so if you ever need a commercial, or a podcast intro, or actually I also do romance narration, it's pretty much my toast and butter, if you're secretly a novelist, which, you know what, probably not, but the offer stands, I'd hate to judge a book by it's cover..." I can hear myself. I hear every word coming out of my mouth and I am powerless over any of them.

"It's *bread*," he says as he exhales with the exhaustion I smelled in the air earlier.

"Huh?" I blink.

"The expression is *bread* and butter." He's shuffling the papers in his folder, straightening them at the corners so they aren't sticking out.

"What did I say?"

"Toast."

"That's the same thing."

"It is categorically *not* the same thing. One is an idiom, the other is breakfast," he says, looking up slowly. He stares at me for a long moment. As flat as the set of his lips and the unmoving line of his brow.

This man, who I don't know, hates me before he's even learned my name. And the one thing about me, (or one of many things about me) is that I *hate* when people hate me. I also hate when they are mad at me. Or when I just think they might be mad at me. Which is unfortunate because right now, it's pretty clear he is most definitely mad at me and *probably* hates me. It's terribly inconvenient, and incredibly unfortunate. I don't need everyone to like me. I just need them not to actively *not*. Which is a distinction without a difference that is currently doing absolutely nothing for my anxiety right now.

"I also work at the coffee shop, the one two blocks down on the corner. Free drinks. For as long as you want. A week, a month, a year..." And then, in a move that I cannot explain except as a Pavlovian response hardwired into me by the years of *Friends* binge-watching, I do the four-count clap from the theme song.

I do it.

Out loud.

In the lobby.

At this man.

His expression shifts. The fury doesn't leave, but something else moves through it. A genuine, bewilderment, almost confusion, as if he's encountered a life form he doesn't have a category for.

"No," he says, the word feeling like a slammed door on the conversation. He checks his watch, bends down to retrieve a paper I must have missed, and tucks it into his folder.

"What apartment?" I ask. "Just tell me your apartment number and I'll cover dry cleaning, I'll drop off apology muffins. I am a pretty good baker, but you also look like someone who eats protein bars anyway so the bar is low."

"The last thing I need," he says, adjusting his folder, stepping over a rogue piece of bubble wrap, "is you knowing where I live."

"That's a little dramatic," I say. "I'm moving into 7B."

He goes very still. Just the smallest micro-adjustment in his posture and I realize he is thinking through his entire morning. He looks at the door. Then back at me. Then at the door again. His jaw tightens in a way that suggests his back teeth could crack if he continues.

"Great," he says.

It is the most exhausted, insulted, expensive-sounding use of the word great I have ever heard in my life. It carries his annoyance as he acknowledges his day has taken a turn he did not schedule. (And from the look of him, there could be nothing worse.)

"I'm trying to apologize," I start.

"I don't need an apology." He turns toward the door. "I need you to pay attention to your surroundings."

The heat crawls up the back of my neck. I am tired. I have underwear on the lobby floor and I am not going to stand here and be dismissed by a man in a suit who has, as far as I can tell, the emotional warmth and depth of a toothpick.

"Hey, neighbor," I yell towards him. "I *was* paying attention!" My voice finds its register and fills the room. He stops. His hand is already on the door, but his shoulders lock and I know he's listening. "I just wasn't paying attention to *you*."

A hair of a second exists between us. Standing amongst the ruins of my things, the artifacts of my life as he is prepared to walk into the bright morning of his.

"Clearly," he says. And he's through the door and gone. Even though the word is heavy, it floats to me on the cold air of the lobby like a final decision on something I didn't even know was a question.

I stand in the wreckage of my 'EVERYTHING' box and the ghost of twelve ounces of tea with the very clear knowledge that I have just introduced myself to my neighbor.

"Welcome home, Lou," I say, to the traitorous rug and the underwear I still need to pick up. "You've officially met the enemy."

Chapter One

EXTRA HOT AMERICANO

LOUISA

The Double Shot coffee shop is walking distance from my apartment, close enough that I can do the walk in four minutes if I'm not stopping to look at things. (Which I always am.) So realistically it takes fifteen, because some days it feels like the whole world exists in these few short blocks, and what a waste it would be for me to walk right by it.

Today, it takes twenty-three. Not because there are new additions of roses for me to stop and smell, but because I've been on the phone with my producer (and friend) Roma, for almost the entire walk.

"Lou, I'm serious, the files need to be in the dropbox by the end of the week." Roma's voice comes through my headphones, with only one earbud in, allowing me to eavesdrop on the lives people are living during their commutes to work. But Roma has been my producer for the last few years, one of the first people I trusted as I became a voice actor, at times acting like a mentor as needed. We eventually became friends as well, but right now, it's not the friendship that had her calling me rather than an equally long voice memo which is usually more her speed.

"I'm working on it, they will be ready for review and pick-ups by Friday," I say, pausing momentarily in front of a bakery window as if the trays of cookies require supervision from my face pressed against the glass. But it will be an inspiration for me when I make my own batch later, even though I haven't quite mastered the pignoli, so sometimes I *do* have to stop in. Antonio, the baker, spots me as usual, with a wave and a motion inside where I know he will offer me my choice in cookies while also telling me about his son (and daughter) in the event I might be interested in either. (I'm not. Since Ben, I haven't really been interested in anyone.) But I just smile, mouth the words *'no thanks'* as a woman brushes by me and opens the bakery door. The wave of sugar and butter escapes into the street and I inhale it deeply like it was escaping just to meet me.

"I think you are stalling because the last round of feedback wasn't what you wanted." She's not *wrong*. The last round of feedback was great for everything except the sex scenes. Any scene where the characters are ravishing each other she called *'distant.'* Every other bullet was about how perfectly I captured them, it was just this. Apparently my inability to convey real genuine passion between two people. (Or more than two depending on the book.)

"I'm sorry, I'll get them over to you."

"This isn't criticism for criticism's sake. I can tell you're shutting down, but I need you to hear me, that this conversation is not me saying you're bad, you have nothing to apologize for, there's no one I'd rather listen to." I leave the bakery window to continue my walk to work. (Or my part-time day job.) The one that allows me the ability to actually talk to people (people not Roma or the voices in my head) and emerge from the small velvet-draped closet I call my recording studio where I spend *most* of my time.

I know she isn't calling to be cruel, her feedback is usually on the nose. Which is why I hate it. Because she's never been wrong before. (Don't you just hate those people?) But my lack of response just gives her the wide open space to keep going, which she does.

"You are technically excellent. You have so much depth, and humor. But when it comes to the spice, that's just not the same as being compelling, babe."

"I'm compelling," I say, with some weak attempt at convincing the both of us. I bend down to pet Mrs. Saraceno's three Pomeranians on their morning walk with Jamie, the dog walker. These fluffy piranhas are a nice momentary mental break for the crippling feeling of inadequacy and disappointment.

"You used to be *more* compelling," Roma corrects gently, which is worse. Knowing like she does that recording, *acting*, as these characters really comes from a part of yourself it's sometimes harder to channel. Do I need to be in a polyamorous relationship with three winged men to be able to convey that strongly? No. Does it help if I'm at least having semi-regular orgasms? Yes. "The last book you sent over, there's more distance, you're farther than you used to be. Maybe not to anyone else, but I've spent hundreds of hours listening to you, I know what you sound like when you're reading like an observer, not the protagonist."

"If I start experiencing it, that's a whole different career that would do better on OnlyFans than Audible, and I'm not sure we're there," I say with more sarcasm than she deserves while beelining it right for the fruit stand where Ramon always lets me nab a bag of cherries to eat for the last block of my journey. (And whenever he comes into the coffee shop I repay the favor with a 'cafecito' as he says.)

Roma sighs, she's coached dozens of narrators through creative crises (and even coached me through a breakup) and now here she is, staring down another one. Creative crisis, not breakup, it's been about six-months since either. "Lou, you narrate smut for a living. You cannot sound like you are standing outside someone else's bedroom door and knocking politely just to sit in the chair and watch."

"Some people are into that," I say just as I reach the fruit cart, Ramon looks up eagerly, clocking me immediately, handing me a small bag of black cherries. Also pointing to bananas to see if it's banana bread week. (It's not.)

"Thank you," I say in a whisper, balancing the two conversations at once, and I can hear Roma breathing, *waiting*. As I take a bite out of an apricot Ramon hands me from the mound because I *'must try.'*

"Are you dating anyone?" she finally asks. I almost trip over the curb in response. Not for lack of trying, it just hasn't been easy for me to find someone willing to spend time to actually build a connection before racing to whatever physical finish line they have. It's almost ironic, the level of emotional intimacy I require before engaging in a level of physicality others can enjoy freely on a Friday night. I'm the person who really means *'come over and watch a movie'* when I ask someone to *'come over and watch a movie.'* I'm *also* the person narrating some of the most graphic, other-worldly romance books currently on the market. (Apparently, sometimes just as a spectator.)

"What?" I ask, with the small hope this isn't going where I think it is.

"It's a simple question," she says, then repeating it. "Are you dating anyone?"

"Doesn't feel like it." There's a pause, not long, just long enough to be loaded.

"Maybe you should consider it," she says.

My laugh in response is thin. "So, you're prescribing dating now?"

"I am *suggesting*," she says carefully.

"As my producer, or my friend?"

"Whichever one will motivate you to get out there... sometimes the well needs to be refilled, babe. Passion is not theoretical, you read enough of it to know that. I'm not saying to go out and just sleep with the first person you come in contact with, I'm saying you tell stories of love and desire, and right now you sound untouched by it." (Ouch.)

I don't have anything to respond, so it just hangs there on the telephone line. It's not like the Ben Breakup was a catastrophic heartbreak, but it certainly reinforced the philosophy I try to live by, which is that things are temporary so enjoy them as much as you can, as long as you can. (Especially with people.)

I pass Howard on the bench outside his building, he lowers his newspaper like he's been waiting for me. "Markets are up," he says. "Bad time to be cautious." Every time I see him he gives me the headlines like a custom news algorithm just for me. Often talking about the stock markets in a way I never understand, but always appreciate the effort of.

"Your horoscope says the opposite," I say. "Same time tomorrow," I tell him in a whisper while handing off a couple of the cherries, as I cover the receiver on my headphones to try and block out the noise to not give Roma another chance to feel like I'm ignoring her. (Which I'm not, I'm just multi-tasking.)

"I don't think it works like that, Rome," I say finally, quieter now as I turn the corner toward the shop. "My personal life should have no impact on my performance."

"No?" she asks, but it's not a real question. "Then why does it?"

I push open the door to The Double Shot, the bell chiming overhead. "I think passion is...earned. It's an investment, it takes knowing someone well enough."

"You sound like a romantic," she says through a soft, sincere laugh.

"I've been called worse." I am a bit of a romantic, maybe not always love-at-first-sight level romantic, but the big, earth-moving gestures? Gets me every time.

I move behind the counter, nodding hello to Chandler as I tie on my eggplant-colored apron, and point to the dangling headphone so she knows I'm on the phone.

"It's not just physical," I add, reaching for a cup. "It's everything underneath that." I stop, because the sentence is about to say more than I want to. "I don't think I've ever really had that," I finish, softer. Speaking now more to my friend than the woman who has single-handedly helped me make the jump from Black Friday commercials to best-selling romance novels.

I pour hot water into my cup, watching the steam rise like it might offer an answer. Roma hums, thoughtful. "Well, whatever it is," she says, pulling the conversation back from the therapy-adjacent place it landed. "We need to find a way to make it sound real again. Go on a date, flirt, fuck, kiss someone you shouldn't. Just, give yourself permission to feel something as Louisa Evans, not just whoever you voice that week, they will thank you for it."

"I'll be done recording tomorrow, I have the dungeon scene tonight." She knows I do. *That's* why she called me now, because later I'll be in the hot and heavy pages of the enemies becoming lovers. We exchange a few more words, and I know throughout all of this her intention is in both helping me be successful and perfect a craft I genuinely love, and also, for me to let someone beyond the first pages of *my* book.

I just stand here, tea steeping in hand. Thinking about what she said, and exactly what I'm going to do about it. Because reactivating a dating app sounds like my worst nightmare.

Chandler is already behind the counter, her hair catches the light from the front windows that makes it feel like it's always golden hour and the rest of the day is just waiting for her to arrive. "Bad call?" Chandler asks, already halfway through making something intricate out of cappuccino foam.

"Not really," I say. "She wants me to *'dial up the passion.'*"

Chandler brightens immediately. "Oh my god, I love that for you. I love that *for me.*" She is the ultimate hype girl. Has been since college, and is by far one of the most convincing people I've ever met in my entire life. It's more than charisma, there's just vibrance that bounces off her in a way that has every single patron tipping 35% when she swings the tablet around for them to pay for their coffee. "I think everyone should have more passion in their life," she says, spooning a little of the coffee foam into a peak.

"What are we making today?" I ask, as I lean over to see what has her so delicately shaping foam with a chopstick and a spoon.

"Working on kittens." Her tongue curls around her top lip in a way it only does when she's thinking, or trying to be very delicate with whatever she's crafting. And I see it, the small nose from a droplet of coffee on the white milk foam. (She *is* an artist.) Though her art is mixed media, and while technically yes, I do believe foam counts as mixed media, she is more known for her large-scale portraits out of whatever the hell she can get her hands on. It's part of why she likes working here, the trash collection, because I don't think it was her BFA that prepared her for cappuccino cats.

I do a totally casual (completely not suspicious) scan of the shop the way I always do, the way *any* normal person does when they walk into a coffee shop when Toby appears from the back, carrying a stack of mugs. "He's not here yet," he says as he pushes his glasses up on his nose.

Toby is getting his PhD in statistics, which means he approaches the human condition as a data set and is focused more on probability than tact. He once told me (with complete sincerity and zero awareness of what he was saying) that based on the frequency with which I change my nail color versus previous months, he had calculated a sixty-three percent chance I was going through something. (He was right.) He is also, inexplicably, one of my favorite people I've ever met.

I think it's because he is the only person I know who is incapable of saying something he doesn't mean. There is no performance in him, no social lubrication or polite fiction. It's exhausting and it's the most honest thing I've ever encountered, and sometimes when the world feels like it's made entirely of people performing versions of themselves (hi, it's me) for each other's benefit, Toby is a relief.

"I wasn't looking for him," I say. (I was looking.)

"You were. You checked the corner table before you looked at either of us when you walked in," he says. He's hyper vigilant like that. He keeps track of *everything*. "But you've got four minutes before he walks in that door."

The corner table currently sits empty but won't be for long. It has been occupied, Monday through Thursday, by the same person since the week I moved in down the street. It's always at the same time, always with the same order, always with posture that's decided the world (and everyone who inhabits it, particularly me) is disappointing. He orders, sets up, works for half an hour, shuts the laptop, and leaves, all before 9 a.m.. We call him *Angry Neighbor™*. (Not to his face, *usually*.) It started after he walked in the first time, about a week after our first (disastrous) encounter and greeted me in the most un-neighborly way possible. With a scowl. I tried to settle up our *'incident'* with a free coffee but he just looked insulted. Chandler wanted to call him *'Hot Neighbor,'* and while she isn't wrong, I refused to concede. At the time, I wasn't sure if he even recognized me, or that just was his face. (Turned out to be both.) I reintroduced myself, and he just said 'I know.' And the name Angry Neighbor™ stuck. Immediately.

He is, technically, my neighbor, the 7A to my 7B with a shared wall and shared contempt that has been brewing steadily since that first chance meeting. Once we were both on our balconies at the same time, and when I waved, he just turned and walked inside.

I know the four minutes have passed when the door chimes, and the atmosphere shifts. I'm not being dramatic, I'm sure you're thinking it's hyperbolic that the air is thicker now, or the notion that all heads turn. But it's just kind of a natural adjustment. The space needing to accommodate a new presence, a tall, brooding, unreasonably attractive, *Large. Americano. Extra-Hot.* kind of presence that didn't occupy space (or thought) a moment ago.

On move-in day, he was striking. (I also technically struck him with lukewarm medicinal tea.) But even amidst the dread of his anger, and my desperate attempt at an apology, I was taken by the look of him. Who wouldn't be? I've read and voiced enough romance novels to know he looked like he could have walked right out of one. He just had none of the charm.

And here he is walking right into my morning, like usual. Always exhibiting the same ultra-controlled energy. He scans the shop, as if he's not going to choose the seat that always seems to be available for him. I sometimes wonder if Chandler shoos people away just to keep it open so she can get a good look at him, which he makes easy for her when he crosses the room to me (okay, not to *me*) to place the order I've already punched in.

Large. Americano. Extra-hot.

He taps his card before I can finish the sentence. He always does, saving himself the trouble of ever having to talk to me longer than necessary. It's transactional, in every way possible. There's not an exchange of words we have that isn't an exchange with purpose. Would never dare a friendly hello just for the sake of it. (I bet Ramon doesn't give *him* any cherries.) His drink is made, he retrieves it with the obligatory 'thanks' and takes his seat like he does four days a week. We've never figured out where he is on Fridays, and it makes Toby insane, like it's his very own white whale.

"He's definitely a hitman," Chandler says. Propping her elbows on the counter and tilting her head toward him. She clearly is fully committed to this theory and will not be accepting counterarguments.

The three of us have worked here long enough to have developed what I can only describe as a shared second sight for other people's lives. I should call them strangers, but they stop being that very quickly. (When we make up stories about them.) What spawned from boredom became something closer to a science and exercise in anthropology and story-telling.

Toby thinks about human behavior in terms of patterns, tracking the orders of our regulars. He can tell you, with an unsettling accuracy, when someone has a new partner, a new job, or a new baby. When a to-go flat white suddenly becomes a flat white and a maple latte, and then after three weeks when the maple latte doesn't continue to make an appearance, we know the relationship was short-lived.

"He's too obvious to be a hitman," Toby says. "Too attractive. It's finance."

"No vest," Chandler refutes. Knowing the Patagonia vest and button-down shirt is a sure fire way to identify a finance guy.

"He's a lawyer," I offer, for the *hundredth* time. "He literally told me the day we met."

"He said he had court, that's not the same thing," Toby says, like he has considered this distinction and to quote him, *'found it non negligible but not definitive proof.'*

"He could've been the one on trial, he has the jaw for it," Chandler agrees. Always interested in supporting the most outrageous of answers. I peer my head around the espresso machine to catch a glimpse of our not-hitman. (At least I hope I'm not living next to a hitman.) The only thing he's responsible for killing is someone's good mood.

"What does that even mean?" I ask. "I didn't think a strong jawline was a prerequisite for being a hardened criminal."

"Clearly you and I are on different parts of the internet," Chandler says through a smirk.

If Toby focuses on behaviors, and Chandler on beauty, I hear voices. (Not like that. Not *usually* like that.) But the voices and sounds from people around me are the sounds that I squirrel away for later in the recording booth for inspiration. Not just how they sound but what they're busy doing underneath what they're trying to communicate. The performance beneath the ease, or the calm driving the chaos. The thing someone is half a breath away from saying, or the words they say without ever voicing them. It is a professional skill and a personal problem that most days I cannot find the fold between.

I grew up fluent in the language of subtext, and like most

things, I can attribute it to my parents. They are just two people who never should have been married, and despite that, have been married for thirty-one years. They taught me the subconscious difference between *'It's fine'* and *'I'm fine.'* The tone that means dinner will be quiet and the one that means dinner will be a vacuum of silence as my brother and I stare at each other trying to make the other one laugh. He always won, which means, I did.

Understanding the dynamics of two people who should have called it quits before I was born made me desperate to be able to feel the pulse of personalities for my own survival. And that extended to my life in a way they have resented ever since. The idea that my investments are in experiences and not a corporate-matched 401k, that my job *'telling dirty stories'* is not one they share with their friends even though it keeps my bills *more* than paid. (And I was able to get a Labubu *and* max out my Roth IRA last year— even if Theo *was* the one to set up my autopay to the IRA.)

But for all the ways they don't understand (or respect) the choices I've made, the great irony is so much of who they are is how I became who I am. They built a life on structure. And in that, I learned to look for the cracks where something softer might sneak out and grow. I became inspired by the wonder of things they never looked for, found my happiness in the small joys they would have (and still do) consider unnecessary. The idea that things don't need to serve a purpose to be loved or felt, and in that, I sometimes feel too much, but it's a worthy exchange.

And yes, I hate disappointing them, I hate disappointing anyone, really. It's the most common, age-old, dynamic to exist between parent and child. (Even though it's different for my brother.) But disappointing myself? That's something I could never live with, so I wake up every morning and make sure I don't.

Chapter Two

JUST ANOTHER PRICK AND A WALL

LOUISA

Roma's notes from the other day live rent free in my head. She sent over some flags and a nine-minute-long voice note, which means it was too much to type and she didn't want me to be able to interject like I could on a phone call. So I listened to all nine minutes, and it pained me to admit she was right. *'Too controlled,'* she said. *'I can hear you thinking about it instead of feeling it.'* (She's always right when it comes to this.) I was too slow (too distant) from the passion.

Fine. Fine. I am living in it. *I am* the passion. I am the passion as I finish up the final chapters of this romantasy series novel that has consumed the last months of my life and which I have loved deeply and will miss enormously, and also need to hand over by Friday or Roma might actually get on a plane and show up at my door. I am the main character. I am Ilaria. And Ilaria wouldn't lie awake obsessing over all the ways she has accidentally annoyed people this week wondering if they are thinking about her. Ilaria is a woman who has been imprisoned in a dungeon by a dark-winged man named Igor, who is objectively her enemy and subjectively the most enticing person she has ever encountered, and she is currently pressed against damp granite with her silk pinned to her skin and her moral compass pointing somewhere it never has before, and she does not apologize for any of it. She does not apologize, she does not spiral, she does not have forty-three browser tabs open. She has one tab open and it is vengeance. (Okay, only parts of me are Ilaria.)

I can do this.

I need to do this, actually, because these are the final chapters of a book I should have handed over last Tuesday. I also have a new book starting next month, this one a Scottish Highlands romance, enemies to lovers, slow burn, wildly explicit, six hundred and nineteen pages. So I can't afford to be behind schedule.

When I tell people I have a recording studio, they usually picture something behind glass, while someone fusses with dials. Maybe a guitar leaning against a stool for atmosphere. (Surprise! I don't play guitar.) When in reality it's a small walk-in closet with deep-wine-colored velvet drapes pinned over sound-reduction foam. I picked *this* closet not only because I had limited options, but because it doesn't share an exterior wall with the street, which is critical for a narrator. It means no sirens, no delivery trucks, no the-city-never-sleeps ambient noise threading itself into a medieval romance and ruining the atmosphere. I spent a weekend lining the walls with acoustic panels, then added the fabric over the top of them, which was technically for vibes but which I maintain also improves the resonance.

There is an Ikea table along one wall, just wide enough for my screens, microphone, and my iPad stand. Plus a hook for my headphones. It is the most efficient use of square footage I have ever achieved, which is impressive given that I'm not known for efficiency, and on any given night allows me to become a medieval prisoner, a woman fleeing a serial killer (also the serial killer), or the narrator of a very tasteful intergalactic why-choose. It's a foam-and-textile-lined sensory-deprivation chamber, purpose built for the professional pursuit of making complete strangers feel things. While they are stuck in traffic or their lives, whether they are lying in a bath or to themselves, maybe pretending to work. Maybe they just need to pretend. These books pull people into places they want to go, and give them things they didn't know they needed. (Me too.)

Sometimes those things are '*I should really buy that Bluetooth blender*' or '*this mortgage rate makes me think I'll be able to buy a house.*' Most of those things are, if I'm honest, '*I want a man with wings and a tragic backstory he refuses to discuss, who has been my captor and is now something considerably worse, to pin me against a cold stone wall in a mountain fortress and absolutely ruin my life while the snow comes down outside and neither of us survives it emotionally.*'

(Same, girl.)

What I did not account for when I was measuring foam panels and debating velvet colors of wine versus burgundy (which is funny because burgundy is just a type of wine) was the *interior* wall.

Now if it was shared with anyone else, perhaps it would not be the issue it is, but this wall in particular is the one I share with 7A. (Aka Angry Neighbor™, you remember him? From the coffee shop? From the lobby? From my nightmares of rabid vacuuming as the most inconsiderate, pretentious, arrogant... I digress.)

The wall must be a single layer of drywall and whatever lives inside it. Insulation, presumably, though this is an older building, so also possibly a ghost of my poor decisions, or a rodent, even a rodent family. Based on available evidence, it might actually be just Hudson '*I don't have time for this*' Ellis's neighborly disapproval, which, in terms of density, is not nothing. But appears to be thin enough to let sound through.

I had, at one point, pushed my wardrobe flush against it as an additional sound barrier, which I thought worked, but left no room for me to breathe. Which was a problem and a panic attack I was going to deal with later, but I was cup-of-tea-to-the-chest *struck* by the realization it didn't even matter when he knocked on my door at near midnight one Tuesday night to tell me he could still hear me. And when I made my case about the wardrobe, he lectured me about how those types of things should be *'affixed to walls for safety.'* Hudson *'I know everything about structural integrity'* Ellis struck again.

I brush away the thought of the man on the other side of the wall, I'm starting early enough that tonight should not elicit the same level of annoyance where he tells me how inconsiderate I am, something he's felt since our first encounter. I settle into my recording chair and pull the headphones on, opening the session file.

"Okay," I say quietly, not to the microphone but to myself. No, to Ilaria, who I need to conjure with some urgency. I have the microphone tilted slightly away, still getting the right levels. "Roma wants passion." I roll my shoulders back and crack my neck. Closing my eyes and waiting for the room to go quiet enough inside my head that there's space for Ilaria to move in and come through.

I try to place myself in the dungeon. The smell of torch smoke and old water. Igor's hands. (Yes, Lou, think about his hands!) Igor, a strong man who has been holding something back for so long, something more than his wingspan, that the moment he stops, it's total, complete, and all-consuming.

"Igor," I breathe into the mic. Unsteady the way Ilaria's voice goes when she is losing the argument she's been making to herself for the last three chapters. Her hands are tangling in his hair, pulling him closer, collapsing the last careful inch of distance between them until there is no more distance and her back is against the wall (literally and figuratively) and with nowhere to run, finds to her absolute devastation and complete desperation, that she doesn't want any. (Take that, Roma!)

I've been at it for twenty minutes when it starts.

THUD.

I stop recording, unsure if I actually hear anything. The

phantom noises sometimes creep through the headphones. Like a vibration of your phone that has you checking your pocket every minute when you're waiting for something, all without it ever ringing.

But I don't hear anything else, so I continue. I reset, find Ilaria again, the damp nature of the setting and the devastation of wanting someone you have excellent reasons not to. I hit record, again.

"Ilaria's silk is pinned to her skin by the heat and sweat between them," I say, in a voice that lives deep below my normal speaking range and above the one I'd use to whisper in someone's ear. "Igor slides a hand up her thigh, the fabric bunching under his fingers, climbing higher, and she—"

THUD. THUD.

Two this time, and I most definitely heard them. Louder and more deliberate than the first. Two knocks on the wall meant to say '*You are an annoyance.*' (I know because he's said it out loud also.) I pull one headphone off my ear and sit for a minute in the tainted silence. This is not new, this is something we do often. It's part of the reason why it takes me longer to finish audiobooks than other narrators. It also is why my editors have to do more to clean up some of the files when he decides to be unrelenting.

Then I reach for the monitor controls, pull up the playback from the previous session, Ilaria's breathy escalation (if you want to call it that) building toward something absolutely filthy, and I turn the volume up. Ilaria's voice fills the padded space, doubles back on itself and becomes enormous with nowhere else to go.

And through the wall, I hear his reply. The escalation from knock (or really bang) to vacuum. It's not just running but *ramming,* which is a new technique he has developed, where he slams the the nose of the vacuum cleaner into the baseboard with a rhythmic, aggressive consistency that vibrates through the drywall and into my foam panels and communicates, very clearly, that he is not actually cleaning. (Though I'm sure his apartment is spotless, he just gives off that energy.) The man is conducting psychological warfare from the other side of a shared wall using a Dyson as his instrument of choice.

I know how this hatred escalated, but I don't understand why. Except that we are so locked and loaded on this mutually assured destruction that he might just be the only person I don't lie awake wondering how to make him not hate me. I did in the beginning, but it lasted about as long as my muffins remained on his doormat before he threw them away. (Not even 12 hours.)

His vacuuming picks up with the background of Pink Floyd being played at full volume. Fine by me, I queue up the thriller-romance I recorded last month, one filled with blood-curdling screams. A satisfying sequence of screams that Roma called '*viscer-al.*' I find the timestamp, turn the volume up further, and with a diabolical smile stretched across my face, hit play.

The sounds collide. (Like we did the day we met.) Ilaria's breathless pleading, a full-throated scream of terror, and whatever is coming from his side of the wall. This is technically nobody's finest moment but is, I maintain, the correct response to the situation. I tried to be friends, but he wasn't interested.

For approximately forty-five seconds, 7A and 7B (us) are having a sound experience that I imagine is very confusing for anyone in the hallway. And is not particularly enjoyable to anyone involved.

The vacuum stops and the silence is sudden from his side, he's adjusting his radar for a direct attack. I wait, holding my breath. I silence my own playback, and in the absence of noise hear the *Jaws* theme song in my mind building the suspense.

Nothing?

Nothing.

Nothing!

I've won this round, Hudson '*Mr. I have a $400 vacuum that I use with the sole purpose of tormenting my neighbor*' Ellis! Take that you bespoke-suited, strong-jawed control-freak.

THUD THUD THUD. (Ugh!)

I completely yank the headphones from my head. The

banging hasn't stopped, it's relocated. It's not the wall this time, but my front door. I stand up so fast, I knock the mic stand with my elbow and spend three seconds catching it before it can hit the table. The whole frantic experience bubbling my anger and the four steps from my closet to the front door powering the rage within me. It's muscle memory at this point. A woman running on adrenaline, chocolate digestive biscuits, and high-stakes, slow-burn smut.

He is still knocking when I reach the door. Hard enough to make the framed prints rattle on the wall beside it. I want to compose myself, but fuck that. (And fuck him.) Instead I just yank the door open, lifting myself on my toes in preparation for the foot he has on me.

He's mid-knock with his fist raised. And the sight of him at close range short-circuits approximately twenty-five percent of my functioning brain (get it together, Lou) before I can marshal the other seventy-five against it.

I know that he is attractive. I have known this since the beginning, since he was standing in the lobby with tea on his suit and tie, steaming fury and heat like a radiator. It's not a secret but it's also not relevant. Because it's the kind of attractiveness that exists entirely separately from whether you actually like a person, (which I don't) and which he has given me no reason to revise. What we have is reciprocal hatred that exists only because he started it and won't let it go. Which *can* be unfortunate, because right now his eyes are so dark that the amber at their core reads like a secret while his lashes are thick and do absolutely nothing to soften the expression currently arranged beneath them. (Because the expression beneath them is not soft, and neither is the rest of him.)

His hair is usually brushed back, but right now it's damp and slightly disordered, pushed back from the shower but not styled. He is wearing a pair of grey joggers and nothing else. (Which feels like an intentional tactic from someone whose body looks like that.) And a single drop of water is making its way down the center of his chest with a sense of unstoppable determination.

Honestly, he looks like the cover of a novel I would narrate. For all the things I hate him for, I think I hate him for this specifically the most.

"Do you not know how to tell time," he says, his voice bottoming out in the depth of it, the one that resonates somewhere below my sternum no matter how much I want to be unaffected by it.

"I can tell time. Right now," I pause, "I know it's time for you to get out of my doorway and march your ass back to your freshly vacuumed floors." My hands find my hips, my chin comes up, and I lift taller on my toes. This is the stance I have developed specifically, for this specific man, in this specific doorway, for this specific fight. (We do it regularly.) To communicate '*I am not even slightly intimidated by you*' in a way that I feel is mostly convincing. (I don't think he agrees)

"Oh, so you just don't care that other people exist. Got it," he says in a patronizing tone.

"I am *painfully aware* you exist. I mean, it's nearly midnight and you've decided now is the *perfect* time to deep-clean your floors."

"My cleaning is your issue?" he says. His dark eyes narrow and the thick lashes drop. He's repeating it to sound ridiculous, because we both know it's not just cleaning, and we know he's doing it with the full intent of enraging me. (And it's working.)

"The *aggressive* midnight cleaning is the issue, yes," I say. "You know, I watch a lot of Dateline. Late night cleaning is usually a sign someone is trying to get ahead of an investigation, ya know? Clean up a crime scene. Can be *verryyy* suspicious," I stress. "By the way, I haven't seen Claire in *months,* hope she's okay."

The picturesque blonde-bobbed woman who didn't actually live here, but I saw frequently enough the first weeks I moved in, to know that she didn't like chit-chat, all I got out of her was her first name and career. (Same as him, except I only got his name because I once got a piece of his mail, and didn't open the mailbox again for three months after that.) It's a wonder they didn't work out. "Do I need to be concerned or did she realize your personality leaves something to be desired?"

The air between us stops moving, his chest stops heaving. Narrating human beings (and not-so-human beings) means I am very good at the moments people try not to have, and this man, who is very controlled in almost every situation I've put him in, is trying very hard to remain that way. But it's the split second before the mask locks back on, when the actual person is involuntarily visible. And I just know it makes him furious.

"That," he says, "is none of your business." I see the thought moving through his jaw, a tightening, a grinding of his back teeth and small adjustment like he's absorbing a hit and choosing not to show it. I shake away the momentary hesitation that I could have actually hurt his feelings, because at this point, fuck him.

"Good."

He fills the doorway in a way that doesn't happen when he's fully dressed. When he's clothed, suited, he's contained. He's organized into something that comes across as powerful, but manageable. Without them he's just... larger, somehow. It's like the tailoring of any clothing has been performing structural function, and without it, the full scale of him is visible.

The air between us shifts like it always does when we get to this part of the argument, the cigarette-after-sex part, where the banter runs out (for now) and something underneath it surfaces for just long enough to be embarrassing.

My eyes accidentally drop to the waistband of his joggers, but his voice snaps them back to his face. (Thank god.)

"Do you realize," he's gruff as he says it, "I can hear every single whimper, Louisa." I don't know how he speaks like that. Where it sounds like every word is its own sentence. *Especially my name.* "Every. Single. One."

"Hmm." I purse my lips to the side. "Maybe," I say, leaning into the doorframe so the distance between us compresses just enough to make my point without crossing into his air as I continue, which is something he very clearly does not want me to do. "The problem isn't that you can hear it. It's what it does to you when you do." Droplets of water crawl down his torso, and the smell of wet hair and a fresh shower sneak their way past me and into my apartment to haunt me later. This is a new tactic for me as we stand nose to nose (not really but close enough in spirit) often enough that it's time for me to try something new. "Because I've been thinking," I continue, "that a man who is genuinely unbothered doesn't march over here in the middle of the night, he just reads his very important," I wave my hand in his general direction, "whatever you do, and goes to sleep. But a man who is—"

His eyes narrow.

"Don't." Singular and directive, I can see his body tighten as he says it.

"What, I'm just making an observation."

"You've done enough of that tonight. So whatever it is you think you're doing, stop." He takes a half-step forward.

"I'm standing in my own doorway, *you* knocked!"

"You're being deliberately provocative." He smirks. "Didn't know you had it in you."

"I don't know what you're talking about," I say as I (proactively) bit my thumbnail. "*I'm* just breathing."

"I've listened to you breathe for months," he says, which is a strange thing to say and which he seems to realize after saying it, because something adjacent to a flinch moves through his expression. "Don't be foolish enough to think I don't know the difference." I feel, rather than hear, the exhale that follows. It's taking him some effort, but he takes another half-step forward.

"Go to sleep, Louisa. Some of us have to be in court in the morning."

"Some of us," I say, "have a deadline."

"Then I suggest you meet it quietly."

"For you? Not. Likely. I hope you like dungeon sex," I say and let the wickedness of a smile spread across my face as I slam the door in his.

I stand in my hallway for a moment with my back against the door and look at my apartment, the prints on the wall and the threadbare rug and the amber glow of the closet light at the end of the hall. My pulse is racing as it always does, and I want to scream. *A real one*, not the thriller-mystery scream. The from-the-gut kind that doesn't solve anything but is the only correct response to every single interaction we have.

But my voice is my livelihood, and livelihood voices don't get free screams without a cup (or teapot) of Throat Coat to follow.

And the last thing I need right now is to pour myself something that would remind me of him. I go back to the closet and put my headphones back on. I rest my hands on the chipboard table and I think about Igor's hands ravishing Ilaria against the stone dungeon wall. But the shape of Igor arrives with wet hair, dark eyes, and a voice I can't shake. I try to replace it with the author's description, with the wings, the mountain fortress, the fictional face of a fully fictional man. And I *almost* have it. I almost have him out of my head and Igor in. (Almost.)

But when I open my mouth and let Ilaria's voice come out, the image I'm working from is wearing grey joggers and nothing else. For the next hour, I try to give Roma everything she asked for, and I hope he hears every fucking word.

Chapter Three

WAR OF THE WALL

HUDSON

Returning to the peace of my apartment is, ordinarily, the thing I look forward to most at the end of the day. Not because I am anti-social. *It's selective.* But I spend ten hours a day being the sharpest person in every room I'm in, it's not arrogance, but the job. It's a billable fact. That takes something out of a person, something only silence and order can return. It's not normal silence, but crafted. In my well-ordered space with no ambient noise or competing sounds, just a clean absence of everything that isn't mine. It is the physical expression of the fact that a mind functions best without clutter.

But for months she has been dismantling it, one recording session at a time.

I change out of the dark-charcoal cashmere suit that I've spent all day in. One that I've had for years and still fits exactly as it should because I take care of things, my body, and my clothing. I prepare something that qualifies as dinner and pour two fingers of scotch, *maybe three,* because the day earned it, *I earned it,* and carry both to the kitchen island where the renovation plans for 8A are still spread from last night. I've done everything right, and it

33

still feels like it won't be enough. I stand at the counter and eat, because eating is not the focus, these floor plans are.

I'm not trying to build more space, exactly, but build the right shape of space. Looking at them now, the idea of combining apartments, mine and the empty one above, I'm not sure what I think more space will solve. It's not like I'm starved for anything now.

The co-op board is still sitting on the approval, everything waiting on them. Waiting on a woman that could be aged anywhere between sixty and eighty-five, and I don't have any indication which way it's leaning. What I *do* know is that Mrs. Saraceno runs this co-op board like she would a small country. The Richmond is her fiefdom, and she makes sure everyone knows it. Which is why I know that if I want the apartment upstairs, she is the domino that needs to fall for the rest of the board to agree. I look at the plans until they stop telling me anything new, I have them seared into my brain as the idea of something I can't let go of until it is unequivocally mine. But I gather up the papers, pick up the laptop, and tell myself it will be a productive evening as I head into the bedroom to settle against the headboard, and shift to my actual job.

Tonight, I have countless documents to read through on a merger I'm leading, and a review of the depositions I have scheduled for next week. With dinner, drinks, and introspection done for the night. I've decided the rest of the evening belongs to work, which is the kind of decision that, in my experience, holds until it doesn't.

It stays quiet long enough that I almost believe tonight is different, having been lured into a false sense of security into the silence and concentration I need. But fifty-two pages in, she starts.

First a vibration in the wall that I might have, in the very early weeks, talked myself out of noticing. Now I notice it immediately, some receptors in me that have been involuntarily synced to the frequency of her.

I have spent considerable effort over the course of my adult life constructing a very reliable filter for what gets through and what doesn't, and it has served me well, professionally and otherwise. I notice what matters and ignore what doesn't. It is a system I have never once had reason to question. *That changed.*

First her voice seeps into the paint, then it smashes through the drywall. And then gradually her actual voice, shaped by whatever character she's inhabiting tonight, gains definition as it crawls through the partition between us. Moving like it has somewhere it has to be, which for some reason, always seems to be my ears.

I read another page, but her voice becomes something that makes the words in front of me stop making sense. Everything I'm looking at loses all narrative momentum. The only concepts being constructed in my brain are the ones she is crafting. The deposition schedule becomes abstract and morphs into desperation of the characters.

This is what I find most unreasonable. Not just the hours or volume. The fact that she finds me. *Every. Fucking. Time.* I have tried earbuds, earplugs, music, a legal history podcast so deliberately dense it should have been impenetrable, and she continues to find the gap between the podcast and my attention and moves in. My brain, which I've spent a considerable amount of time training to concentrate under conditions that would constitute a hostile work environment for most human beings, simply stops cooperating. *Abandons me completely.* Through a wall, apparently, and into a dungeon I now have an involuntary working familiarity with.

I close my laptop and stare up at the ceiling. This can't go on much longer. Except I know *she* can. This is, I think, for what must be the hundredth time, not sustainable. I am a man who requires sleep, focus, the ability to wake up, go to the gym, without being kept awake listening to her performing muffled orgasms. I require the basic human ability to sit in my own bedroom and read without my concentration being dismantled brick by brick, *or word by word.*

When she first moved in and told me she was a voice actor, I had assumed this meant commercials. Maybe I would hear her when whatever streaming service I'm watching decides that my premium subscription isn't premium enough not to have commercials anymore, and therefore requires me to upgrade. Which I do, *again*. But what it actually means, in practice, is a woman moaning at a level that would alarm anyone who didn't know the context, and frankly still alarms me even when I do. Sometimes I think the crescendo that comes through has the sole intention of aggravating me. All because I was rude to her the day we met.

I know she isn't doing it to me. But I also *don't* know that.

I turn the volume up on the podcast versus the winged captor I'm being forced to listen to against my will thanks to my neighbor in 7B. But somehow now I am half listening to both, with the podcast losing ground by the second.

I take the earbuds out, and stare at the wall, that is, the only thing between me and her voice, and doing an insufficient job of it.

The day she moved in, I had been having a good morning. This is the most important contextual fact, and I would like it on record. The most important part, I'd say. My statements were prepared, the discovery was organized. And I was wearing my *'lucky'* tie. I don't typically believe in things like that, signs and superstitions, but this one tie has produced me more victories than anything else. Even though I am the common denominator of it. After the pattern emerged, I reserved it for the most critical cases. It never let me down. *Until that morning.*

I had left early enough to avoid the elevator bottleneck that happens when everyone's morning schedules converge. I narrowly avoided Mrs. Saraceno. Claire and I managed not to fight that morning about the same things we had been arguing about on loop. *See what I mean? Lucky tie.*

And then she came tumbling in.

I clocked it all in the second before impact and had approximately enough time to register that there was no version of this ending well before I was doused in something that left me pungent and smelling like licorice. *I fucking hate licorice.* Ruining my blue silk tie and staining my white shirt. I left early enough to avoid the bottleneck, but not to double back to shower and change. So I made the game time decision to keep going, and just praying to god the smell would dissipate. *It didn't.*

Next is the part I have replayed more than I should have and continue to hold against her, because she gathered my papers with the frantic good intention of someone trying to fix a thing they can't fix, and she handed them back to me in a stack that was, on the surface, orderly. At least by her standards. I took them. Tucked them back into the folder, and hurried out the door.

It wasn't until I was standing in front of a judge. I flipped open the file I shuffled all the papers into. Smack dab between the financial reports to be used as evidence was a page from a script or a manuscript. Some paper that had been living in her box alongside everything else spilled out on the floor. And what was on it: a graphic detail of a sexual encounter between a human woman and a creature with three tentacles all being used for different *pleasure* that I genuinely did not know how to process in the thirty seconds I had before I needed to continue speaking.

I froze. And as I stood in a courtroom trying not to gag from my tea-soaked tie, with a page of alien erotica where my closing argument should have been, I fumbled. All the people in that room saw it. My girlfriend at the time, Claire, saw it, and it became a story that followed me for weeks afterward, like nicknames in boys' locker rooms. Where suddenly everyone has an incredible memory for this one thing you wish they would forget.

I recovered because I always recover. That is, if nothing else, a thing I know how to do on my own with no help from anyone. But when I came home that night, I had to grapple with the fact that she is now the one on the other side of my wall. I stood in my kitchen holding the tentacle novel pages, even reading them. It's not that I can't see why someone would enjoy it, but today it was the thing that threw me off my game. I tried to determine the correct response to the situation. Do I return them, burn them? Finish reading them? What I did know, returning them required a conversation I'd already had too much of that morning, and I could not bring myself to get tangled in another fruitless exchange with that chaos. It was hard earlier, her standing there in daisy-embroidered denim, looking at me like we are two entirely different brands of adults. And I already had more contact with this woman in one morning than I had with almost anyone else in weeks and all of it had been negative. So I grabbed the *titillating* tentacle pages and taped them to her door. I never asked if she received them and she has never mentioned it. But I know she did because days later, I heard her recording them, like it was nothing.

She eventually found out I am the one on the other side of her wall, and now that interaction remains the foundation of every one since.

The shower, I decide, is my only option tonight. To stand under the coldest water I can tolerate for as long as I can. Which accomplishes nothing except making me colder, more awake, and somehow more aware of her voice that I can still hear even from here. I know that's not true, but once she's in, *she's unshakable.*

The first night it happened, I turned up with some concern. It wasn't sexual moaning, I would never have showed up for that. But a fight so violent it was either that or call the police. When I showed up at her door, she was obnoxiously proud of the small space she had built out. Showing me every bit of padding and drapery, explaining how I shouldn't even be able to hear her. But as evidence indicated, I very much could. And to this day, months later, that hasn't changed.

In my head she has implanted herself from repeat offenses. And while I know it's not possible, it feels like her voice comes through the plumbing just as easily, dripping from the shower head with every spray of water. She is everywhere. I press my hands against the stone wall of my shower and hang my head low, letting the water run itself down my body trying not to imagine exactly what it is she's trying to evoke. *It's clearly not working*, so I am just standing in a cold shower like an actual schmuck.

She doesn't shower with such misery, I know this because the architectural geniuses put a large window in her bathroom that she leaves perpetually open. Which means, I know when she's in the shower. *Fucking great.* I'm sure the office building across the street gets a good view. I also know because she actually sings, and if my balcony door is open, her voice strolls right in like it's been invited for dinner.

I scrub my hands across my face, through my wet hair. The steam filling this space is from me, fuming with the thought that this girl can be so wildly ingrained, uninvited, in my brain that the classic *'cold shower'* did nothing.

I yank on a fresh pair of joggers and hope I've given her enough time to finish. But walking back to my bedroom wall, she is going full force. And apparently, so are her main characters.

I form a fist and slam it against the wall, right where I know she is. But she just turns up the volume. I *'knock'* twice. She just plays a scream that cuts through every room of this apartment. It's a deliberate escalation, a conscious decision to take what I've just communicated and reverse it, to tell me, through the medium of her screams, that she has heard me and has chosen to do the opposite.

Every escalation I take is equally matched or exceeded, and we have found ourselves in a standoff that will soon impact the entire floor, not just units A and B.

I cross my apartment in the dark, out the front door into the hallway, and I bang on her door with the full intention of saying something that I will have prepared by the time she opens the door, because right now, my feet made this decision before my brain was consulted. So I have to manage it while standing on her *'Hello Sunshine'* doormat.

The neighbor across the hall opens his door. He is a small man, mild-mannered, who should be, by any reasonable logic, on my side. But I also couldn't tell you his name if I was on trial and I know she picks up his groceries for him. I know because he mentioned it in the elevator, twice, and it appears to have constituted a binding agreement of loyalty, he didn't shut up about what a 'neighborly' thing it was to do. And because of that, I know he looks at me monitoring the situation on behalf of the wrong party.

I hear her footsteps as she makes her way to the door, and they are not the footsteps of someone who is ready to let this go. They are quick, forward-moving, and fueled by something. I think it's rage. Me too, sweetheart, me too.

The locks disengage.

The door opens.

And there she is.

It's beauty that doesn't need to announce itself and therefore arrives when I haven't prepared for it. And fuck, am I not prepared for it now.

The chin up, the widening of her eyes, the way her jaw sets. She believes she is right and is prepared to be right at any volume necessary, which I will admit is professionally admirable, but personally catastrophic. Her hair is half-captured, her eyes are bright and already loaded, headphones hang around her neck, and she is lifting herself on her toes, which she does when she's preparing to fight with me. So I straighten my spine to stretch every inch of myself in the frame of her door. It's the only leverage I have.

In a meeting, in court, I am never underprepared. I don't show up without knowing what I'm going to say and why, what every possible response is, and how I'll meet it. That's the standard, *that's the fucking floor.* But here, in this hallway, the floor is lower. I manage with what I have.

'By the way, I haven't seen Claire in months, hope she's okay.' Great, now she thinks my relationships merit a Dateline level investigation. She mentioned my girlfriend, *though the word girl-friend is only still applicable with ex as the pre-fix now*, so casually. *Why wouldn't she?* I watch it cross the air between us and I make

the accurate and instantaneous read, she doesn't know it's loaded. She is not cruel in the calculated sense, I know enough people who are that I can recognize it. She is, *if anything*, the opposite of calculated. She is a person who fills silences by instinct, and this one has misfired. She just doesn't know it yet. Because someone who bakes *'apology muffins'* doesn't scream intentionally cruel. *Sometimes she just screams.*

But she says it, and it lands. I organized almost all of my life to be impressive and almost none of it to be known, because my grandmother is the only person who ever did the latter without requiring me to earn it first, and I spent long enough trying to earn affection from two people who were too busy to prove they were winning. The problem, the one I have not resolved, and which Claire hammered in any chance she could, is that no one ever gets close enough to know me. Certainly not close enough to unravel me, except for one notable, loud exception.

Claire ended it by saying that I wasn't available in any way that mattered. She was right. And I had no interest in fighting it.

"That," I say, "is none of your business."

I step forward, keeping one foot on her doormat because it's the last piece of the self-possession I have. I came out here already losing, but she can't know that.

She slams the door in my face hard enough to rattle the frame, and while I won't admit it to anyone else, it rattles me.

Chapter Four

BAIT ARM AND SWITCH

LOUISA

"Hold it!" I yell, as my shoe is tucked under my armpit, sliding my key into the lock as I'm closing the door. "I'm coming, just one... more... sec!" I hop towards the still-closing elevator on one foot as I try (poorly) to slip my foot into my shoe as I do. Just as I manage to sneak my body into the elevator, barely scraping the closing door that is past the point of caring about any obstruction, my shoe does *not* make it onto my foot and instead lands in the space between the inside of this elevator and the floor we were just on.

I grab for it in horror as the door shuts and crushes my sneaker. "Quick! Press the open button!" I say in a frenzy as I try to decide whether to grab for the shoe or reach for the button, but it's too late. I just watch my pink Chuck Taylor slide along the side of the elevator door until it gets stopped at the top, folding at the toe and struggling to be sucked through to the other side where it's stuck.

Standing and spinning, I knew before I saw him who it was willing to abandon me to my fate. The scowl on his face is full of disgust as he glances down at my socked foot, and shakes his head in admonishment. (Trust me, I feel dumb enough for the both of us.)

The elevator door makes a crunching, wheels on steel coming to a halt, kind of noise. I can hear the deep breaths of rage emanating from him. Angry Neighbor™ will always do whatever it is to keep his Angry Neighbor trademark. It would have been no effort for him to just hit the button, or even just hold the door.

But no.

Not him.

Definitely not for me.

It's not his breathing that makes the ground we are standing on sputter as the elevator comes to a screeching halt. I grab the rail, mainly because I don't know what else to do.

"We're stuck," I say, a little too enthusiastically for anyone's benefit and far more than the situation warrants. It's definitely nerves, because what goes up always does come down, or whatever they say. And I'd really like to not plunge to my death with someone who takes any opportunity to remind me what an inconvenience I am to him.

"Clearly," he replies. Because *clearly* it would cause him physical pain to have an interaction with me that isn't just pure annoyance. He presses the 'HELP' button repeatedly, causing the buzzing ring to reverberate through both of us. I'm not sure what it's supposed to do besides *'call for help,'* but does that mean someone is waiting to answer the phone? Does it automatically call a fire department? Is it just a placebo effect?

Staring at the display indicating we stopped somewhere around the sixth floor. Rest In Peace, Left Foot Pink Chuck Taylor, you were a loyal support all these years. And the thought makes me laugh. (Wrong move apparently.)

"What could possibly be funny." His tone is sharp, coarse, the words are being pushed through gritted teeth behind lips I doubt could form a smile. And it strips the smile from mine. He presses the door-open button, it lights up, but does nothing. The breath he lets out in return is the most exasperated sound that fills the entirety of this small space with all the hot air that must fill that (well-shaped) head of his.

"Lots of things," I say as I step closer to the wall of buttons, and he jumps out of my way faster than you would imagine someone could move while confined to an elevator. "Right now, I think the elevator eating my shoe for breakfast is at least a *little* funny."

"Some of us have places to be," he says. Like always, wherever he is going, whatever he has to do, is the only thing of importance.

"You think I raced in here because I wanted to start my morning with cardio?"

"Skipping down the hallway *isn't* cardio."

"How would you know, you give off more *'a round of golf with the guys'* kind of vibe." The corner of his mouth does something I have never once been responsible for before, which is pull in a direction that is not downward. I wouldn't call it a smile, but it's loaded. And the sound that escapes him is barely the chalk outline of a laugh. (But I'll take it.)

"Don't worry, I get my heart rate up just fine," he says, and the meaning is filthy, written across the white teeth that sneak out from the grin. Not only is his sex life *not* something I worry about, I've seen enough of his comings (wrong word, Lou) and goings to know even if that is his only cardio, he's doing just fine.

"Gross," I reply, though if we're honest, the shape of him tells me that there's nothing gross about it. I shake the thought from my brain where it wants to squirrel itself away for later (Roma would thank me), but I won't let it. He's hard enough to get out of my head when I'm recording lately, the last thing I need is actual traction for these thoughts that don't do me any good. Unrequited lust doesn't work out well for the unrequirt*er*.

He's looking at his phone, trying to make a call, but the no-signal message keeps flashing. And I can feel the intensity in his eagerness to get the fuck out of here. (Same.) If he could go back in time sixty seconds, I'm pretty sure he would take the stairs. I press the 'HELP' button, it buzzes and lights up but does nothing. I press it again, and again, and okay, again. (Just for good measure.) Maybe what I'm doing is more of a button smash.

"I already tried that," he says, holding his phone up to the corner of the elevator, hoping for a bar of service to save him.

"Yeah, but maybe it just needed a little extra *umph*." *Smash. Smash. Smash.*

"I don't think *pizazz* is going to save us." The emphasis on the word pizazz is meant to be insulting, dripping with sarcasm aimed right at me. I'm not insulted by pizazz; frankly, he should have more of it.

He's dressed for a work day, or dressed like every day I've assumed he's gone to work. So much about him I just piece together with Chandler and Toby as we craft the most interesting hypothesis about him, never knowing more than his actual coffee order, his address, and his general *'I hate the world'* energy. Except today is Friday, so I don't know for certain *where* he is off to because it's the one weekday we never see him at The Double Shot.

I wonder if he can *feel* me roll my eyes. I hope so, but if not, I turn to face him as I do it so that he has a clear view of my defiance. Which is ironic, because as much as I like to live by the rules I make, I also hate hate *hate* being the reason anyone hates me. Except for him. Because I've given him ample opportunity, I've left more than one basket in front of his door full of apology muffins, I'm-your-new-neighbor focaccia, and even the I'm sourry-dough loaf. No success. They ended up in the trash while still warm. Some of the few words he's spoken to me, were to get me to stop leaving him baked goods.

We're stuck somewhere below our floor, so I hit the seventh floor button, maybe that's what's needed. A reminder to go home, back to the start, like a little elevator reset. Since I can't turn it off and on again, the way I fix anything else electrical in my life.

"That's not going to help." Each time he speaks I can feel my cheeks flush the same way I can see his nostrils flare. Our eyes locked on each other, I don't reply. He's right. It doesn't help, but maybe it was the wrong floor, maybe 6 is the answer. Without breaking our gaze, refusing to concede whatever staring contest we are both too petty to lose, I slide my hand over just one button.

"Don't," he says, cold as ice.

I hit the button for the sixth floor and for a moment think I hear something, but it's not this metal box we are in, suspended in the air. It's him, growling out his frustration as he slams his hand over the buttons. "You're going to make this worse." But when he pulls his large hand away, it is him who ends up pressing multiple buttons, leaving them illuminated as we remain frozen in the air. "Fucking great."

With that, I slide myself down the wall and take a seat in the corner. No point in standing. I've made my best attempt at getting us out of here. I just cross my legs, one foot in nothing but a sock, and I plop my bag on my lap. Rummaging for the muffin I was going to eat on my walk to the coffee shop to stop me from grabbing a *cornetto* from Antonio. (Who am I kidding, I would have eaten both.)

Hudson is standing at the opposite wall, leaning against it. Pretty sure he's trying to will himself into a jelly to melt through the wall, negotiating with physics to try and escape me. (Good luck.)

"Do you want half of a muffin," I ask. No idea why, except if we are going to be stuck here, might as well. He cuts me a glare and just shakes his head. Guess a *'no thank you'* would be too much to ask for. He is genuinely missing out, which I hope he knows on some level, even if it's buried under six feet of contempt and *bespoke* suiting. Fine, his loss is my muffin. (*Not like that.*) I take a big bite of the streusel topping. *Too* big of a bite, one that in ten-second retrospect is far too ambitious. But as I do, the clump of cinnamon sugar hits the back of my throat and I start choking (figuratively.) I want to be clear, I can still breathe. Everything is fine except that I am now coughing up muffin in what can only be described as a dramatic display that is doing absolutely nothing for my case that I am a competent adult woman who has her life together. (Which I do, sometimes.)

"I'm fine," I choke out (literally) in a rough voice dry from too big a bite of my breakfast. "Don't mind me, just dying over here."

"You're talking," he says. "Clearly not dying."

"Too bad for you," I say between coughs as he does something unexpected. He reaches into his bag and pulls out a sleek black water bottle, silently extending it to me. My eyes narrow skeptically, but my mouth is too dry to refuse. "Are you poisoning me?"

"Yes," he says, his face and tone equally deadpan. "I poisoned the water, got you stuck in an elevator, and now I'm trapped here with both the murder weapon and the body. Masterful." I just shrug and take the bottle, holding it in my hands, considering, still coughing up apple cinnamon muffin.

"I didn't say it was a good plan."

"Drink," he says with a voice deep and impatient. I take a sip from the bottle, ice cold, like him. Eventually, the coughing is controlled, and I hand it back to him. His hand wraps around it so easily it swallows mine in the process, but he just pulls it out of my grip and quickly tucks it away. (No lingering touches here.)

As the minutes tick by, he remains standing. Maybe it helps him feel hopeful that we haven't been in here as long as it feels. I just hope the usuals don't worry about me. Ramon will have a bag of cherries waiting, and Howard will be waiting to deliver the headlines. Not to mention Chan and Toby, who I actually *am* supposed to meet for my shift. It's not that they can't handle it, I just don't want them to think anything is wrong.

"We aren't going anywhere, you might as well sit down."

"I'm fine," he says.

"You've been standing for like, twenty-five minutes."

"I'm aware," he clips.

"But, it's like you're waiting for a train or something, it's making me feel like I should be standing."

"*I'm* waiting to leave. If you want to wait like that," he tilts his head down where I'm sitting, "*you* can."

"You *can* relax, ya know."

"What makes you so sure," he says and I wonder if that's humor behind it. Feels optimistic to think so. I'm not sure what compels him to listen to me. In fact, I'm not sure I would actually *call* it listening, but he joins me on the ground with his legs outstretched, nearly long enough to encroach in my space, no longer worried about staying on *his side* of the elevator.

"Next time, put your shoes on before you leave the house."

"Next time, *you* do the neighborly thing and hold the door." I don't know what it is that makes every interaction with him so tense that I channel some version of a heroine who doesn't actually care what the world around her thinks. And part of me likes it more than I should admit.

We hear the call from outside, some local-accented fireman, promising to come and get us.

"You managed to turn this into a hell of a morning," Hudson says to me incredulously. He leans head against the wall and forces his eyes closed hoping for peace we both know he won't get from me.

"You're seriously blaming me for a bit of bad luck? We should be grateful, we don't know why the universe needed us to get stuck, or even whose bad luck we borrowed, because maybe they just really needed a break."

"That's right, you *like* bad luck." He picks his head up slightly to pin me with the darkest stare, one that I try my best not to fall into. But the depth of his eyes is beyond coal, and yet, much like it, there is the smallest ring of fire trying to burn through his irises.

"Where are you going this early anyways? It's Friday."

"I know what day it is, Louisa." He says my name in a way no one else does. Most people opt for *Lou,* but also because he won't look anywhere but directly at me as the syllables form on his lips in a way that feels criminal to hear alone with him in a confined space. (I've been reading too much.)

He looks like he could be readying himself to say something, but as he does, the elevator door cracks just the smallest amount, letting the outside hallway light into this space my eyes had adjusted to. The firefighter, whose name I learn is Bill, works as I talk, maybe because we are both trapped. Me in this elevator, him in this conversation. He lives outside the city with his wife and four sons. (I'm serious.) Two of whom are single. (I'm really serious, also not interested.) I hear Hudson huff in reply, probably because Bill doesn't offer up any daughters. The doors are cranked open and we're assured we'll both be fine, even though I can now clearly see the sixth-floor landing that is just about three feet from the elevator floor.

I look at Hudson, whose face is stone cold with aggravation. I guess the casual conversation I made as Bill (and the others) worked their magic to pry the door open just annoyed him even more. He's never been one for small talk. (Obviously.) Being forced into it while trapped in a hanging metal box with me? That might actually be his worst nightmare.

"Lou, honey," Bill says. The sweetness of adding *'honey'* has more to do with whatever they teach firefighters to help calm people down than any real term of endearment. But I like it all the same. "You ready to slip on out?" he asks. And for the first time, I'm staring at the opening, we're between two floors, and will need to quite literally slide out of the elevator (that is still suspended), and I am unable to imagine anything other than my body getting sliced in half.

"Wait, actually, I—I don't think I'm ready," I say nervously. As Hudson, even from a seated position, looks down at me.

"It'll be fine, honey, now come on, feet first, and I'll catch you on this side," Bill says. But now, the *honey* is not doing what I need to sweeten the fear I am overcome with. A fear I didn't even realize I had.

"It's just a little too *Final Destination* for me. I think, maybe,

I should just stay here until the elevator gets fixed. I mean, we bonded, it would be rude to leave her while she's stuck like this!" I am spouting absolute gibberish, and I know it when out of the corner of my eye, I chance a look at Hudson, whose face is dripping in judgement. Maybe it's satisfaction that this could be my payback. Being split in half by the elevator that made him late for... whatever it is.

"What if we start with your friend, you'll see it's nothing to be worried about." I let out a laugh that came from somewhere deep within me, I would feel bad except a similar sound also escaped from him, knowing, like I do, for all the things we are—neighbors, enemies, coffee patron and barista, narrator and complete noisemaking asshole. (We are *not* friends.)

"That's a great idea, he should totally go first!" I say with an enthusiasm at the idea that one, I don't need to go, and two, he would be the one to get sliced first.

Hudson's face is on mine as he shakes his head an infinitesimal amount. Lips pursed together, he drops his bag to Fireman Bill and slides his body between the opening. Landing with a thud on his own two feet, not needing anyone to help *him* down. The length of his legs doing all the hard work. I crook my head to see what's going on, he's just shaking hands with the firemen. Bill tries coaxing me again, but this fear I didn't know I had is keeping me stuck in place. (Just like the elevator.)

And then I hear it, the tone that has no patience, and no interest in prolonging this experience. "Louisa," Hudson says, as if that should be enough of a summons. We can see each other through the forced-open doors. His eyes narrow, and maybe it's the recent (one-sided) trauma bond, but it doesn't look like anger. I hear the exhale, the one that every time tells me the depth of his lungs in a way I didn't expect to care about.

He steps up closer to the elevator floor, he's tall enough where he can see in, about a head higher, giving him a full view of me. He does something surprising then, reaches an arm in, lays it on the elevator floor.

"How about this, if you get sliced in half, you can die knowing I lost a limb." I scoot towards the opening, not sure in what twisted world that's a good deal, but the tone in which he said it was stripped of anger, and just offered the smallest flash of decency I didn't know he possessed. So much so it has me inching closer. "Come on," he reinforces.

As soon as I slip my feet through the gap between the elevator and the seventh floor, he wraps his other arm around my legs, the bait arm, that was meant to be the offering to the elevator gods, grabs my waist. "Duck" is all he says with sharp direction as he feeds my body quickly through. I close my eyes for a split second of movement, and when I open them, I'm held in his arms, surrounded by firemen.

It happened so fast, but we aren't moving quickly now. Both just a little bit frozen as the only thing suspending me in the air is him. And while I'm held against his hard body, the hold he has on me is cradling in a way I don't have the time or health insurance to fully unpack. I can feel the rise and fall of his chest, and he's looking at me with a momentary sense of tenderness that I wish I could bottle for the next time he does something to make me hate him.

He smells like peppermint and subtle cologne, not in a *trying-too-hard* kind of way. More like he has good dental hygiene and a signature scent. As I take a deep breath of him, his arm releases and my feet swing to the ground. He clears his throat and walks down the sixth floor hallway to the staircase, without another word, to escape me and this morning for good.

Chapter Five

ORGY DEN DENIED

HUDSON

After starting this morning from hell trapped in an elevator, I missed the most important standing meeting of my week. *I'll hear about that later.* I'm sure of it.

By the time I get into work, I am so behind schedule and so many degrees off from the axis of myself that every encounter I have from the door to my office is short and annoying in a way that makes even me hate myself a little bit more. But the part of myself that operates best was left on the floor of that elevator as soon as it came to a stop. And I know it even in the smallest way that I set my coffee cup on my desk with more force than necessary. Or the way my attention drags before locking in on the topic.

Of all the people to be stuck in that elevator with, it would be her. Of course it would be her. In her mind, the universe is giving me some grand reason I needed to be late. Or *my favorite* explanation, that *'someone else needed a good day.'* It's not the first time she's used that exact ideological belief to try and talk me off the ledge of a disastrous morning. Never in my life have I met anyone so far from any version of reality I exist in. I almost, *almost* envy it.

She arrives everywhere like a desirable disruption, half-dressed, *or half-shoed,* in mid-motion, incapable of moving through a space without leaving some degree of chaos behind. A trail of rainbow sprinkles left in her wake. She lost a shoe, stalled the elevator, and talked the entire fucking time. Like we weren't hanging between floors with no clear exit strategy and I wasn't suspended on the wrong side of my own sanity. And as she was frozen in that elevator, it took all I had not to just yank her by the ankle. I should have walked away, left it to the professionals, I couldn't fucking help myself.

All because, apparently, *the universe* had plans. Lucky me. But I don't believe in the universe as an acting force. I believe in cause and effect, poor timing, and the mechanical failure of an old elevator that the building's maintenance log has flagged twice in the last eighteen months, which I know because I read the maintenance log as part of the co-op board minutes, because that is the kind of person I am.

Through the glass walls of my office I can see the open-plan of the law firm churning with well-paid purpose and associates bent over monitors with poor posture and the belief that sleep is a lifestyle choice. *I remember those days.* I turn my back to the sound of billable hours and face the window and city below. This is a city that rewards people who are willing to work harder than the person next to them. I am and always have been. It has gotten me here and I intend it to get me further.

"Hudson Ellis," I answer the phone before it has a chance to get to the second ring.

"Ah, Mr. Ellis." The voice on the other end has never been in a hurry, except now, when she clearly doesn't want to be speaking to me despite being the one who called. The pause that precedes her sentences is heavy with the fact that she had no intention in speaking them to me and was prepared to leave them recorded in a specific sequence, and now has to have a conversation, something she confirms. "I was hoping to reach your voicemail." *I knew it.*

"You've reached me instead, Mrs. Saraceno." I set my coffee on the desk. "What can I do for you?" What I can do for her, as I have been doing for the better part of six months, is jump through whatever configuration of hoops she has decided are relevant this particular week to my application to purchase the unit directly above mine, 8A. The apartment whose previous and still technically current owner relocated to Scottsdale before ripping the place down to its studs. No drywall, no floor finish, raw beams and exposed wiring and the cold skeletal openness of a space that has been stripped of every decision anyone ever made about it in preparation for a blank slate of new ones. Knowing full well that blank slate will require a blank check for someone to complete. He accepted my offer in principle before the co-op board's supreme leader made it clear, in no uncertain terms, that their approval was not a formality. A mistake I should not have made. Resulting in me being no better than a man who bought his plane ticket before confirming he had a passport. *Idiot move.* I know better than to assume anything is settled before it is signed, I'm a fucking attorney. A mistake I'll never make again.

I bought 7A four years ago. Corner unit, three bedrooms, with eastern-facing windows that matter enormously in winter when the light can still find its way in. I used that year's bonus to buy it, which tells you two things: what kind of year it was and also what kind of decisions I make. Calculated without emotional decisions.

What 7A and 8A could become, together, is the thing I've been seeing for the last two years. The same footprint, stacked. Connected by an interior staircase, which structurally can be supported, I hired contractors to confirm. And the current owner, an architect in a former life, drew up the plans. It would take two years of work and a significant investment. I've done the numbers *several times*. I have an actual folder in my home office that contains all the architectural plans, the contractor quotes, the board application materials in multiple unsuccessful drafts, and a running document of every objection Mrs. Saraceno has raised and the legal counterargument for each.

I have counterarguments for everything. *That* is not the problem.

The problem is that the board has five members and four of them are, on any given day, potentially reasonable, persuadable. Board politics are not unlike litigation in this respect. You identify who you need to build your case, you address the objections before they become objections. I have done all of this many, *many* times. And I've done all of it correctly. *But Mrs. Saraceno remains.*

One vote by one little old lady. The vote she has cast against me at every interval and will apparently continue to cast until I satisfy criteria she has not fully articulated, only implied, across a series of interactions that I would describe as professionally painful and that she would probably describe as thorough and necessary.

She has all the time in the world to go in circles on this. Whereas I am also heads down on one of the biggest cases of my career.

"The board met last week," she says. The shaky quality of her voice is age, not uncertainty. She is not uncertain about anything. Especially not this. "We've been discussing your application again."

"I see." I don't see at all. I have no clue why this has dragged out the way it has. The request isn't unreasonable, I went through the co-op board bylaws and there is nothing that prevents it. This is preference and preference alone.

"We cannot allow the transaction to go through." No apology. She stopped apologizing for the rejections because she isn't sorry at all. She's actually pleased with herself. Deciding to stop performing the courtesy that neither of us is fooled by. I can respect that, technically, while still finding it deeply irritating in practice.

I close my eyes, setting my phone on the table as I rub my temples, taking a slow four-count breath in through my nose, as a way to keep my shit together, which I know I must, because the second I let loose, I can kiss 8A goodbye for good. Each round she has a different reason, be it permits or financing. Both of which I managed to quickly convince everyone were not viable concerns. But this is a new round of bullshit. I slowly exhale as I lean back in my chair. The leather gives as it is expensive and well-used, and the motion buys me two seconds of silence in which to run through my options and next steps.

I've read all the building's governing documents. *Nothing there.* There is the precedent set by the last two purchase approvals, *but that won't help.* The specific language of the co-op agreement regarding board discretion and the limits thereof. It all protects the board's decision making power. I have read all of it. I have read all of it more than once. I know the edges of my legal position, and if I wanted to fight Mrs. Saraceno through official channels, I could. It would require a reasonable argument that her repeated rejections constitute an abuse of discretionary authority. But as ridiculous as I have found each rejection, she has been within her rights. It would be an effort that costs us more money and gets me no closer to the resolution of what I want.

Because even if it did work, Mrs. Saraceno has lived in The Richmond for longer than I have been alive, she has an extensive social network amongst its residents, and will absolutely outlive me. Some wars are not worth the ground they're fought over, even when you're right. Which means I need her to say yes. Not to be forced to..

"What is it this time?" I keep the gritted teeth out of my voice. *Mostly.*

"The Richmond is *not* a building for investment portfolios."

"Right," I say with a firmness she needs to understand. "I'm not building a real-estate portfolio. I fully intend to live there, you know this. You've seen the plans." It feels like she is just trying to run out the clock as we do this dance. I presented the plans to the building two rounds ago. So she is either senile, or intentionally being obtuse to wear me down. Fine by me, I've gone up against much worse, and I can go for hours.

She shifts her reasoning at that, without acknowledging it. "Well, It's a larger unit, there are a limited number in the building of this size, you're already in possession of one. It should go to someone who intends to make the most of it, not—" She pauses to carefully choose her words in the most unrushed way possible. Forcing me to sit in silence on the edge of my seat for whatever excuse she is about to deliver. "A bachelor play pad."

A laugh escapes me, which could tip my hand that she's gotten to me, because it's a completely ridiculous notion. "I don't know what's more ludicrous, the decision or the reason. I've owned my current unit for years, I'm trying to expand that, not turn it into some kind of orgy den."

She gasps and then there is a cathedral-type silence, that would have anything echo off the vaulted ceiling and be considered a confession. Perhaps I've gone too far. *Orgy den might have been over the line.* The line she already had imagined with her stress on the term *bachelor.* Maybe imagining I'll center the design around a large hot tub to hand out roses with every failed date.

"Mr. Ellis," she says, her voice climbing in octaves as she does. "This is precisely what I mean. These units should encourage families into the building, but you want to turn it into some big, wild... sex space!" And I'm not exactly sure what she's envisioning, *sounds worse than a hot tub,* and I definitely don't want to find out now. "Yes, you've owned 7A for years and in that time, you've never attempted to contribute to the building community. The only thing we know about you besides that your maintenance checks are on time and clear is that we've observed a considerable rotation of... guests." Another pause as she builds *her* case. "You had that lovely girlfriend for some time, but since then, the comings and goings at all hours—"

The mention of Claire, twice in a week when we broke up six months ago, feels great on this morning already from hell. The fact she happens to be clicking her heels somewhere outside my glass door doesn't help my tone. But our relationship ended and since then, sure, I've leaned into the fact that I am single.

"My personal life—" I begin, having heard enough.

"Is entirely your own business," she says pleasantly. "Which is why I haven't raised it formally. I'm simply expressing the board's feelings about the application."

"The board, or you?"

"*We*," she stresses, "feel that a second unit, at this time, would be better suited to someone else." She takes a breath that carries satisfaction. "You understand, of course." Her tone is ever so slightly more sweet, but the intention isn't.

From the outside of my fishbowl office, I look like a man having a calm, professional phone call. From inside myself, I am doing something resembling a controlled forest fire.

Having paced outside my office long enough, Lucas seems to decide there is no phone call of mine he wouldn't be allowed to interrupt. *He's not wrong.* He enters without knocking, which is a habit I never corrected from him. He's the only one with the free-entry pass. And everyone in this office knows it.

He drops into the chair across my desk because unlike me, he is a man who is comfortable everywhere he goes, which is either a personality trait or a consequence of being genuinely liked by most people he encounters. *Probably both.* He peers over my desk at the phone to see who I'm so entangled in conversation with, the question on his face prompting me to respond.

'Apartment.' I mouth to him.

'Neighbor?' he mouths back. Asking about the *other* thing about my place of residence that keeps me up at night. *Literally.* I just shake my head, and get back to the pressing issue at hand.

"Is there anything that can change the board's position?" I say. Lucas nods, arriving at an understanding of the situation, knowing well the rounds of this fight. Now just listening to this conversation in a way I may be able to have him debrief with me afterwards. I speak slowly, intentionally trying not to scare her more than my 'bachelor ways' seem to. The way you approach a negotiation when you've identified the only variable that matters but need the other side to say it out loud. A pause gives me hope she may finally say it.

"I'm not telling you how to live your life," she says. Beneath the frailty of her voice is a woman who has no problem telling people *exactly* how they should be living their lives. She knows which doors she's slamming in my face, and which she's leaving unlikely but still slightly ajar. "I'm simply explaining where we are."

She hangs up.

Lucas and I are left sitting here in the momentary silence of the ended phone call. We went to law school together and he is, without qualification, the best lawyer I know, which is not something I assign carelessly. *Careless isn't a word anyone would use to describe me.* He is also the kind of person who remembers your coffee order, knows *your* assistant's children's names and birthdays, and can walk into a room of strangers and leave with three people who would do him a favor. These are not skills I have. I have other skills people find valuable. But somehow, I also have Lucas.

"That went well," he says with some humor. Knowing by the way it ended it remains an open wound that I won't let scab over. Anytime it does, I just return ready to pick it off again. To an actual disadvantage for myself. At this point, I could buy a house somewhere on the outskirts of the city, a vacation property, or hell, sell my current apartment and just buy something else, not worry about any of this. But this apartment has been the first thing in a long time that is a challenge, an investment that would allow me to actually reap the benefits of my hard work.

"She compared my reno plans to an orgy den, so I'd say so."

Lucas is doing genuine work not to smile at that. "And you said?"

"Technically, I said *orgy den* first, so nothing helpful."

He does let it out now, large and childlike, laughing my name out of his wide smiling mouth. "Hud." Even in the middle of this shit-show co-op board coup, he is always positive. A pragmatic optimist. He usually attributes it to his wife, but I've known him long enough to know, it's him, too.

Lucas married Paola three years ago, which is relevant only because it did change him in that marrying the right person does. Not something I have experience with. *Except watching him.* It settled him without weakening him. It grounded him in a way I see every time I'm with them. He comes back from lunch slightly later on Tuesdays because he calls her on his walk and they get lost in each other as he takes the same laps around the block and she laps him in conversation. She is a woman who has never let him know a moment of peace, and he drops to his knees in gratitude for any chance he gets. He has a photograph on his desk that is not a formal portrait like so many of the partners here do, show-casing their families as part of their success. He refers to her in conversation with the unconscious frequency of someone who has reorganized their whole frame of reference around another person and finds this completely unremarkable.

But it's remarkable from where I'm standing.

"Here's the thing," he says. He leans forward, elbows on knees. The posture that means he's about to say something I won't want to hear.

"You've lived there for a while."

"And?"

"And your relationship with your neighbors is—" He waits for me to complete the sentence.

"Functional." *Save for one.*

"Do you know any of their names?"

"Mrs. Saraceno." I smile at him sarcastically, because I know what he's doing. Leading me right to the fucking point. I'm the horse he's leading to water, and he might be the only person that can make me drink it.

"That's because she's actively stopping you from getting what you want. That's not the same thing." He gives me the look he's given me since law school to prepare me for landing point. "You don't make it easy on anyone, Hud. You're not warm." He doesn't hold back, like the implication that I'm cold and distant is something he has teed up to tell me for some time. Like it isn't something I've heard firsthand from nearly every failed relationship.

Part of the reason Claire and I were so well-matched was just that. She's equally harsh, ambitious, and self-involved. *Or so I thought*. Months wasted, at least that's what she said when she broke up with me, only for us to continue to interact on the daily as we both are constantly vying for the same cases.

"I'm not trying to be warm. I'm trying to buy an apartment." I let the false smile pin my cheeks as I flutter my eyes, mockingly. To which he rolls his. *A very adult exchange.*

"You could buy any apartment, renovate a fixer-upper and get your hands dirty anywhere. You're only hell-bent on this because you're being told no, so now you're trying to prove a point. Thinking you'll be able to build a home in a building full of people you've made no effort to know. And you're surprised that no one wants to do you a favor." He shrugs. "She doesn't know you. All she knows is what she's seen."

"There have not been *that* many guests." I say under my breath. Knowing that if I wanted, it could have been more. But it's been a very respectable, totally normal amount of *guests.*

"I'm not judging," he says, throwing his hands up in defeat. Maybe just conceding for my own comfort. Because as the most brilliant legal mind, he knows when to let someone sit with what he's said, and that is exactly what he's doing.

He sees when my eyes focus on something over his shoulder, and doesn't pretend not to turn and look, and he sincerely waves at her as she passes. *Perfect fucking timing.*

Claire smiles at Lucas, not at me. She wouldn't waste her limited resource of social niceties on me. Why should she? Why should anyone? Our relationship ended six months ago, but not before the entire office decided I massively fumbled the bag.

Lucas heads back to his desk but not before telling me the real reason he popped his head in, that Arthur wants to see me. Something I feel he should have led with. He's waiting in his office when I round the corner. That isn't unusual, Arthur is Managing Partner of this law firm, which also makes him my boss. What *is* unusual is that he isn't alone. From twenty feet away I can see her. I should have known this was where she was heading. Claire is seated across from him, posture effortless, one leg crossed over the other. She understands she's always being observed, keeps herself composed because of it, and has decided that works in her favor.

"Hudson," Arthur calls, gesturing me in. I school my expression before pushing open the door as he motions me to the empty chair next to her. "Good timing," he says like he wasn't the one who summoned me. Having engineered this to look like a coincidence. "I just got off the phone with Hugh Sterling. This merger, I hear it's getting messy." Don't I know it. I've been pouring myself into the pages of this acquisition masquerading as a merger for weeks, and the family at the helm of the company isn't making it easier, but this is what they are known for. Most of my communications run through two of the sons, each with a cushy job of their own. *Like I said, they aren't making it easier.*

"Claire," I say evenly, with a tone of emotional unavailability she'll recognize and will later use to validate her decision.

"Hud," she replies, just as neutral, except she holds on to some of the old familiarity of a nickname.

"We're having Claire join the team working on this, it's too critical for us not to throw our best at it." I don't bristle. Other men might be offended at the implication that *she* is the best. But she's definitely one of them. It's one of the things I respected about her from the start, and my respect doesn't expire the way other things do. She's a force in any room. But both of our priorities were outside of each other, always. Which dressed on me, looks emotionally unavailable, and on her, stubborn and unyielding.

Arthur looks between us. "I want to be sure, given your history, there's no conflict."

"Not a problem for me," I say. And it isn't, especially because I won't relinquish this over discomfort.

"Great," Arthur says.

"I told you, Arthur, we are both professionals," she says. She takes a sideways glance at me that is beyond subtle, but even I know there's an ounce of gratitude in it. Because while I'm not giving up this case, the truth is, I doubt they would ask me to. There's more than enough work for her to step in, and it's good exposure as she fights her way up a much harder ladder than the steps I get to climb.

We spend the next thirty minutes on numbers, voting rights, proxy exposure. She's sharp, efficient, exactly as I remember. When she reaches across to pull a document toward her, the light catches her left hand and that's when I see the ring. It's emerald cut and substantial, catching the sun and refracting it back against the bare skin of her legs. It shouldn't matter, we ended for reasons that made sense. She wanted depth I couldn't manufacture. I wanted compromise she wouldn't offer. *Clean break.* The only sting I feel in response is ego, I'm smart enough to know that, but not brave enough to admit it to anyone but myself. The only thing we would have been good at: drafting the prenup, because we both know it never would have lasted.

When she leaves, Arthur leans back in his chair and looks at me the way he has looked at me since I was twenty-five years old and convinced I had nothing left to learn. *Here it comes.* He's been my mentor for years, the first partner who took a risk on me. In ways I would never articulate, he became something close to the image of father I imagine others had. Steady, demanding, ever present. *Which is how I know he's not my actual father.* He has children of his own, *grown* children not far from my age, which is maybe why it feels like it. Like one of those monkey families in the zoo that takes in an abandoned baby and raises them in their image. Except in this case, the zoo is a top law firm, and at the time, the baby monkey was a twenty-five-year-old man just passing the bar exam.

"You didn't know," he says.

I press my lips together and shake my head once. "No."

Before I muted her on social media, I saw the strategically shot photo with a corner of a man's hand with a large AP wrapped around his wrist while holding a wine glass. I knew then she had moved on. I want to say I'm happy for her, but is anyone really ever happy when their ex moves on? She won, *quickly*, someone chose her in a way she made clear I would never have. All I've collected in the time since our breakup is an enemy in the form of an old co-op president who seems to be tracking my sexual encounters.

"It won't impact anything, Arthur. Trust me," I say, and I know he does. "I've worked too hard to let anything or anyone distract me now." There's emphasis, making sure he knows there's nothing to worry about.

"I know that," he says gruffly, and more parental than boss. With it he lets out a soft huff and his eyes soften slightly.

"I'm glad she's happy" is all I say. Whether it's true or not, he doesn't push the topic anymore. It's a door slamming three rooms away. I hear it, might wonder momentarily. But it has no real impact on me, except knowing now that the door is closed.

Chapter Six

____

MY EXPIRED LIFE

LOUISA

My couch is a Facebook Marketplace find that cost me two hundred and forty dollars and the dignity-loss of Chandler and I loading it into a borrowed van at eight in the morning on a Sunday while Jason, the man I bought it from, stood on his porch with his cup of coffee, watching, offering no assistance whatsoever. (Jason, if you're reading this, I hope your coffee was cold.) Even still, I love it with a disproportionate ferocity that has nothing to do with its actual quality. It has lumpy stuffing with one armrest that sits slightly lower than the other. Plus, it's a forest green that lets me pretend I'm just a girl living in a cottage in the woods decorated by moss and knit things. I have dressed it up in every throw pillow I've ever impulse-purchased, some embroidered with funny sayings, or my favorite, the one with a corgi on it. (I've never in my life had a corgi, I'm not the Queen of England.) The way I love this couch is more to do with the fact that it's mine, it has only lived here, in a place that is mine, in a life I built from scratch and am extremely attached to.

Friends is on, not because I'm paying attention but because the laugh track is like a lullaby, there is a lot of comfort in watching people navigate their lives with more chaos than competence and somehow always land on their feet. (I usually land face first.) I know every episode, every beat. I clap every time during the theme song. But the light from the television is soft in that 90s sitcom glow, transforming these friends into more than just background noise, but a nightlight in my small space.

Ross and Rachel are currently in the middle of something I can narrate back to front, and I am paying zero attention to it because my thumb is doing the thing my thumb does on Saturday nights since Roma's advice, which is scroll left with an automatic rhythm that has long since stopped requiring any conscious participation from me, but is going through the motions anyway.

Way too many men holding fish.

An *unreasonable* number of men holding fish.

I don't know when this became the dominant visual language of male romantic availability, but I want it on the record, whoever is maintaining the record (Reddit? Is that you?) that this is not working on me. There's a man on a mountain. A man at a wedding that is not clearly enough not his wedding, which raises more questions than it answers. A man with a dog, which is the only profile that gives me genuine pause, not because of the man but because of the dog (which is a corgi and could fulfill the pillow prophecy), but the dog looks like he deserves better than to be used as romantic collateral. I swipe left on the dog's owner with some regret (for the dog.) There's someone who says they are *'fluent in sarcasm.'* Another bio that just says *'I dare you.'* Absolutely not.

The screen refreshes, my thumb stops. (So does my heart and perhaps the rest of my cardiovascular system.)

The profile is as severe as the man himself. No fish, no mountain, no borrowed dog. Just a high-resolution headshot in a suit that I know from firsthand experience costs more than my monthly rent, against a background that is a wall of books. Dark eyes, and lashes, which, even in a photograph, come through. His distance from me is listed in a measurement so small it's a joke, which I also knew, because he is approximately twenty feet away through a wall and a hallway.

Hudson Ellis on this app is not something I needed to know tonight or any night, or ever, really. This profile confirms what I suspected but didn't know with certainty besides Toby's 'Relationship Status Drink Order Model' that he is single. Like not just casually available, but on-the-dating-apps level single. The tall, glamorous (lives her life with more competence than chaos) girlfriend, Claire, really is out of the picture.

Which makes me feel better about using him while recording. It's not been consciously, or at least not entirely consciously.

I swipe left. (Hard.)

Harder than necessary, if I'm honest. There's no one here, so I'm really only making the point to myself. And with that he disappears into the profile graveyard with the fish men, and the mountain man who wants someone *outdoorsy,*' and the man whose dog deserves better, and I put the phone face down on the cushion beside me and throw a pillow over it. Instead, I just stare at the television to tell myself firmly that there is no universe, not one, not even the weird ones, in which that would be anything other than a catastrophe.

The notification buzzes through the pillow I thought was necessary to hide the screen that momentarily held his face, and makes the whole cushion vibrate.

"Louie-Gooey!" Theo is grinning on the other end of Face-Time and it's clear he's on the comfortable side of several pints of Guinness. Behind him I can hear the ambient noise of a London street at closing time and laughter of people singing something that I can't identify but which is definitely being performed with more alcohol than skill. His face is flushed and his hair is doing the thing it does when he's been running his hands through it, which is a habit he's had since we were children which means he's been laughing a lot.

"It's Saturday night," he announces, as though I might be unaware of what day it is. "You need to be doing something more age-appropriate than sitting in the same flat you're in ninety percent of the time."

"It's not ninety percent," I say, I'm defensive because we both know he isn't that wrong. "And I'm working, I had a full day."

"You're in your pajamas."

"These are lounge clothes."

"You Americans and your 'lounge clothes,' but those are pajamas." Since he moved back, he's always teased me about being his American sister. Something he never saw himself as, but what I always desperately wanted to be, and in all ways except the occasional swear word and my pilgrimage to the specialty grocery for the specifically imported beans, I am.

"Piss off, they're comfortable," I say, looking down at the oversized t-shirt printed from some museum gift shop.

"The accent always comes back when you're annoyed," he says, with a laugh and the cheerful accuracy of an older brother. "It just appears, like a little Union Jack. Pop. Hello, I'm British and I'm irritated."

When my accent forcibly evaporated when I was a child, he clung to his for as long as he needed. Until he replanted himself back in 'his homeland.' (We couldn't be more different.) The vowels that sit slightly wrong, the words that arrive in the wrong order. He kept his deliberately, clung to it the whole time we were in California like a flag he was saving to plant when he got back to his real life, which he always knew was there. I didn't know where mine was, I'm not really sure I even know now. But so far, this is closer than anywhere else.

No one I meet now even knows that there is backstory as to why sometimes in frustration or panic my words sound a bit closer to a transatlantic accent. Everyone just assumes it's the voice-acting of it all. Not knowing that my passport is a little less bald-eagle and actually has a unicorn on it. (Which, to be fair, is perhaps the only thing that makes me want to keep it.) Hints of my accent only come out now, when I'm talking to my brother.

"Only with you, dear brother," I say. He laughs and I let

myself smile at it, because Theo's laugh is one of my favorite sounds in the world, always has been, because he doesn't hold anything back. When we moved here, when I was nine and drowning in the misery of being new and different, it was Theo's laugh that I always followed home. He was fifteen and decided before he ever set foot on the plane that he was going back, which he did a year and a half later. He carried his accent like a shield because he knew he'd need it later. I didn't know what I'd need (I still don't), but he has always let me stand behind his armor with him while I figure it out. Especially against Mum and Dad.

"Happy belated birthday, Louie," Theo says. His voice fills every invisible crevice of my apartment with sincerity and the nostalgia of our shared childhood. Even though, despite the same house, our childhoods couldn't have been more different. "Have you checked your mail?" he asks, with the tone of someone who already knows the answer.

"The mail is fine" (I hate the mail and he knows it.)

"Lou."

"It's a system, I swear!" I say. "The system is that I check it when it becomes urgent." The real system is that I leave it until the mailman writes me a threatening note that he sticks to the front of my mailbox.

You know who never gets Post-it Notes about *exceeding mailbox capacity'* or *'ceasing to deliver?'* (Of course you do.) 7A. In fact, the last time I was at the mailbox doing my clean out of miscellaneous garbage coupons and loan pre-approval looking for my car registration, he strutted up to his mailbox, walking right by Mrs. Saraceno and I without even so much as a hello, not even that pursed lip smile that you do when walking down the hallway and someone is walking towards you like a game of human chicken.

He retrieved his totally respectable amount of mail, and walked out of the mail room without so much as acknowledgement I walk on the same earth. He seems to save that for late nights when he shows up at my door to remind me that I am the bane of his existence. (And not in a good *Bridgerton* way.) Mrs Saraceno and I just stood there chatting as she told me all about her newest addition, the chocolate Pomeranian she's naming Hermes. (Who definitely bit me when I went to pet him, but I didn't have the heart to tell her that.)

"That's why you never responded to my birthday card."

"You sent me a birthday card?" I lurch forward and practically bring the phone to my nose with skepticism. But he just breaks into laughter, his friends on the street around him break into a chorus of happy birthday. (Which was last week.) My birthday came and went with cake, *Friends* in the form of Ross and Emily's wedding, friends in the form of Toby and Chandler, and streamers that are still hung up behind me.

"You would know that if you just checked your mail." He says the last three words with individual, pointed weight.

"I'll check it tonight," I say, mostly to make him stop. He does this regularly. Calls me to remind me to do the things that many people just do naturally. Make a doctor's appointment, renew your car registration, check your mail... It annoys me at my core, mainly because it feels like some kind of personal deficiency to operate in the adult world. Our brains just never worked the same, and doing a task as simple as checking my mail can feel like I'm holding my hand over the hot burner on the stove, telling myself to lay it flat. I just... can't.

"Tonight," he repeats, like a verbal contract.

"Tonight," I respond, my eyes bulging hoping to emphasize the 'I got it' that I'm not saying. (And praying I actually do, got it.)

The call winds down with an update on our parents, Dad's new woodworking phase, Mum's book club, the general comfortable retirement of two people who have decided that England suits them and always did despite their stint in the States. And then, with the intention of trying to sound subtle, when in fact he is just drunk and interested, "How are things at the coffee shop?"

The pause before *coffee shop* is infinitesimal and damning. What he's actually asking about is really a who.

I just roll my eyes and start talking about Toby's new tracking of almond versus oat milk selections and how it might indicate political party. But Theo is very clearly uninterested, his focus is singular, and it's not Toby's alternate milk model that he's curious about. Finally giving him the small morsel he's after.

"Chandler is fine, she has an art show coming up," I say. I don't exactly know when they started this game of long distance flirting, but I get to play middle man while they pretend that's not what's happening because it 'logistically doesn't make sense.'

"I'm asking about the coffee shop generally. You know I have an interest in small businesses."

"You have an interest in three things, Theo. And two of them are rugby." I hear a call from his friends as they stumble their way down the street.

"Goodnight, Lou." He's still grinning when the call ends. The sound of Chandler's name is usually enough to tide him over until we speak again.

The paper chains and streamers from my birthday are still pinned to the ceiling, I keep meaning to take them down and keep not doing it, both because they make me happy and because taking them down would require getting on a chair and I haven't been in the mood for the level of follow-through.

I told Theo I'd check the mail tonight, which means I have to check the mail tonight because he will call me tomorrow to confirm. I am a bad liar under normal circumstances and a catastrophically bad liar to my brother, who has known me since before I even had a personality to hide things behind. Leaving me no options but to get up. I find my shoes, one under the couch, one somehow in the kitchen, and I take the elevator down to the mail room where my mailbox, sure enough, has the aggressive OVERSTUFFED Post-it stuck to it. (Rude.)

I pull the small door open and an avalanche of envelopes and catalogs and what appears to be a rolled-up magazine unfolds itself into my arms. I gather it all against my chest, it's physical comedy. As I am the master of this exact problem and I'm now suffering through it. Even by my standards, this is a lot of mail.

Upstairs, I clear the coffee table and sit cross-legged on the floor and begin to sort. Utility bills on autopay (Good job, past Lou.) I set those aside. Credit card offers, no. (Good job, current Lou.) A catalog from Restoration Hardware, which arrives because of the afternoon Chandler and I spent sitting on cloud couches we can't afford and apparently gave them my address, which I do not regret because even though I love the green, lumpy one I've got, those couches were transcendent. (Maybe for future Lou.) A birthday card from my brother makes this all worth it.

But what's behind it has me stop.

The envelope is white and bureaucratic, my full name is visible through the plastic window, Evans, Louisa J., printed in the font of government correspondence. Which if I had any doubt about, the return address in the upper left corner in small, unambiguous letters confirms it.

USCIS. United States Citizenship and Immigration Services.

Strange, I think. My father always handled these things. It was his visa that carried the family when we moved here, and then mine evolved with me, student status growing as I grew, and I signed whatever forms arrived, vague and unexamined, and assumed it was all fine. He's in England now, and has been for two years. They encouraged me to return with them, the doubt and criticism I could support myself on my own was the main reasoning.

I read it once, quickly, because my instincts (which aren't always great) immediately flagged it as important, before my brain even had the space to catch up.

Then I read it again, slowly, with deliberate attention, trying to locate the part where this isn't as bad as it looks. But I don't find that part. In fact, the more I read it, the worse it looks. And Theo's birthday card isn't enough to pretend otherwise.

NOTICE OF EXPIRATION OF STATUS.

The language is bureaucratic and cold, designed to communicate facts without implication of feeling, which has the paradoxical effect of making the feelings hit harder because there's no softening in the words to absorb them.

Nonimmigrant status expired. (Like milk?!)

Derivative eligibility terminated. (Derivative of WHAT?!)

Unlawful presence. (I'm against the LAW?!)

The phrase sounds meaner than it has to. *'Unlawful presence.'* As if I am an intrusion. As if the years I have lived here, the life I have built here, the specific geography of my entire adult existence, is something happening without permission. *I HAD PERMISSION!* I have a job, and a driver's license, I even pay taxes!

But the expiration date is in the past. I read it again, thinking I've made a mistake, (which I clearly have) but it's not my reading comprehension that's in error. The date on the letter is over sixty days old. It has been sitting in my mailbox between a Restoration Hardware catalog and a credit card offer for sixty-something days, and I have been living my life, unlawfully.

'Failure to comply may result in formal removal proceedings.' I know they don't mean black tie.

My breathing changes and I see it coming from a mile away. The panic rolling in, something tightening in my chest that has nothing to do with my lungs and everything to do with the word removal sitting on the page in front of me. I open my laptop because this feels like the kind of emergency that requires a larger screen.

I type with shaking hands.

'Punishments for overstayed visas'

'Is the government mad at me for overstaying my visa'

'What happens if you overstay a visa'

'Resolution for overstayed visa UK national who didn't know they overstayed their visa and are very sorry'

'What is unlawful presence'

The results repeatedly wash over me, like I am caught in the crashing and receding roll of a wave on the shore. I'm drowning in all the information. I don't know what half of it means, I just know they are not kind. Reddit threads full of horror stories and 'ask a lawyer forums' with disclaimers and worst-case scenarios. Someone's blog post titled *'What I Wish I'd Known'* that I click on with desperate hope but it makes everything worse. The internet, it turns out, is not the place to go when you need reassurance (surprise!) The internet is the place you go when you want to confirm that everything is as absolutely catastrophic as you suspect. And it is delivered in real time by strangers who want you to know they've been through worse.

I reach for my phone, Chandler is the first on the list of SOS phone calls. But she doesn't answer. She almost always answers, but unlike me she has a functioning social life and a lower threshold for staying on the couch, so she is probably out experiencing the real world while mine crumbles around me. That or she's in her studio, hands covered in paint, and she's watching my name flash across the screen, but will call me back as soon as her hands are clean of the acrylic.

I call Theo back. It rings four times and goes to his voicemail, which means he's either back inside somewhere loud or he has succumbed to the Guinness.

Finally I pull up my parent's number, it sits on my screen waiting for me to hit *call* with the same judgement they'll have when they answer. And unlike my first two attempts, despite the time difference, I know they will. But with that, I also know what that call will produce, it's not comfort, not warm, unconditional *'everything will be fine, Lou'.* They would work backwards from the issue to find the moment of irresponsibility, to find my failure. (No need, I've already done it.)

My search has gone from *'can I apologize to the government'* to flights to London Heathrow, thinking maybe I save my parents the trouble. But in the split second it takes for the flight prices to return, I realize there is nothing for me in a country I don't know.

Sitting on the floor with the letter in my hands, I think about my life here, the irreplaceable texture of it that has been quilted over the last decade and a half. What I stitched patch by patch, where I have been (slowly and sometimes even in the wrong direction) becoming who I actually am.

And that's when the tears come, not gently. They overtake my entire body, possessing every extremity and organ I have. They involve my shoulders and chest and with ugliness because I am genuinely frightened. I cry because I don't know what to do, which is a feeling I have had before and have always found a way through, but this time the not-knowing has teeth in it and it has taken a bite.

The one thing the internet has said repeatedly, I need a lawyer, a really fucking good one. I know exactly one lawyer and the last time we had a voluntary conversation it ended with me slamming a door in his face, and the time before that ended the same exact way. He also (god help me) might be my only option.

I stand up and hurry past the mirror, because I know what I look like and I don't have the emotional reserves for a confrontation with myself. I take the letter in both hands, and walk out (run out) my front door in my pajamas and I knock on the door of 7A. And because my body has apparently decided the act of knocking was the last bit of scotch tape holding this operation together, I completely collapse into hysterical tears as soon as my hand leaves the wood.

He opens it faster than I expected like he was awake and sensed an emergency. But maybe that's just how severely he reacts to everything in life.

The first expression is one I know, it has greeted me in every doorway we've ever stood in. The scowl isn't fully formed across his face, but the muscle memory of hatred has it shaping into place. But then he sees me, and suddenly it's something else, the sharpness washed away by something I have not seen on him before and don't have a name for yet.

"I– I need a lawyer," I say, and my voice comes out broken,

nothing like the voice I use for anything. Not work-Lou, not coffee-shop-Lou, not fight-with-Angry-Neighbor™-Lou. Just me, completely frightened. "I think I'm a fugitive... or I'm about to be. The timeline is ambiguous, and the letter doesn't exactly say. Maybe it does," I'm aware I'm not making sense. I keep going anyway because I've started and stopping feels worse. "I checked the mail. Which I know, I know, I should have checked it sooner, it's my fault, I know it's my fault—"

"Louisa." His voice is sharp, authoritative, but surprisingly, not cruel. "I can't understand you. Breathe." Despite his best intention, that does it. It's the thing that unravels me into a complete puddle of tears and strung together words.

"I, I am breathing..." (I'm not)

"You're not." And then, before I register what's happening, he steps back from the door and for all I imagined him to do, to yell at me, to tell me to go home, he says the two words I didn't expect. "Come inside, whatever this is, it won't be handled in the hallway."

Chapter Seven

DID I SAY FRIEND?

HUDSON

The knock at my door is a handful of raps, quick, erratic, and uneven. I check the time on the microwave, later than I would have expected a knock from anyone. And the rhythm is too frantic to be a return guest. I cross the apartment and open the door.

The woman in my doorway is not recognizable, even though I know her. Same face, considerably fewer defenses. Smaller, somehow, though not in any way a tape measure would catch, but compressed. The way a person gets when something has gotten to the part of them they don't show people and they are left alone, standing in their own fears. Her face is blotchy and her eyes are glassy with the tears that haven't finished falling, and she doesn't reach up to stop them. She is too overwhelmed by whatever has thrown her at my door to care.

The grip she has on the paper in her hands is alarming. It's crumpled between them, but she's holding it so tightly, I'm not sure how she even knocked.

'I need a lawyer,' she said. And the words come out fractured in a tear-blurred rush. Pieces I'm expected to put together.

"Louisa." She keeps going. I try to strengthen myself to get her to listen, because I can't help her like this. I don't even know what's wrong like this. "I can't understand you. Breathe."

"I, I am breathing…" she says. Looking at me with eyes wider than I've ever seen them. The depths of brown I never noticed. For once, the thing in them is not anger or hatred at me. She doesn't look at me with the same resentment and loathing she normally does. It is plain fear, undisguised, with no performance in it. And she's staring at me like I've said something in a language she didn't know I could speak.

"You're not," I say as I step aside. "Come inside. Whatever this is, it won't be handled in the hallway."

It's never a good thing when someone shows up with a paper in hand claiming they need a lawyer. At least she isn't covered in blood. But something crosses her face, surprise, maybe, that I didn't say something that sounded more like me. Her breath hitches once, twice, and I step to the side to hopefully ease her in.

She's never been in my apartment, which is maybe a good distraction for her, as it has her eyes moving over everything, giving her something to do that isn't crying. Under different circumstances she'd be ripping into me with a critique of the space, but she's too overwhelmed. I'm almost sorry to be depriving her of the opportunity. *Almost.*

I guide her to the armchair with my hand at her back. She is warm through her sweatshirt, and is wound so tight I can feel the tension. Her whole body has been held at a high frequency and she hasn't been able to come down from whatever this is. I crouch in front of the chair so I'm below her eye line.

"I need to see what you're holding," I say. "I can't help if I don't know what we're dealing with." She looks at me and extends both hands, the paper between them, like she's offering something she's been gripping so long she's not sure she remembers how to let go. I smooth it flat across my knee and read it once, quickly, the professional scan, the source, the date, the citations. Then I read it again slowly because the first read told me something critical I'd like the second pass to contradict. But it doesn't.

The expiration date is already past.

Something tightens in my chest that has nothing to do with the letter, but the trembling in front of me. I didn't know she could unravel like this, every interaction I have reminds me how she lives her life like a ball of yarn already rolling down the street as someone chases after it trying to spool it back into a sphere. Just warmth and noise that tangles around everyone it touches. Tripping them up in all the ways they never see coming.

But this is different. This isn't the chaos she is comfortable in, this is something that has scared her, *genuinely*, down to the bone and deep in her soul.

"Could I—" She stops and tries again. "Do you maybe have… a cup of tea?"

I look up, catching her round, watering eyes.

Her multicolored nails are shades of purple and neon green that alternate across her fingers. Currently digging hard into her own palms all because her hands don't know what to do with themselves now that I've taken the one thing she'd been holding together with what appears to have been sheer force of will.

"What kind?" I ask, knowing that I doubt I have ever kept tea here.

"Anything." It's barely above a whisper. "Anything warm," she clarifies.

In the cabinet, behind the spices that are never used, is a box of Sleepy-Time Chamomile. While the water heats in the microwave, I read the letter again with the learned, focused attention I practice daily, rather than whoever I was a minute ago. This isn't my area, about as far from it as one can get. I jot down some notes on a legal pad in the kitchen as the microwave plate spins.

I steep the tea for six minutes, which is the middle of the directed range, and I return to the armchair with a warm beverage and better understanding of the situation. I resume my position in front of her, holding out the mug, waiting for her to take it.

Her fingers close around the cream stoneware and I feel, for a moment, the warmth transfer to her cold hands against the hot ceramic, the small visible relief of it.

"I'm not this kind of lawyer, Louisa," I tell her. I keep my voice level. Level is what this room needs right now, and if there's nothing else I can do, I can give her that. "Mergers and acquisitions, hostile corporate situations. Not immigration." Her face does something terrible and surprisingly, that does something terrible to me. The last composure she was holding dissolves like cotton candy.

And through a stuttered sniffle, "But I don't know anyone else." The words are very quiet and very honest and they very honestly hit me harder than they should. Her breathing changes, I can hear it picking up. It's shallow and rapid, it's her nervous system responding to a genuine emergency. Her hands tighten on the mug, but even that doesn't prevent the trembling as they do.

"Louisa." I put my hands over hers, both of them, and they disappear under mine completely. She takes up so much space in every other sense that the smallness of her actual hands is shocking. I haven't touched her since I pulled her from the elevator, spent exactly ten seconds holding her in my arms in a way that felt more dangerous than the elevator itself. Just being in my grip I felt the natural warmth her body emanates, and I had to put her down and walk off before I walked her into my apartment, and then, the bedroom. It was a ridiculous thought, and I couldn't let it fester.

I can tell from the state of her, one I know from my own experience, that this is a panic attack. I don't get them often anymore. But when I was a child, after my parents' divorce, from time to time I would feel the slow roll of anxiety build within my chest until I broke out into full-blown panic. It means that I can see it on her face as her hands tremble.

"Feet flat on the floor," I command. My tone is clear and direct as her eyes are frantic, looking around the room nervously between blinking back tears. "Louisa, do as I say." I take the mug from her grip and set it on the small table at her side. "Feet, flat." She uncrosses her ankles, putting them flat against the rug, not arguing or hesitating at the direction the second time. I take her hands and put them on her thighs, leaving my own on top of them to steady her shaking.

"Eyes on me."

She looks at me. Stunned, but trusting. Though she has no reason to, and she's never trusted me before.

I take a slow, deep, practiced breath. I watch her try to mirror the rise of my chest and fail. Her breath catching halfway. "It's okay," I say, as the tears stream down her face and her lungs fight for every bit of oxygen she's trying to claim. "In through your nose." I inhale so she can see my chest expand when my lungs fill with air as my nostrils widen taking it in. "Long and slow," I say slowly.

She's watching so intently, her chest moves up and down in a frenzy as I'm trying to get her to follow me. Finally, she does it. A breath longer than a hiccup and her shoulders lift with the effort of it.

"Hold," I say, and she freezes. I count in a whisper with small nods. "One, two, three, four. Now out through your mouth." I round my lips with exaggeration and she does the same. The exhale is shaky on the way out, uneven, but it happens.

"Again." Her hands under mine shaking just the smallest amount less. Her chest moving with just a bit more consistency. We sit in my apartment doing this, her in the armchair and me crouched in front of it with my hands over hers and the chamomile tea steaming quietly next to us, until I feel her hands stop shaking all together. Until the breath comes in properly and goes out steadily and the space between them stops being erratic. The quality of the look in her eyes shifts as the panic settles, looking less desperate. She's herself the way a city remains after it's been ravaged by a storm.

"Better." It sounds like an assessment, not a question. Her nod is small in response. I was telling the truth, this isn't my kind of law, but the feeling that I can't do anything is not one I am comfortable admitting. "Okay, from the beginning." I say.

And she does. How she came here as a child carried on her father's visa who came for work. How the status evolved with her through school, the extensions granted, the paperwork that always seemed to sort itself through the machinery of her father's oversight. How he went home two years ago and took with him, apparently, the working assumption that someone was still handling it.

She tells me the story, about a little girl who was moved away from her home, only to make a new one. That now, she's all alone, and saddest of all, how her parents will have *expected something like this'* which she says without self-pity, in a tone like she's reporting a weather forecast, and she's accepted it. It's actually heartbreaking, because I realize I know absolutely nothing about her. I never even picked up on an accent, let alone the fact she's practically as alone in her life as I am mine.

I listen without interrupting, which is something I'm able to do well. My grandmother always said the most expensive thing a person can do is start solving a problem before you've finished hearing it. Even though it's taking every ounce of patience I have to not jump into action now.

When she finishes, she takes a long sip of the tea and looks at me with the eyes asking to confirm what she's most afraid of. I have an honest answer and an unusual resistance to delivering it. Overcome with the strangest concern it's going to hurt her, which is not something I've previously considered in the context of this woman.

"This letter," I say carefully, "is the preliminary notice. Which means there are probably additional letters, at minimum one, that would have come after this. Terminating your status formally." I watch her absorb it. "When you get home tonight, you need to go through all of the mail."

She closes her eyes for one moment. "Of course there are

more letters." I've just told her she has to go through the most unimaginable haunted house of her own making.

I stand, which brings me back to my full height, and she looks up at me from the armchair with an expression I haven't seen from her before, something open, and uncertain, and younger than she usually lets herself appear.

She is quiet for a moment. "Can I ask you for something else?"

"You can ask." And I just hope whatever it is can be as easily found as that box of tea because I have this completely unreasonable desire to solve whatever problem I can for her.

"Can you put on *The Greatest Showman*?" She says it quickly, like she's expecting to be rejected. "I just, I don't want to be alone, and whenever I feel bad, it's the only thing that helps. I even taught myself the choreography from the last song a few years ago. I saw someone do it online, and I'm not very good, but my anxiety was really bad for a while. So I'd put it on and do the steps until my brain had something to follow. Kind of like what you just did, with the breathing, ya know? Something physical, with a pattern. I don't need to do the dancing, I just—" She stops herself mid sentence and redirects it. Her eyelids look heavy with regret for even asking. "Never mind. It's so stupid, I shouldn't have asked." She moves to stand, to hurry off like a bother, but I just reach for the remote control.

"Sit," I say, and she does. Every bit of vulnerability she offers is followed by the shadow of self-deprecation that could only be painted by someone's family. It's why I put on the movie. Not out of softness, out of recognition. I can't fix what's happened, but I can give her this.

The opening song swells and fills the apartment and I watch her shoulders drop a fraction. She sinks back into the chair, closes her eyes for a moment, and though I expected them to re-open with tears, when they do, the tightened worry of the last hour is gone. Postponed until tomorrow.

The music moves through the apartment. I don't watch musicals, I am definitely not learning their choreography. But as it plays, the sound is familiar, not because I've ever seen it, but because of the frequency with which I've heard it coming from her apartment, and given what she's just told me, my ribs crack open a bit more.

My back is to her as the movie continues to play. I've gone back to the kitchen island to do some research. Which is why I barely hear the whisper when she says it. "They just expired my life."

I walk back over to her, and she's standing now as the final credits roll.

"It's your life, no one can take it from you." It's the most cordial conversation we've ever had, because desperation makes people set aside all types of things. "I'll be honest, it's not nothing," I tell her. "But tonight there's nothing more that can be done. Go home. Get some sleep, I'll make some calls."

"But you said you can't help me." It's said through the smallest yawn, as she wipes a straggling tear from the corner of her eye.

"Doesn't mean I won't try."

When she leaves, I don't return to any of the plans I originally had for the night, instead I flip the page on the yellow legal and hit dial on my phone. Lucas answers on the second ring, of course he does. His voice is thick with sleep but not bothered, it's a quality of friendship I don't acknowledge my gratitude for enough but am constantly aware of.

"Hud, what's on fire?"

"I need a favor." I am already pacing, across the living room, through the dining room, around the kitchen island, the circuit I do when I am thinking hard and moving is the thing that helps it. "An immigration attorney, someone with success on overstays."

The silence on the other end is long. I doubt it's because he's fallen back to sleep. From somewhere behind him I hear it. A sleepy laugh of his wife, Paola. "Is that your girlfriend? Tell her not to call so late." He responds with a laugh and soft affectionate whispers of his own.

"Go back to sleep, my love, I have some business to take care of." They have the easy affection of two people who have been choosing each other long enough that it has become the constant state of their lives rather than something they have to think about doing. I'm the guy who has to think about it, and still falls short.

"You there?" he asks, tone a bit louder than before, meaning he relocated to his home office to give his sleeping beauty the respite. Or save himself the mocking. The quality of his voice adjusts to the seriousness of the call.

"Yep," I say quickly. As I keep adding thoughts to my list.

"Okay," he says, and I imagine him like me, with a notepad ready to write out every critical detail. "What's going on?"

"I have a friend, a British national. Overstayed derivative status after aging out. Sixty days post-deadline, preliminary notice received. Likely a formal termination letter in the same stack of mail." Giving him all the same information I have. "I've just emailed you a photo of the notice."

"Sixty days?" he asks, confirming what I think he knows well enough.

"Sixty days," I reply.

"Okay, so here's the deal, Hud. That's not a hurdle, it's a brick wall." I run my hands through my hair, closing my eyes to listen more closely to what he's saying. As if by closing my eyes, I'll be able to hear something different, with more clarity, more of a solution. "I did work on a case like this years ago, when an executive's visa was revoked after unauthorized travel. I can give you the name of someone who can take a look, he'll handle a messy one. But I'm gonna be honest, he's going to charge you out the nose to tell you exactly what I'm about to."

"Which is…"

"The options are essentially nonexistent for an overstay. They are cracking down on things like this. One, she can leave voluntarily. She'll have to accept a multi-year bar on reentry. Maybe this can be negotiated, but it's not hopeful. Two, she ignores it and stays, gets caught, ends up with a ten-year bar. Three, she finds an employer to sponsor her, but given what you've shared, she sounds too freelance for that to be an option, so that's not promising."

"There has to be something else, man." I'm beginning to feel as defeated as Louisa looked. There are so few things in my life I haven't been able to lawyer my way out of. Hell, most of the time, it wasn't even my law degree that solved the problem. It was just the fact that when I set my sights on something, I made sure that something came to fruition.

"You know as well as I do there is one more option," Lucas says, and I stop moving. "Adjustment of status through an immediate relative. Marriage to a US citizen. It's the only mechanism that automatically waives an overstay and clears unlawful presence in a single instrument. Everything else is appeals and negotiations and hoping someone gives you a window that's already mostly closed." Another pause. "It's a silver bullet. But she'd need to already be engaged, or pretty close to it."

My pacing feet walked me right to my bedroom, staring at the wall. The wall that separates my apartment from hers. The wall that has been, for months, the border of our particular war. She is on the other side of it right now. Lucas has inadvertently set me up with one solution to many problems, not just hers. Mrs. Saraceno thinks I'm just looking for a bachelor pad? What better way to show her that's not true, than a wife. Having Louisa as my on-paper spouse isn't a bad idea for either of us. And I bet Lucas knows it.

"Did I say friend?" I say, "I meant fiancée." The silence on the other line is a man who knows me well, and is proving it by not saying the obvious thing out loud.

"I thought you did."

Chapter Eight

YOU'RE PROPOSING, WHAT?

LOUISA

Sundays at the Double Shot belong to a different species of person entirely, they are not the Monday-through-Friday crowd with their cortados and their laptop bags. They have somewhere to be in eleven minutes and despise every one of them. Sunday is for the leisure caffeinators. The ones coming from yoga smelling of Palo Santo, or a meetup of two old friends trading dog-eared paperback books. It's for the slow crowd. The jazz-listeners and the newspaper readers. And it is for at least one person too hungover to realize I've given them whole milk instead of skim. (Oops.)

Normally, Sundays are my favorite shift. The pace of it, the way the shop sounds different when it isn't running at full tilt, running less like a machine and more like a living room. I pretend Ross, Monica, Joey, and the whole gang are tucked away on the sofa, and this is Central Perk. I'd like to be Rachel but I've been told I'm more Phoebe. (I'm probably Gunther.) I take a kind of sustained joy from this job that I have never been entirely able to explain and have long since stopped trying to justify to people (my parents) who think it should be temporary. Sundays are also days without Angry Neighbor™ and his four-word, always rude coffee order. As if tipping well cancels out that he never once said hello. I'm not sure what to call him now. I could just drop the 'angry', but it might have been a fluke because the shock of me turning up the way I did was so jarring he became the only thing left when the surprise drained him of all other emotions. He became decent. Kind, even. I don't know what to call it yet. I also don't know what the motivating force was that had me believing he was someone I could turn to. (Desperation.) He put on *The Greatest Showman* and didn't rush me out the door. Whatever marble of empathy he keeps tucked away in his pocket, he let me hold last night.

I'm not even sure I should be working. I think that's what the letter said. But I've been working all this time and no one has noticed. I do need the money, especially if I need a lawyer. (And not the neighborly kind.) So today, I am hiding in the back, cross-legged on the floor with my spine against a massive bag of roasting beans, which gives new meaning to the concept of a bean bag chair. (Less comfortable but smells incredible.)

The events of last night have left me feeling like less of a person and more of a live wire, stripped of insulation, exposed to air, vibrating with a current I don't know what to do with.

"Drink this." Chandler appears from somewhere and deposits a cup of tea in front of me, dropping down beside me on the floor, back against the bean bag, the apples of her cheeks flushed pink from the slow Sunday morning 'rush' that has just petered out. Her auburn hair is up in braids today, which showcases her bone structure. She is, even on a Sunday morning behind a commercial espresso machine, unreasonably beautiful.

"Toby's got the front," she says. "It's the lazy-latte crowd. You hide as long as you need." I stare at the surface of the tea she handed me, like the tea leaves might have something useful to tell me. (They don't.)

"I don't know how I could have been so stupid," I say. It is the thought that keeps surfacing, the one I keep trying to release and keep finding at the top again when I look.

"Stop," she says, firmly and without heat. "We are not doing that today."

"It's true. There's no magic wand that makes this all go away…"

"It's also completely useless information that serves no purpose other than making you feel worse, which you don't need any help doing." She turns to look at me with the same expression she has since I've known her. The *'we've got this'* face. If I'm considered type B, she's type A and a half. She's not disorganized, she doesn't hide from her mailbox, but she also does not plan her life beyond necessity.

She showed up at my door first thing this morning because my late night missed call *'gave her a bad feeling.'* (She was right.) I didn't get into all the details. I just said my paperwork is all a mess, that I don't understand what's going on, and that I need a lawyer to help me figure it out. I think I blocked out the reality of the situation, the actual expiration of a life. And after talking to Angry Neigh—*Hudson*, I understand even less. So she just got a bulleted, nonsense version where I showed up at his door (true) and he made me a cup of tea (also true) while he looks into whatever legal documents I need.

She bumps my shoulder with hers. "Tell me again what he said."

"Well, I collapsed myself into a total puddle on the doorstep like an absolute maniac. Turned up in my pajamas, had a complete breakdown in his foyer, and forced him to let me sing along to *The Greatest Showman*." She always liked him, but is also kind of known for liking terrible men. Then again, she says that's how she knows he is actually just a *'complicated soul'* underneath all that tailoring and terror; if he was actually a bad guy, she would be in love with him.

"He was…" I search for the right word and find it is not one I have previously associated with him. "Calm, very calm. It was disorienting." He wasn't just calm, he was calming. (Maybe that's what was disorienting.)

"So, his magic wand," Chandler says, holding her hands in front of us, stretching them out to indicate size. "How big, say when."

"It wasn't like that," I say as I slide down the bean bag. Her hands continue to distance further and further from each other. "I'm not above covering you in this tea."

"You would never waste tea, that's why you folks were so upset when we dumped it all in the harbor."

I elbow her and when she laughs I feel something loosen in my chest that has been clenched since the minute I woke up. That's her magic wand. Always able to get you to smile no matter the scattered pieces of your life or devastation of the day. Which is not a small thing. And that sound can drown out anything for at least a little while.

"But he said he doesn't deal with this kind of thing," I tell her. "He said he'd make some calls but..." I shake my head. "It felt like niceties, not a plan."

The back door swings open, Toby's glasses slightly askew. "You should probably come out here." Chandler hops to her feet, brushing down her apron, ready to man the register. He shakes his head, the glasses wobbling on his nose "Not you. Lou." A pause. "I'm pretty sure Angry Neighbor™ is here for you," Toby says to me. I pin the paper cup between my teeth to hold it as they each offer me a hand to pull me to my feet.

The three of us are at the porthole window in the kitchen door, faces stacked, peering through the small circle of glass into the shop. And sure enough, there he is.

"That asshole Beetlejuiced us, we said his name too many times and voilà," Chandler says.

"He's here. On a Sunday," Toby specifies.

"For... me?"

It's not the crisp four-days-a-week Monday-through-Thursday of his utterly predictable routine. Sunday, he has never once been here on a Sunday. He has taken a seat, collected his americano, and he is looking at the porthole because he knows exactly where I am.

There's no way he could have *'magic-wanded'* this away, definitely not in the twelve hours since I saw him last. If anything, he's here to tell me off, like he should have last night. To tell me not to expect anything from him. That it was some kind of weakness, remind me that the only thing we share is insulation and irritation, not friendship. Which would be fair. We've existed with this rage reciprocity for long enough to know what it is and what it isn't. And just because someone shows you a little bit of kindness in a moment of desperation, and just because he is currently the person I'm conjuring when telling stories to the microphone to dial up the passion that is lacking from my actual life, well, all of that has nothing to do with our actual relationship. That's just because of proximity, and well, the fact that his face looks like that.

"He knows we're watching," Chandler whispers.

"He always knows," I say.

"He's not in a suit," Toby observes. "I didn't know he had other clothes, I don't know what to think about this."

"I bet Louisa knows what to think about this…" Chandler smirks something wicked as her eyebrows shoot up on her forehead.

We all look again, Toby is right. (Always.) He's in a navy sweater, dark jeans, the Sunday version of a man who still manages to look like he has somewhere to be even when he demonstrably doesn't. If he did, he wouldn't be sitting there and staring at me. Absent of the suit but still clothed may be the most dangerous persona he possesses. Without the suit, he's just the person underneath it, which is larger and appears warmer, which makes it considerably harder to be furious with him for reasons that feel like the memory of the grievance, rather than any real issue. (Even though he is undoubtedly here to be furious at me.)

He picks up his coffee and takes a sip without looking away

from the door. Then, unhurried, he raises one finger and does a slow, deliberate beckoning motion. We all drop from the porthole to the ground like he didn't just call me to him. As if we can pretend we weren't seen.

"The audacity," Chandler dramatically breathes. But she says it with profound admiration.

I retie my apron twice before I go out. I don't know why. It doesn't need retying. I'm not even really working. My hands just need something to do while my brain scrapes up the motivation to walk across the shop and sit down across from him.

He watches me cross the room. Doesn't look away, doesn't do the polite thing of finding something else to focus on while I approach. (Because he's not polite.) He just watches, and when I pull out the chair across from him and sit down, he looks at me focused because he's already thought through this conversation and knows how he intends for it to go. (Which makes one of us.) I'll just wait for him to tell me *how inappropriate it was to turn up last night, that there's nothing he can do, and he wouldn't if he could, that he's filed a complaint with the building and I'm being evicted.* (Okay, that last one might actually be a stretch.)

"You're here on a Sunday," I say, because it is the most neutral available observation. And better than talking about anything I cried about last night. Mostly because I don't want to cry again now. Despite his more casual attire, it looks like he has been awake for a while, like he has been working for a while. Monday through Thursday I know his routine, first because he is here, and at night because I can hear. But today? I didn't even know people like him existed on a weekend.

"So?" he responds. Genuinely dry, like it's the dumbest question I could have asked. Back to the tone of all our other interactions.

"You're never here on Fridays or the weekend," I say, while picking the chipped polish off my thumb nail. Bright blue I did this morning, but by the time I walk home tonight it will be gone and I can layer something else over it like a makeshift tie-dye. "Saturday and Sunday, makes sense, because you aren't a *weekend guy'* but where do you go on a Friday..."

"I'm aware of my own schedule, Louisa." The espresso machine hisses somewhere behind me, and it sounds like it could be hissing my name like he is. Chandler and Toby are definitely watching this for different reasons from different hiding spots behind the counter, both with a good view.

"I called someone last night," he says, and the shift in his tone is subtle but immediate.

"A date? *An escort*?!"

"A friend," he corrects, not taking the bait of my desperate distraction of any mention of last night. At some point between me leaving his apartment and now, while I was sitting on my living room floor opening every letter that looked important and then lying awake staring at my ceiling rehearsing catastrophes, he was on the phone with people. *For me.* Because he said he would and apparently he is, among other things, a man who does exactly what he says. "He and I spent this morning on the phone with an immigration attorney he knows." Hudson continues. "He handles situations like this one." His voice is low and measured, preparing to deliver information that matters as I feel my stomach sink into a part of my body I didn't know it could inhabit because of news that's only been half-received. Waiting for the other shoe to drop. In this case, expecting the shoe to be thrown at my face (or maybe eaten by an elevator) with *'There's nothing I can do. Pack your bags and never contact me again.'*

"And..." I say carefully. Both because of the rest of the sentence and the person delivering it.

"Your options are severely limited." It's said without apology, no sympathetic preamble or cushion to absorb the blow, because he is not a man who delivers difficult news softened into something more palatable, especially for me. My feelings would be hurt if he wasn't so consistent.

"But there are options?" I say it as a question. "The word

options implies, well, options." (Not just a *'See ya, Lou-ser!'* that I'm expecting.)

"You can leave voluntarily and accept a multi-year bar. You can stay and get caught." My face pinches with each 'option' he presents. "An employer can sponsor you, but given your employment situation, you're not considered exemplary by the relevant definitions," he says so cleanly, no editorializing. The facts in a line, I can imagine him for a moment in a courtroom laying out information just like this. Undeniable.

Not considered exemplary is perhaps the meanest way to phrase it I could have imagined. But neither the bureaucracy nor my brooding neighbor care about feelings. I've heard it my whole life from teachers, coaches for sports I never was good at (obviously), and of course, my parents. I know that's not what Hudson means, but it doesn't make the idea of *'unexemplary'* sting any less.

Maybe I'm not exemplary in the ways my dad was, the way that had us all moved here for his career. Or the way Theo is on a rugby pitch, truly being fawned over by hoards of people. Maybe that's why I like to perform privately behind the sanctuary of a closet door and only involve myself in other's lives when invited through their headphones. Because they never really know it's me. And even still, I am not exemplary, whoever I'm portraying is.

Maybe the United States government is right, I don't have anything to offer this country or anyone in it. It's a terrible thought, even worse as it becomes the thing I feel undeniably, that the place I have called home longer than anywhere else, where I got my first period, had my first kiss, my first job (and maybe last) could have deemed me unworthy of my life here because I am not 'exemplary' by a standard defined by some legal code for capitalism.

"So..." I drag out, doubtful of what he could have to offer. I try to jump to the end, the way I always do, before someone else can hand it to me. "I should start packing."

He shakes his head, slowly, just once. Cautiously deciding how and when to deliver what will clearly be a knockout punch.

"There is an option."

Singular.

He picks up his coffee, takes a sip, sets it down like he needed it to prepare for what comes next. Something is happening in his expression, not discomfort exactly, but a careful arrangement that suggests this next part is being handled with more deliberation than anything he's said to me before.

"What exactly are you proposing?" My hands come up to cover my face, trying to limit the embarrassment of him watching me fall apart twice in the last twelve hours. I don't need him to be the audience for this misery, and I don't need the criticism for it.

His hands close around my wrists, not quickly in a way of reprimand, but slowly as one brushes hair from someone's face. (I really read a lot of romance novels.) His fingers wrap around my wrists, and I'm reminded how large they are. He draws my hands down with the same firmness I felt from him last night. The message in the movement is clear, that he has decided I can't hide, and he will sit here as long as I need to accept that truth.

"Perfect question," he says, with a broad, almost comical smile across his face. "Marry me." The words are a quiet impossibility that for a full three seconds I don't process them. They arrive as sound, as a vibration of his voice and my brain cannot fathom what they actually mean.

"I... I'm sorry?"

"Marry me."

Repeated with the same calm, smile less prominent now. But said as plainly as he did the first time, as if he is just simply reminding me. It is the most unhinged sentence, truly bonkers question that has ever been spoken in this coffee shop and possibly even in this zip code.

"I can't marry you." The words come out slightly strangled.

"Do you have someone else ready to sign their name on a marriage license?"

"Well, no, not exactly, but—" I regroup my thoughts, the end of the sentence, as he just stares, waiting. "You definitely don't want to marry me."

"Sure I do," he says dismissively. And now I am knocked back. More and more confused by the second.

"Hudson," I say, and realize it might be the first time I've used his name in conversation. "We can't share a wall, you think we can share a life? You've told me on more than one occasion that I'm an inconsiderate—"

"I know what I've said." His reply cuts me off. "And I'm not talking about a life. I'm talking about solving a problem. There are logistics to sort out. But we would keep it up long enough for everyone to get what they want, eventually get a divorce, less than a year if we move quickly, and then we go about our lives."

"What problem could I *possibly* help you solve?" It's not rhetorical, I'm incredibly skeptical that there is anything I could do for him. Why in the world would this man be sitting across from me in a coffee shop on a Sunday proposing marriage? He said it himself, I'm not exemplary and everything in his life seems to be. Unless the problem is introducing color to his wardrobe or how to record an audiobook, I don't think this is anything I can specifically *help*.

"Having a consistent companion for work events would be helpful," he offers, watching and measuring my face based on his reply.

"I'm sure you have no trouble getting a date."

"That's true," he begins. "That's not all." Like that was the toe he dipped in the water. Some kind of foreplay to warm me up to the real ask. "In order to purchase a unit in The Richmond, you need approval from the co-op board. I have plans for the apartment above mine, but I've been denied. More than once." We both happen to glance down and realize my wrists are still wrapped in his hands, holding them steady. I yank them back, thinking how uncomfortable he must have been. He uses his now free grip to slide his phone across the table toward me and it looks like blueprints, the plans he must have. (Seriously, what's that like?)

"Why?"

"They want to reserve it for more serious residents, families." There's a small tick in his jaw, the same one that I have watched from behind the coffee bar for months. "The board's president believes I'm too much of a bachelor, *her word*. She doesn't like my lifestyle."

"I can see how your general," I wave my hand in his direction, "might clash with any living situation where you have to interact with other people." He shakes his head the smallest amount and a hair that is typically brushed back from his face falls gently. "You're being cock-blocked by the co-op board and you really think a wife fixes that?" Out of the corner of my eye, I see Chandler practically climbing over the counter to try and eavesdrop.

"Fiancée, initially." Completely matter of fact. "Then, a wife. Mrs. Saraceno wants a family man with roots, and you." His eyes find mine, and it's as if I can't look away. "You want to remain in this country."

It is the least romantic framing of a proposal in the history of proposals.

"You said you weren't an immigration lawyer."

"I'm not. I do mergers, and I am very good at them." His jaw does the thing, the slight tension, the tick. "You need citizenship. I benefit from the illusion of stability in my personal life."

"And what happens if we get caught?"

"I lose my law license," he says, without flinching. "You get deported. Significant fines for both of us." He's somehow unfazed by the severity of what he just said.

"You say that like it's a reasonable risk."

"I'm a good lawyer, Louisa." It's said without arrogance, as a fact, and that makes me believe it even more. "And you perform as other people for a living, which means you are, by profession, a convincing liar." Somehow in this conversation, I've seen more of him than I have in every encounter we've ever had. I wouldn't call him vulnerable right now, but he is definitely more of a person than just the villain next door.

And somehow, that became my best option.

"Between the two of us, I think we can manage to convince one co-op board and a handful of immigration officials that we're married."

"Yeah, but can we convince them we like each other?"

"We will be like every other married couple then," he says and it sounds like he's speaking from experience.

"How romantic."

Chapter Nine

A RISK AND A LIABILITY

LOUISA

We agreed to meet to discuss the details, because he made it clear, there would definitely be details and we need to *'align on a plan.'* (It sounded like a threat.) Which he then communicated to me by saying (I'm paraphrasing here) *'come over at seven, we'll work through everything then.'* Not *'if you decide yes.'* Not *'assuming you're on board.'* Just seven, dinner included, and bring nothing but yourself. (Implied) He didn't even laugh when I asked him for his address. He ordered another extra-hot americano, two-coffee Sunday (which is new information for Toby) and left. Walked right out the door and back into the Sunday morning, like he hadn't just proposed marriage to me in a coffee shop. Like it was a scheduling matter rather than the single most insane sentence anyone had ever directed at me in my entire adult life.

Chandler slid in next to me as soon as he left, very quietly and with tremendous restraint, asking if I wanted to talk about it. I didn't, because I didn't know what to say about it, mostly and because of the horrible, annoying, completely presumptuous fact that he had already known I would say yes before I had finished thinking it to myself. He probably knew before I sat down. He built the next move on top of the assumption without waiting for confirmation, like he knows the foundation will hold.

The most horrifying part of all, the part that has been living deep in the base of my throat since? He's right.

I was going to say yes. I *am* going to say yes.

Because when you're hanging on the ledge of your life, and someone offers you a hand and a plan, you take both. Even if the hand belongs to Hudson Ellis and the plan is fucking insane.

I left The Double Shot, proposal in hand, anxiety in gut, and spent my afternoon submitting auditions for a stack of non-fiction titles I've been sitting on. Non-fiction is fine. Non-fiction is good, actually. It's earnest and useful, full of harrowing true-life accounts and real people who have successfully figured something out and want to be helpful about it. Characters who exist in the actual world, who made decisions under real pressure and came through the other side. Which, given recent events in my life, feels aspirational in a way I genuinely need right now. (If they did it, so can I. *Right?*)

The thing is, I am better at fiction. (Or I thought I was.)

A romance novel when I have climbed the rising action, and two people who have been furiously denying their feelings for three hundred pages are finally ready to combust. Is there a better feeling? (No, there isn't.) The moment it stops being subtext and becomes holy text, the moment the careful restraint collapses and takes everything with it? I live for that, it's the part of this job that I would do for free (you know what I mean) and in the early years, essentially did. (Sometimes it actually seemed like I was paying them.)

Non-fiction doesn't have that moment, not in the same way. And following Roma's recent (accurate) deeply burrowing-into-my-brain feedback, I've been even more aware that the passion I need to be delivering is lacking some of its former conviction.

The other problem with non-fiction (and I say this with the utmost full professional respect) is that nobody is using wingspan as a euphemism for dick size. Nobody is discussing wingspan at all (maybe a biography on the Wright Brothers), and no one is talking about dick size, period. (Except in an LBJ biography I read once, I'm serious.) The only wingspan I can think of right now belongs to who I am trying to accept as my soon-to-be fake-husband.

So I log the hours in the booth. Record the auditions and send them off.

By six-thirty I've also done a completely productive (and not at all spiraling) amount of light Googling about expired visas. The internet, as always, knows everything and absolutely nothing simultaneously and makes you feel horrible about both. I close seventeen browser tabs without reading them and call that enough preparation for the day.

I show up at his door at seven on the dot. I knock, and he pulls it open like he was already in the hallway, waiting. (Of course he was.)

His apartment smells, as it did last night, like a decision was made and bulk purchased, a curated scent like a five-star hotel. It's not like next door. My apartment is a rotating cast of Home Goods clearance-shelf candles that occasionally create something interesting and more frequently require damage control in the form of another, stronger candle. Today we're working with Pear Pancake, a combo that even at the time I bought it, gave me pause. (But curiosity won out.) This is, as a metaphor for the two of us, so on the nose it barely qualifies as a metaphor at all.

"Come in, sit," he says, already turning back toward the kitchen island before I've fully crossed the threshold of entry. He's different than he was last night, likely because he expected me at his door tonight. Every conversation we have that isn't immediately adversarial catches me off guard, and when it inevitably devolves into the state of reality we know, it's stubbing my toe on a piece of furniture I should have known was there.

I don't sit, I mosey. Circling the far side of the counter instead, trailing my eyes over the kitchen that is pristine. Funny because I've definitely heard him using a blender at two in the morning when I was in the middle of an emotionally devastating breakup scene. You know what doesn't work in that scene? That's right, a blender. At a completely unreasonable blender hour.

"You don't have any appliances," I say.

"They're in the cabinets."

"Who would put their toaster in a cabinet?" I say as I open one to see if I find the right cubby. (I don't.) Just perfectly stacked tupperware, all with matching lids, meanwhile my tupperware collection has been gathered from takeout containers and creates a plastic avalanche every time I open the cabinet door.

"People who don't want to look at a toaster," he says like this was self-evident.

"I've never once thought about *looking* at a toaster..." I take another step and pick another cabinet to check. (Again nothing.) "So what do you do when you want toast?"

He stops straightening what is already straight on the marble island in front of us, and looks at me for the first time since I walked through the door. "I take it out of the cabinet." His face looks offended at the question.

"And then you just... put it back?" My search for the hidden toaster has been unsuccessful so far. (Haven't found this mysterious blender either.)

"Where else would it go?"

"On the counter, like a person." He points diagonally and downward from where he is. I grab the cabinet handle and pull it open for the big reveal.

"AHA!" I exclaim like I found it on my own.

There are six binders lined up in a row. (Who even has six binders lying around?) He has clearly spent his intervening hours doing what I can assume he does with any problem: organizing them into submission. Which should by any right be annoying. (It is, and it's also kind of extraordinary to see his brain work.)

"Your status is already expired," he says, anchoring us to the only thing I know. "An immediate marriage to a citizen, with an application for adjustment of status filed concurrently, addresses the unlawful-presence issue." He looks up. "But only if it's handled quickly."

"How quickly is '*quickly*'?"

"City clerk's office for the license Tuesday. Married by the end of the week." I stare, mouth agape. I don't think I can pull together a grocery list as quickly as he has planned our wedding. (Who am I kidding, I never make a grocery list.) I can't tell whether this is impressive or whether it is the single most alarming thing I've ever heard.

"This week," I repeat, just for clarity of the thing I already know.

"Yes."

"But, Tuesday is in two days."

"I'm aware how calendars work."

"Ass," I say. And it's a flicker of the relationship we actually have. The one where he is a sarcastic asshole, and my existence just annoys him. But I might see the corner of his lips flicker in hopes of being invited to smile, just waiting for a reason, and the subtle warmth of the insult might just be it.

"We'll review these folders together, then take them home to study." He's already sliding the first folder toward me. "Dinner arrives in fifty minutes."

I hoist myself up on the counter and swing my feet. He crosses the kitchen to me in two strides, and now, standing next to me, we are eye level for the first time. He takes my hand in his, and places the other on the small of my back.

"Down," he says flatly.

"You invited me over for dinner and then ordered in?"

"I'm not known in the kitchen for my culinary skills." A small guided push to get me off the marble. He doesn't release my hand until I've landed on my feet. I just sigh at him in response. "Down first, offended later" he says. (What a buzzkill.)

"What are you known for in the kitchen?" My question results in a look from him that actually seems to bloom something devious, so I clarify. "Culinarily. I mean culinarily."

"Scrambled eggs," he responds with the same dry effect he brings to most things.

"I love scrambled eggs," I say under my breath. (And to myself.)

"I heard that." He takes a seat and slides a bar stool out from the island for me. "Sit here so we can begin," he says, like someone's governess. I sit, fold my hands on the marble, and look at the row of folders. I feel the disorientation of being in the most organized room I have ever been in, while entering the most chaotic possible arrangement with the most controlled possible person.

He grips the seat of my stool and slides it closer to him in one smooth motion. I whip my head to him. "Next time," he says, "ask nicely, and I'll make you eggs." And he casually glides the first folder toward me like there's nothing out of the ordinary in this exchange.

A lot of these documents and rules I couldn't understand even if I had a law degree and a translation guide. My name appears in them several times, which is strange, seeing your own name in official documentation. But it's no problem for him.

"The narrative," he says. "We stick to it, no matter what. We've been seeing each other casually for six months. Occasionally still seeing other people. We tell the truth wherever we can, but six months ago we started spending more time together, hiding it from everyone. The friction of being neighbors became—" he pauses, choosing his word carefully "—complicated. We eventually fell in love. I proposed. We've kept it quiet because I had just gotten out of a relationship when this started."

"So had I," I say. "Right before I moved in." He looks up and something shifts almost imperceptibly in his expression, not surprise exactly, more like a piece of information slotting into a place he didn't know was empty. But like with most things, he clears his throat and continues.

"Then the story writes itself. Tell your friends we've been involved for a while. That the fighting was complicated feelings we poorly managed."

I look at him for a long moment. "You want me to tell my best friend that our mutual hostility was actually just pent-up sexual tension."

"It's the most believable part of the whole story."

"I can't lie to Chandler." He might think it's a non sequitur but it's been all I have thought about all day. The thought tucked underneath every other thought, just a face pressed against a window staring me down. "You aren't lying to *your* friend," I say with some strength. It's clear that he considers this before he speaks again.

"*My* friend is also my lawyer, *your* lawyer. What I tell him is protected to an extent, and even so, we both know better than to outright call this what it is. He may strongly assume, but he has plausible deniability, everything he has been told is above board."

I wonder if it's hard for him to lie to the only people he has. And in reading through the folders, I understand the people he has (like me) are in limited supply. The fact that his closest friend (also his lawyer) only *'strongly assumes'* makes me wonder who holds all of his secrets the way Chandler has held mine. I never thought much about his backstory. Honestly, I didn't even think he had one. Maybe in some ways I just assumed the Angry Neighbor™ is who he is to everyone in his life. But the way his friend, (who I've learned is named Lucas) jumped into action to help, to help me, someone he doesn't even know just because of who asked him, tells me that to a select few he is worthy of the most loyal of friendships.

"Isn't it hard for you to lie to people you love?" I ask him. Kicking my shoes off, and pulling my feet up underneath me on the stool.

"No, because I'm not." He keeps writing notes across the papers in front of us. Things to come back to, things we need to do, memorize. I don't know how he's multi-tasking so effectively, then again he seems to do everything so effectively. When I try to multi-task, I get one thing half-done and eventually just lose interest and move to the next.

"Is that some kind of legal loophole?"

"If that's what you need to call it. But just because you can't tell someone the whole truth, doesn't mean you have to lie."

"What does that mean?"

His dark eyes hide under dark lashes, and still I feel like he can look right through me. "I want you to tell her the version of events that protects anyone from being asked to lie under oath." He holds my gaze as he speaks, it's convincing. "There's a difference between a cover story and a lie. The first one keeps people safe, doesn't that matter more than someone's feelings?"

"That is a suspiciously convenient distinction."

"And," he begins, shifting his body, stretching his arm across the counter bringing our torsos closer together, the *pent-up sexual tension*' on full display. (Might just be me.) "Tell me you haven't thought about it?"

I have thought about it. Every time I turn the page of a new script and someone releases a throbbing member or pins the feisty protagonist against a wall, I have thought about it. But that is obviously not what I'm about to say to him.

"I'm told hate-sex is a thing," I say instead. Because I've never had it and because no matter how much he has been wearing me down with this organized, amber-lit, scrambled-eggs charm, he has made it consistently clear that whatever *complicated feelings*' he's had have never been in the direction of affection. (And even less directed at me.)

"Right," he says. Just that. But his eyes stay on mine for a beat longer than the word requires, and there is something in the category of suspiciously convenient distinctions that he is not interested in addressing.

I reach for the folder labeled *Hudson Personal,*' which he has pinned under his arm. He keeps it there, not moving, just watching me with that small trapped smirk, like he's waiting to see what I'll do.

I yank it toward me.

The stool tips.

For one lurching second I feel myself going backward, and then his hand, each time larger than my memory of it, splays across my back and pulls me into stability. We are close and the folder is pressed between us. Like some kind of college drinking game where you can't let it drop. He blinks the moment away, takes the folder from between our torsos. Sets me back on the stool and returns to his seat with composure.

"Homework," he says, sliding it back to me, reestablishing the boundary as if it wasn't the only thing (besides his general disdain for me) separating us a moment ago.

This folder is different from the others we've looked at. It reads less like legal documentation and more like a private investigator's dossier, all his precise handwriting in the corners. His mother's maiden name. His grandmother's name, photos of them together. (She's still living) The schools he attended, the years, the extracurriculars. (Debate team, *of course.*) His coffee order. (Which I already knew.) His deodorant preference. Daily vitamins. His political affiliation. (Don't worry.) A hatred of reality television. A preference for lamps over overhead lighting, which explains why his apartment, for all its minimalism, always sits in soft light that feels counter to everything you would expect of him. That is (against my will) surprisingly comfortable to be in.

I get to the next line, and my head jerks up. "Nerds Gummy Clusters."

"Yes."

"Your favorite candy is Nerds. Clusters." I punctuate the end of the sentence for emphasis.

"And?"

"You don't really give off Nerds Clusters energy." I tell him. He doesn't hop down from the stool, because he definitely doesn't give off *'hop'* energy either. But he steps away from the island and walks towards a drawer in the corner of the kitchen.

"What energy do I give off?" Not a question, a dare to pass judgement. He's rummaging through a drawer, which also takes me aback, because as much as he doesn't seem like a sour-candy guy, he *definitely* doesn't seem like a guy who rummages.

"The kind that suggests the reason you use Sensodyne toothpaste is because the most dentists recommend it." A pause precedes the smirk pulling at his lips, as he turns around and slides a bag of Nerds Clusters across the counter.

"Why would anyone choose a toothpaste that isn't the most recommended?" This smile that he seems to let escape is a habit I never imagined. "The Nerds are non-negotiable," he says rejoining me in his seat as he tears open the bag and pops a few in his mouth before offering them to me.

"I didn't know this was a negotiation," I say, taking some.

"What is it you want, Louisa?" He says my name casual and commanding, like he's used to it, which makes one of us, because I am not.

"I'm just saying, I would have come with a list of demands," I say.

"Do your worst." It's delivered in a tone that is deep and challenging.

"No more interrupting my recording sessions," I say, with conviction I am proud of. "I record at any hour. You get earplugs."

He narrows his eyes. It looks less like annoyance and more like he's re-evaluating something. "Fine. No screaming past midnight."

"Same goes for you," I say with full eye contact. "I'd prefer not to hear your guests while I'm trying to sleep."

"I wouldn't do that," he says, and the face of annoyance returns, almost looking insulted. He takes a steading breath, preparing himself to deliver something I think we both already knew but hadn't said out loud yet. "No dating, no other partners. We can't risk it. It would nullify everything. So if you have anything *going* on with anyone," he says, but he must know that if I'm saying yes to this, then clearly I don't have anyone else.

He has suddenly introduced new words into his vocabulary,

and every time he uses them it comes through at a different frequency than all other words in the sentence. We. Us. Some combined plural state that didn't exist twelve hours ago that feels like a glass door I keep walking into. I should know it's there, but every single time my heart jumps as if to say, *'Did you hear that'* and each time, I pretend I don't.

"You gonna be able to last?" I tease. It might be easier for me, I've been single for half a year now. But my single and his single look very different from everything I've seen.

"Usually," he says with his eyes locked on mine. Before shifting back to the negotiations I'm sure he is going to draft into a contract. "You're officially my permanent plus-one. Every dinner meeting, colleague's wedding, or fundraising gala. You're there with bells on," Hudson says, adding another requirement to the ever-growing pile.

"I LOVE bells," I begin excitedly, "I don't know if you remember at the building Christmas party, my skirt had—"

"Wasn't there." (Of course he wasn't.)

"You really should be more neighborly, you might not have to enter into a marriage just to get an apartment," I tease.

"We are getting married, it isn't a marriage. It's an arrangement."

"Good, because I'm keeping my apartment." He hadn't implied I wouldn't, but I say it anyway because twenty-four hours ago I couldn't have described who I am or what I'm doing and I need to hear it out loud. "It's got my studio and it's the first place I've ever seen myself staying longer than six months."

"On paper, fine, but you'll need to spend nights here, especially in the beginning so that it's believable. Too many people in this building pay attention."

"Then I get my own room... and bathroom."

"Obviously."

"And, no lying," I say. The irony of a statement that's only needed because we are entering into an agreement that's built entirely on a lie. "To each other," I add quickly. "The government, and everyone else we know, fine, yes, necessary, that's the whole point. But you and me," I point between us, "I want the truth."

"Okay, Louisa," he says. It looks like he might want to disagree, maybe refine the point with another clarification between a cover story and a lie, but he doesn't. "Between me and you, no lying."

I put out my hand. (A handshake is the right move, right?) His eyes drop to it for the splittest of seconds before dragging themselves back up to my face, but then he slips his large grip into mine. It doesn't move the way a handshake should, but his hand is warm and certain, even without the symbolic up-and-down gesture meant to indicate the *'binding agreement'* of this thing.

We spend the next half hour on the small things. The specific, granular, intimate details that any real couple accumulates without effort. His preferred side of the bed, *the left*. I tell him mine. (The middle.) I tell him about *my* favorite snack, which requires a bit of a drive to procure and which I am both willing, and now apparently required, to make for him to try them. I tell him about Theo, and about my parents. Not just the move and the parts that got us here, but the underbelly of it. The dynamics that don't fit on a legal form, but my husband would know.

He listens without checking his phone, without formulating his response while I'm still talking. Just absorbing it. It's attentive in a way that looks practiced but no less sincere.

"I never noticed an accent," he says, when I finish.

"I don't really have one, I grew up here. Whatever's left is more about the house I grew up in than the country." I sit up slightly, offering him something. "But sometimes, when I'm very tired, or drunk, or talking to my brother, the occasional word slips out."

"Now that you mention it, I always thought it was weird you told me to *'bugger off'* once," he says. "I assumed you were method acting."

"Oh yeah, also sometimes when I'm angry," I confirm. He lets out a breath, resigned to the fact that even if it's easy to momentarily forget, our interactions have never looked like this.

The doorman calls, there's a knock at the door, and Hudson returns with two pizza boxes. He sets them on the counter between us, and I am, completely against my will and better judgment, unreasonably charmed. (Stop being so easily impressed, Lou!)

And then, he opens the top box and I see the logo.

"This place is my favorite."

"I know," he says, taking a slice of pepperoni, which is also the reason this place is my favorite, small, crispy, and a generous amount of pepperoni.

"We haven't even gotten to my folders yet."

"You order it once a week. It's not the closest, it's not the highest rated." He glances at me sideways. "Process of elimination."

I've dated men who didn't know my coffee order after three months. Hudson learned my beverage before I knew his name. (Oops.) He seems to absorb information differently, knowing parts of me just from proximity and a single day of preparation.

"What happens when the interview comes, if they ask me something I don't know."

"Whatever happens, I'll handle it." There's a momentary beat, and I don't know why, it makes me believe him. He says it with such assurance. Like he has thought through every risk, '*whatever.*' Which is why every question I've posed, he already has an answer for.

There are so many what ifs with all of this. *What if I forget something? What if they don't believe us? What if we can't survive being in the same apartment? What if the visa is denied anyway?* For every question I ask, he has a prepared answer.

We eat the entire box of pizza as he answers every version of '*what if*'... except perhaps the most important. (Also the most unlikely.)

"What if," I say, "you fall in love with me?" He looks up,

working out how to treat a question like that. The kind that sounds like a joke but has a room behind it. "I've seen enough rom-coms to know how this could go."

"That's a risk you'll have to accept," he says.

"And what if," I say, more quietly, in the key of *this is obviously hypothetical*, "I fall in love with you?"

The corner of his mouth flattens. He looks at me with the full, focused stillness that is overwhelming to me, but I can't break the contact of our gaze. The quick electric current normally pulsing between us, slows so he can answer.

"That," he says, "would be too big a liability." The words don't carry cruelty, they arrive honest and unapologetic, the way most of his words do, which has always been easier to be angry at than to sit with. I look at the shape of what he's actually said, which is not that won't happen but that will be a problem if it does.

"Fine, I won't fall in love with you." (Easy enough, right?)

Chapter Ten

LICENSE-TO-WED DAY

LOUISA

Bathroom mirrors like this are designed to show you where you missed a spot shaving even though you've already left the house, point out the mustard stain from your cafeteria lunch that you didn't notice, or confirm that yes, that *is* your first white hair, what an ideal time to find it. Fluorescent lighting is a beacon for every single flaw you'd managed to forget about and illuminate it with the enthusiasm of a prosecuting attorney. (Who some people might be in here preparing to face.)

I have been standing at this public bathroom sink for seven minutes, I know because I have checked my phone once a minute, and each time I have put it back in my bag without doing anything useful with it, like texting Chandler, calling my brother to come get me like it's a party in high school where the girls are being mean and the boys are being forward, or even Googling whether it is possible to dissolve a marriage-license application before the ink dries. Technically we haven't signed anything yet, I could totally walk out of this bathroom, past the suits (lawyers) and silks (brides), past the clerk's window that smells like wet umbrellas and bureaucratic resignation, and just... keep going. But I don't want to go anywhere, that's the whole point.

I look at myself in the speckled mirror, which makes this reality look just a little bit worse. The eyelet sundress, embroidered daisies, puff sleeves, ruffled hem. Chandler said it was a must. (I already had it.) *'You're getting a marriage license,'* she said. *'You're not renewing your gym membership.'* She believes even the smallest moments deserve to be dressed for, which is very Chandler and also the reason I am currently standing here in something bridal-themed while my stomach performs a slow, sickening bungee jump in the direction of my feet. (Ready to fall right out my butt.)

Even dropping my gaze a fraction of an inch would require me to acknowledge the dress and that would have me acknowledge—

The heavy door swings open and in bursts a gust of air from the hallway and deeply intertwined laughter accompanying it. I've been standing here long enough that more than a dozen people have come and gone. And I am a ghost in the background of everyone else's traffic tickets and *I do*s. (Including my own.)

Two women tumble toward the sinks like they've been laughing since before they got here and will still be laughing well after they leave, which is the kind of energy I would normally immediately want to be near. The taller one is in a cream jumpsuit, lace bodice, silk legs that move like water, a bouquet of dahlias in one hand and a Trader Joe's tote in the other, which she is currently excavating with the bouquet hand in a feat of coordination that I find genuinely impressive. She produces a lipstick from the bag, and hands it off. Then, in one continuous fluid motion, spears a loose ash-blonde curl back into her updo with a bobby pin and pops open a tin of Cinnamon Altoids, tossing a couple in her mouth.

I watch them through the speckled silver of the mirror, the filter of age and water spots, and still they are radiant in a way that has nothing to do with the lighting, because the lighting in here is genuinely criminal.

I watch all of this happen the way you watch someone parallel park perfectly on the first try, with complete admiration (jealously) and just a little bit of personal shame and your own deficiency. (Again, jealousy.) I want to talk to them, which is not unusual, I want to talk to most people, it is my greatest, and most unrelenting quality. Because they are the main characters of this movie and every frame is theirs. While I am Woman at Sink Number Two, the blur in the background that the editor almost cut. I am not the main character, I never am. I can voice one, but never, truly, be her.

Not the way these two are.

The brunette, in a floor-length lace gown with a leather jacket slung over her shoulders like she refused to completely surrender to the occasion, leans toward the mirror and applies the lipstick, one so dark it could only be described as oxblood if you were being generous and kiss of death if you were being accurate. Her new wife (or maybe soon-to-be wife, I'm making it up without Toby and Chandler, so your guess is as good as mine) watches her do it the way people watch things they can't believe they get to have. Like she's checking, quietly, that this is still real. (What is that like?)

I genuinely can't fathom it as I am about to enter an entirely fake relationship, with a very real problem.

My stomach does another bungee jump, harder this time. I am either about to faint or hurl the breakfast I pretended to eat. Either way, I'm gripping the sink for dear life. But them? These two probably had some big, sweeping proclamation of love, a proposal where they could imagine their futures, ones they've discussed in fantasy while tangled naked in each other, not just agreed to for logistics. I've barely had a day to decide what to do, and I've just handed my future over to someone whose reason for ensuring its success is so he can have a date to a few parties and qualify for a bigger apartment.

Our priorities couldn't be more different, but what we do share is mutually assured destruction if this fails. Which means, as far as the rest of the world is concerned, *we're in love*. Not the reality, where we are the abject opposite.

But I can recognize what this look is between them, I've read it described endlessly. I know it because I have read it out loud in a soundproofed booth (depends who you ask) and made it sound like the most inevitable thing in the world.

And I have never had anyone look at me like that.

Not Ben, certainly. Ben was charming in the beginning, which works until it doesn't, which in our case was approximately eleven months longer than it should have. Who said *'I love you'* early and often with the same energy he brought to *'I'll be there by eight and I definitely didn't forget.'* (He always forgot.) Who I moved in with weeks after meeting him, with the breathless, *stupid* optimism, because I confused momentum for intention.

Then after months of wondering if I was talking to a wall that just learned to nod, I sat on his floor at three in the morning having a panic attack while he slept. That week I learned about the apartment at The Richmond and I moved days later. And suddenly, it became a place I saw myself, not just the place I had a few drawers assigned.

The Richmond, however, also came with Hudson Ellis.

Who is, at this exact moment, somewhere on the other side of this bathroom door, in a queue for a marriage license, checking his watch, waiting for me.

The thing I keep not-thinking about (liar), the thought I keep picking up and setting back down like a cup of tea too hot to hold, is that Ben never knew me. He always ordered from whatever the top-rated pizza place was, even though their sauce was too sweet and their pepperoni was large and never crispy.

Hudson, who has not once been anything other than a thorn in my side since the day I moved in, knew my favorite pizza place and not because I told him. Because he paid attention to my silence. For reasons I have no capacity to worry about right now, but still.

He made a full dossier of a person and handed it over like a key, it's not out of love, I know that. (Obviously.) But here is the thing about being protected by someone who is doing it for their own reasons: the outcome is the same. That's what matters here. It's the same reason I haven't given Chandler, Theo, Toby, anyone in my life I care an ounce about, the full, honest story about our proposal, because while I can't swoop in and save anyone, I can protect them from the mess I am making.

The brunette in the leather jacket catches my eye in the mirror. She has the lipstick done now, dark and perfect, and her wife is still looking at her with an expression I will let fill my mind when recording a love scene later.

But, the sound of his throat clearing cuts through the romance as the door cracks open, and there he is, or rather, there the shadow of him is. He stays hidden behind the heavy wood door, but even under the cruelest of industrial lights, his outline is visible on the wall. The sharpness of his jaw, of his nose, he's here to remind me that it's time.

"Our number is coming up," Hudsons says. Not with any excitement, just as if he was ordering a ½ pound of extra-thinly sliced roast beef from a deli counter. (Which *is* his preference on deli meat, it was in the folder.) He calls for me through the door matter-of-factly, task-oriented, because that is exactly what we are here to do.

With that, my new sink-standing friend pops the top on the Altoids and extends them to me. "Make sure that kiss is spicy," she says, with a wink. I take the mint, square my shoulders, and look at myself one last time in the foggy, speckled, horrifically unflattering mirror.

"You are going to be Hudson Ellis's wife," I tell my reflection. My reflection looks like she needs a moment, but she doesn't get one. (And neither do I.)

This is a building that has witnessed too much paperwork to

feel anything about any of it. Which is fine, because I feel enough for both of us. (Mostly anxiety.)

Hudson is already back in the queue when I find him, looking like this is just another appointment for him. (I guess it is.) Charcoal suit, because of course, collar precise and expression neutral, bordering on brooding, probably because even if I am dressed bridal themed, he is just doing this on a scheduled lunch break.

"I was having a moment," I say as I step next to him in line, we're already near the front. Meaning another *moment* and he would be stepping up to the window without me.

"We don't have time for moments."

"Noted," I say. "I'll be sure to schedule them with your assistant moving forward."

"You're fidgeting," he says. His hand finding the small of my back, guiding me forward in the queue, and I can feel the tension in his palm. The slight pressure that means settle, and I know this because I have been studying his hands for approximately seventy-two hours, even though this isn't the moment they are going to start quizzing me. His hands, and what he does with them, also isn't likely on the question list. When you marry someone (even fakely) you need to understand the full vocabulary of them, and his hands are, it turns out, a full language I'm becoming fluent in. And he doesn't even know he's speaking it.

"I'm allowed to be nervous on my wedding day," I say.

"It's not your wedding day. It's your License-to-Wed day. Different thing."

I stop moving and he nearly walks into me as I whip my face to stare at him. "Was that a joke? Did you just make a joke?"

"I don't know what you're talking about." He continues us forward as we are only one number away from next up.

"This *wholeee* time, you've had a funny setting, and you've been withholding it!" I wonder if he can see the joy on my face from this revelation.

"Keep your voice down," he says, but the corner of his mouth hasn't settled. It appears and then gets managed back into composure with ease like he decided that humor is something he only allows himself in very specific conditions. I am apparently one of the conditions, though perhaps only today, on our *'license-to-wed'* day.

"Do others know about this?" I'm practically giddy in a way that is distracting me from the ridiculousness of where we are currently standing and for what purpose.

"A select few," he says dryly.

"I don't even know what to do with this information... Wait," I practically scream with excitement. "What other settings do you have besides grumpy and funny? Is there a third, oh my god, is there a whole dial of options?! This wasn't in the file."

His hand slides from the small of my back up along the curve of my spine with a slowness that feels like it's drawing electric from my skin, and he leans down until his mouth is close enough to my ear that I feel the warmth of it before I hear the words, in a voice I have only previously heard through drywall and in the unhelpful early hours of the morning. (Or in my imagination.)

"If you're good, Louisa, maybe you'll find out." And that shuts me up, which I know was his intention, because he's used this tactic before. (Though not so bluntly.) But for all the tension that exists between us, it's a fine line between *turned on* and *I hate your guts*. (At least for me.)

Fine, there's at least one more setting of Hudson's personality that I will never get to fully experience.

The line moves forward and I wonder if all these people love each other. I wonder if people are looking at us and wondering the same thing. Or maybe that's just what love looks like from the outside, two people moving forward in the same line. Trying to get to the final goal of completing paperwork and getting a stamp of approval.

"Names," the clerk says, without looking up from her screen. She seems like she has been entirely unbothered by any human drama that occurs on the other side of her plexiglass window for the last thirty years and intends to remain so. And just like he promised (did he promise?) when asked a question, he takes it.

"Hudson James Ellis and Louisa James Evans," he says, answering for both of us.

The clerk looks up. Just slightly. "Huh," she says. "Look at that. Meant to be." Like this was a momentary break from monotonous stamping of licenses and instead checked some version of a bingo card she plays by herself behind the plexiglass. And then she just moves on.

While James is *now* a cool-girl celebrity name, for me, it's the name my father was never able to give the second son he wanted. So they settled for it being my middle name.

"First marriage for both?" the clerk asks.

"Yes," he answers again.

Hudson doesn't flinch as she asks clarifying questions, not to confirm anything for immigration, just to complete this transaction. His hand finds mine on the counter. (For the audience, maybe for my nerves.)

"Groom on the left, bride on the right," she says as she slides a form through the plexiglass slot. He fills out his side with a quick, aggressive hand. I expect him to slide it to me, but he doesn't. He just moves to the right. Filling each box with as much confidence as he did his own, handing me the pen to sign, which I do, and then slipping it all back to the clerk. (Almost like I contributed.)

"Everything seems in order," she says. Slamming the stamp down to indicate by the state and this random government employee, we can be married. "Congratulations," she says, entirely dry and devoid of any real celebration, already looking past us. "You have twenty-four hours before you can legally marry. The license is valid for sixty days," she says, a rinse-and-repeat button she hits with each new couple she calls to the window.

And that's it. We step away from the window and the state has decided that we are a legal possibility.

I don't know what I expected to feel. Something, surely. But the lobby just continues being a lobby, people with their own forms, their own appointments, their own reasons for starting their day in a building that smells like damp wool. The world doesn't register the seismic shift of me (Louisa James Evans) becoming a legal possibility in the context of him (Hudson James Ellis.)

But here we are.

"Should we kiss?" I say. I don't know why I say it, the nerves, probably. The cumulative weight of the last few days pressing up against the absurdity of the moment, looking for somewhere to go.

"Now is not the time, Louisa," he says, his tone is short and flat and clicked back into the Angry Neighbor™ I know.

I don't decide to do this before it happens, but I step into him. A hug he is not offering and has never offered and would probably not have predicted as an outcome of this particular errand. I just wrap my arms around him, carefully, with gratitude, as my cheek finds the lapel of his jacket. And he doesn't move at all.

"Thank you," I say. I probably should have said it sooner. I know he says there are reasons this benefits him as well, and yes, I'm sure I will have to pay the piper when the time comes. But for now, we are here for me.

Then I feel it, the exhale, a long and slow one released against the top of my head. He pulls me the smallest possible increment closer, it's the split second tightening of a hug being returned.

"Louisa," he says, into the crown of my head. I tilt my chin up to see him looking down at me through his lashes, a setting on his dial I haven't identified.

He clears his throat and steps back, gently. Reaches into his jacket pocket and holds out a key. "Here, you'll need this."

Chapter Eleven

SOMETHING BORROWED

LOUISA

Chandler drags me to Timeless Velvet, a vintage store that we frequent, usually more for a retro knit, or a fun piece of mercury glass which one day might give me lead poisoning.

It's walls of old lace and florals, and smells like that, the memory of someone's grandma's garden. Not any one particular flower, but the memory of a garden once tended, now just the fragrance untethered from its original source. Grandmas also notoriously douse themselves in any floral scent they find, so it may actually be *that* I'm smelling. While the rack of sequin pants near the window catches the afternoon light and throws it back across the hardwood floor in tiny fractured pieces, little disco planets orbit nothing but my feet.

We are on a very distinct mission. Having worn my one wedding-adjacent outfit earlier. (Still wearing it, actually.) But that means that when we show up to the Justice of the Peace's office, I'll have nothing to wear that isn't in my usual wardrobe of clothing. It's not that I'm looking for something that screams *bride*, because I most certainly do not. But I think for the purposes of

Immigration, having the look of someone happy to be getting married definitely won't hurt.

"What about this?" Chandler holds up something that is more sleeve than dress.

"No way, I like my arms," I say, as I do a serpentine motion from fingertip to fingertip. "I don't think that's me." She agrees with a nod of the head, holding the length of the sleeve against her arm to assess.

'What about this?' is about the only question she has really asked me today. Here's the thing about Chandler: she is genuinely trying. She drove us here in her car (which means I now have a perfume of acrylic paint and Febreze) and she made a playlist for us to listen to on the drive over to *'hype us up.'* (Which ran the gamut of everything from "Marry You" by Bruno Mars to "January Wedding" by the Avett Brothers. Subtle, huh?) Which, I'll admit, even knowing full well this is a completely fake marriage, it worked more than it should. She had a lot of questions, even doubt when I first told her. She didn't understand how everything changed overnight. But she's someone who loves to believe in love, so that is what she's choosing to do. And now, she's moving through racks of dead women's wardrobes without asking the question I think she is absolutely dying to ask.

'Are you sure about this?'

Perhaps she's holding herself back in an attempt at self preservation. (Or maybe blind faith in me, because I think she's perhaps one of the only to have it.) Really, it's because the love she believes in above all else? Our friendship. She has decided that what I need right now is not the question, but the company.

Which makes the fact that I have not told her the entire honest truth even worse. I told her the version that protects her (just like Hudson said) and I think it held. I think she believes me, or believes in me, enough.

My phone vibrates in my purse, and I pull it out to retrieve a message from my soon-to-be husband. (I'm trying on the term for size like I am these dresses.)

ANGRY NEIGHBOR™

Dinner when you get home

(I really need to change his contact name.)

The word home hits with some discomfort. He deployed it so casually, as if we've been sharing one for years, when in fact all we are sharing is an agreement, and previously it has only been a wall and resentment. As if this is just the natural order of things, him thinking about dinner and me being the person he thinks about it for.

Maybe it's strategic, for the paper trail. *'Look, here's the text message where I asked my wife about dinner, see the timestamp, see the domesticity of it.'* That would be him, intentionally, logically, thoughtfully doing everything he needs to make this appear legitimate.

"How about this one?" She holds up a long cotton gown, doing a light spin with it to showcase its flow, but I just shake my head and the boho nightgown goes back on the rack. It could have been cool with the right accessories, maybe even a flower-crown. But I don't think Hudson screams *floral guy*, a preference for things much more purposeful. It also could have washed out my skin and made me look like a Victorian child that died from cholera and came back to haunt him from the grave.

dinner sounds good :) working up an appetite trying to find the perfect outfit for our wedding *bride emoji*

ANGRY NEIGHBOR™

Wear whatever you want, Louisa

Daisy crown it is

ANGRY NEIGHBOR™

I'll call the florist

> What are you planning on wearing, suit, suit,
> or suit

ANGRY NEIGHBOR™

You ruined my favorite tie, so that's out

> You have a favorite tie? That wasn't in the
> folders

ANGRY NEIGHBOR™

Retired it after an unsanctioned licorice tea
baptism

(Oops.)

> Pickings are slim, I might need to borrow it

ANGRY NEIGHBOR™

Just wear your overalls

"This one?" Chandler asks again, pulling my attention from the texts, which were alarmingly normal. (Despite the fact we were talking about our wedding.)

Each time Chandler asks my opinion, it's just slightly more defeated than the last. She holds up a silver sequin jumpsuit that's magnificent. (For someone else.) Then a white tulle dress, three sizes wrong, but she held it up with such excitement and hope that I instinctively said yes just to make her happy, but even that went back to the rack.

With each possibility pulled from the rack, I stood in front of the small mirror in the dressing room and looked at myself in other people's histories. Every time I did up a bow or a button, or Chandler pulled up the retro-zipper (even did up the laces of a corset), I felt like I was wearing a costume. And the small voice in the back of my head relentlessly continued to point out, it's because I am.

I am dressing up as someone's wife.

I have known this from the beginning (seventy-two hours ago), but what is coming into focus no matter how vintage (discolored) the mirror is, is that I don't know that I *want* it to feel that way.

I run my fingers along the rack across the silk and polyester, across something stiff that might be brocade, all of it so dense with accumulated occasion, other women who stood in other mirrors and decided yes, this one, this is who I'm going to be at this moment. (Not me, not yet.)

All it took was a single form and a rubber stamp to say we are eligible to get married, to get married to *each other.* Shows how little they know about either of us, but we walked out of there with a license to wed. And by we, I mean Hudson, obviously he is the one responsible for it, because as we've learned I am not to be trusted with important paperwork.

I slide over another section of hangers, the pink taffeta is enormous and ridiculous and parts the rack like it's been waiting its whole life for an audience. While I know with certainty it's the farthest thing from a wedding dress I can imagine, I split the hangers on the rack to see it properly, parting the pink taffeta sea. It requires a level of center of attention I'll just never be comfortable with. Even on my fake wedding day. (Or I guess it's a real wedding day, fake marriage.)

But there, on the floor, having slipped from its hanger and given up on being found, is a soft cream-colored dress bundled on the floor. Small and overlooked in the way that things become when they've been waiting too long. I crouch to pick it up and it unfolds in my hands, awakening from hibernation.

"Chan." My voice comes out quiet, afraid someone else might claim her before we've even gotten acquainted. "I think I found something."

I hold it out in front of me, it's short, kind of mod. Not traditionally bridal, but in the right color scheme that will work for a courthouse wedding. Maybe in another life it was a cocktail dress, hanging on the body of someone glamorous hosting a party in their very mid-century home. It has clean lines, but also, there's humor, like we are sharing an inside joke.

Chandler's head appears from the dressing-room curtain, one shoulder bare, the velvet drape clutched to her collarbone, clearly not dressed but too excited to wait to see what I may have found. The excitement she may hear in even the whisper of my voice begins to dissolve the held-back question of hers, turning it into something that looks more like hope.

"Hold it up!" she says excitedly. (See? Hype girl.)

I grip each strap and lift it against my torso. It smells like it has been here longer than it lived in someone's closet, who knows how long it was in a puddle on the ground, whatever life it had before this shop, it has long since finished remembering. The color is a soft cream, whether by design or by time I can't tell, but it's beautiful all the same. There are small pearls flooding the hem that break out into clusters traveling upward, fanning out across the base of the dress like something growing, thinning as they climb until they dissolve midway into plain satin. And like a snow flurry across the landscape of pearls, the softest single feathers sprout. Not boastful, but a gentle, joyful reminder that this monochrome dress is anything but dull.

Chandler is very still. "Oh," she says, just that. But it's her face that gives her away. My hype-girl stunned to silence, and we both know this is it. I look at the dress in my hands and think about the woman who wore it before, whoever she was. Maybe I will make her proud.

———

The key is new enough that it still catches slightly in the lock, the way new keys do before they've learned the shape of where they live. (It's me, I am the key.) I push the door open with my shoulder, the bag with the dress tucked against my chest

He's already here, in the kitchen where he seems to spend most of his time, which is ironic for a man who isn't known for a lot *'culinarily.'* He doesn't look up when I come in, but he also doesn't look surprised, like the sound of my key in his lock is already a thing that makes sense to him. He just learned a new word, and suddenly it belongs in the vocabulary of his life.

I don't know what to do with that thought, so I put it on the shelf next to the toaster. (The *cabinet*, sorry.)

"What are you making?" I ask, dropping my purse on the entry table. (Bad luck to put it on the floor.) But the dress bag stays in my hand.

"Scrambled eggs," he says, with a quick glance over his shoulder to see me, getting ready to crack one in with flawless timing, even though I'm no less than twenty minutes later than I said I'd be. (And he seems to know it.)

"In a pot?"

"Talk to your countrymen about that." I hop up on the counter and kick off my shoes, which I know he hates, which is exactly why I do it. I swing my legs and his jaw tightens at the sight of it. But he's carefully scrambling eggs in a way he can't abandon to push me down. (Again, the reason I do it.)

"Gordon Ramsey," I laugh, "screams at people for sport, so I'd choose your allies carefully... Actually, he might be right up your alley."

The corner of his mouth tugs on his lips, wanting to release a smile, one he seems to let sneak through. I watch it happen and look away before he can catch me, because the minute he knows I get joy from something he does, I'll never see it again. He plates the eggs and takes them to the island. He has a perfectly good dining table, even though I doubt he ever uses it. And yet, it remains set like he needs to be prepared for some kind of impromptu dinner party. (I doubt the guests I've seen are here for dinner.)

"If you want dinner, you have to get down," he says. I consider arguing (for about three seconds), which is about how long it takes the smell of perfectly made scrambled eggs to dismantle my entire position, so I hop down. Some battles aren't worth it, they are worth exactly one plate of Gordon Ramsay eggs. Which are, I'll admit (with great reluctance), perfect.

"Okay, these are actually good," I say, as I take another bite of the soft, folded eggs.

"You sound surprised."

"I am surprised. Pleasantly." I take another bite. "I know you said you could make eggs. I didn't know you meant you could *make* eggs."

"Those are the same sentences."

"It is categorically not the same thing," I say, borrowing his own words, in a voice meant to mock his own. And this time the smile doesn't get managed. It runs right through the front gate of his control, just for a second, real and unguarded, and I feel it land without permission (his or mine) somewhere in the center of my chest.

He picks up his own fork and doesn't say anything, and I let him not say anything, and we eat. This is new, not just the eating, we have eaten together before. But that had purpose and agenda and somewhere to point itself, this is just dinner, or breakfast. (It's breakfast for dinner, which I love.)

"What's in the bag?" Not asking it as a question, exactly, even though it is and his inflection should go up at the end, but there's no oral question mark, he asks questions like they are facts he's decided to surface. I look at the dress bag I draped across the stool next to me.

"Nothing." I adjust it to make sure it stays balanced. "Just a dress."

"For Wednesday."

"Ready to put the *wed* in Wed-nes-day" I say.

"Technically, the *wed* is silent," he counters. And the more we speak I can see how quickly his mind moves. He sets down his fork, wipes his hands as if he's about to do something precious, looks at me, and says two words. "Show me."

"You don't want to see a dress."

"Your wedding dress, I absolutely do." He's watching me,

waiting, and he looks like he has the patience to wait me out, which is annoying because he is very good at waiting and I am very bad at being waited out. Especially as the amber at the center of his eyes catches the lamp light and it always feels like I can see it move, see myself in the reflection of it. Until he blinks back into himself, and remembers he was supposed to look away.

I unzip the dress bag, exposing it, and in this light it's just as beautiful as when I saw it the first time. (This time much less crumpled on the floor.) The pearls catch the light and throw them back in small soft pieces. And he looks at it with a focus that does not perform the casualness it probably should. Instead I see his throat bob, as he swallows hard. Pressing his lips together.

"Good," he says, reaching for a glass of water.

"Glad it meets your approval," I say to him. "Don't worry, I think you're *beautiful*," I whisper to the dress as I tuck it back into the hanging bag.

"So do I." His voice is lower, softer in tone, saying nothing else, and yet, it feels like more.

After dinner he rinses the plates (of course he does) before putting them in the dishwasher, and as part of our arrangement marriage (get it, like arranged marriage?), I agreed to sleep here, consistently. I'll use my apartment for recording, for anything else, but given the attention to detail he lives his life with, and the intensity with which Mrs. Saraceno watches his front door, we knew this was the best option.

I am trailing behind him the way I do when I'm somewhere new and my feet are more curious than the rest of me. (Who am I kidding, I am also curious.) We walk through the main space, past the dining room that is probably lonely and jealous of the kitchen island, and down the short hallway that leads to one of the three bedrooms. Stopping in front of the door.

"Your room," he says as he joins me at the door. "Go on, open it."

I turn the knob and I step inside, and he's behind me.

This room looks like Nancy Meyers designed it on a really

good day after a phone call with someone she loves. (And a glass of wine.) The duvet is botanical, subtle soft greens and creams that sneak through, a whisper of something growing in a place where nothing is supposed to grow, which feels, now that I'm standing here, like a description of exactly what is happening in this apartment. The windows are offensively large, and there are curtains, not just blinds. This room is designed, intentionally. I won't say for me, but he definitely made sure any guests (that don't spend the night in his bed) have somewhere comfortable to drift off to sleep and dream. (About him.) We share a wall, this man and I, this is the same building, on the same floor, he and I have to take the same elevator, we have shared plumbing! I live in a small, makeshift one-bedroom, and he lives like this?! (Well, not like this, this is for *guests.)*

This whole room suggests thoughtfulness, not in utility but real, sincere comfort.

He's standing in the doorway as I mosey. (As I do.)

"Did you always have this duvet?" I ask, examining the botanical print as I run my hand across it, and it's fluffy and soft in a way I want to be swallowed whole. I wonder if this is what his bed is like, the kind of multiple-marshmallow-level duvets that let you sink into them. (He doesn't give a *'sink into a bed'* vibe.)

He lets a breath pass between us as I drag my hand around the bed, walking across the room where there's a perfect reading chair and ottoman, and a throw blanket, which is the first one I've seen here. (He also doesn't look like the *'I get cold, pass me a throw blanket'* kind of guy.)

"No."

"Hmmm," I say. Just that, because if I say anything else I will either laugh or cry at this situation, and I genuinely don't know which, and neither seems appropriate right now.

He didn't do this to make me happy, I know that, for whatever internal jury is currently deliberating in my brain. He is a master of strategy.

"I couldn't listen to you call my decorating style 'institutional' again," he says like it explains the thoughtfulness away. (I did do that, didn't I.) "Bring whatever you need," he says. "Books, clothes, whatever makes it work. Your apartment next door will be yours, but we will call this our bedroom to anyone who asks."

I turn around to look at him as he's leaning against the door-frame with his arms loosely crossed, and he looks almost (almost) relaxed, which is so rare on him it reads as a different feature entirely. (I wonder how to get him to the *'relaxed'* setting, that feels like a good one to know.)

"Hang your Wednesday dress in the closet." There's something about the casual way of him that warms me and I'm not prepared for it. My Wednesday (aka Wedding) dress has about seven days to pull herself together. We may have made progress today with the license, but we have a week before we stand in front of the Justice of the Peace to make it official. So I have one week to stop looking at him like that.

Chapter Twelve

YOU HAVE A GRAMS?!

HUDSON

She hasn't moved into the *'guest'* room officially, but each time she comes over, which has been every day since Tuesday, she brings more things over. One. At. A. Time. We agreed, she'll live here while we do this song and dance for Immigration and *everyone else.* And last night is the second night she's spent here, but I think she's waiting for the wedding to make it *'official.'* All the paperwork is ready, it was just getting an appointment, which we secured for Wednesday, less than a week away.

The longer we can make it seem like she's been living here, the better. And while it would be easy enough to keep her next door, there's something comforting about her under the same roof. Though I wouldn't admit that thought to anyone but myself in the shower, and even then, that's not the thought of her I have as I turn the water to ice to try and shake it out of my head, and well— enough, Hudson, *enough.*

While immigration interviews are intense and require a level of intimacy like *'what color is your husband's toothbrush'* and *'how many pillows are on the bed,'* the proximity of her here, in my apartment, *in my home*, is intimate in a way no one else has been.

Which is saying a lot, considering the *'guests'* I have usually don't sleep in a separate room. If they sleep at all. Which is ironic because the only time Louisa really spends here is to sleep.

Her bedroom door left ajar, yielding to the hallway, *to me.* Strange that now, even asleep, she isn't trying to put every possible lock and barrier between us. Open just enough to let the air move, not enough to be an invitation.

I'm not lingering.

I was passing by.

The distinction matters less than I'd like it to, given that I've stood here longer than passing requires. But there's the smallest light creeping out from the crack in the doorway. Too warm for a phone screen, too low for a lamp. I shouldn't look, but against the better judgement I used to have, *the same judgement that seems to have flown out the fucking window when she showed up at my door,* I tilt my head slightly to catch a view through the sliver of space left open.

The night light is small, from the far corner plugged into the wall. And for some reason, that makes me smile. She doesn't hide her vulnerability, at least not well. But she's open to everyone she encounters. There's no one she meets whose name she doesn't learn, on the chance they may see each other again. And when they do, they greet her like an old friend. And yet, here is this small hidden thing that no one else would know. Just me, lucky enough to see it. A quiet, private vulnerability plugged into a corner. Whatever the reason, habit, comfort, or fear, it's a secret she hadn't thought to hide from me, or perhaps she just didn't think I'd be looking. *Which I shouldn't be.*

I feel like a thief, standing here in the hallway, stealing a glimpse of her that doesn't have a witty comeback, that isn't filled with her resentment of me.

She's kicked the blankets half around her feet. Twisted in a way that makes sense for her. A large t-shirt swallows her torso as she's asleep on her stomach in the middle of the bed. Her hair hides most of her face except her full lips, which are popped open, much like the door, just the slightest amount, like she's waiting for something. Or, just that the drool on her pillow needed a way to escape. Her ass is covered only by a pair of underwear that I'm doing my best not to have seared into my memory, but I know I'll be unsuccessful.

The look of her is incomparable, sexy in a way she has no idea, in her most natural form. And the smell of her sleep punches me in the face right where I'm standing. The realization that I have no sense that can suffocate anything my senses have consumed in the last minute.

'Enough,' I tell myself, in just a fraction of a whisper for the third fucking time. I tell myself that a lot recently. I need to wake her up, that's why I'm standing here, not just as a creep. But it's Friday morning and I, no, *we*, have a schedule to stick to. She just doesn't know it yet.

I step back from where I have become too comfortable in the doorframe stealing the glances of her, now steeling myself back to a place of composure. Pretending that my pants haven't tightened due to the swelling of my cock thinking about her, something I'll have to deal with later. I just take the deepest breath I can as I run my fingers through my hair, regaining the distance we need to make this work.

"Louisa?" I say her name, gentle as a question, as I knock on the door. Though historically gentle has never been the dynamic when my fist hits the woodgrain of a door, or wall, between us.

I can hear her scrambling in the sheets, frantic and a little confused. But I've stepped out of view. Her groggy voice coming through, "Wh-what?"

"Can I come in?" I ask, though it's minutes too late for that.

"Sure." The shuffling of the blankets, her pulling them up over herself, providing a semblance of modesty. As I push the door open, she's sitting upright in bed. The comforter pulled up almost to her neck. The pillow crease on her face. And eyes that look like she's trying to blink herself into alertness while her brain is buffering on. And I think my face betrays me with a smile, based on how she responds. Which is warm. She's that kind of person, maybe more flower than person, and when you show her warmth she blooms in your direction for you to experience the beauty.

"What's up?" she says, as she's brushing the hair and sleep from her face in equal measure.

"We've got somewhere to be," I say. "Can you be ready in twenty minutes?" She just looks at me. "It's casual," I add. Her eyes are large and filled with the question and then eagerness of *'what the fuck is going on?'*

She comes out forty minutes later, changed into a pair of jeans and a striped cardigan, her hair is tied up and brushed out of her face, which is strange when she so often has it down. She looks like, I'm not entirely sure, but it's not the her I'm used to seeing.

"It's Friday," she finally says. As if this explains it. *Which it does*. But I'm not about to admit that to her, yet. When she has directly and *indirectly* asked me about my Friday morning routine more than once. Though never did I think she would be a part of it.

"I have a calendar, Louisa" is all I reply. Taking the last sips from my coffee mug before dropping it in the sink.

"It's early," she says as she checks her phone. It's earlier than most people would wake their fake fiancee without a pre-agreed upon reason. "Is this like—" she stops, starts again, "are we going somewhere for Immigration? Should I have prepared something?" Her face looks almost concerned, so I respond quickly.

"No."

"Then what... is this, like...a date?" Her voice sputters out somewhere between confusion and disgust. I laugh in response and see her face pinch in insult. Noted, *not funny*.

"If you consider breakfast with my grandmother a date, sure." Her face shifts from suspicion into something else. The surprise blooms across her high cheekbones, along with the smile that rounds them. It looks like actual excitement, joy even. And then she turns her back to me, because her face can't hide that she's pleased, and she would hate to give me the satisfaction of show-ing it.

She hurries to the kitchen, pouring herself a cup of coffee. Which is interesting because I can't for the life of me figure out the variable between when she chooses coffee and when she chooses tea. *I will though.*

"Bring it with you," I say, stepping next to her to reach for the cup and transfer it into a to-go thermos, with a secure lid. "We can't keep Grams waiting."

"You have a Grams?" she says, like it's the most interesting thing she's learned about me yet. That the studying of files about my first pet, or who I lost my virginity to, this was the thing she hadn't considered, despite it very much being a part of the documents.

"It was in the packet," I remind her. Because not only do I have a grandmother, I spent most of my childhood with her as Mom and Dad were more focused on *'winning'* than ever being a parent to the only *'asset'* they had to share post divorce.

"Yeah, sure, you have a grandmother. I got that part... but you said GRAMS. Like a cutesy grandma nickname, I know you have a grandmother." She stiffens her tone with the important clarifica-tion that she apparently needs me to understand. "I just didn't know you have a Grams!" She doubles down on the point like there's a distinction. Which in her mind, I guess there is.

"You'll like her," I say, holding the door as we make our exit.

"I already like her," she says with a devious smile. "Anyone with the patience to spend time with you voluntarily, that's someone I need to know."

She lives exactly twelve minutes from us, on a tree-lined street in an independent-living facility that is really more senior-citizen condo than anything I would have considered a nursing home. The building itself is old red brick, quiet and substantial, which I always feel represents the dignity of the people inside well. Part of why I chose it.

I don't talk about my parents, and it's not an accident. It's a decision I made early and have maintained with consistency. The facts are available in the folders I gave her, names, dates, the broad strokes, but the folder doesn't have the texture of it. The weight of being the one thing two people couldn't agree to share because they despised each other so deeply.

But she needs to know, not only because it's context for Immigration, they won't ask, not at this level. It's that Grams will assume she does, and the gap between what Grams assumes and what Louisa knows will be visible to both of them immediately.

So here I go, knowing the conversation is timeboxed to the rest of this drive, which has exactly nine minutes left.

"You know my parents divorced when I was seven." I keep my eyes on the road. "My father left first, *technically*. New city, new life, new family. Even though I think the new family actually preceded any real departure. My mother stayed for a period, but staying physically isn't the same thing as being there." Louisa's body shifts slightly as if to indicate her attention is on me, while I am focused on this drive. *Even though I could do this drive with my eyes closed.*

"She was so burned by him that I think I became the part of her life she couldn't look at without seeing him in it." I slow at a yellow light. "She went on a lot of *'journeys of self discovery,'* which was just an excuse to run away. Each time leaving me with Grams." She lets out the smallest *'mmm,'* and it sounds sympathetic, which is not the goal of this.

"She remarried when I was eleven. Moved out of state. And made it clear that she had found the journey that was right for her, and I wasn't a part of it." Louisa is quiet. I can feel her eyes on me, if I were to turn my head, they would find each other and we would be locked in a stare.

"Grams took me in. I don't think she was given a choice, exactly, but she never made me feel that way. I had stayed with her every school break before that, every summer and weekend, and then just permanently. I lived with her until I went to college."

"What was that like?" she prompts. Not aggressively to dive

deeper into the ugly details as much as a soft nudge to learn more about my childhood.

"She made breakfast every morning, came to every debate tournament, was in the front row at every graduation; at every meaningful event in my life, she's had a front row seat," I say, and realize there is a significant one coming up, that when we make our way to City Hall for our appointment, will be notably absent from the list. *But I don't say that out loud.*

"She taught me bridge," I say, because this is safer ground. "Said it would teach me to pay attention to what people weren't saying. To communicate with a partner without words. We still play weekly."

"Did it?"

"I'd say yes. Past relationships would probably disagree." Claire said something close to this verbatim in the one of the last conversations we had. She wasn't wrong. Knowing what someone isn't saying and doing something useful with it are different skills, and I've historically only been good at one of them.

Louisa makes a small sound that isn't quite a laugh. "I don't know how to play bridge," she says. And from my peripheral vision I can see her picking at the edge of her purple nail polish, which she does when she's nervous, maybe nostalgic for something she can't put her finger on. "Maybe she'll teach me."

"Yeah, maybe." The thing I don't say, that I have no business thinking, let alone breathing into this small space between us so it can buzz around this car like a trapped bee, is that I would like that. The image of Grams teaching Louisa bridge is something I want to exist in the world, in my world.

"What about your father?" she asks. "After." It's the follow-up question that on any given day would have said there's a fifty-fifty chance of answering, and I find that with her, today, in this specific twelve minutes, the odds shift.

"I spent a lot of time waiting for him," I say.

"What does that mean?"

"He was always elsewhere," I say. "Even before." The resentment I've processed. *Mostly*. What remains is cleaner, flat disappointment in two people who could have chosen differently and didn't, abandoning me out of spite for each other. "I waited for him to be proud of me, or choose me, in any way for a long time. No matter how much Grams hated him, or how disappointed she was in her own daughter, she never let it affect me. She made sure I got his birthday card every year. Always waiting with my pile of birthday presents with twenty dollars in it. Eventually I realized they were never from him at all. That's when I stopped waiting. My mom was at least there when I was growing up, until I became the memory of all she didn't want to be around. At least her birthday cards were really from her."

"That's a lot." She says it and it's validating. She's not using it as justification to explain anything about me away, just acknowledging this part of who I am.

"When I stopped waiting," I continue, because there's no reason to stop now, "things got easier. You can't be let down by someone you've stopped expecting things from." I say it the way I've learned to tell myself doesn't have the weight of old resentment dragging at its edges. It took longer to achieve than I'll tell anyone. But it's true now, or *true enough*. "Grams is the reason anything about me works," I say. We're a block away, meaning I get to conclude this dive into my childhood. "Everything that functions. Everything I've built. It maybe started because I wanted to impress them, to be the thing so undeniably successful they would be proud and regret leaving. But then it became about her. She was the only person who pushed me without an agenda. The only one whose investment in me had nothing to do with what I'd eventually be able to do for her." I pause as I follow the traffic lights, each red stop light gives me a minute to pause, and decide if I should continue. "I'll never be able to do enough in return. I know that. But she's close, and she's taken care of, and I show up every Friday for breakfast."

She doesn't try to fill the space with noise, or fix it, or reflect it back at me with therapeutic phrasing. She just holds it with me for the last half block.

"Hudson."

"Mm."

"You're enough."

Two words, quietly delivered. I don't respond. Not outside my own brain. They are words I never admit to myself and certainly have never heard spoken out loud, only ever received from Grams in the form of action. But there's something different to hearing something spoken.

I pull into the small lot and cut the engine off.

"Ready?" I ask.

"Since the second you said Grams," she says. And she's out of the car before I am.

Chapter Thirteen

HOPELESSLY ROMANTIC

HUDSON

"You must be Louisa," she says, before I can open my mouth. Grams has never waited for a formal introduction when a direct one was available. She extends both hands and Louisa takes them in both of hers with the easy warmth she gives to everyone. Everyone, I've noticed, except me, or the version of me she constructed before this week started dismantling it.

"I've heard so much about you," Louisa says. "Can I call you Grams?" It's such a sincerely sweet question that I'm glad it's not directed at me. And I know the answer. She has been Grams to anyone close enough to me to know her. Which nowadays is really only Lucas and Paola.

"Only if you want me to answer." Grams says it to Louisa, but the look she slides to me over her shoulder is one I've been on the receiving end of since childhood. I give her nothing in response. This is also a language we've been speaking for thirty years.

The dining room at Highland Place has high ceilings and good light, because its residents need it to read the menus, though the staff knows Grams's order and mine without asking. Louisa asks the server about the specials. I come here weekly, and five minutes after Louisa meets her, I now know that her name Tiff is *not* short for Tiffany with an *'a'* but *Tiffiny* with an *'i'*, which is *why* she goes by Tiff. Louisa has all this information before we even have waters on the table. Louisa asks Tiff what she thinks is best, listens with her full attention, and orders it. When the food comes out, it looks better than what I ordered.

I sit across from them both and become, within seconds, an audience.

This is not a complaint. Far from it. They begin with weddings, not ours, which I'd called ahead to navigate so Grams wouldn't surface it cold at the table, but my grandparents'.

"The year was 1959," she begins, and Louisa is enraptured as she pops another piece of squared cantaloupe in her mouth. It's a story I've heard enough times to recite. They were going to elope, but at the last minute decided not to. They didn't want to run off and get married in secret, even if people objected. She tells Louisa about the dress she made herself from a pattern because the one she wanted cost thirty-five dollars she didn't have. My grandfather in his father's suit, too broad in the shoulders. Her sister picking flowers from a neighbor's garden the morning of, without asking. All of it told with the happiness of someone who has never once resented the imperfection of it.

Louisa absorbs every word. Not politely, *genuinely*, leaning forward, asking for more. She asks follow-up questions about details Grams hasn't reached yet, which requires Grams to double back, which she seems delighted by. I watch Louisa give this woman her complete and total attention and I think about all the times her voice came through the wall between our apartments and I made myself be annoyed by it, because the alternative was something I didn't have a plan for. When here she is, delighted, on a Friday morning, with a mediocre breakfast, completely enthralled by my grandmother.

"What are your plans, my dear?" Grams says, so crisp and intentional. She has never stirred a pot she didn't mean to stir. "Shall we make it a big affair?"

Louisa's eyes find mine across the table. Panic as she calls in the agreed-upon lifeline.

"Louisa's family is in the UK," I say, smooth and immediate. "We're going to the courthouse." I look at Grams with the expression that means, *I know exactly what you're doing.* She looks back with the expression that says, *'I don't care.'*

"Don't let him tell you he can't afford something if you want it," Grams says to Louisa, ignoring me. "Look at this nice place he keeps me. *He can afford it.*" She pats Louisa's hand. "I'll even throw in thirty-five dollars for a dress, if you need it."

Louisa laughs, and it's the realest one I've heard from her, and fuck if it isn't something I need to hear again. Which is saying something, because she is not a person who laughs quietly, or by half measures. This one comes from somewhere deeper, not just the air in her lung, but deep in her person. This pulled some version of genuine joy that feels too intimate to experience. It's different than the ones she uses in conversation, those are warm and easy, distributed freely to anyone in her radius. But this? She didn't plan. And that's why it overtakes me.

I have spent six months being annoyed by this woman. I have a list, a mental one, itemized, with supporting evidence. Filed actual complaints. All the escalations and midnight doorway arguments that I told myself I was winning, and which I was, objectively, losing in ways I didn't have the vocabulary for yet.

I told myself the sound of her through the wall was an inconvenience, so many times and with such consistency that I believed it, the way you believe anything you repeat enough.

But right now, the only thing I want repeated *is her laugh.*

"I appreciate that," Louisa says, patting Grams's hand before turning to look at me. "I already bought a dress. Though I *have* had a front row seat to his finances lately, and between the Nerds habit and the eggs for dinner—" the smile she gives me is nothing short of diabolical "—which have apparently gone up in price— I'd say thirty-five dollars might actually be what we're working with for the flowers." It's sticky with sarcasm as it drips down each declaration.

"The flowers," I say, "are handled." I take a sip of my coffee. Louisa looks at me for just a heartbeat longer than the joke requires, then she turns back to Grams.

"I actually never wanted a big traditional wedding." The word traditional sounds different coming from her. The idea of it, handed to her early and then quietly set down. "I never really wanted traditional *anything*, honestly. I'd absolutely trip over my own feet walking down the aisle and take out whoever was waiting at the end." She turns to me then, with a smile that is warm and shockingly playful, and for me. "Isn't that right."

I hold her gaze. "With a cup of tea in hand."

"Exactly," she says. "And no one there to catch me."

"I'd catch you," I say. It comes out like a fact, which, I'm realizing, *it is*. But if there's something I learned six months ago, it's that I should have dodged the tea, and caught the girl.

Grams watches us with the face she used to wear when I'd come home from school and try to pretend a day had been fine. *She was never fooled then, either.*

Louisa looks at me like she's deciding whether to say the thing or the *other* thing, she picks the other thing.

"I *have* always liked the idea of the people you love most in a room," she continues, "celebrating something as rare as finding the person you love most in the world. I think that's why I love a sitcom wedding episode on television. There's always the formula. There's this core group of people who've watched the main characters fight to get to each other. Something always goes wrong. Someone always does something that redefines what seemed possible. And everyone who loves them gets to be in the room for it."

"You're such a romantic," Grams says. Not an accusation, just a statement delivered with something that looks very much like recognition.

"Hopelessly," Louisa says. "And sometimes more than is good for me."

After breakfast, we head to Gram's apartment, and I become even more peripheral to the conversation than I was. I want Grams to like her, she already likes her, I can tell. And Louisa needs this too, in a way I don't think she'd name if asked. And one I hadn't considered, but I'm glad of it now. She's been alone here longer than anyone should be, and not just physically. She told me some of it, not in those words, but in the spaces between the ones she used. The geography of her family that loved her in name but not practice, never being what they wanted from birth. Except of course, her brother. Whom she loves, just at a distance.

Grams knows something about filling that distance. She's been doing it for me for thirty years. I watch Louisa settle into the wingback chair with ease, and I slip quietly down the corridor to get the *other* thing I came for.

Grams's bedroom is exactly as it has always been, no matter how many times she's moved. The mahogany vanity table positioned under the window so the morning light hits the mirror at the angle she requires. Her hand cream and the small glass dish for rings when she applies it. A photograph of the two of us I don't remember being taken, which is my favorite kind. And the dark-green jewelry box, gilt edges worn soft from decades of handling.

I called her yesterday. Told her we were coming, told her I wanted her to meet Louisa, and there was a pause on the other end that was not surprise but recognition.

"I've been wondering when that was going to happen," she said.

Not whether. When.

She never met Claire. I didn't bring her. It took weeks before she even realized my Friday mornings looked different than every other day. I told myself it was because things were uncertain, because we were still figuring it out, because the timing wasn't right. All of which were true and none of which were the reason.

The reason was simpler and less flattering: I knew what Grams would see, and I wasn't ready to hear it.

I lift the lid of the jewelry box. The velvet envelope beneath the tray is dark burgundy, thinned at the fold from however long it's been waiting there. I can feel the shape of it through the fabric before I open it. It was my grandfather's first significant purchase. He bought this ring on a payment plan from a jeweler and proposed again, the year after they were married, when he could afford it. He stood in the kitchen of the apartment where they lived with their daughter. One oval ruby, deep red, set in a thin band of yellow gold that's been worn smooth and bright by sixty years of daily life. It's not a diamond, it was never meant to be flashy. It was meant to be real, because it's the only kind of beauty that holds up over time.

Ironic if you think about it, the *reality* of this artifact to symbolize something so real, slid on the finger of my fake wife. It doesn't matter to me how fake this marriage is. The reasons behind it are *real*, and that has to count for something.

Grams wore it every day until her fingers made it impossible. Then she kept it in this box, in this envelope. And when I called, she offered it to me. Demanded I take it. *'I always thought I'd give it to you when the time came, and then, I worried that when the time came, I didn't know you would be there to greet it.'* I stood in my kitchen and didn't say anything, just accepted the same truth about myself that I've been told, *and I've known,* for some time. Which was its own answer. She knew, because she always knows. After thirty years of watching someone build walls, it gives you an excellent understanding of where the doors are.

From the sitting room, I can hear Louisa's voice. Not the words at first, just the cadence of it, the rise and fall, the rhythm that I know now means she's doing something more than speaking. It's something I have no trouble recognizing through walls. She's reading, out loud.

She's taken one of Grams's books, the historical romance I keep saying I will read just so she has someone to talk to about it.

Apparently Louisa has. And she's reading it out loud, doing the voices with full commitment, her audience of one not diminishing her performance. If anything, it's amplifying it.

I stand in the doorway of the bedroom for a moment, not going back yet. I know why she's here, what I'm giving her. It's paperwork and a fiction we have agreed to maintain for however long it takes.

Here is what she's giving me, and what she is giving me is so much more than a fucking apartment.

I close the bedroom door quietly behind me and walk back down the corridor. I join them, and Louisa is perched on the edge of the armchair with the book open in both hands. Grams is in her usual chair, turned fully toward her, hands folded, entirely captivated. Louisa is mid-scene, and she doesn't look up when I appear.

But Grams does.

On Wednesday, we have an appointment at the courthouse. Someone to sign a certificate. That's all it is.

But it doesn't have to be only that.

I cross to the small settee and sit down, and I don't interrupt her, and I don't look away. She continues reading through the end of the chapter.

Grams holds Louisa's hands when we leave. "I've waited a long time to meet you," she says it directly, I don't think Louisa realizes just how literally she means it. Louisa bends down to kiss her cheek and her hair falls forward from behind her ear and she doesn't fix it and Grams reaches up and does it for her, tucking it back, holding her face just a second longer.

The drive home is quiet, peaceful. I called the office and told them I'm going to be working from home today, delaying my start, because we ended up spending more time with Grams than just a few chapters.

A ring is in my pocket that she doesn't know exists. She thinks we're getting married on Wednesday. We are. *That* part will be true.

But all week I've been making decisions based on what this arrangement requires. What it needs to look like, what it needs to hold up under. But now? There's something I have to do, and I can't justify it for strategy alone. I've tried, and the justification doesn't hold.

My future wife, I think. Nods off in a twelve-minute drive back.

I sit with it in the dark of the parking garage, in the quiet of a car I'm in no hurry to get out of. But I do eventually, because no matter what, I can't stay suspended in this moment. She doesn't even realize it is anything more than a nap in the car. I walk around to her side. I open the door carefully, and I say her name, and I watch her come back to herself— slow and blinking and completely without defenses.

Enough, Hudson. *It has to be enough.* But even I know, standing here, that I'm fighting with a wall, my own, one I put up, and one she has no problem fighting her way through.

Chapter Fourteen

THE STARS REWRITTEN

LOUISA

I'm standing here, in my wedding dress. Although, not a wedding dress, technically. The woman at the vintage shop never called it that. It had no tag, no provenance, no record of what occasion it was originally made for, or who wore it, or whether she was nervous when she slipped it over her head. (Because why would someone be nervous in a beautiful cream-colored dress?! Don't ask me!)

It's a short, structured satin cocktail dress in a soft ivory, and yes, the cream may just be age, but it's beautiful because of it, and right now, against my skin, it's perfect. Even Hudson thought it was *good* when I showed him.

The back drapes low, gathering into a cascade of fabric that looks like it is meant to be cradling my shoulder blades, because while from the front it is high at the base of my neck, the back is low and deep. I bought this dress not just because it was forgotten on the floor, but because the hem has humor and beauty at the same time. The details trailing off as they climb the same way I sometimes just wander off midway through a sentence once I've said all I need to or get distracted.

It wasn't born to be a wedding dress. And I don't think I was born to be a wife.

But here we both are.

Being the thing we need to so we can exist in the world rather than stay hidden.

A string of pearls sit at my throat, another purchase from the vintage shop, this one an impulse buy at the counter. (Makes sense for an impulse wedding.) A simple strand that's luminous from having absorbed decades of other people's happiest occasions. (I hope they don't absorb too much of this one.) They match the detailing at the hem of my dress in a way that feels less like coordination and more like the dress and the pearls already knew each other in a past life, like they are old friends who planned this reunion and I'm just lucky to be part of it.

I certainly didn't plan it. I've never, in the history of my life, planned anything that went this well by accident (or even on purpose), which means it is most definitely a sign. And I absolutely love signs, especially when they are conveniently on my side.

I swipe another coat of mascara over my lashes. My hands are steady (which surprises me) and my heartbeat is not (which does not.) I place my hands flat on the marble counter of his (well, my) bathroom sink and in the silence of his space, I can hear him without him even being here. Just somewhere knocking on the door of my mind, getting it to settle.

'In through your nose.' I take a slow breath, filling my lungs and holding it there as I count to four in my head.

'Out through your mouth.' I round my lips and exhale.

A much easier, much more doable in public way to counteract the anxiety that creeps in more often than I like to admit. But I don't think I can break into the choreography from *The Greatest Showman* while standing in front of the Justice of the Peace. Right now, the anxiety is telling me that this ruse will have us both found out. It will result in a fine I can't pay, and being returned to the rainy land of Yorkshire puddings. And for him? He agreed to do this for his own reasons, and if I mess this up before I've completed the end of the bargain, not only can he be arrested, but he'll lose his dream apartment. (Priorities, Lou. *Priorities.*)

His text had arrived as soon as he left this morning. The plan had been to meet at the courthouse for our wedding appointment this afternoon, but something changed.

ANGRY NEIGHBOR™

Meet you at the apt. We'll go together.

(I really, *really* need to change his contact info.)

I had stared at my phone for minutes, typed and deleted multiple responses but just sent *'okay'* instead. Because I have learned that arguing with Hudson Ellis results in me saying more than is helpful, him saying exactly as much as he intends, and the gap between those two things is where I find myself in the most trouble.

I pick up the small beaded clutch with my lipstick, my phone, a tin of cinnamon Altoids, and the folded piece of paper I've been carrying around since the city clerk's office with the list of things I need to remember about him as if someone could quiz me at any second.

I check my phone for the time, I have a few more minutes before I have to leave, my shoes already by the door. (Learned that lesson the hard way, I'll put them on before I walk out.) But in the breath before this big thing, before I slip my feet into satin and head out to sign my name on the dotted line for my future, I find myself walking through this apartment with a different lens. There's no music, not really. Just something soft and cinematic playing in my head as my fingers trail over cool marble counter-tops, skim the backs of chairs, trace the edges of carefully curated, monochromatic art lining the hallway.

Everything about this place is so him. Controlled, intentional, and just a little cold. I never noticed how little of him actually lives here. (Maybe I never looked closely enough.) Even as I moved myself in, there was space for me because the deepest parts of a person's life that should be here aren't. And I wonder if he keeps them anywhere, or if Grams is the real keeper of who he is.

My feet carry me, of their own traitorous accord, stopping just short of his bedroom door. The one he always keeps shut, the one boundary in an apartment that otherwise feels like a show-room. The secrets of my soon-to-be husband sit just on the other side of it.

This is a line, isn't it? He's welcomed me into this space, formally, for purpose. Like everything else he has, functional. And the guest room I'm in (whether he fully admits it or not) I know he updated it for me. Not just white linens, but something that he looked at and thought would make me happy. (Or at least might make me stay.) But before we say *'I do,'* my hand holds on the black doorknob, because if there's one thing we've been painfully, meticulously clear about, it's lines.

The marriage is fake, the whole thing temporary, that means the terms are clean and absolutely no personal entanglements. *'That would be too great a liability.'* A liability for him maybe, but I don't think of feelings as a liability. Especially not curiosity.

"Of course," I mutter to myself, fingers more tightly gripping the brushed handle. "No problem committing fraud, why draw the line at a bedroom door."

The handle turns too easily. Completely unlocked and feels like a mistake by someone who I don't think could make one. Or, if it's a pre-marital test, I've failed anyway. So I push the door open just enough to slip inside, as if opening it any more would be greedy.

His bedroom is a more relaxed space than anywhere else in this apartment. It's still minimalist, but there is warmth here even in the neutrality of the space. Pausing at the bookshelf, the photographs of parts of his life he never talks about, tucked away here in the most private of places. A young Hudson at what looks like a debate podium, too serious for his age. (That tracks.) He and Grams at a table somewhere, mid-laugh. (That feels familiar.) One I don't recognize of a woman with his jaw who must be his mother, younger than I imagined her. These are the things he keeps in the most private room. The things that only make it as far as the place most people never see. Like something he only reserves for people who make it past the deepest level of trust.

I stand in front of the shelf for longer than I should. I've narrated a hundred scenes set in rooms like this, the private space of someone who doesn't let people in, the moment the protagonist finds the hidden self of the person they've been misreading.

Standing in his bedroom in my wedding dress, I think, *'I'm working on it, Roma.'*

I can hear footsteps in the apartment. My heart (and stomach) lurch. He must be here already, waiting. And about to find me in his room. Two things that would seriously aggravate him. (Not the vibe for my wedding, no matter how fake it is.) But if he's here, I must be late. Slipping out of his bedroom, running towards the front door. And much like the first day, I crash right into him. This time, without any beverages or boxes, but my arms land around him as he catches me in his chest.

I peel my face back from his jacket and look up.

Hudson is dressed in more than something from his usual grey or navy work-suit rotation. Not a tuxedo, but a crisp black suit with a stark white shirt unbuttoned at the collar. Which is a detail I will recall once I put some distance between myself and this moment, when I am not standing in this hallway looking at the man I spent so many months tangled with in this personal-grudge match. His neck isn't tied in some large knot in a silk noose.

I can feel his eyes on me as he sets me back on my still-bare feet. He looks surprisingly relaxed standing very still. But his expression isn't normal, and as his gaze crawls across my body it does something I've never seen before. He doesn't manage it back to neutral.

"In a rush?" Hudson asks in a way that is not the usual conde-scending, but dipped in the smallest humor. Recognizing, perhaps like I do, the irony that if this were a real wedding, if any of this were real, it would be a full circle moment. So reminiscent of our first meeting, disheveled, contentious, that it would bring a smile to both of our faces.

"Being late is a terrible way to start a marriage," I say as I straighten myself.

"Good thing, this is just a wedding."

"Pretty sure this is just a trip to City Hall," I say. Hurriedly I put on my shoes, soft pink slingbacks with bows on the toes, concerned that without any buffer minutes, I might actually make us late to our own wedding. (Or whatever we want to call it.) Pulling the slingback around my heel has me lose my balance, and I nearly careen forward, but Hudson's hand juts out, gripping my hands where they were already desperately looking for something to grab.

"You have to stop doing that," he says. "I won't always be around."

"Well, lucky me, I have you for now," I say as I check my reflection in the hall mirror, tuck the brown wave of hair behind my ear.

If anyone were to see us right now, they wouldn't doubt we are a couple. We look it, from head to toe. Except he's watching me with this new expression I cannot read, and never imagined on his face. Not one of immediate annoyance or hatred. His stare drips down slowly and his lips part as he comes to stand behind me with only inches between us. It is not a large movement. It is barely a movement at all. On anyone else I would miss it. But in a short time, I have become very aware of the movements of this man's mouth. (Damnit, Lou.)

"It's time," he says, calmly, soothingly, as we make our way out the door, into our fake future. And somehow in that register, with that look on his face, it doesn't feel like just another schedule item at all.

The elevator doors open and in flawless silence, he extends his hand out to me. Slipping my hand into his and stepping in. But rather than heading to the lobby, he hits 'ROOF.'

"If you're taking me to the roof to murder me," I say. "They will never sell you that apartment."

"Louisa." My name forms on his lips in a low tone that rumbles through me. It hit me the day we met, also. But that day, he wasn't saying my name. The only words out of his mouth were dripping with annoyance. Now, if I didn't know better, I'd say they are dripping with something wetter than desire.

The elevator climbs and so do my nerves until the doors open to the stairwell to take us the last few steps to the outside. His hand hasn't released mine as we climb the five steps together, him leading me each step of the way.

"What are we doing up here?" I ask. "What about our appointment?"

"Cancelled it," he says flatly. Concern is a pit deep in my throat and it's expanding each time I try to swallow it down. Nervous that somehow I had made a mistake or misunderstood. That it's another thing that got lost in a stack of mail I'm too nervous to open.

"What do you mean you cancelled it? Did I do something wrong? Did I miss something?" The spiral is immediate and I cannot stop it. "You said we were on a strict timeline, you said—"

"I know what I said." (Of course he does.)

With his other hand he finds the bare skin of my back in the low drape of the dress, and I feel every fingerprint of his as it settles there, warm and certain. Not feeling foreign the way I imagined his touch might. I feel the moment he registers the goosebumps and chooses not to mention them, which is somehow more devastating than if he had. Because of course, we both know despite the outfits we put on, or the physical reaction I may have, no matter how important it is, it isn't real.

"Was I late?" I ask, quieter now. "Is it... is it my fault?"

His eyes narrow as he steps deeper within my space. We are on the same inch of floor as he looks at me and doesn't move, our feet are an alternating pattern standing on the same highline.

"The only thing," he says, low and close, "that is your fault

—" his middle finger traces a line down the column of my spine and my next breath does something embarrassing "—is how fucking beautiful, you are, in your dress."

We're standing at the door of the rooftop, and I feel my mouth open with something to say but no words to come out.

"Are you ready?" he asks. I look up at him somewhat confused, and he takes my silence as agreement. Pushing open the large metal door to the roof as it screeches in celebration of a visitor.

His hand is on my back, we step forward, and with each step further into the open air, the illumination of the hundreds of candles comes more into view.

Suddenly, the rooftop feels less like a place that existed and more like a secret someone built just for this moment. The harsh, industrial edges and cement ledges, the hulking metal vents and the pipes that would never be called romantic, have been softened into something sacred. By him. Every surface possible to hold light does. Pillar candles casting long, golden shadows that flicker and breathe against the cement walls. Around their bases, around everything, white daisies bloom in delicate rings, their petals catching the glow so they look almost luminescent, like they've borrowed the light from the flames.

Clusters of votives gather in small constellations scattered intentionally but effortlessly mirroring the stars above, as if they simply appeared there a billion years before. Candlelight traces the edges of the rooftop, lining the ledges in shimmering rows that echo the city skyline beyond. All the flickering light blends into the world around us, until it becomes hard to tell where the city ends and this begins.

The quiet hum of the city exists up here with warmer air and the glow of starlight. Distant traffic, a faraway siren, and the low, constant pulse of life below, but everything except my heartbeat feels muted. And his pulse, which I can feel so long as his hand is in mine. Like the rest of the world has stepped back to give us space to exist.

As the candlelight dances, trying to reach the stars that inspire it, this almost feels real. The makeshift aisle does not scream *fake marriage'* but *'grand gesture.'*

It's not an aisle runner, but a carefully folded drop cloth from a renovation. Maybe it was up here already, clustered in a forgotten corner. (That makes me like it more.) It's lined on both sides in petals and candlelight, and leads towards the far end of the rooftop, a larger space with a gathering of six chairs.

Chandler is here, both hands pressed over her mouth, mascara already making its exit. Toby's face says he has been sitting on information for longer than was comfortable. Lucas ,Hudson's friend I met briefly to discuss some of the legality of my immigration case, and his wife, Paola, are here. She might be the most inarguably beautiful woman I've ever seen in my life, or maybe that's just because of how her husband is looking at her. She's sitting there with her hand on Grams's arm. And Grams is looking at me with equal parts warmth and an *'I told you so'* that you're only allowed to claim when you've lived a certain number of decades.

But most special of all, despite the lagging wave of excitement, propped on a chair beside Toby, a laptop screen glowing in the candlelight, my brother, Theo. (Though it's weird his laptop self isn't *'sitting'* next to Chandler.) His face is slightly blurry and slightly flushed because it's late there and I assume this was not on his original plan for the night. But he sees me see him and through the screen I feel the hug of my brother three thousand miles away.

"What is all of this?" My voice comes out too small for the size of what I'm feeling.

"You should have a wedding," Hudson says, close. "Regardless of the reason for the marriage." I turn to look at him. My eyes are collecting the tiniest bit of tears. "I'll meet you down the aisle," he says. Walking off, taking a few long steps to cross the space where his friend joins him in standing.

Chandler appears at my elbow. Any doubt she has about our love story, she seems to have pushed aside, by this display. She presses a small bouquet of daisies into my hands, loose and simple, held together with a length of blue fabric that looks like it was cut from something else and makes the entire bouquet smell like licorice and cloves.

Across the roof, he's standing and the illuminated path is ready to guide me to him. His eyes are locked on me, not just in the soft glow of candlelight, but the warmth of people who know and love us. It's hard to believe that none of this is real.

Music suddenly comes through speakers I didn't even know were here. I recognize it immediately. No lyrics, just an orchestral version of a song that I curl under a blanket to regularly. He knows this, I've told him. (He's seen it.)

I take a deep breath in through my nose as the music builds.

As the music ascends, both in melody and volume, he nods at me from six feet away. With my bouquet in hand, and fake fiancé waiting for me, I start walking. Each step requires me to remind myself, this is all an act, because with each step I take, he takes the shape of someone I feel like I've known, a future I'm committing to for real, not papers.

I know what this is. (I know what it isn't.)

I just wish the rest of me would consult the part that knows.

But Hudson doesn't look away once. Doesn't break eye contact. In fact, a smile spreads across his face as he watches me get closer and closer. It's only then I realize, it's because I am (unknowingly) mouthing the words to "Rewrite the Stars."

When I reach him, we are standing so close as the song fades out and we are just left in each other's shared breaths.

"I love this song," I say.

"I know" is his only reply. And there is a light chuckle from the people who surround us. Chandler takes my bouquet, releasing my hands from their task of gripping something. Resulting now in an absence of what to do with them. But his are extended to me so subtly, that I can slip them into the partnership of his grip. Standing here in this well-crafted ruse, the photographs will appear far from fake.

Lucas clears his throat. "We're here," he begins, looking out at the assembled group and city beyond, all of which has been brought together into something extraordinary by sheer force of intention, "because these two people have made a choice." He looks back at us. "A legally binding one, which I can confirm is entirely in order." A small chuckle moves through the chairs. They all had doubts about this. But Hudson and I agreed, no one can know the depth of the truth. So any suspicions are reduced to a bit of laughter that Lucas waits to pass. "A choice that, above all the paperwork, is the most important one of all. It's the choice to love."

Lucas turns to me.

"Louisa, do you take Hudson, to be your lawfully wedded husband, to have and to hold—"

Lucas's voice reaches me through a significant amount of interference, drowned out by my own pulse. (Mostly.) And the terror of standing here with my hands in his, in front of the people I love, saying words I have narrated in every register and had started to doubt I'd say out loud myself. Saying them now and not being able to tell (and this is the part that frightens me) whether the terror is because they're fake or because I don't want them to be.

Hudson's eyes find mine and stay there. I watch his lips count, barely moving. Not visible to anyone around us. One, two, three, four. An exhale through his full lips. The instruction he gave me, again in a moment I need it most. I follow him, and it begins to settle me.

It's Lucas clearing his throat that breaks us from our concentration.

"I do," I say, quickly. My answer is rushed, either honesty or panic, and tonight I can't tell the difference. Because I don't know how to take my time with this, so I might as well just spit it out. The answer he needs from each of us to sign, seal, and deliver this wedding as legitimate.

"Hudson." Lucas turns to him. "Do you take Louisa—"

"I do." Before the sentence finishes. Before Lucas has arrived at the part that requires an answer, Hudson has already given one. (A legally binding one.)

"I knew what he was going to say." Our friends laugh. *Our* friends. I wonder how long I will think of things in terms of *our*. (Less than a year if we're lucky, he said. Just as long as we need to.)

Lucas has known Hudson for years, maybe that's why all he says in response is *'Good.'*

The rings are in Hudson's jacket pocket, already there, already decided, because of course they are, because he doesn't leave anything to chance, and would never ask me for help. His hands carefully shift as to not release both of mine that have been held by him since we came face to face at the end of this makeshift (very real) aisle. He holds both of my hands cradled in his right palm, and is careful when he slides a small ruby on my finger. So much more careful than his usual self, or the usual version of him that I've known. It's like the care itself is the point. When the ring reaches its new home, he doesn't release my hand immediately, just runs his thumb across the stone that now sits centered below my knuckle. As if he too needs the reality check that this isn't reality. A small, deep-red ruby, held up by a soft cool-gold band. This isn't the Cracker-Jack-box ring I thought it would be. Not even an Amazon cubic zirconia. While Grams had made the joke about what he'd be able to afford, I don't think any of what's happening affords me any kind of proper jewelry. Especially not something that looks like an heirloom, not a purchase. He can see the question in my eyes, or maybe on my lips, as I open my mouth to ask. But his lips give me the smallest wink as his eyes flick towards the chair to his left, where Grams is sitting.

And when I slide the simple gold band on his ring finger, his eyes are unwaveringly watching my hands as they do it. Like he needs to see it happen to believe it has. (Maybe that's just me.)

"By the power vested in me by this great state," Lucas says, composed with the same gravity he has when delivering a closing argument before court (I assume), "and by the internet's most well-reviewed and entirely legitimate quickie-wedding-officiant.-com," a sound moves through the chairs, "I now pronounce you—"

He doesn't wait for the end of it.

His hand comes up to my jaw, fingers curling at the base of my neck, and pulling my face close to his. Our lips can feel the warmth of each other, but not the agreement to meet yet. It's a fraction of a second that we are suspended. As the prequel of his kiss hangs above my lips, he says, "I know what he's going to say."

And he kisses me.

It's not restrained, or careful. Not the performance of a kiss for a paper trail, but a real one, in this very fake *'I do.'* He's present in a way I didn't imagine this could be, that *anyone* could be. As his mouth parts mine, I stop performing, I stop narrating in my head, I stop doing anything except kissing him back, which I am, so completely, that I'm overtaken by it.

His hand spreads across the low drape of my back, warm against my skin, pressing me closer, and somewhere behind me, Chandler stops pretending to be quiet and Paola says something to Grams, and Theo, on a laptop in London at whatever hour it is there, makes a sound that carries across the distance.

When he pulls back, his thumb stays at my jaw.

"Now is the right time."

Chapter Fifteen

HE LOVES ME... NOT

HUDSON

The guests leave the way good guests do, without needing to be asked, probably why they are the only ones who earned invites. Lucas with Paola, his hand at her back the way it always is, the unconscious touch that happens when someone has become so habitual to your body that your hands always know where to go. He offered to drive Grams before I asked, or maybe Grams told him to. Chandler cried through the departure the way she cried through the ceremony, with full commitment to the emotion. *Impressive.* She closed the laptop screen on Theo somewhere in the middle of a hug, which means his last image of his sister's wedding night was the inside of Chandler's elbow. *I think she did it on purpose, and I don't think he minded.* Toby shook my hand once, said something I didn't fully catch about being an outlier to a data set, and left.

These are, *apparently*, our people.

I ordered pizza for the group that we ate on the drop cloth I'd unfolded back into its full width. The aisle doing double duty. Surrounded by the guttering remains of a hundred candles and what I can only estimate are several thousand daisy petals, and the city below us like it didn't notice what just happened up here.

I expected her to leave with the others. Or shortly after. To brush the petals from her dress, reclaim her shoes from wherever she'd abandoned them near the end of the aisle, and take herself back downstairs with some version of *'well, that was something.'* That is the reasonable outcome. That is the one I had prepared for.

But she didn't. I don't know why I'm surprised, when there is no decision I can expect her to make, that she does. Rather than retreating downstairs to separate bedrooms, she sat back down, legs stretched out and shoes abandoned somewhere, face tilted up to the sky. Checking, *I think*, to make sure the stars didn't rearrange themselves in the minutes she looked away.

I won't pretend I minded.

"He loves me," she says, with great ceremony, plucking the first petal from a daisy she picked up. The petal drifts to her lap. "He loves me, *not*," she says with emphasis this time. Another petal. For a while, neither of us say anything. She just plucks the petals, each one meant to indicate more than it has any possibility to know. But the silence we sit in isn't resentment, it's peaceful. And the look on her face, it's the precursor of a laugh, as she leans her back against the concrete wall, even letting her head roll back against it.

She looks at the bare stem for a moment like receiving the exact verdict she expected. Then she sets it down, picks up another one. *Not plucking petals this time, she already has her answer.*

After listening to her and Grams yesterday, there was no world where I could rob her of the gesture, *no matter how crafted*, of this moment. I might be an asshole, but I'm not *that* asshole. Paola was too eager to help me turn this space into something special. Then I just had to convince Chandler, *which was easy enough*, though she seemed genuinely shocked when I showed up in the afternoon with the request. I asked Chandler about any family for Louisa, knowing that Lucas and Paola are the closest family I have besides Grams. I asked her to call Louisa's brother, the only one she seems close to. And Chandler didn't seem inconvenienced in the slightest.

When all is said and done, her first wedding should be special. One day, she'll plan a real one, pick a DJ, a ring, but she will have this memory not as plainly as we signed the documents at the court, but amidst all the pretend we're doing, this could feel a little real. And for me, my only wedding will have been special. Grams will have this memory, and so will I. And when the ink is long dried on the divorce papers, this will have been enough.

She was mouthing the words with each step closer to me. It looked like a private prayer, some small act of rebellion against the cold, hard facts of this arrangement. Taking steps toward an unreal future, one we just can pretend exists for long enough for us to get what we want.

"How long did all of this take?" she asks eventually, gesturing at the rooftop, though I knew what she meant.

"I had help," I respond, not eager to give away more than I have tonight.

"That's not an answer."

"It's enough of one." *Or so I thought.* But she picks up her head, a daisy chain she strung together as we sat here now atop her soft brown hair. As her eyebrows are high on her inquisitive face, I concede to my new wife. "I got the key to the roof this morning, Paola picked up the flowers, and Chandler handled the candles."

"You didn't have to do this," she says, and I think it sounds like guilt more than gratitude.

"No, I didn't."

"It's all so much more than I expected, more than necessary."

"That's where you're wrong," I say it simply, because it's true. It *was* necessary. The reasons are obvious and also, separately, none of her business at this point. "It was a good wedding."

"It was a really good wedding," she says, pausing momentarily, weighing the rest of what she says. "Ya know, for a fake marriage."

Fake indeed. But looking at her in the shimmer of star and candlelight, twirling a daisy between her fingers, as the ruby ring continues to catch my eye as a reminder that even if this is fake, so long as we are in this, she is my wife.

I'd heard *The Greatest Showman* more times than I had realized prior to the night she showed up. I'd never seen it, so when the sound would come through the walls almost once a week, I could never place it fully. Until she sat in my chair, watched the whole thing front to back, and sang herself through what looked like an anxiety attack. It was the only thing that made sense for her to walk down the aisle to. *Assuming she would be anxiety ridden the whole way down.* The traditional wedding march for our nontraditional wedding felt inappropriate. Not because this is some great whirlwind love story for her, but because of everything she is; boring would never be a word used to describe her. In the plainest versions of herself, there is no part of her that is anything less than fascinating. That fact is no doubt what got me here.

And when time came to kiss her, it was every late night moan I swallowed down as she crept through the walls and lodged herself deep in my brain. I used that to fuel every shower thought of her I'll have from now through eternity. The feeling of my fingertips against the bare skin of her back, unlike anything I could have imagined, the softest nectarine, and I feared pulling her too close would bruise her just as easily.

But as the *I do*s reached up to the sky, and Lucas declared us married, I realized she didn't just walk down an aisle, she walked right through the walls I've spent years building, leaving nothing but the raw, unfinished truth behind. And as we sit here, it's more poetic than I consider most things to be.

Somewhere mingled amongst the occasional siren or laughter on the street below, we do something we never have. We have a conversation. Without purpose, just casually strolling through the corridors of each other without an agenda. No logistics or timeline. No reviewing facts we'll need to perform back at each other for strangers. Just talking.

"You really drive an hour for a cookie?" I say through a laugh as she tells me about a specialty store that carries imported items from the United Kingdom. "I thought you were more American than that."

"What's that supposed to mean?" She points the tiny daisy at me like a weapon, it's about as threatening as she is. "I'm sharing. This is called sharing, Hudson."

"I know what it's called."

"Oh so you just don't know how to do it." She tilts her head. She's watching me clearly to indicate that this has not been an equal round of information. "You've been very quiet on the *contribution* side of things."

"I've been listening."

"Not the same thing." Her voice sounds coated in champagne, which went well with the pizza. As is evidenced by the empty bottle that rolls away at our feet.

"I could argue otherwise."

"You can argue anything, you went to law school. Though," she pauses as she narrows her eyes and purses her lips. "You probably could before that." Her daisy weapon waves like she's using it to convince me. This is, *apparently*, serious. "It's technically our wedding night," she says. "Tell me something."

"What do you want to know?" I ask.

"Everything," she says simply, like that's a reasonable answer. Who am I kidding, she doesn't care about being reasonable. And then, at my expression, refining the ask. "Okay, fine. Tell me one thing you haven't told anyone in a while."

The request calls to some childhood version of myself, someone I wasn't prepared to have to look in the face. I turn it over in my mind, knowing there's the obvious deflection. I can say I'm a private person, which she already knows and doesn't find interesting or acceptable. I can tell her about some failed relationships, which may remind her why she should keep her emotional distance. Because eventually I'll put the wedge between us anyway. There's the version where I give her something true but small, a calculated disclosure that satisfies the requirement without actually costing me anything.

But I look at her, so full of interest, not judgement.

"I wanted to be an architect," I say. Her face opens.

She sits up straighter, moves slightly toward me, I don't think she notices she does it, closing the distance between our shoulders to approximately nothing. "Reallllyyy." She drags the word out.

"When I was young."

"Why didn't you?"

"I liked the idea of it," I say. "But I was good at arguing, I liked winning, and I liked feeling like a winner. It didn't matter if I enjoyed building things or playing with Legos, I had skills I was good at, the practical decision became obvious." A pause, I could leave it there, it's more than enough. But there's no one else here and we've already started down this road. "I also went into law to impress my father, it was something he couldn't do. Then I did it to spite him. Neither reason held up, but by then I was good at it, so." I shrug ever so slightly. It isn't a sob story, I didn't give up something I pine for. I like my career, my life choices. But there's an element of creation that I used to think about as a child that I don't get to experience now.

"You can be good at something and not want it," she says.

"You can also want something and not be good enough for it." She considers this, and I can see her deciding not to push it, which I appreciate more than I tell her. Because so much of who we are to each other has been to push. Though, *not like this.*

"Is that why the apartment?" she asks instead. "The renovation?"

I hadn't thought of it that way. Or I had, and filed it in the same drawer where I keep everything I don't want to look too closely at. "Maybe."

"Hudson." She says my name in a tone that means she thinks I'm being deliberately obtuse. *I am.*

"Probably."

She smiles and it's a smile I haven't seen in weeks, the kind she gets when she's convinced she bested me, one I've only seen standing in her doorway right before she slams it in my face. She just leans back and holds the daisy up above her face, examining it against the sky.

"I wanted to be a marine biologist," she says. "Because I once saw this documentary about octopuses." She pauses as her eyebrows knit together in thought. "Octopi?" Another pause. "I refuse to look it up, they both sound right."

"Octopodes is technically correct, octopuses is fine."

She drops the daisy onto her face in exasperation. "Octo-PODES?!" she stresses. "PODES," she says again. "God, I would have made a terrible biologist." She laughs, and so do I. I don't think it's a sound I've ever heard before, our voices sharing something like a joke, not at the other's expense.

"It's Greek in origin, not Latin. The *i* plural doesn't apply, but octopuses is correct enough."

"Of course," she says with sarcasm and acceptance. She removes the daisy from her nose. "Surprised your childhood dream wasn't to be a pedantic asshole... Oh, wait, you did that." *There it is.*

"Why no octopodes?" I ask.

"I was six. Marine biologist felt like the exact opposite of where we lived. Somewhere the skies were always grey, and life was boring. By nine, we moved to California. So naturally, then, I wanted to be an actress. By twelve I realized I don't like being the center of attention, *hate it actually,* so acting, at least the way most people do it, was not for me."

"You hate being the center of attention, had me fooled," I say.

"Do I?" she asks.

I just shake my head the smallest amount. Because while she garners the attention of every room she's in, it's not of her own doing. *At least, not in that way.*

"But yeah, I hate it, I can't even order fajitas because they just call attention to you. And it's such a shame, because when Chandler and I meet for our Tequila Updates—" she says it like it's a ritual I'm supposed to know. *I don't.* "Matteo, the waiter, he always says the fajitas are the best thing on the menu, but I just can't bring myself to do it." She sighs to herself, some inner battle between being her truest self, but also, not being too loud while doing it. "One day maybe, I'll care less, but for now, I prefer acting in private and will make fajitas at home."

She's so open in a way I've never experienced, it's no doubt why every time she walks down the street it's like an opening to a Disney movie. Everyone just knows her, because she lets them.

"And how did you get into—"

"Taunting you all night long?" she teases.

"Exactly what I was going to say." And she doesn't know just how true that is.

"When I went to college," she pauses, "*that was an experience.* There was nothing I liked enough. By then, Theo had moved back, *more like ran back,* so I was just floating about," she waves her arms, "like an octopode." She cuts me with a look, but I shake my head at the incorrect use. But I think she can see as the corner of my mouth pulls into a smile she has total control over.

She brushes it off with a laugh. "Eventually I found this. That wasn't the end of wanting anything else, but it was the only thing I wanted consistently."

"And the coffee shop?" I ask, wondering about her finances in a way that isn't actually my business.

"I do well enough that I don't need to be a barista, but I like people too much to only talk to myself all day." It's the most insanely clear thing she could have said. I've seen her around people, how she lights up, lights them up. With each question about their pets, their children, and their childhood hopes and dreams, she leaves them with a sense of warmth and wonderment, and sometimes even a basket of muffins.

There's an intimacy between us we haven't shared, maybe drawn out of us from the events of tonight. At least, drawn out of me. But this is just the beginning. We have too much time remaining locked in this agreement for me to be careless about it now. Never being known for my emotional investment in relationships, this is the one I can't risk.

"So," she says, the question is thick with the air around us. "Now that we've technically committed to *death do us part*'... What's next?"

"We can begin your paperwork immediately, and from now till the end of this thing, we have to be prepared. Between Immigration and Mrs. Saraceno, no one wants this to work. So we will have to be the image of a happy couple the second we step outside."

She sighs, larger than I would expect. "And how long *'till the end of this thing,*'" she asks. Maybe that was the wrong phrasing, but it's another goal post, one we both agreed to. No reason to sugarcoat it more than I have.

"Depends, could be up to a year of documented cohabitation, joint bills, shared grocery lists, photos, and social outings. All building to the series of interviews for both of us."

"A year is a long time," she says, almost sounding concerned. "It's a long time to not, I mean, I'm not exactly swiping on the apps regularly, but you–"

"Me, what?" I ask, a little harsher than I need to.

"Well, you are," she says.

"I saw you, too, Louisa," I reply and her eyes widen. The night she came up on the app was shocking, and at the same time almost surprising that it hadn't happened sooner. At the time I thought I had no reason to swipe, I could just walk the few feet next door. But I didn't. Her profile was clear, she was looking for a relationship. *Who knew it would be a marriage.*

"You said we can't date other people," she says, and there's a question in it.

"I know what I said." And I meant it. It adds a layer of complexity we don't need. It also means I'm effectively taking a vow of celibacy. "Don't worry about me." I reinforce my earlier stance on it. "Unless," I let the word drag on. "You're thinking about your own *needs*." I don't hide the grin that spreads across my face as her cheeks blush.

"I can manage *my* needs just fine," she snaps.

"Well, Louisa," I say, slowly, "if that changes, come to me, first."

It is perhaps the dumbest thing I could have said, and I've said an increasing number of reckless things lately. Maybe it's the champagne, or it's the fact that fourteen days ago I was conducting psychological warfare through drywall, and tonight I married her on a rooftop, and somewhere between those two events I appear to have lost the ability to manage what comes out of my mouth when she looks at me like that.

She looks at me for a long moment, maybe deciding what to say. "For what it's worth." She pulls her knees up to her chest, crossing her arms atop them and laying her head down. "You don't have to worry about me, I can't do casual." She takes a breath. "I like to actually have *feelings* for the people I'm with, you know, the ones *not* scripted." She adds the clarification as if it means something more. It also explains why I've never seen anyone sneaking out of her apartment the next morning. *Even after I've heard moaning through the walls.*

"Good thing we're married," I say.

She needs feelings to give herself over to someone, meanwhile I give myself to people specifically so I *don't* have to feel anything more than the pleasure you feel with someone in your bed. *And even that has been harder to satisfy lately.*

We are, I think, looking at her in the candlelight, the worst possible combination.

And yet, here we are. Husband and wife.

"How long?" she asks, breaking us both from a set of different thoughts entirely. It's not a sad question, probably the opposite, eager to know the shape of the thing she's agreed to.

"Long enough to be convincing," I say. "Short enough to be clean."

She nods slowly, like she's measuring the distance between those two things. "And after?"

"After some time, we will file for a no-fault dissolution. You'll get your residency, and I'll get the apartment. And then go back to being strangers." I say, and her face looks more resigned than I would have hoped.

"We weren't exactly strangers," she says as she's looking at me through thick lashes, and thicker intent. *I doubt it's the one I feel.* "Maybe at the end of this, we can at least be friends." And it's the sweetest sentiment I can imagine.

"Yeah, maybe" is all I say. But she is friends with everyone, every stranger on the street. Whereas me, as evidenced by the people at our wedding, my list of friends is few and far between. Even fewer when you consider the list of people I dated. That's just never been a superpower I've had. For her it might be the minimum, but for me it would be the most.

And then she does what she does, which is accept what she's been given and look for something to appreciate in it.

"We should go down," I say.

"Okay," she says, soft and sweet. Pausing just a breath. "Before we do, can we sit here just another minute?"

"Yes, Louisa."

She tips her face up to the sky one last time, I don't look up. I look at her. The bare daisy stem she set down earlier is still in her lap. *'He loves me not.'* The conclusion she arrived at, with great ceremony and genuine investment, on her wedding night.

One more minute becomes several. I don't correct it. But we do eventually retreat behind our separate bedroom doors, this time, under the same roof.

Chapter Sixteen

I'M A MARRIED WOMAN

LOUISA

My phone has three missed calls from Roma and I know what they're about. (It's absolutely why I'm avoiding them, and my phone in general.) The files I sent before everything imploded into paperwork and chaos, the ones I recorded in the weeks after she called and told me the passion was gone. The ones I recorded (if I am being completely honest with both of us) with the shape of him in my head after a face-to-face one night.

I have been a professional for long enough to know that Roma's feedback is always right, and recently that feedback requires me admitting that I am the cuckold in the chapters I'm narrating as I watch rather than experience. So I let her call go to voicemail a third time, and I get up from this bed that is newly mine to make a cup of...tea. Yes, I think this is a tea morning.

I play a game of Go-fish with his cabinets looking for his kettle. None in sight. His espresso maker is perhaps the only appliance that he allows to live exposed to the outside world and sits on the kitchen counter. Sleek and flawless. Fine, morning latte it is. But one of the first things I'll move over is a kettle, because microwave tea is a travesty.

I listen to the voicemail while the espresso hisses into a small glass as I steam the milk.

Roma's voice comes through, brisk and satisfied (not what I was expecting) and very caffeinated. (Okay, *that* I was expecting.)

"Whatever you're doing," she says, "married life agrees with you." A pause. "Also, your instinct on the chapter pacing was correct. Keep doing whatever—*whoever*— you're doing."

I put the phone face down on the counter.

Ha. Married life. I told her about the nuptials, had stuck to the same story we've given everyone else, and she didn't even ask a follow-up question besides about my next recording plans. And now, I see why, clearly thinking this will be the thing that reignites the passion she felt I was missing. (In the words of Alanis Morissette, isn't it ironic?)

Sure, does Hudson have something to do with it? Maybe. But not because it's passion, because I was channeling the rage that buzzed between us. Rage that just happened to look like him bare-chested in my doorway, or like our bodies pressed together as he asked me if I'd *'thought about it.'* And I don't know how to tell her (like everything else) this, too, is temporary.

It's not anything sustainable, not any real intimacy which doesn't just spawn out of nowhere, certainly not just saying *'I do.'*

Even though the wedding (Say it, Lou, *our* wedding) was single-handedly the most thoughtful thing anyone has ever done for me. Not the marrying part, though being saved from the U.S. government will certainly be at the top of that list also, but the wedding. The thing he didn't need to do. And did, for me.

I make my latte (no art because Chandler isn't here) and I take it on a tour around the apartment that is his and also now mine (and also not mine in any way that will outlast the paperwork.) But he's doing this for his own reasons and they all come down to what is right upstairs. In some ways, I think USICS is going to be easier to convince than Mrs. Saraceno and the co-op board. Especially because it sounds like he hasn't made the best impression. I'm not sure that I can help besides check the box that says *wife.*

Because I've never been anything impressive to anyone. (Go ahead, ask my parents.)

And as for Roma, she might think the explanation for whatever is now coming through in my recordings is just *'married.'* A box checked. (The explanation is not married.)

The explanation is that I have spent years narrating other people's passion and somewhere along the way stopped being able to feel it as anything other than language. Beautiful language, delicious, tantalizing, language I *love*, but language all the same. Words arranged in a particular order to produce a particular effect. (Like the ones I just used. But saying tantalizing, and being tantalized are not the same.) But somewhere in there, what I stopped feeling, and what stopped being conveyed, converged. And that is the problem she thinks *'marriage'* has solved.

I just understand something now that I didn't before. About the last inch of distance that is both nothing and everything as his lips consumed mine after an abrupt 'I do,' and the goosebumps ripped down my back as he touched me, it didn't feel like an arrangement. It doesn't feel like a marriage either, but it does feel (at least for now) like the way I can record things that aren't *'A Modern History of the Postal Service.'* (I still submitted the audition just in case.)

I spend the morning moving, because apparently marriage is just a lot of logistics. (At least this one is.) Waking up this morning as a Mrs. should be nothing except adding a syllable to an honorific I never use anyways.

The newspapers would say it was a casual, intimate, *surprise* affair. In reality, no papers were written about it (we aren't exactly wedding-announcement people) and it was intimate because, well, we don't have a lot of people between us. And it was a surprise because I didn't see this coming. (Any of it.)

I woke up the morning after our night under the stars (just call it a wedding, Lou) in my new bed with a headache from all the champagne and a pepperoni-oil stain on my dress from the pizza. I went back up to the roof to see the graveyard of our nuptials, all the candles that had been lit gone, maybe by Hudson, he seems like he'd be conscious of fire safety and not wanting to leave behind a trace of what happened. He just woke up and went to work after some forensic-level cleaning of a romantic affair no one has record of besides a few cellphone shots because there isn't even melted wax left upstairs.

There's nothing different between us except the paperwork we signed and a conversation that didn't result in me calling him an arrogant asshole and him calling me inconsiderate brat. (That really happened.)

I'm on my fifth trip between apartments, waiting for Toby and Chandler to show up, when Mr. Ambrose, my eighty-six-year-old neighbor, stops me, the pile of my clothes wrapped in a blanket still in my hands. (Because why would I pack a box to walk a few feet?)

He has been orchestrating a deeply charming long-game of flirtation with me since about the third day after I moved in. It doesn't mean anything, because no matter how playful he may be, he's told me enough stories about his marriage to his wife, who passed away years ago, that I know this is just a game to pass time. He jokes of *'if I was forty years younger,'* and I just reply *'then you'd still be too old for me.'* He always laughs, then invites me in for tea, introducing me to new flavors whenever he picks one up he thinks I might like. Which we share while he shows me pictures of his grandchildren that don't visit and I end up fixing his TV remote, because his *'Smart TV is the dumbest contraption he's ever seen.'*

Today, he catches me, from his door, in his usual brown cardigan, and it looks like it's been his favorite since the Carter administration. (Who am I kidding, I would totally buy it at the thrift shop.)

"Going somewhere?" he asks.

"Moving day," I confirm, from behind the pile of stuff.

"I'll be sad to see you leave, Lou, but I expect a forwarding address," he says.

"Oh! Easy, it's erm— well, the same exact as the current, just, a different apartment. 7A rather than B." I adjust the pile of clothes in my arms, as he clearly has no concern for how heavy knits can be.

But there's a pause as I see him wrestling with the realization.

"You don't mean, *Ellis's* place?" he says, with just the slight inflection of an impossible truth forcing it into a question.

"I sure do." Another pause. Longer this time. So I finally give up and drop the makeshift blanket-bag full of laundry at my feet.

"If you were looking for a roommate, I would have loved the company," he says with more sadness than maybe he means to let through. I don't doubt it, and honestly, a daily tea time with Mr. Ambrose in exchange for the occasional *'how do I FaceTime'* support isn't a bad deal. (Just not the deal I need. Then again, if he was forty years younger…)

"Mr. Ambrose." I put my hand on my hip and look at him with what I hope conveys both the affection and regret I have for the rejection. (Though he will never know the depths of regret I truly feel.) "I'm a married woman now."

He stares at me, frozen in his doorway.

"I'm sorry?"

"Me too," I say under my breath as I snort a laugh that does not convey *'newlywed'* the way I want it to. So I switch to the thing every newly married woman does, and just extend my left hand to wiggle my ring finger, with the ruby that sits atop it. "Married." His eyes land on it, and me, with a weight of disbelief. (Same, honestly.) "It's new." I hurry as if the recency of it explains anything more than timing.

"To—" He stops, looking directly at the door of 7A, which I currently have propped open with a shoe, and then looks back at me. "You married Ellis?"

"I *sureee* did." (That sounds natural, right?)

"*Hudson* Ellis?" He says the full name as if maybe a different version of the man will materialize if he's more specific, maybe I'll clarify a different broody, rude man. Not the one who we all collectively seem to feel is the same Angry Neighbor™.

"One and the same."

Mr. Ambrose is quiet. He's been to war, and somehow this seems to be the most shocking piece of news he's ever been asked to absorb.

"Well," he says, finally, but has no end to the sentence, so just nods quickly to himself as if he's convincing himself. (Again, same.) "I have that wagon for groceries, let me get it for you." He grabs the trolley which does meaningfully speed up the processes. Rather than me walking armfuls of stuff between the two doors. And he stands in the hallway and chats to me as I go back and forth. Never daring to set foot inside Hudson's apartment. (I get it.)

I've moved nearly all my stuff into the guest room, which is because it's bigger than my living room. I discover this on trip nine, when I finally stop moving long enough to stand in the middle of it and actually look. The living room of 7B could fit inside this room with space to spare. I have been living for almost a year next door in a bedroom space roughly the size of this room's closet, sacrificing my own closet in the process.

I sit on the edge of the bed, I left it unmade when I climbed out of it this morning, but it feels like I'm doing it a disservice, so I quickly straighten the duvet and throw all the pillows (for design not function) back on the bed. It's not exactly the way he had it, but he isn't sleeping in here, so it will do.

The light is different here at midday than it was this morning when I woke up. It feels magical in a way I didn't think he would subscribe to. Then again, he's smart, practical, thoughtful. And my comfort in sharing a space will benefit both of us if it means I'm not constantly running back next door. (This bed is too comfortable to run back next door.) Even if it feels like I'm cheating on my own apartment.

I should make a list. It's the thought that arrives every time I am confronted with a large, unstructured task, that never amounts to the bullet points it should. But there's so much to do, items to unpack, things to organize, a system for the closet. I should find some kind of order imposed on the chaos of my belongings now distributed across two apartments like I exploded gently. (I do not make the list.)

What I do instead is lie back on the cloud like duvet and look at the ceiling of a room that is mine (for now), knowing it is temporary, and making the decision, the Louisa James Evans factory default that has gotten me through every ending I never saw coming (always my fault) to just enjoy it while it's mine.

You can be terrified and still show up with a smile, I do it every day. Even on the bad-luck days there's a reason to smile, because the more I do, the more everyone smiles back at me. Creating this Ponzi scheme of happiness that works. The smile is real, by the way, the terror is just also real. They're not mutually exclusive, they just take turns being louder. So the more I can find joy in all the things that might not last, that's usually what drowns out the rest of it. (That and Hugh Jackman.)

Right now, in this room, in this light, the terror is very quiet. (And that is terrifying for a different reason.) I am somewhere between a guest and not, which is maybe the most honest thing I can say about all of this. Not quite belonging, not quite visiting. (Doesn't that just sum me up.)

By the time Chandler and Toby get here, I've made more progress than I thought I would. Chandler walks in first, and I watch her face take in the full tour of the apartment in seconds, she's not subtle about it. (She's not subtle about anything.)

"Lou," she says, stepping into the main room. Where the kitchen breaks away with the large marble island serving as the anchor to the space.

"I know." And I do, it's actually laughable.

"How is this even the same building?"

I walk towards the large windows, where they slide open to a balcony that has a view of the surprisingly quiet street we live on, despite being in the city. Sliding open the glass doors, and somehow the space becomes filled with even more light.

"I'm just saying." She follows me out towards the balcony, leaving Toby behind us in the apartment, as she just sinks down onto the concrete floor, and I join her. "No wonder you married him. If I saw this apartment, I also would have jumped his bones."

"That's not exactly—" I begin, but stop myself as she narrows her eyes with skepticism. "Yes, exactly, bones *jumped*." I don't know how much she will believe all of this, she seems to go back and forth between the romantic who wants everyone to fall in love, or at least fall into bed, with someone, and my best friend, who has doubts. But what Hudson said is true, and I've put enough people in jeopardy by just existing. I'm not going to ask someone else to lie for me.

Toby crosses the living room, where his glasses are pushed up his nose like he identified a research opportunity and will not be derailed by crown moulding, but eventually joins us on the balcony.

It's a large space, surprisingly, and has seating, but for some reason we all are more comfortable down here. It's the reminder that while we aren't *that* different in age, Hudson aged very differently. At one point, he went out and bought patio furniture while I don't have matching sheets, which is a style choice. (Although I do here.)

Toby leans over the railing, looking towards the windows and my side of the building exterior. All of which are smaller.

"Is that your apartment? I don't think I ever noticed that window" he points to the one between the spaces of our balconies. Realizing he's never seen it, probably because he's never been behind the shower curtain in my bathroom.

"That's just my shower window," I say almost comically, like it's an obvious thing, as Chan nods her agreement. "Weirdest design detail ever."

We spend some time catching up, which is funny because it's only been a few days, but apparently a few days is enough for The

Double Shot to have generated a full season of content without me. We eventually moved to the patio furniture, and when we surrendered to it, we spent another ten minutes being annoyed at how comfortable it was. The sun settles lower over the city, and we settle lower into the cushions, and for a while nobody says anything that requires a real answer. Until Chandler sits up straight, reinvigorated and ready to explore.

"Let's look around," Chandler says, hopping to her feet with excitement

"Well, the kitchen you've seen, the living room and dining area you've seen, he has an office, a guest room, and—"

"The primary," she says.

"—is fine, it's just a room, Chan."

"Come on, I'm nosey, let's see it," she presses.

"She's suspicious," Toby corrects.

"There's nothing to be suspicious about," I say, standing and brushing my hands down the front pockets of my overalls. "Down this way, there's a bathroom, behind that door is his office, he never uses it, he seems to like standing at the counter more." Somehow the natural understanding of him slips out, and they don't question it. "That's a guest room," I say. Hoping the curiosity doesn't extend to a room that should be of no interest. Even though that guest room is absolutely the primary bedroom, and *I* am the one inhabiting the guest room.

We cross the apartment, where everything has a place, and the temperature of the thermostat and the signature scent are in a long-term relationship.

"And here is the bedroom," I say as I push open the door. It's covered in bags and piles of clothes I moved over, and still have the long ordeal of hanging up in the shared closet. (Because that's what married people do.) He has some suits in the walk-in, but the rest of the space will be mine, and we will say just like everyone does on any HGTV house-hunting show, that I have *'too much stuff'* and *'need all the space for my shoes.'*

"He doesn't leave a toothbrush out," Toby says from the bathroom. A large ensuite with a tub and separate shower, and two sinks set into a marble different than anywhere else in the apartment. "The counter is immaculate except for your bowls of stuff."

"And? His toaster has also never even seen the light of day." Chandler scampers in to join him, as her reflection in the mirror catches mine. The collected crystal dishes from thrift stores is now how I keep my toiletries, including makeup, and all the perfume samples I've collected. A game of perfume roulette every morning when I dig my hand into the bowl and pray to the Bloomingdale gods to bless me with something that doesn't smell like baby powder.

"There's nothing on his side of the double sink," Toby looks back at me, now the more skeptical of the two. "Most couples, when they cohabitate, show an increase in counter clutter."

"Who is operating this thing," Chandler asks as she leans closer to him and taps him right in the middle of his forehead.

"Hardy-har-har, very funny," Toby replies.

"He's just, very private," I say. "About the bathroom. It's a thing."

"Tell me more about this *thing*." Chandler's head cocks to the side, trying to get more info out of me, on either side of the double entendre.

"A tidiness thing, you know how he is."

"I knew how he was at The Double Shot," Toby says. "I have a half a year's worth of data on how he takes his coffee, I don't actually know him at all, not besides a phone call to your wedding."

"He also hasn't been in lately," Chandler says, and she looks at me and her face is doing the opposite of playing innocent. (Of course.)

"He's probably just—" I start.

"Changes in routine following a significant life event are expected," Toby says. "But the pattern break preceded the wedding by days. Which suggests the variable wasn't the marriage." Chandler rolls her eyes, even though I know she secretly loves to watch his brain work.

"We've been busy," I say.

"I'm sure you have." Chandler pulls her teeth under her lip playfully as she arches an eyebrow in my direction.

Chapter Seventeen

I LIVE HERE

LOUISA

We hear the front door open and I check my phone for the time, he's home early. Not early *early*. But earlier than I expected him to be.

"What do we do?" Chandler asks in a frenzy and Toby makes a confused face.

"What do you mean, I live here, you're allowed to be here," I say. (They can totally be here, right?) I pull Chandler with me. "Come on, you should get used to spending time with him, outside of handing him a coffee." She cuts her eyes back to me now, knowing full well she hasn't seen him in days, and now, it seems, doubts she will outside of being with me.

When we emerge from the bedroom, he's still standing in the entry way, his finger looped into the knot of his tie as he loosens it from his neck. In his other hand, a large brown bag of takeout.

"You're home," I say, walking up to him quickly, knowing I have spectators who already seem to be collecting data and compiling a case (maybe just one of them.) I rise up on my toes and kiss his cheek. The corner of his mouth twitches in reply.

"I live here." He clears his throat, surprised by the guests, the performance, and well, maybe even the questionable judgment that got us here.

"And you brought dinner?"

"Indian," he specifies. "There's more than enough, stay." He looks over my shoulder towards my friends making the offer, speaking louder so they know the invite is for them.

"Absolutely," they reply at the same time. Chandler is not interested in the butter chicken, but maybe buttering him up to see what else she can piece together. And Toby will be more than happy to run it through some mental model of his to tell me that the likelihood of these nuptials being successful is nil. (I already know, trust me.)

"I can take this," I say as I grab the bag of food and bring it to the kitchen. He just follows my steps, taking off his suit jacket and rolling up his shirt sleeves. We leave them in the living room, and I lower my voice to a whisper so the sound doesn't carry through the open space. "I didn't know you were going to be here."

"I *live* here," he repeats, as he grabs a can of sparkling water from the fridge.

"Right, duh, obviously, I just mean, I was moving in all day, and they came by to help." I start unpacking the bag of takeout, container by container. "Although, now that I think about it, they didn't really help at all," I say much louder with the intention of Toby and Chandler both hearing it.

She just blows me a kiss. "I'm helpful in other ways," she says.

Hudson leans against the island so his back is to them when he says, "It's no problem, Louisa, you live here also." He grabs a samosa from the bag on the counter, and reaches for dishes to *actually* set the table, not just the staged placemats that are already there waiting their turn.

"This smells great, I love Indian food," I say.

"I know," he says under his breath.

I don't know when I became a person who eats takeout out of anything other than the container it came in, but here I am, legally bound to it. Chandler put herself well within questioning distance, and I know this was not an accident. Toby on the other hand, he will just quietly observe, eventually telling us his findings, but for now is just here to enjoy some vindaloo. (My favorite.)

"So, Hudson," Chandler kicks it off, with the pleasant tone that screams of a not-so-hidden agenda. "How did you two actually get together?"

Hudson passes the vindaloo without looking up. "I thought Louisa might have covered that." As he takes another bite of food, perhaps in the hope it will spare him the questions.

"Lou has been a little vague," Chandler says. "But I'm a details person."

"She's really not," I say.

"I am for *this*." She cuts me a look that tells me she won't let up.

"I'm also a details person," Hudson says cooly as he settles back in his chair. He's argued cases in front of actual judges, he shouldn't find a twenty-nine-year-old with a gel manicure and a hidden agenda remotely intimidating, but I sure do.

"We were—" I begin, as he is watching me with easy composure, waiting for me to toss him the ball, to tag him in coach, or whatever other sports reference I'm not equipped enough to make.

"The answer about how we got together," Hudson says, knowing that my reply fizzled out on the line. "It isn't interesting." It's delivered flatly, but somehow he manages to sound earnest. "We spent a lot of nights at each other's throats, there's always been tension there. We just didn't immediately call it what it was." He's able to lie so smoothly, though to him, he wouldn't consider this a lie at all. "We were both *just* coming out of relationships." Chandler rolls her eyes in response, knowing exactly who he's referring to, and wanting to make it known that now, even months later, she still has a disdain for him. But Hudson just continues, "Everyone assumed we hated each other, Louisa is such a relationship girl, and I have never been a relationship guy," he says, looking over at me, delivering the final blow that lands this as *authentic.* "So neither of us was entirely sure how to announce it."

"Right," I start.

He hangs on the breath, giving me space to answer, but I don't. "Given the circumstances," he continues, "of how we met. Which were, by most measures, a disaster. And the months following, which were—"

"Also a disaster," I offer.

"Characterful," he says. "I was going to say characterful."

"He wants to say disaster," I correct.

"Well, you did earn me one of my worst days of my professional career." His tone corrects from the flat narrative one he's been using, to the sharp one he uses for me.

"So you decided to return the favor that night?" I retort. We have clearly diverted topics, this one far more honest than the previous.

"I was still trying to get the tentacle porn out of my head and the smell of cloves off my chest," he says, eyebrows pinching together, exposing the wrinkle that lives between them. Chandler makes a sound that is definitely a laugh but she converts, at speed, into a cough to hide it.

"We both know I tried to apologize for that," I say quickly.

"Right, because muffins left outside someone's door like a baby at a fire station is an acceptable apology."

"Survey says?" I look to my friends at the table hoping for the support, where Toby is shoveling food in his mouth and Chandler is wide-eyed.

"Calm down, Steve Harvey," Hudson says, as Chandler's hands just go up in a *'don't look at me'* motion. "The point," he says, taking control of this before it goes somewhere he can't navigate, "is that telling people felt—" I see him searching for the word. "Complicated. Because how do you explain falling for someone when the falling looked, from the outside, like hatred, before we could even admit it to ourselves?"

"There was always tension," I jump in. "I just didn't know

what that tension meant at first." As I say it, I worry that it sounds true, even to me. "And because of the timing, I didn't want it to be colored by the idea of it being a rebound." It's hilarious, actually, knowing that Chandler would have hooted and hollered if I told her I had a rebound. (Roma, too, honestly.)

"So the letter came," Hudson says, bringing it back, which is something I didn't expect him to do. "And when it did, I couldn't lose the person I'd spent months being an idiot about."

I choke on my rice. (Not metaphorically.) A genuine, undignified, wrong-pipe inhalation of basmati rice that requires me to press a napkin to my face and spend three seconds coughing into it while Hudson passes me a glass of water.

I am performing being his wife while he is performing being my husband while my friends sit across the table and watch, one of them already emotionally invested in it being real. This is, objectively, a very manageable situation that I have completely under control. (Not one bit.)

But even knowing this is him putting on a show, the words take me aback by the sheer impossibility of them. And I wonder if this is obvious to everyone. Because if we can't even get past the *'how did you get together'* part of the story, we have absolutely no hope to prove to Immigration (to anyone) that we are happily married.

Under the table, I find his foot with mine and press down with what I intend to be a warning but what he takes (apparently) as an invitation, because his other leg shifts and traps mine beneath it. Calm and strong, and he doesn't look at me as he does it, just reaches for the naan. I drop my hand under the table to try and free my ankle from its cage, and he just swats it away, a smirk pulling on the corner of his lips. (And that makes me want to punch him right in the balls, or, *well*, I can't think about the other thing it makes me want to do.)

Chandler is watching us wordlessly, but for the first time in nearly ten minutes, Toby speaks.

"Statistically, relationships that originate in conflict have—"

"Toby," Chandler snaps.

"—have a lower success rate than those beginning in—"

"Toby!" I'm the one who snaps this time.

"I'm just noting the data doesn't indicate success beyond the two-year mark when you factor in normal divorce rates, family dynamics, the nature of the beginning of the relationship," he continues, unfazed as always. Never really understanding why people don't seem to feel as drawn to the numbers of things as he is.

"The data," Hudson says mildly, taking his glass of water back from me, "can take the night off."

Chandler continues with her round of questioning as she pushes food around her plate. He answers, charmingly, eventually releasing my leg from where he held it long and tight enough I was beginning to feel pins and needles. Hudson answers like he's being deposed, or maybe like someone who is used to doing the deposing and knows exactly how much rope to give. Finally, she asks how he knew. He doesn't ask what. He says *the immigration letter changed everything practically.* There it is, the rope. Not too much to hang ourselves, but just enough that someone might think we could. "But the rest, my feelings, changed earlier than that." She asks what he means by the rest and he looks at me, briefly, and says, "Ask Louisa."

"Do not ask Louisa," I (Louisa) say emphatically.

"Magic-wanded those problems away." Chandler grins, finally satisfied. Taking a sip of the wine Hudson opened when the conversation took a turn into an interrogation.

"What about work," Toby asks, shifting gears. "What happens with work?"

"Well, I won't be able to work at The Double Shot until this is all sorted, but I can keep recording, and that's going well," I say.

"Better than well," Hudson corrects. "She has three books releasing this month." I do, he's right. Even amidst the *find your passion* and my auditioning for non-fiction in the event I never do, I have three books coming out, and already am booked out for the next months with new recordings.

"How would you—" I start, low enough that only he can hear it. He moves closer, the corner of his mouth looks like it could be reaching for mine, but I won't let myself believe it. Instead it's the almost-smile that gets settled back. (Even though it still exists in his eyes.) Chandler and Toby are having a sidebar conversation about something far less interesting than whatever is on the tip of his tongue, and with his eyes on me, mine drops to his mouth as it forms the words.

"If you think," he says, as his voice drops a step lower, "that I don't know exactly what my wife is doing, you're underestimating how closely I pay attention to you."

Chapter Eighteen

KERMIT THE MUG

HUDSON

I'm dressed for the day, standing in the kitchen, staring at the shelves in the cabinet that actually shocked me when I opened it this morning. In the last weeks, she moved in the small things as well. The quiet colonization of objects you don't notice until you do, and then you can't remember what it looked like before. Who am I kidding, *I noticed immediately.*

The mugs are the worst of it. There are too many. There is no logical reason for the number of mugs currently occupying this cabinet. They are stacked, *if that's the word*, in a way that suggests pure optimism is keeping them in place. They don't match. They don't even attempt to. Different sizes, shapes, colors, some with sayings, some with drawings, some that appear to have been formed by hand in a moment of artistic passion and complete disregard for symmetry or function. I think one of them has actual holes like Swiss cheese and was put here just to taunt me. *No need, sweetheart, you walking around in just the 'sleep shirt' you call pajamas is doing that more than well enough.* It hits her mid-thigh, I've seen her less clothed in public, but there's something about the way she just wakes up and hops on the counter, bare legs dangling, that could send any man over the edge.

I shake the thought, and look back to the bright collection of misshapen pottery where my four cream stoneware mugs used to be. Seriously. How does *one* woman have so many mugs? How many cups of coffee can she even drink? Is she hosting a daily tea service for eight that I'm not aware of? Does she cycle through them without washing them? Is there a system here that I'm simply not seeing, or is the absence of one the point?

I pull down a mug that looks mostly normal.

That is until I set it in front of me. It's a frog, not *decorated* with frogs, not printed with a small tasteful frog somewhere near the handle. It's actually shaped like one, the handle is a lily pad, the body is green and slightly lumpy in a way that suggests the sculptor was either very committed to the bit or had never seen a mug before. *It has eyes.* Bulging ones, that are staring at me from the rim with a blank serenity that it has accepted its fate to be filled with boiling liquids.

I stare back at it. Locking eyes with the vessel for my coffee was not on my list of things to do today. But that list is becoming more untenable the longer she's here. And we still have a long way to go.

"That one's mine." She doesn't look up from where she's sitting, folders spread open on the counter, with a yellow legal pad where she's actually taking notes. She's already been at it for twenty minutes, cross-referencing notes she's made about my life against the actual facts of it with the intensity of, well, *me*, studying for a bar exam. Given the circumstances and what's at stake, it's not an unfair comparison. *I'm impressed.* I'm— well, I'm a lot of things.

"I can see that it's yours."

"He's Kermit the Mug." I look at Kermit, and he looks back at me with his terrible, lopsided, empty clay eyes.

"Terrible," I say. With the sneaky suspicion that this may be the source of my nightmares tonight. Who am I kidding, I know what will occupy my dreams.

"Don't be mean to him." She turns a page. "If you hate it, just use a different mug." I turn to face her, holding it out in front of me, assessing it for history, chips, maybe seeing if it was once a boy turned into a mug by a witch who cast a spell on a castle. *That would explain it.*

"Did you make it?" I ask, skeptical, and her eyebrows shoot up as soft brown hair falls around her face. "Sorry," I add, "*him.*" Because that one look made it feel necessary.

"No, I bought him off a street vendor named Lara, she was Turkish, she made the most beautiful pottery." he starts off the story as she does everything, with a smile across her face and complete disregard for the time or any schedule I might be on, naming every character, including anyone in the background, because she feels they deserve to be seen. "—I went back weeks later, but she was gone, so I never finished the set."

"Bummer," I say. And imagine the *'rest of the set'* with some actual fear. I put Kermit the Mug on the counter and take down one of the matching set I've had for years, parting the Red Sea of mismatched ceramics to find one with no engraving, no face, and doesn't say *'Mug Lyfe'* on it.

I pour a second coffee without being asked and set it near her elbow, and she pulls it toward her without looking, as I fill it with milk and bring out the teddy-bear bottle of honey. Don't ask me. She drinks coffee, tea, drip, matcha, lattes, it's like each day she throws a dart at a board, or spins a wheel to make the decision, whereas every morning I wake up and start my day with the same order. At least I did until she moved in. But when I pour myself a cup, I do the same for her.

She crosses her arms and lays her head atop the open folder on the counter. When this started, she mocked my preference for printed materials. All of which I will shred when this is done. But it's better than being glued to a screen, and the way she doodles in the corners is ironic given the seriousness of the situation.

"I'm studied out," she stresses, her muffled voice trapped in the folded cavern of her arms.

I take a sip of my coffee as I lean against the counter. "Prove it."

"Hudson James Ellis," she says into the countertop with a scoff, likely at the coincidence of our shared middle name that everyone else can call fate. "Born September 9th, 1989." With the first driver's-license-level information confirmed, she sits upright on the stool, cracks her neck to each side, and tucks the loose hairs behind her ears, though they remain defiant as they fall immediately. She looks at me like she's preparing for something competitive, a glint in her eye that's a challenge I crave.

"Columbia undergrad, Columbia Law School, it was good for you because you passed the bar on the first try, which you don't talk about, but I know you think it makes you better than other people, *definitely one.*" I don't react, even though I want to.

"You take your coffee black at home," she goes on. The casual use of the word *home* is something that is more and more frequent now. "But it's an Americano, extra-hot, when you're out. You had one of those hot-dog dogs growing up named Nathan,. Your first kiss was when you were a sophomore in high school to Charlotte Hartley, *that one was honestly a surprise.* The timing, I mean, I assumed it would have been earlier." I raise an eyebrow, but she doesn't stop, and doesn't look away.

Good.

"Your parents got divorced when you were seven, which pretty much stunted who you are and your ability to commit to anyone." She pauses. "Or anyone *real,*" she clarifies, because this, right here, what we are doing is about the largest commitment one can make. She seems to be enjoying herself, which regrettably, makes me enjoy myself.

"Your first car was a used Volvo because you considered it extremely sensible," she continues, warming up again. Building as I've heard her deliver powerful monologues, this time, *about me.* "But after you made your first real *'I'm a big deal'* money, you bought yourself a brand new one. Same brand, slightly less sensible."

Not inaccurate.

"You use an Old Spice deodorant, but one that smells like lavender which, also a surprise. And you don't have any known allergies, but you have that thing where you think cilantro tastes like soap. You have strong opinions about everything, so strong they border on political, and when you're thinking really hard about something..." She trails off and I don't move.

"You stand exactly the way you are right now." The last two words are said with overwhelming pride and accomplishment as she points the glitter pen at me with her big eyes narrowed to victorious slits in my direction.

"How am I standing?"

She dramatically looks me up and down. "Like you're waiting for the part where I get something wrong so you can point it out." It's annoyingly accurate. I was, on the edge of every word, waiting to correct her, but the thing she doesn't see is how impressed I am that there's nothing to correct. The coffee in my hand is good, so good, I use it to swallow down the very accurate assessment of me.

I don't confirm or deny any of this, which she *correctly* interprets as confirmation.

There's a shift in her posture that's subtle, but there. Her spine straightens. Her shoulders pull back just slightly. It's pride. Not the way most people have it, it's not loud. Not obnoxious. Just... present. *Like she is.*

She's done well.

She knows she has. It swells me with pride and fear at the same time. Something about the way she looks at me like she's figured something out makes my pulse quicken in my chest. Because I know how this goes. I know what happens when someone starts paying this much attention to me. When they start noticing the small things, the parts you don't offer up willingly. It always turns into something else. And I am, historically, not built for the part that comes after that. Part of why this agreement is possible, because there's no one who has loved me by choice, not really, that didn't recognize how little of me they knew. That didn't lob the term *'emotionally unavailable'* as they walked out the door I held open for them.

I set my mug down.

"That was thorough," I say and she smiles at that. Not wide and over-exaggerated, but enough to show she heard it, and she liked the praise.

"I've been studying," she says, capping the pen dramatically for effect.

"Good girl."

Her eyebrows pull together and the smile on her face morphs to something else. She won't name it, and neither will I. So instead I finish my coffee, rinse my mug before putting it in the dishwasher, and head to work.

Chapter Nineteen

LOUISA

The chair makes that awful plastic-on-linoleum screech as Hudson pulls it out and sits beside me, like the building itself is objecting to our presence.

"Okay," Hudson says. He's prepared for this, mid-process and ten steps ahead. The way other men prepare for triathlons. (Note to self: ask Hudson if he has done a triathlon.) "We start with the I-130 and the supporting affidavit. Then, I have the financial co-sponsorship form, already filled out, you just sign at the bottom."

"You filled out my forms?"

"You don't have a great track record with paperwork."

"Presumptuous," I mutter not so quietly under my breath.

"You're welcome," he says.

"Sorry, did I say presumptuous? I meant asshole."

"Wow," he says, completely unbothered. "I didn't know you Brits pronounced 'organized' like that. Cute." He pulls out the paper and hands me a pen. Tapping his long finger on the dotted line where I'm meant to sign. Scrawling *Louisa James Evans* on the line before looking at it a second longer and adding a quick *Ellis* to the end of it. There's something about the way he does

198

things that's not just organized, but inevitable. Like even if I didn't sign it, the pen would somehow sign it on its own just to keep things moving because *he* said so.

Hudson takes the paper back without comment, already stacking it with the others, and on to the next thing.

Of course he is.

When they call our number the anxiety begins to build. I wish I could say it's exciting. It's not even really fear. Just an awareness of every single nerve ending in my body suddenly remembering they exist. Waiting to be told what kind of reaction to have. (I wish I knew.)

The clerk (Deborah, according to her lanyard) looks at us, a completely unhidden assessment of the two of us. Her eyes move from me to him, back to me, taking in the differences, the similarities (wedding bands is about where it ends), and whatever invisible checklist she's running through in her head; she's marking things off.

I wonder what she sees. (If she sees it immediately.) If she has a mental stamp of FRAUD she just slammed against my forehead.

But she accepts the first form Hudson hands her without question. I always thought the DMV was bad. This? This makes that scene in *Beetlejuice* look like a dream. Not because of the people in the waiting room, we're surrounded by them, all kinds, all stories, all sitting in the same awful chairs under the same flickering lights. I want to talk to them, and what brought them here, what they left behind, what they're hoping for. But Hudson was more focused on paperwork than making waiting-room friends. (Boo.)

"Do you have the original certificate?" the clerk asks. Hudson doesn't hesitate, opens the folder, finds the right tab, and pulls another sheet, and slides it across her desk.

Deborah says nothing, so I say nothing.

My leg, however, did not get the memo. What started as light shaking is beginning to become a non-stop bounce, and I wonder how long before it gives me away. Before they realize I'm a fraud, he's helping a fraud, we could never be married, and they arrest me. The anxiety in my chest is blooming, but I'm trapped in this chair until we finish this transactional *'the United States government does not yet consider that you are a person'* paperwork. Any second now, they're going to stand up, walk around the desk, ask us to come with them, and suddenly this becomes a different kind of room for a different conversation.

I feel his hand come down on my thigh. Pressing it down, stopping the jittering from continuing. Not aggressive, but firm. (Like everything he does.) The bouncing stops, not because I told it to, because he did.

I spend our entire time here watching the clock behind Deborah's head, because there are only so many times you can read the laminated posters about penalties for immigration fraud, what to do if you suspect someone of immigration fraud, and of course, job recruitment. Every poster begins to feel more and more personal.

I'm on maybe the fourth or fifth document when I finally pause. It's not anything dramatic (maybe it is), but the pen didn't run out and no one walked in to arrest me. I just simply looked down at the paper with a little more clarity, and saw for about the dozenth time today, our names together, printed in that standard government font, clean and official, and entirely without sentiment.

Hudson James Ellis and Louisa James Evans.

Right next to the box checked 'spouse.'

The word is there in its little bitty box like it means nothing, because to the form it doesn't. It's just a category in someone's database somewhere, and yet, somehow this is the moment it finally clicks into place. The gravity of the situation. Not just mine, but his as well.

"Louisa," Hudson says, as it pulls my attention away from the hyperfixation of something that won't do me any good now. His hand is still on my leg, maybe the only thing keeping it steady, as his finger taps against my inner thigh. A quiet, gentle rhythm like he's counting me back into the room.

I don't know how this can feel so intimate, when it's all paperwork. How the government, which doesn't care about my feelings, looks at the two of us and goes *yep, you both are legally bound.*

I've been other kinds of intimate with people before, I've shared beds, even a toothbrush holder, I've told people things I hadn't meant to, laughed when things weren't funny, and I've stayed when I should have left. (Clearly.) I might not always find passion easily, but there are intimacies of friendships, and even what I thought might have been love, that I've shared with people in my life. But when the time came and I needed someone to stand next to me at an altar and in a room like this, I can't think of anyone else who would have even considered such a thing. And I don't think I would have been able to say yes to anyone but him, knowing his investment is transactional. It's the one thing I can't mess up, because he hated me from the start.

It's a deflating thought, the slow air seeping out of a balloon versus a balloon being squeezed so tight, it pops. But there's something underneath it that makes me want to laugh. Because how in the ever-loving fuck did I end up someone's wife.

Not just someone's. *His.*

I look at Hudson as he's trading papers with Deborah, sliding our IDs across the desk. It's contractual for him, a dance he knows steps to. His jaw is slightly set, he's dressed for work, and he's getting through this as quickly as possible. If I'm smart, I'll do the same. But smart is not something I'm often called. Each time signing my name, appending the new last name that I haven't taken more legally than updating my instagram. (For show, obviously.)

With that, Deborah, who does not go by *'Deb'* (sorry), takes a large stamp and presses it into the ink before bringing it down onto our application. (Not my forehead.)

"Are we approved?!" I say, excitedly. Okay, sure my hand

hasn't had to sign that much paperwork maybe in my life, but this wasn't nearly as hard as people make it out to be.

She laughs. (Okay, maybe not.)

"Step one, Louisa," Hudson says, a voice low in my ear. Somehow finding its way to speak to me even with the background noise of dozens of papers and people all around us doing the same thing.

"We will contact you about the interviews, any questions?" she asks, typing something quickly into her computer and eager to dismiss us.

"Um, what questions do I have…" I think out loud. "What. Questions. Do. I. Have." It's almost a nervous little jingle as it comes out of my mouth.

"None," he says smoothly. "Thank you." He collects the papers, pulls my chair back before I can even process that I should stand, his hand settling at the small of my back as he guides me out of the chair, out of the space, out of the room.

"Hey, what if I have a question," I ask him as his hand on my back guides us through the fluorescent government-building hallways.

"I'll answer it."

———

The restaurant is loud in a good way, you know the kind that means people are enjoying themselves and the music, and kitchen is just a backdrop to that. I invited Hudson to join us for lunch and our 'Tequila Update' but I knew he wouldn't for two reasons. One, he doesn't eat lunch, and two, he spends as little unrequired time around me as possible. He did tell me to *be brave and order the fajitas* before he got into his car and headed back to the office.

I've barely sat down before my shoulders drop the six inches from where I felt them hanging from my ears. "I need a big one."

"Pretty sure you've got that at home," Chandler jokes as she flips to the back of the menu to pretend to make a decision about something she definitely already decided before we walked in.

"I mean a margarita," I say.

"Ahhh," she theatrically says, always one for a little bit of gossip. Even when I wasn't dating, she loved to hear the salacious details of whoever I'm narrating, it always makes for fun margarita conversation.

We have a usual booth by the window, it's also in our favorite section because in all the time we've been coming here, Mateo, the server, has completely gone along with the fact that we are fully invested in reaching the bottom of the bottomless chips and salsa. (Which of course, we never do.) The margaritas usually take up more real estate than we anticipate.

"Good afternoon, ladies, my name is Paul, I'll be your server, can I get you started with anything to drink?" I look up from my slightly sticky menu where I had been mulling over what flavor sugar-tequila mixture I was going to go for today, when the unfamiliar voice interjected.

"I'm sorry, and I don't mean to be rude," I begin.

"Yes, she does," Chandler jokes.

"But we were hoping to sit in Mateo's section, is he here? Is this not his table today?" I ask, hoping Paul can see that it's really nothing personal.

"He no longer works here, but I'll be glad to take care of you." Ugh. Last time we were here, he was telling us all about his sister's gymnastics competition. How am I supposed to know how it went? I shake away the fact that I'll just have to accept it.

"I'll have a mango marg, please and thanks!" Chandler orders, knowing Paul is surely just as capable. He put down the chips and salsa with the same enthusiasm as Mateo always did.

"I'll do the same."

The margs come out, the chips and salsa are replaced for a second bowl, and we put in our order for lunch, late lunch. Closer to dinner. (I did *not* get fajitas.)

"So," Chandler says, "How's it actually going?"

I drag a chip through the salsa. "Which part?"

"Being married." Chandler props her chin in her hand. "Like, day-to-day, because it all happened so fast, Lou, and you know me, you know I'm supportive, and I get it, I mean, I've seen him, but it just went from nothing to somethin' *real* fast."

"It was always something, Chan," I say, and it doesn't feel like the lie it might be. "You heard him at dinner."

"I heard him, but now I'm asking you."

"He's different from anyone I've ever been with." And that is a truer statement than anything else I could have said.

"I figured, I mean, when he called to help with the wedding, I was stunned. But he was so specific, he had everything thought through, flowers, music, all of it." I'm drinking down the last drops of my mango marg, and definitely ready for another one considering the topic of this conversation. Trying not to fixate on just how much he did, even though he was ready to dismiss it all to Chandler and Paola.

"He's very specific," I say, licking the salt from the rim.

"Would you tell me the truth?" she asks, staring at me in a way that fills me with self-doubt.

"About what?" I ask.

"All of it. If, well, if you weren't happy, or if something is wrong." She almost sounds sad, and that makes me sad. I didn't want to lie to her. Then again, I also didn't want to lie to the government. But I also don't want anyone else in a position where they could get into trouble for me. So, I pack it away, think about what Hudson said. I don't have to lie, I can just tell the part of the truth that's the safest.

"I am happy," I say, "but I'll be happier with another drink."

Chandler's phone buzzes on the table, and I see the name flash across the screen, along with this face beneath a red circle with a slash through it. We both look at it as her eyebrows shoot up.

"Now, Chan...I guess the question is, would *youu* tell *meee* the truth about why my brother is calling you?" I cock my head to the side, playing coy, because she has refused to admit what everyone around her has seen from the beginning. That the two of them, no matter the literal ocean that is between them, cannot stay away from each other.

She flips her phone upside down, pretending that by not seeing it, it's not real. But just because it's facedown on the table does not mean the phone stops ringing. But that's not how problems work.

Chapter Twenty

HUDSON

"I have three work dinners in the next six weeks," I say. "Andrew's wedding, *you don't know him,* and," I check the date on the calendar again, "a silent auction in June."

She looks up, eyes wide and cheeks hollow. This was part of it, she knew it, but maybe she thought there was more time before I'd call her up for duty. So far it has all been submissions of paperwork. The application for purchase of apartment 8A happened four weeks after we said *I do.* I even included her name on the application, which will improve optics for Immigration.

But she has a way about her in the morning, no matter how routine this has become, that I find distracting. I think because she listens with her entire self, like whatever you're saying has her full attention whether you've earned it or not. In a room full of lawyers, it'll be the most dangerous thing she walks in with.

"The silent auction is part of the foundation attached to the client we're meeting for dinner. Don't let it fool you. It's not altruism."

"When is it ever," she says as she sips from her mug. Our

mornings have become a routine of discussing the logistics of shared life. She's picking at her nail polish, subtle but nervously.

"They're not interrogations," I say, trying to assuage some of the nerves she seems to have. "The partners know I'm married now, their wives will be there. It's the kind of thing—"

"That someone's wife attends." She completes the sentence and nods quickly, resigned to her fate, like she knew the bill was coming but still flinches at the total. "Right, okay, yeah, of course I'll be there." I can see the wheels turning behind her eyes, thinking through what exactly it will mean.

"Tonight."

"*This* tonight?" The shock nearly knocks her off the stool.

"What other tonight could I mean?" I don't think she hears the laugh in my voice as I take another sip of coffee.

"I don't know, tomorrow's tonight? Next week's tonight?" She's absolutely rambling some kind of frantic nonsense. "You should have led with that."

"I'm leading with it now."

Tonight's dinner has been on the calendar for weeks, and having Louisa in attendance is more important than ever. Because to men like Hugh Sterling, who you marry is about as much of an accessory as anything else. *And his sons are no better.* All but one I hear, who walked away from this in favor of a quieter life. Which, from everything I've seen of this family, strikes me as the most intelligent decision any of them has made. Lucas was closer to their account when it happened, and from what he says, the family nearly split from the whole ordeal. Probably why *this* merger has them all at each other's throats, PTSD from the last time a deal like this nearly took down their empire.

"It's a big client, my boss and some colleagues will be there, but so will Lucas and Paola. You'll know them."

She stares up at me. "What am I supposed to wear?"

"Whatever you'd normally wear."

Her arms are crossed across her terrycloth robe with an expression that fiercely communicates that *'whatever you'd normally wear'* is not remotely helpful guidance for a dinner with the senior partner of a corporate law firm and a client whose family is currently the subject of a merger negotiation, and often Page Six.

"I'm known for a lot of things, Louisa. Women's fashion isn't one of them," I say through a smirk. She doesn't miss the intent, but is too focused to respond directly.

"I'll call Paola." Of course she will. Louisa wasted no time making Paola her friend, because Louisa wastes no time making anyone her friend. "Because there isn't something *I would normally*...that's the point," she quips.

I've met her friends, her colleagues, and I know what she means. The people I surround myself with professionally have a different kind of polish, the kind that comes from decades of measuring success in shiny, reflective ways. But Louisa's success is a different metal entirely. It accumulates the way the darkening on a silver tea set does, not a flaw, or something to be corrected. The evidence of the *life* of the thing. She isn't waiting to be polished into something. She already is something, her desperation to stay here proves that. I mean, why else would someone go so far as to marry an effective stranger, especially one you loathe.

"Some people," she says, in a tone of profound reasonableness, *which is clearly an act,* "give someone more than eight-hours notice for an event that requires a person to find a dress and build an entire personality for an evening."

"You have a personality." A massive one. She's a color wheel of emotion full of the most nuanced tones I didn't even know existed.

"I'll need a *different* one."

"No, you won't." She's not anything like the rest of them, and for that reason more than anything, I don't want her to be anyone but herself. "I'll pick you up here, at six."

———

She comes out at six on the dot, which is a surprise that I didn't account for, because I factored in the Louisa time buffer of twenty minutes.

I'm sitting in the living room, a room that has gained more colorful decor in the last months, and as I notice every throw pillow or knickknack she brought into this space, each one seems to fit in a way that indicates the space was being held for it. As her bedroom door opens, she is draped in something the color of deep plum and dripping with a beauty that I've never seen her have. It catches me off guard.

Her hair is up, tightly pulled back and pinned. I heard her getting ready, the same video playing over and over. It's smooth and contained and unlike her in every way that matters. I can tell it doesn't fit, as she keeps checking it in the mirror. She looks like she prepared for an inspection.

"Do I look okay?" she asks me, looking for an approval that feels deeper than this one outfit. I take steps to stand near her.

"Turn around," I say.

"I can change, I have another option…"

I place my hands on both her shoulders and turn her to face the mirror that hangs in the hallway. She resists for a second, squirmish, but stills as I exhale. I see she does the same. Nodding to herself, gently, a subtle count of four all while her eyes are locked on me.

I find where she's tucked and hidden the pins in the folds and twists of her hair. I am aware of her in a way I was not prepared to be, the warmth of her neck, the small escaped pieces of hair at the nape that the pins never captured. There's no less than a dozen of them, I keep pulling them out until I find the one that has been doing load-bearing work for the whole structure. I take them out one by one and set them on the hallway table, and when the last one goes, I work my fingers into her hair at the base and shake it loose the way the wind might, gentle and thorough. The way she always seems just a little windblown, like she came in from some-where more interesting than wherever she's really been.

My hands are not delicate in the way the situation requires. I work through the length of it once, redistributing, settling it back into the more natural state of her, one that I recognize. And one it's growing harder for me to ignore.

She steps back into me, the shape of her body soft against mine. She goes very still. Thinking, like I am, that this surreal closeness is the comfort we have to avoid in each other. Because too much is at risk. My body twitches and the front of my pants feels fuller as the scent that radiates from the nape of her neck climbs upward and becomes the only air I can breathe.

The hallway is quiet and suddenly has a different weight and texture than it did only two minutes ago. My hands are still knotted in her hair, which I remove with an unhurried motion. My thumb drags down the column of her neck. I am not going to make this into something, I am going to put my hands back in my pockets and say something, *anything*, because the silence of our stares as she stands in here in that dress is going to make me more ill-prepared for tonight than any tentacle porn.

"Better," I say.

She turns around, eyes large, and the plum of the dress pulls a similar color from the depth of her irises that I'd only ever previously considered brown.

Her face is painted with an expression trying to multitask, the resentment that normally freckles her nose is tucked behind the reflections of curiosity, looking at me in a way she never has before. *For a long moment, or perhaps a moment too long.* Something snaps her attention, and her eyes narrow with an amount of doubt she's let slip more than once.

"Was it that bad?" She exhales the question with a resignation that makes me sad for her. It's not coming from this, but my guess is the hundreds before where she's felt like she wasn't enough for the people in her life, the unrelenting disappointment she felt from her parents. She looked stunning, perfect. It was jarring when she first stepped out of the bedroom. But she looked like a perfect stranger.

"You weren't yourself." I tuck a loose tuft of hair behind her ear, leaving the rest to fall around her face in the way it does naturally, with pieces that wave and brush her shoulders.

"Kind of the point."

"Not for me, it isn't," I reply, hoping she can hear in my voice just how honest I'm being. We are sharing space much more than we have been, and the tension between us is palpable in a way it's never been tinted before. Now without the drapes of anger to hide it, *I am in significant fucking trouble.*

She asks me questions on the drive to the restaurant, the kind that always fill her mind when she's about to meet people. Pure, kind curiosity. *Also nerves.*

As we walk towards our party, she slips her hand in mine, delicately, but confident in its place. The timing reminds me of the intention of the show, so I wrap my fingers with hers. As I see the table of my colleagues, I lean down ever so slightly to whisper to her before the moment is too late, because from everything I've gathered, situations like this are unnatural for her. "You're smart, you're funny," I take in a breath of her, "beautiful," I exhale. "Be yourself and they'll never fucking see you coming." I know I've said the right thing, maybe for once, when her shoulders drop where they had been lifted in a state of anxiety.

"Be myself, or be your wife?"

"Lucky for me, tonight, that's the same thing."

Arthur stands with enthusiasm when we arrive, which he doesn't do for everyone, which means he's been looking forward to this. He gave me shit the day I returned to work wearing a wedding ring. The next day, waiting in my office, was a check and a sterling-silver picture frame as a wedding gift with a note that said *'you should have invited me.'* It now sits on my desk as a reminder, picture and all.

"Hudson." The back clap and handshake before turning his full-attention to Louisa. "And you are the reason this one has suddenly become something approaching bearable to work with."

"I don't know that I would *ever* call him *bearable*," she says.

"We're making forward progress, but I'd say we're still pretty early in negotiations." Even though she's nervous, her voice is packed with the sunshine she expels freely. And Arthur's face responds as I've seen everyone's do in her presence, just opening, becoming somehow more alive just by her attention. The attention of most, particularly those in this room, puts people on the defensive, but not hers. Because it looks far more like interest, genuine, compassionate affection. Even if the crux of the comment was roasting me for my lack of friendly nature, there's something in the manner of her that envelops anyone she's talking to.

"Well, let's just say it's more than anyone has managed in years," Arthur says, and the look he gives me is one of approval. "I like her," he says to me, as though she isn't standing directly beside me.

"She's aware," I say, and she just responds with a smile.

The Sterlings arrive last. Hugh, the CEO of the Sterling Group, *and his family,* his two sons, Alfie and Cal. Something has always felt strange to me about grown men who are exclusively referred to by nicknames. They both have high-ranking titles in an organization they've inherited. Alfie looks like he has spent his life being the son of the money rather than the earner of it. While Cal, I imagine, must be short for calculated. I've never had an interaction with him where he wasn't clearly attempting to shape the conversation in a very specific way for his advantage. And in the time I've been on this account, his opinions have been more shrewd and two steps ahead than anyone I've worked with, *including his father.*

Cal is seated next to Claire, strategic, whether on her part or his I'm not sure. *Even though her fiancé is casually on the other side of her.* She measured the geometry of the table in advance. She is as she has always been. Polished, tall, and statuesque, in every way.

Louisa walks up to her, gives her a hug. I know they had met, but with Louisa, meeting someone and knowing someone are pretty much the same thing. She asks how she's been, *and means it,* compliments her dress, *and means it,* congratulates her on her engagement, *and means it.* And Claire does the same. She takes her hand, and with a sincere sense of warmth I've never seen, congratulates her, *us,* on the wedding.

Meals like this are common. Meant to instill confidence, as we all drink overpriced bottles of wine, and I watch Arthur's cholesterol increase by a dozen points with the slab of steak he orders.

Louisa ends up next to Alfie Sterling. I did *not* arrange this and I cannot fix it without making a scene, which I am *briefly,* genuinely tempted to do.

Alfie leans toward her like he has decided she might be interesting. I give it thirty seconds before she has him completely.

She's got him in ten.

Where most people would cower, or concede to their seatmate, I watch as she charms him. Pulling out honesty that I didn't think possible from the man who ordered for his wife and told a dick joke within thirty seconds of his arrival, *which is coincidentally how long he lasts in bed.*

That is a dick joke.

I watch as he becomes a realer version of himself, even involving the woman who he has exclusively referred to as his ball and chain. *Yeah, he's that guy.* They fall almost immediately into a conversation about something I can only catch fragments of from where I sit. She is making him laugh, and it's making me fucking crazy.

"That's exactly the problem with—"

"The Hamptons, I know." She says it like she's finishing his sentence because she already knew where it was going, which she probably did, because she listens to people in a way that means she already knows what they'll say before they say it. It's infuriating. It's the most disarming thing I've ever watched another person do.

She leans back towards me, and I lower myself so her lips are at my ear.

"I've never been," she whispers and I can feel the victorious grin that spreads across her face, even though it's hidden in the crook of my neck. Alfie says something else to recapture her atten-tion. *It's fine.* This is the point. This is why she's here.

This merger for the Sterling Group has not only been my primary focus for months, it's a path to partner and to really carve myself a seat at Arthur's table for the rest of my career if I want it. It's complicated for reasons that predate me that include board approvals and proxy voting members, the fact that multi-million dollar deals like this one always feel like there's some kind of hidden liability baked in, especially for companies where nepo-tism is key. But I'm good at my job, and this will be a big feather in my cap. Hugh Sterling isn't here to talk about the deal that he knows will be done one way or another. But as he and Arthur are deeply engaged in discussing the future, as present as I am trying to be, it's the conversation next to me that has my attention being peeled away. Something about the sound of her voice is able to cut through all the layers of the people around us.

Arthur asks something to me that snaps my attention back. But the thought lasts approximately three seconds before Louisa laughs again, and anything not related to her is ripped from my mind. I am more than peripherally aware of her, even while she is next to me, that she is somehow not near enough.

By the third course, Alfie has landed on the topic of the silent auction. Meant as a way to sponsor their arts and music founda-tion. I told her about it as part of the run-through for tonight. I, *of course*, am attending, I have for the last years as long as I've worked with them, or even adjacent to them. Arthur always buys a table to show the firm's support, and this year, I'll have a date.

"You'll both come, obviously," Alfie responds with such assurance, answering the question that wasn't asked to him. I know it's just pandering, the way he is, but dear god, I can't stand him.

"Of course," she says, touching my arm.

Alfie is looking at Louisa like she's the best conversation he's had in recent memory, *which I'm sure she is,* and the thought is followed immediately by another thought I refuse to finish. I grab the seat of Louisa's chair and slide her the six inches closer to me. Is it territorial? *Sure.* Do I care? Not in the fucking slightest.

Her head spins to look up at me, as she is now nestled closer to me, she can undoubtedly feel the breath I expel with each word in response.

"We'd love that," I say.

She turns back to Alfie like nothing happened, but her shoulder stays against mine.

Neither of us moves.

The end of the dinner happens the way these things always do, with the handshakes and cheek kisses, the social administration of departure. Arthur shakes my hand and pulls me in for a hug, all setting him up to articulate the thing he's had tucked into his pocket behind his pocket square all night. Just how pleased he is. "You've always shown up, but this is different." He looks between us with deep satisfaction, and a part of me hates myself for how much validation I get from this man.

I collect Louisa's wrap from the coat check as we walk out to the valet. "You survived," I say.

She shrugs into it, into *me.* "Turns out being your wife isn't the worst thing that's ever happened to me."

"High praise."

"Top ten, maybe." She starts walking toward the car. "Don't let it go to your head."

I don't say anything.

But it goes straight to my head.

Chapter Twenty-One

NOSTALGIA TAX

LOUISA

The clock on my dashboard is six minutes fast, a temporal hallucination I refuse to correct because some days those six minutes are the only thing keeping the rest of my life from totally going off the rails. (And it doesn't always work.)

I'm thirty-five miles from home on a pilgrimage for the *chocolate* digestive biscuits. (The local grocery import aisle doesn't stock them anymore.) The justification I've built for this trip is airtight, the specialty shop is the only place within a reasonable (kind of) driving distance that carries the version of a smokey Earl Grey, and the clotted cream that when I put on the scone I make later, will make *my*—erm, *our* apartment smell like a kitchen I only half remember from my childhood. I don't cling to a lot of my childhood, definitely even less before we came to the states, but there's something about the nostalgia of baked goods. That's the justification. The other reason (that I will admit to myself in this car alone) is that the last few months have involved so much newness that sometimes I need the smell of something old just to confirm I still exist as myself, separate from everything I've agreed to.

The drive is long enough that I've played Roma's voice note, twice. (And the new Noah Kahan album.) She left it this morning while I was recording. Eleven minutes, which means she had too much to say for a text and too much tact for a phone call she knew I'd have to fake my way through without lying directly to her face. (She knows my face, even when she can't see it, she would know.)

'Okay so I've been sitting on this because I wanted to be sure before I said it out loud,' Roma begins, giving me a grace period to prepare. *'But I've listened to the last files back to back and Lou, I don't know how you did it, I genuinely don't, and I'm choosing not to ask, but whatever it is— it's back. Not just back. It's different. It's so much more. You're not narrating two people anymore, you're making us all live it.'* She goes on, tells me about a new series, a protective author who wants a call, and the three non-fiction auditions she gently (not so gently) brushes aside. She's not wrong. I submitted them as a backup plan, not a real one. *'Romance is your home, babe. You can visit anywhere else you want. But this is where you live.'*

I laugh to myself (okay, maybe I cry a single tear) because it wasn't long ago I didn't live in the books I was reading, and I wasn't going to be able to live in my home. It's just taken a few months, and my once-grumpy-neighbor-turned-husband.

When I pull into the parking lot, there's more commotion than I would expect for a mini mall with nothing more than a British grocery store, a laundromat, and a bookstore with a *'Going Out of Business'* sign that looks like it's been in the window a lot longer than it would if it were actually going out of business.

A police SUV has their lights pulsing between red and blue, flashing and reflecting against the windows of the laundromat. They've blocked in a sedan and the officers are aggressively leaning toward the driver's side window, with posture suggesting a question that has no good answer. I feel a brief, sympathetic beat in my chest, remembering the cold sweat of my own traffic stop last month. I still maintain that I wasn't actually speeding, but none of the classic damsel-in-distress maneuvers had worked for me. I didn't cry, I didn't flirt, I just sat there, gripped by a profound sense of annoyance that my day was being hijacked and I would then have to show up to some government building for traffic court. (Don't ask me what happened next, but it's in a folder in Hudson's desk drawer.)

But today, the annoyance isn't mine to carry. Today, I am a woman on a mission for digestive biscuits, and I can just hope that they also have a lawyer fake-husband to take care of their ticket.

I ignore the siren-light disco and pull open the heavy glass door of the specialty shop. When I walk in, the bell above the door gives a pathetic, tinny chime, and the woman in the back matches it with a "Be right there, dear."

I'm here on a mission, in and out. I tell myself. Even though it wouldn't be the worst thing to pop into the Going-Out-Of-Business-Bookstore before I head home, ya know, perhaps to keep them in business a touch longer. I grab the Union-Jack-painted basket, and head to the corner to grab the goods. Got it!

"Back again so soon, are we?" Mrs. Clarkson coos. She's hovering near a display of prawn cocktail crisps, flavors that feel like a fever dream to the uninitiated. She can't be more than sixty. She's mentioned that she and her husband moved here to be nearer to their son. And they just couldn't live without the tastes of home. Lucky for me. We've *'hobnobbed'* before, a terrible pun I only allow myself because it's also a top-tier biscuit, but today, she decides to break the cardinal British rule of Mind Your Own Business.

"I've been meaning to ask, dear," she says, squinting at me over her glasses. The ones that can't escape her neck if they tried, strung around her with a simple chain that dangles by the sides of her face. "Where exactly are you from? You've got that nowhere-in-particular lilt, but every now and then, a vowel escapes and I just can't place it." I offer her the very practiced, easy smile and answer I've perfected for every date I've ever been on. Which, honestly, few and far between.

"I've been here since I was a child," I say, reaching for a tin of smokey Earl Grey. Didn't need it, but not going to leave it behind. "The original accent got buried under a decade of trying to fit in, I suppose." Explaining that there's nothing more than small nostalgia back in the UK, and thanks to her, I can buy nostalgia, sometimes it's just at a premium price.

The accent has been long since demoted to more of a tool. And in my line of work, the British inflection is my superpower. I can turn it on like a faucet, sharpening it so it sounds like I've *received pronunciation.'* Elongating the vowels until I sound like I should be narrating a documentary about the Tudors. (If there's smut that is. Because I don't know if you heard, but I'm back, baabyyy!) But here, standing in front of the Hobnobs and the Ribena, I keep the accent tucked away.

I see the stacks of British candy and grab bags of Percy Pigs and Flying Saucers. I add them to the pile of stuff that amounted to much more than the biscuits I came for. I can just hear him now. *'Percy Pig is a ridiculous name for a candy, Lou-i-sa.'* Because he always says my name, he wouldn't dare waste a syllable. And then I'll tell him that it's *'no worse than Nerds,'* which are like his holy grail of sweet-treat. (He wouldn't call it that.)

"Actually, these too." I toss the Wine Gums in with the rest. I don't particularly like Wine Gums. They're not sour enough to be interesting and they're not sweet enough to be worth it. They exist in a middle ground I have never found compelling, but I know someone who will. (Even if his preference *is* for Nerds.) *'It's nothing,'* I tell myself. (Out loud and under my breath.) People pick up things for people they live with; if we were roommates, it would be totally normal. (Whatever you have you tell yourself, Lou.)

I think I've been telling myself I'm still on solid earth, that the terror I feel is just the anxiety of everything we're doing this for. I pretend the way I listen for the sound of his key in the lock has everything to do with the performance of cohabitation and nothing to do with me. That when I picked up his brand of sparkling water at the grocery store last Tuesday without thinking, I was just being practical. But I'm standing here with bags of candy on top of my favorite things, and the honest version of what's happening is that I know him now. Not in what he's listed, but in a way I've figured out. And the thing I know most about him is that letting anyone know him, *honestly* not just truly, is not in the cards. (Not by accident and not ever.)

So I look at the Wine Gums, a candy I only picked up because I can picture exactly the face he'd make trying one. (And I want to see it.) The way he'll pop it in his mouth and spend three seconds deciding if he likes it before saying something dry and conclusive (maybe insulting), like it's a verdict. The way he won't concede, not immediately, but he will finish off the bag. Then he'll ask where I got them, so he can add them to his grocery list. The grocery list he always asks me if I want to add anything to.

'Romance is your home,' Roma had said. (Yeah, okay.) I've narrated enough people who want things they can't have. I know how those stories go, I know exactly how they go. I've voiced them in countless accents and numerous different sub-genres. (Hello, alien smut.) But those are fiction. And this? This is faker than fiction and somehow doing more damage.

This is proximity poisoning my ability to see him without caring.

Because here's what happened: it was supposed to be simple, because we didn't even like each other (right?), let alone have any real affection for one another. But we've lived together now, my apartment is only there serving as an office. And we went from enemies, to husband and wife, to roommates, and in the cracks of all those might be a friendship that scares me more than I want to admit.

We became something that exists in the inbetweens, like the doorways we'd face off in. I don't have a clean word for it. What I do have? Clean laundry. He just did it, with his own. (Separating items that he thought should be dry cleaned, of course.) But he didn't separate our laundry before putting it in the wash. Just, combined it, like that's a thing we do now, like there's a *we* that does laundry together. Like the idea of sorting my clothes from his was a step that simply didn't occur to him because the category of *mine versus yours* has started to blur at the edges.

We might have separate bedrooms, but the separation of our lives is blending together dangerously. And for everything he sees, I don't know that he sees this. (While I am pretending not to.)

Hudson is someone who pretty much up until we said *I do*, had a rotating door of guests. Now, he washes my socks. I think about that sometimes, and then I think about him, across the apartment, in the middle of a big bed, in a bigger room. He's probably reading something dense and useful and not thinking about me at all.

But I lie awake in the room he furnished for my comfort, staring at the ceiling, slipping my hand under the covers and between my legs, and I think about him. Who has made it extremely clear, in the most honest and unapologetic terms, this is not real. Despite what he said. (Trust me, I think about it more than I should.) It's not about being single, but if *it* becomes too much, I should come (*word choice, Lou!*) to him about it. What a thing to say on your wedding night.

His feelings for me? Would be a *'risk.'* Well guess what, I'd risk it. But that's the thing, he can control that. (Must be nice.) My feelings? Those would be *'too great a liability.'* (Like the rest of me.) He said it with such truth, without apology, which is somehow the most devastating delivery method available.

And I am terrified. Not of the feelings, exactly. I've had feelings before, I'm a person who feels things at full volume with no volume control and I've survived all of them. (Up till now.) What terrifies me this time, when the paperwork clears and the interviews are done and we file the dissolution and go back to being the people who share a wall and nothing else (if I even can), Roma is going to call me and play back my recordings and say *'what happened, you've lost it again, where did it go?'*

And I know, I'll have left it with him.

I'm standing at the counter as Mrs. Clarkson touches my hand gently, I don't know how long I've dissociated into this spiraled state. I pay what I call the *'nostalgia surcharge'* on a few of my favorite items, Hudson would call it an import tariff, and push through the tinny chime of the door.

When I step outside, the SUV is gone, though the sedan is still there. The driver likely having gone back inside the laundromat, taking whatever ticket they were written, and going about the rest of their day just slightly more annoyed.

I just clutch my bag and get into my car six minutes in the future.

Time to return to my fake life. With very real feelings.

Chapter Twenty-Two

DOWN TO THE STUDS

HUDSON

All the paperwork was submitted *for both of us*, pretty soon after we said *I do*. We checked that off the list, immediately. *I'm the only one keeping the list.* She has access to the shared note that I keep in my phone of all the items we need to satisfy, but I doubt she's ever opened it. I'd even synced her calendar to mine, which was a bold and useless move considering she viewed the concept of *'time'* as a loose suggestion rather than a linear reality. Looking back, I'm lucky she showed up for our wedding. The only clock she's aware of now, the countdown doomsday divorce clock, that she'll occasionally ask about. Curious what's next on the list of requirements, and how much longer we stay together.

She stays here every night, which has been helpful more than once when Mr. Ambrose knocked on the door first thing in the morning, which you can't convince me wasn't a tactic. Though now, I think he just likes coming by for tea. *Which they do twice a week.*

This morning she's dressed like she's going to court *or a funeral,* she does that. To her, they might feel like the same thing. She dresses like she thinks she is supposed to, consulting Paola often, as someone she thinks knows the ropes. As Louisa is trying to play a part she hasn't quite rehearsed in a costume that doesn't fit. Sometimes it's endearing, like how a kitten trying to roar is endearing, but in every other way, it makes my chest ache with aggravation. This morning I grabbed a patchwork cardigan on our way out the door, just so there could be some of her, even in the most drab of situations.

We step back into the apartment, our trip to Immigration this morning to submit some additional paperwork. Nothing substantial, but I wasn't going to send her alone. *Not a chance in hell.* We sat there in the waiting room, she said hi to Deborah, who processed our papers last time. Despite the women's effort to not remember anything or anyone about this job, she did wave to Louisa.

We got in and out quickly, got an official agent assigned. We weren't gone long, but the entry hall still smells like her when we get back. The perfume and shampoo combination of fresh fruit and baked goods. Lingering from when she left just hours before, waiting for her to return. Who am I kidding, *waiting to fucking haunt me.*

"Well," I say, checking my watch because *one* of us has to acknowledge it's the middle of the day and time is very real. "I need to get back to the office." She makes a face at that, disappointed in a way I wasn't expecting. "What?"

"Nothing, I just was thinking." She purses her lips to keep them from transforming her face into a smile. *And I am a fucking sucker for it.*

"I like thinking," I say. What I really mean is *I like hearing what you've been thinking,* which sometimes she does without me asking.

She releases some of the tension in her mouth, letting the happiness that bubbles out of her escape. She's balancing to take off her black buckled heel, so I offer my hand for stability. Which she takes without any caution. Just naturally slips her hand into mine. Even though she doesn't say anything, there's a peace offering in it, as we've found in many small things recently.

I think she's beginning to realize just how much I'm willing to do to stabilize any part of her life she needs.

"You should play hooky from work," she says, like it's an entirely viable option.

"I can't."

"Can't or won't," she presses. "I met your boss, and he *loovveeeed* me, I bet he'd be okay if you said you needed to spend the day with your *wife*." She emphasizes the word, and she's not wrong. Arthur was enchanted by her and has made more than one comment about how he'd like to see more of her. I *do* have things to get to, work to do. But I can always do that tonight in bed when I am stuck staring in a game of *'don't blink'* with the ceiling, unable to sleep. She sees my hesitation, that I'm thinking about it, and uses this as the final strike. "You're not *that* important, Hudson. The world won't stop spinning if you're offline for a few hours."

"What did you have in mind," I concede.

"Well, you know what's at stake for me, *husband,*" she stresses comically, like it will help her make her point. "How about you show me yours?" She can see the look on my face, as her cheeks bloom pink, flushed. "What you plan to do with the apartment upstairs,. After all, *it will be our home*," she clarifies, not to imply anything more.

It's strange for someone to express interest in me, besides Grams and Lucas that is. But she does, *always has*. Asking questions with such genuine curiosity of knowing someone. Be it the doorman, whose name I learned is Oscar, or to the fruit-stand man, Ramon, she tells hello whenever she walks down the street. And now, just by knowing her, they say hello to me, too.

"Fine," I say in a deep, resigned register. "But if I get fired, or the world stops spinning, we're going to have to downsize."

"Deal," she chirps. "We've got a perfectly good one-bedroom right next door." I can't believe she would mean it, we might be living together, but we don't even share a bathroom. She keeps herself sequestered to the other side of the apartment, we just meet in the middle for dinner or details.

She kicks off the second heel and stands a few inches shorter, looking up at me with that terrifyingly bright curiosity. "Finally," she says, slipping her feet into a pair of Birkenstocks that were by the door instead.

We take the elevator up to the eighth floor and walk down the identical hallway, right to apartment 8A. It has a lockbox on it, but I know the code, unlocking the door, and pushing it open into a shell of a space with the smell of drywall and dust.

Right now, it's a hollowed-out ribcage, just a skeleton of wood framing and studs, waiting for me to build its heart. Louisa wastes no time as she drifts through the open floor plan like she's already haunting the place, something I know she will do long after this is all done. But there is something giddy about the way she moves through, imaginary.

"What's this going to be?" she says as she stands in what used to be an office. There is still some framing of the former walls, a pair of French doors standing where they once served a purpose, but she's standing in what I'm planning to be the new primary bedroom.

"Well, from here." I take steps towards her, grabbing her hand to drag her with me towards the large arched windows at the opposite end of the room. "To about here," I say, "will become the main bedroom."

Light floods the space and washes over her, casting our shadows long against the unfinished floors. Shadows of us that stretch and appear closer than we could be. Maybe in the alternate universe they exist in, they find happiness in each other more than we do. *Or at least, it's reciprocated.*

"Wow," she says. She seems to realize her hand is still in mine, slowly pulling it away as she opens the window and leans her head down. I reach out and bunch the fabric at her back in my hand, holding her in with my feet planted firmly in this future I plan to build.

She drifts back into the center of the main room, spinning slowly, looking perfectly ironic against the unfinished industrial grit.

"This could be a library wall," she says, her voice echoing through the empty space. She traces a finger along a support beam as if she could already see the mahogany shelves that would be there. "It could have one of those rolling ladders, I think I'd spend half my life just sliding back and forth."

She can see beyond the layout of the rooms, but as she looks around, she's able to see more than even I can. She does this with most things, most *people.* I watch her with my hands shoved deep in my pockets. "Ladders are dangerous, you'd probably break your neck trying to reach for something." Doing what she did, and not calling attention to the reality that by the time the bookshelves are built, the ink on our divorce will be long dry.

"Ladders are *fineee,*" she stresses, like I'm dismantling her dream.

"Fine, then *you* are the danger." *I know how true it is.*

She rolls her eyes, as if our first encounter isn't confirmation of her clumsiness. No doubt our dynamic has shifted, almost uncomfortably, in a way that leaves us both unsure of the roles we are supposed to fill. *Besides husband and wife.* But this is a moment where we both are seeing flickers of that same friction coming through. Igniting something familiar, and comfortable for each of us.

She spins on her heel, and in doing so, catches it on the unfinished floor and nearly goes down. I jump forward to grab her hand, to stop her from falling.

"You had to be right, didn't you," she says with sarcasm.

"You had to prove my point," I reply.

"It's the shoes," she says as she kicks the sandals off her feet, off to the side where she will surely forget them.

"Louisa, don't. You could step on something."

"Why are you such a grumpy old bugger?"

"Would you look at that, the Brit has made an appearance," I say with a laugh, and she smiles at it, as she hops off to another area *definitely* riddled with old nails, dust, and chips of plaster. I don't know what's on the floor up here, but I know her bare feet shouldn't find out. "Seriously," I say. As I pick up her shoes from where she had kicked them off. "When was the last time you even had a tetanus shot?"

"I got one when I was a child, I'll be fine," she says as if it's that simple. She just tiptoes herself farther away from me, almost dancer-like to music she has playing in her brain. With her Birkenstocks in hand, I follow her into the next room, or what will be the next room when there are walls.

"Well, you're supposed to get them every ten years, so be careful," I stress.

"Who says?!" she turns to face me, as if I'm making it up for my own health.

"I don't know, medical professionals?" She just shrugs it off, unbothered by the fear of lockjaw from stepping on a rusty nail. Do I know if that's a legitimate concern? No. But it's categorized as one of those fear-mongering things Grams told me as a boy, that now I think about more than I should.

She pivots her direction, and the conversation, to an area that would be ideal for a large closet. But she has other ideas. "And *this*," she raises her arms above her head, making a gesture and swirling the air around her. "This will be my recording studio. I can actually have one with a window so I don't get claustrophobic, but it would be a proper one, actually soundproof. You. Are. Welcome," she points her finger at me with each word.

The sound that lands at her feet is not a laugh as much as a loud, disbelieving *'Ha!'* I lean against a stack of drywall, and try to look bored while my pulse hammers in my chest to a rhythm that is becoming increasingly hard to ignore. One I don't really *want* to ignore.

"Closet not cutting it?" I ask smoothly, pretending entirely I have not heard her paint herself into every corner of this space.

"Well," she begins with her hand perched on her hip. The ruby sitting on her finger catches my attention every time she moves. "I'd like not to have any more noise complaints filed against me."

My shoulders drop the smallest amount. I *did* do that, more than once. Each time the complaints were dismissed, likely because while I only have enemies on the co-op board, in her short time living here, she made actual friends.

"I haven't made one since you moved in, and you know it." Which is true. In the beginning I thought staying away and just having someone else handle it was the best option. Until it turned into this challenge between us. This warring dynamic that had us nose to nose once a week. "Why was recording at a reasonable hour never an option?" I prompt, knowing full well that if that were the case, we likely wouldn't be here. I wouldn't have, well, I wouldn't have done a lot.

"I was still working at The Double Shot," she begins. And I see her shift her face, knowing that since her visa, she is in limbo in more ways than one. "I also work better at night sometimes, because some scenes are just *night* scenes, ya know?"

"I really don't, but I'm sure you're about to tell me."

"Like, a meet cute, sure, that can be recorded sun up. But when he's got her on her knees and is slamming himself into the back of her throat, that's just not a daytime scene..."

I choke on air, or my thoughts, or whatever the fuck it was that she just said like it was a completely normal string of words in casual conversation. "You okay over there?" She cocks her head to the side as she crosses her arms in mockery.

"No," I say, and I don't think she realizes how honest I'm being. "What do other voice actors do, torture their neighbors like you do?"

"Believe it or not, my goal was never to *torture* you. At least not in the beginning. But in my current place, or—" She pauses, realizing she doesn't actually live in her *current place.'* "Well, in 7A, the closet is the only space that actually deadens the echoes. Ideally, an actual booth is the way to go. But that's a big purchase, and I didn't think I had the space without totally rearranging my furniture, so I've made due with a bunch of heavy fabric and a prayer." I look at the raw space, imagining her tucked away in a corner of my life.

"I'd say you've more than made due, because I've heard every *'oh god'* you've *prayed* since you've moved in." She takes steps towards me, still on her toes, because in her mind it's less surface area of risk for stepping on a nail.

"And *I've* heard every one of yours." Her tone is harsh as she meets my gaze. "Did you think that wall was one-way? It's not just your late-night vacuuming I can hear, Hudson." The warmth she'd brought into this room, the light she'd poured into the conversation with her, imagining a future we both know we are on a countdown to conclude, dims. I don't respond. "Right" is all she says. Her smile turns brittle, and I watch it crack into the disdain that I can still elicit. "God forbid I disturb the activities of your bedsheets, the way you enjoy interrupting my actual *job.*"

The air is stripped, the draft in this open space becomes the harsh reality of who we are.

She grabs her shoes from my hand, and stomps off towards the door. Sawdust and silence left in her wake, and the incredibly painful fucking irony that once again, I am the successful author of my own demise, watching her breathe in the dust of a home that will never be ours. Some people are their own worst enemy, she is when it comes to managing anything that requires her opening a mailbox. But me? I am the consistent conductor of my own contempt in a way far worse. Managing to snatch defeat from the jaws of a genuine moment between us. Every. Single. Time.

I watch her as she walks away, each step purposeful and strong, moving her farther and farther from me, with an angry stride probably running through the list of ways I'm the asshole she believes I am. No amount of fake interior design, *hell even a fake marriage,* can change her mind.

It's the tiniest, microscopic stutter in her next step that has me narrowing my eyes to focus more closely. Her rhythmic, steady pace turned to a lopsided shuffle, not putting pressure on her left foot as she hurries out the door, and I behind her.

"Louisa," I call after her. But she tosses a wave over her shoulder at me as I follow her out the door in a few long steps. She's pressing the 'DOWN' button ferociously, trying to call the elevator more quickly, but that's not how it works. The black dress she's wearing is a shroud to the pleasant afternoon we just killed. *I killed.*

When the elevator doesn't arrive with the speed she had willed, she turns to march down the hall towards the stairs. Just one flight down, under normal circumstances, would be no big deal. In this case? Still fucking barefoot? Absolutely not.

Her hand is on the doorknob to the stairwell, but I stop her. I see the way she is shifting her weight. She's uncomfortable. "Would you slow down," I say. It's not a question because I don't want her answer. "You're limping."

"Fine, okay? I stepped on something. Do you need to be right about *everything*?"

"Yes," I say. Which isn't actually true, but in this case, had she just listened to me and not traipsed around without shoes on in a literal construction zone, this wouldn't have happened.

"Congratulations. You win. You were right."

"Show me," I command, putting my hand on her waist and spinning her to face the wall. I reach down and grab her by the ankle, she bends her knee and exposes the bottom of her foot to me. We're in the hallway of the eighth floor, and if anyone were to see this, I wouldn't hurt our *'we're a real couple'* story. But it also wouldn't make sense.

With her foot in my hand as she balances like a flamingo, I see it, the splinter that looks to be about a half-inch deep into her skin. I press my thumbnail into the base of it, to see if I can push it to the top of the skin, but it's really in there.

"Can you walk?" I ask as I lower her foot back to the ground.

"I was walking just fine before you stopped me," she snaps.

"Liar."

She moves to take a step, a determined, painful step, and I see the wince she tries to swallow. There's no blood, but it's deep and could get infected if she doesn't get it out. No matter how much she wants to pretend not to be bothered, the way she curls her toes and pinches her face tells me everything.

"Come on," I say, scooping her into my arms. It might seem dramatic for a splinter, but pain is pain, and having her this close, tucked against the steady, betraying beat of my heart, it's clear I have agreed to a different kind of pain entirely.

As I carry her a handful of steps to the elevator, I can feel her body relax the smallest amount, but I don't let myself imagine it's comfort. I'm staring at my own reflection in the mirror of the elevator door, the reflection a mockery of who we are, as she softens in my hold. My face remains a mask of stoic indifference, even with the urge to drop my lips to her temple, just once, just to see if she tastes like the sunlight in the life she imagined for us upstairs.

The door retracts with a soft *ding*, revealing Mrs. Saraceno, staring at us, a gargoyle clutching a grocery bag, a small fluff of a yapping dog at her feet, and a look like she's been waiting for a reason to be offended. *Which from our history, I usually give her.*

"Newlyweds," she mutters under her breath. It sounds more like a curse than a congratulations, and the sick, twisted truth is how accurate it feels. I have been bewitched, and in this brass lined box, lowering us just the one floor, it's the jolt of genuine terror that I never want to be released from this spell.

Chapter Twenty-Three

NOT A DOCTOR, A BOY SCOUT

LOUISA

Hudson sets me down on the edge of the large soaking tub in my room, the guest bathroom. The porcelain is cold as it hits the back of my thighs, I lean back against the tiled bathroom wall as he takes a seat and stretches my legs out and drops them into the tub. Guiding my feet into the warm, shallow water of the filling tub that he has just turned on.

He leaves me in the bathroom alone, and while I have complete control over myself, I don't move. Instead, I let the water rise to the middle of my calves. Hiking up my dress higher on my thigh so it does not fall in.

When he re-enters the room, he joins me on the edge of the tub, turning off the warm water, as we both just sit here in silence. His moods land between silent and surly; sometimes within that pendulum swing, he takes a detour into a moment of humor, or compassion. I've seen it more than once. Each time while I am surprised by it, it also feels like the truest version of himself.

Hudson rolls up the sleeves of his shirt, folding them up to his elbows, exposing the veins on his forearms. Sometimes I look at him and I think he could have been a lumberjack as much as he could have been a lawyer. Just in need of a flannel shirt and some wood. (Don't think about his wood, *Louisaaa*.) But in all seriousness, there's a way about him, that even now, like this, he feels more rugged than who I see head off to work every morning.

He drops his arm into the water and I watch the ripples off his forearm spread as he moves his arm, reaching for my ankle. His fingers wrap around it as he pulls it from the bath and places it on the folded towel atop his hard thigh. He's unfazed by the water, still not having said anything, just moving through the motions of this totally not-normal task as if it was something he had scheduled. My leg stretched between us, a line of vulnerability, which I've reached out with too many times. He can't keep being the one to fix my problems. It's far more than he signed up for. (Than either of us signed up for.)

Spending time with him upstairs felt like getting a peek into his brain. The parts of it that hold a dream motivating enough for him to enter this crazy arrangement with me.

His hand is holding my foot as he retrieves the tweezers he went to grab. I can feel the pressure of his thumb into the ball of my foot. Pushing the skin harder and harder, rhythmic, I don't know if there's any progress. And while it doesn't feel great, the piece of wood he's trying to force through a minuscule hole in my skin, the way his hand wraps wholly around the arch of my foot as he works methodically, feels too intimate for what we are.

I snapped upstairs, and while it's all rooted in the reality of who we were prior to all this, karma clearly repaid me the second I stepped on the splintered wood and it went right into my left foot. And whatever I was annoyed about upstairs, I'm already busy lying to everyone else about how I feel about him, might as well lie to myself about it also.

I watch as he dips a washcloth into the warm water and holds it against my foot. My foot twitches in response but settles comfortably back into his grip. His gaze is focused on the splinter he's working on, but his eyes flicker up to mine in the smallest breath between seconds. Locking on me from under his rich, dark lashes, makes the view almost perverse. (For me at least.) Before using the tweezers, trying to needle out the tip of the splinter from my foot.

"You're good at this," I say, trying to claw back some of the tension that tightens the air between us. "Like, *really* good."

"I've been told." His lips taunt me as they pull into the smallest smirk, his eyes narrowing to match. (Arrogant ass.)

"I'm sure," I reply, knowing that I doubt he's ever *not* been good at something. "I'm not like that you know," I say as I can feel the warmth of breath land on my skin he's holding close to him.

"Like what," he asks under his breath, clearly focused not on the conversation but engaging just because he's got my foot hostage, and he knows I'll be a lot more agreeable if he goes along with it.

"You obviously have been successful at everything," I begin as I lean back into the wall, trailing my fingers across the surface of the water. "I'm good at some things. Lattes, amazing. Voice acting, great. Making conversation with people's dogs, or remembering someone's birthday, there's no one better. But the important things? The kind that makes you valuable to society, I've never been any of those." For some reason saying it sounds much sadder than I expected it to. "I'm not *exemplary.*" (Not to people, and not to the government.)

"You're kind," he says plainly.

"Lots of people are kind," I reply.

"No, they're not," he says with such certainty, as he looks at me to convey the truth in it. I wonder if he's including himself in that. Something tells me he is, even though his actions remain some of the most generous I've experienced. His eyes drop back to the task at hand.

"Is there a secret medical degree I missed while doing my *husband homework*?" He laughs at that, but I can see the smile exposing his teeth from here, even with his face tilted down.

"No, just a Boy Scout."

"A *Boy Scout?!*" I don't know why I sound shocked. "In the little neckerchief and everything?"

"Yep," he confirms.

"I'd pay good money to see those photos."

"Never gonna happen," he says under his breath.

"Grams will show me," I retort. (I know she will.) He scoffs at that in reply, probably because he also knows she will.

"Even got a few badges." His tone is darker, thoughtful, deep in the own recesses of his past. "After the divorce, I thought if I prepared for everything, it might make a difference." His voice is soft and low. Rolling across the bathroom tile as he continues. "I learned how to treat a snake bite, to tie knots, to build a fire in the rain. I had this idea that maybe, *just maybe,* if I was useful, maybe they'd want me." It's a glimpse into a part of a complex relationship he shares in slices. And I'm frozen from it. Any witty remark, anything I thought I might have for him, dies on the tip of my tongue.

"It didn't work," he concludes. The honesty is a physical weight, it's as if because we are physically close, in this intimate moment, that he has safety in sharing more.

"My dad would have been happier with just Theo," I say, offering him a little bit of myself in reply. Somewhere in the middle we're able to meet, find this terrible common ground we share.

"I doubt that."

"I just am not someone he understands, and he never wanted to. He wanted another son, but didn't get one. I got a middle name and became the constant disappointment he ignored. So I guess together we can unpack the age-old question which is worse, never being around physically or emotionally."

"I've been told I'm emotionally unavailable." He says this like a warning, the one he repeats back to his usual (or former) *guests.* But we're already married, and I don't expect him to be *emotionally* anything. Despite the fact sometimes it sneaks out.

"That sounds like a choice." His hand stops moving, maybe

because I said something he's heard too many times. (Or not enough.)

"I hate this, you know," I say, quieter than anything yet. His hand is back to applying pressure to my foot, not stopping, just listening.

"What," he says. Perhaps because there are so many things he imagines I might hate about this.

"That you always have to come fix things, that I *come* to you to fix things." I pick at the edge of my glitter nail polish. "My dad did that. Made himself the only solution to every problem I had. Every mess I made. Even if I didn't think it was a mess, just... my life." I pause. "At first it felt like love, ya know, like someone was paying attention." The water has gone lukewarm as I drop my fingers to play in it. "But eventually I figured out it wasn't really about me at all. It was about control, about being the one who got to decide when I was okay."

Hudson doesn't say anything for a moment. His thumb presses into the arch of my foot, steady and slow.

"I'm not your father," he says finally. Not defensive.

"I know, Dr. Freud." I say it with a touch of humor, hoping to bring us back from the depths we just dove.

"Told you," he says. "Not a doctor. Just a Boy Scout. Do you want to know my favorite badge?" he asks, and it's such a bizarre question, I straighten, eager to answer.

"Was it—OUCH WHAT THE FUCK!?" In the split second from when he asked it, he pressed the splinter through the soft skin of my foot and pulled it out with the tweezers.

"Don't be such a baby." He holds it up between us, the wooden spike pinched between the prongs of the tweezers. His voice returns to the place that keeps him even-keeled. And as for me, I'm unsure of what to do with any of it.

Chapter Twenty-Four

CO-OPTED MY HEART

HUDSON

She has become the sole focus of my day. Even as I am sitting here at this round table, waiting for Mrs. Saraceno to pass judgment. It's funny actually. How this little older lady has become the single most frustrating hurdle I've ever experienced. Really think about that, on any given day I am dealing with the loudest, most abrasive, cutthroat attorneys, business people, and somehow, this woman is the worst of the worst.

She treats this co-op board like it is the inherited right of her lineage, divine providence from God above. At every turn she has been the voice that rejects the application for sale, and the subsequent plans for renovation.

Board meetings are held in the multi-purpose space of this building, a rogue piece of confetti implying the last use of this room was something that looked more like a gender reveal. She's positioned directly across from me, with two other resident board members on either side,. One of them lives on my floor. They really are the most neutral obstacle one could encounter. It's her and I locked into this death spiral of board approvals.

"Mr. Ellis," she says, steepling her fingers in a way that is actually villainous before folding them into each other and placing them on the stack of papers in front of her. Very clearly my most recent board application.

Her hair is perfectly coiffed, Louisa told me she has a standing appointment, something I guess they covered in one of their casual hallway chats. And her tweed jacket does not indicate a profession, but a luxury shopping habit.

"We've reviewed your application once again." It's said in a tone as flat as you can imagine. Not giving away the ending means she can keep me here on the hook for as long as she wants. I don't miss what looks like the whisper of joy on her face at the use of the word *again*.

"I appreciate this group's time on the matter," I offer. Hoping some gratitude might further this more than it has in the past. I have everything I need to make this case. Financials, architectural plans, anything anyone *else* would need to get this approval. This isn't even the first time such a request has been made. In fact, Mr. Rogers, *seriously, like the neighborhood's Mr. Rogers,* did something similar three years ago. *I have that readily available also.* But Mrs. Saraceno's issue was never the plans themselves, it has been and remains with me.

"And, we've also had the opportunity to get to know your wife," she emphasizes, indicating the only thing that has changed between the last application and now. Within me, there is a shift, the same one there always is when someone mentions Louisa. "We have found her to be.... well, quite unlike you." I don't flinch, it's true and the best compliment she can receive, especially from this crowd. I press my lips together into a clearly forced smile, the compliment for Louisa wrapped in an insult to me, but I don't care. If Louisa's charm is the key to unlocking my renovation, I'll take it. I'll take anything. "She's even shared you'd offered to support this board with any legal guidance or contract negotiation we may need."

Of course Louisa found the thing they would want from me, besides just my money, *which really should be enough,* and extended a peace offering I never thought to.

"Anything you need," I say, knowing this clearly seems to be of interest to them.

Mrs. Saraceno looks to the two board members on her left, who nod in a synchronized, bobblehead fashion. "Then the board has decided to approve your application for the upstairs unit. You can proceed with the purchase and subsequent renovation." The relief should be instantaneous. It should have felt like crossing a finish line I've been sprinting toward for years. She folds her aged hands and places them on the table, waiting for me to kiss the ring. *Which of course I do, metaphorically, with a gross display of gratitude.* It's clear that the gratitude I need to express is to Louisa.

"You can go," Mrs. Saraceno's voice breaks the thought I've become tangled in. Her tone shifts from flat to terrifyingly pleasant as I push back from my chair, not needing to stay now that my business here is complete.

"Now, on to our second order of business. The sale of apartment 7B." She pulls a second folder from beneath the first. This one was thinner, but as the delayed impact of the words land, and the sight of Louisa's unit number is confirmed, all the blood in my veins rushes to my heart. I return my ass to the seat with a curt "I'll stay" back in her direction. She doesn't acknowledge it, just proceeds.

Louisa doesn't own her apartment, but she's told me more than once how it was *'serendipitous.'* Her word, not mine. Our meeting, her next door, all of it, does sometimes feel that way, though that's not what she meant. For her, it was the perfect size, the perfect location, and the perfect amount of independence. It was also her stipulation as part of our agreement that she get to keep it. I'm not trying to displace her from her home when all this is done. *Doesn't matter if I'd rather her stay.*

"We have received formal notice from the owner of 7B,

they've decided to put the unit up for sale, effective immediately. Per the bylaws, the board has the right of first refusal, but we've decided to waive it in favor of an open-market listing, allowing it to be sold immediately as the tenant is none other than Mrs. Ellis, whose residence since marriage has been 7A. We foresee no reason this should not be a swift sale."

The room seems to tilt, this will break her heart. Her space has been her safety net, one she wove together herself. More than that, this apartment has been her *home*. She even told me she had talked to the owner about purchasing it herself.

"Wait," I say, my voice sounding tight, even to me. "The owner is selling, now? It was my understanding he planned to sell it in a few years."

"Ah, yes, we spoke to him about that, but given *your* plans, it seems unnecessary now," she says as a slow, shark-like smile spreads across her face. "After all, you've just been approved to double the size of your own residence. Surely your wife has no need for a separate lease now."

Inadvertently, in getting what I've wanted for so long, it's come at the expense of Louisa. The approval for the upstairs purchase, the victory I've been chasing, tastes bitter now that I know the cost. The arrangement we made, the tidy temporary deal we'd struck, had this flaw. And I totally fucking missed it.

I straighten in my chair, calming my voice to convince this board. "7B was my wife's home, before she was mine. She has a right of first purchase the owner verbally extended. I'd like to honor it."

"Mr. Ellis, we cannot allow for another purchase of a unit on your behalf. This is a co-op, not a monopoly." The handful of other people at this table all nod in agreement. It's been Mrs. Saraceno and I in this death spiral for so long, I forgot anyone else was even here.

"You all know her," I say. Trying to sound like a man making a reasonable point rather than what I actually am, which is a man who has run out of ways to pretend this is about anything other than *her*. "You know how much this space means to her."

I turn to Mr. Ambrose. "She's carried your groceries once a week since she moved in, and the only time you FaceTime your grandchildren is when she comes over to help you." His lips press together, not disagreeing.

I shift to Ms. Aguilar, seated directly beside me. "When you spent three weeks in Europe on your eat-pray-love journey, or whatever you called it, Louisa watered your plants. Even bought you a new one because the snake plant *'looked lonely.'*" A pause. "Her words," I say quickly and clarifying.

I turn back to Mrs. Saraceno. "And you." I say it with more aggression than is helpful, but marginally less than she deserves. "When your—" I gesture at the yapping fluff in the stroller, "—was sick, she made dog biscuits. And when you were in the hospital with pancreatitis, she not only visited you. She brought scones to the nurses." I let that sit for a moment. "This apartment means something to her that predates me, I want to make sure it remains hers."

If that apartment sells, she won't just be moving out of my apartment at the end of this, she'll be moving out, gone completely from my life. And while there may have been a brief moment in time when I thought I'd rather her be gone, now? I can't imagine not seeing her *even* in passing. No matter how painful it will be to see her move out and move on in all the ways I wish I was able to give her, I can't just let it happen.

"I'm sorry, Hudson," Mr. Ambrose says, speaking for the first time this meeting. "She's been a wonderful neighbor, she's a lovely person. But that doesn't change anything."

The sound of my own heart beating in my chest with guilt is only drowned out by the screaming in my head. Rapidly thinking through every alternative.

"If there is nothing else, I move to adjourn," she says, as the small group around her hums and nods in agreement.

"Actually, one more thing..."

———

I have to tell her. Not just about the sale of the apartment, about all of it. The other thing, underneath every decision I've made since I've met her, that I've been calling strategy, practicality, *a fucking liability,* when it has never, *she has never been,* not once, any of those things.

My phone goes before I've finished the thought.

"Yeah," I answer.

"Where are you?" Lucas asks urgently.

"Wrapping up the co-op stuff," I say. "What happened?"

"Cal fucking Sterling." Lucas, for all he is, reserves a swear word for only the most critical moments, which tells me everything I need to know. "He made a move this morning, it's aggressive and it's going to hold up the whole acquisition if we don't get ahead of it."

"I'll be there," I say. It's fine; by lunch we will have figured out whatever move Cal made and how to ensure it doesn't turn the whole deal into a house of cards. Just means that the morning conversation I had motivated myself to have I now can chicken my fucking way out of. Again. *This time, worse.*

I pull out my phone and type quickly before I can think too carefully about it.

Co-op board approved the purchase

I look at it, and quickly send another that says *'heading to work for an emergency, we should talk about it when I'm home.'* It's insufficient for everything it has to carry. But it's true, and it will have to hold until I can say the rest of it properly, in person, with her looking at me so I can watch her face when she understands what I mean.

I take the elevator down and by the time I hit the lobby, her response has come through.

LOUISA

Congratulations, you won't have to deal with
me for much longer! :)

Little does she know, I'd like to deal with her for the rest of my fucking life.

Chapter Twenty-Five

LOUISA

Coming home to this apartment rather than the one right next door became easier than I thought it would. In the beginning, muscle memory would take me to 7B, but the more nights I spend here, the more it becomes second nature. Now, months later, my feet step off the elevator (with both shoes) and walk me right to this door.

My arms are practically screaming for help as I fiddle with the doorknob trying to get my key in without putting down the bags of groceries I just carried in from the car. My phone is wedged between my cheek and my shoulder, which is making the grocery-bag front-door one-handed act even harder.

My father booms through the phone, the kind of fully British voice they would assign to a bulldog in a kids movie.

"The recklessness of it, Louisa," he continues, as he has, and I just "mhmm" every so often like I have since I was fifteen. (Even before.) We've never seen eye to eye, I don't think we've even seen face to face. But the incredible irony is the reason I'm even here is *him*. We moved to California when I was a child, *for him*. I could have grown up with the accent, the wellies, become the version of a daughter he imagined. (Not really.) Even though I can't imagine any version of myself being that for him, knowing I'm not Theo.

Instead, he gets this. "I always knew you were out of control, but to hear you've tied yourself to a stranger, for a bloody passport?"

Theo texted me as soon as it happened with just three words. *'They know. Sorry.'* Which is the most efficient possible warning and also arrived only seconds before my father called, which is not enough time to prepare for anything but is very on brand for the way my life has been going lately. Apparently the name change on Instagram (which I did months ago), finally made its way through a game of telephone that apparently involves no less than four of my mother's mahjong friends, one of whom follows me for reasons I suspect has more to do with the why-choose romance series that I put out last year. (But she'd never admit that, definitely not to my mother.) They called Theo first. (Obviously.) He tried to calm them, even mentioned the status, trying to find a practical argument, one that requires no emotional investment and simply asks them to consider the logistics of their daughter not being deported. My mother, I'm told, had feelings about finding out from Instagram. My father just said he *'has been waiting for something like this.'*

I doubt I've ever existed a day in this world, whether it was the tattoo I got at seventeen or my choice of career at twenty-five, that didn't come with a postscript from my parents about what they would have chosen instead, and was then passed through the filter of what it said about them.

"You've made a mockery of things," he continues.

"Dad, please," I say as I finally manage to push the door open, shuffling quickly into the kitchen and hurriedly dropping the grocery bags on the counter, the bag of cherries rolling out.

All the while the tears he always triggers build behind my eyes, begging to be released. I pull the phone from my ear, switching to speaker and laying my cheek and arms across the cool marble while he continues to prattle on.

"You've always had your head in the clouds, and this is where it gets you. You, and your choices, continue to disappoint me."

I can tell when he enters a space I'm in, because his body always shifts the air around me, it did long before now, and I don't think that will ever change. But I can hear him, taking direct and predatory steps towards me, where my face is splayed flat on the cool counter while my father hangs there, waiting for me to respond. But instead, Hudson picks the phone up off the counter.

"This is Hudson Ellis," he says in a deeply authoritative tone. His eyes staring into mine in a way that has me peeling my skin from where it has been. And I can hear the scoff on the receiving end, my father, annoyed.

"I don't know what you both are playing at," my father begins before Hudson cuts him off. He made it about as far as understanding that his daughter got married, and wasn't clever enough to find out *who* she married.

"She's not *playing* at anything, and so long as she is my wife, her choices aren't your concern." There's a stunned silence on the other line, a silence in all the years of my life I've never heard my father succumb to. He's not a bad man, he just would have been better without a daughter. He likes things in a certain way, people to behave a certain way, and no matter how much I tried when I was young, I never could. "You can call back when you can say something nice, or to congratulate your daughter on her *very real and extremely happy marriage.*"

He hangs up, sets the phone back down, and just begins to move about the kitchen putting the groceries away. As if it didn't happen.

It's not what I was expecting him to say. The room feels ten degrees hotter, and I don't stop the tears that rim my eyes from falling. Hudson has become the person consistently coming to my rescue, and I have spent the last few years on my own, and in all the messy parts of myself, I didn't need rescuing.

Hudson doesn't say anything to make it better, he just acts. His broad back is to me as he unpacks the groceries, washing fruit and putting it away, but I think I can see the smallest relaxing of his shoulders when he retrieves the bag of Nerds Clusters. I can almost feel the way his smile is broadening across his face, despite it facing away from me. As he just tucks the bag of Nerds into *his* everything drawer, and continues on.

"Tell me about your day, Louisa," he says, commandingly but wrapped in compassion.

"You don't want to hear about my day," I say through a small sniffle left over from the call with my dad.

"Yes, I do, I want to hear everything." He means it, somehow.

"I spoke to Roma today," I start. It's a strange conversation, one I don't actually think he cares about, except for the fact that it *feels* like he does. He tucks a loose strand of hair behind my ear, a prompt to continue.

"What else?"

"I went to the grocery store, then the farmer's market," I say, the words spilling out because he was right (like fucking always.) I need to talk. I need to drown out the sound of my father's disappointment. (And my own doubt because of it.)

"Did you get your cherries?" Each small question is a gentle nudge.

"No," I say as I cry. "Ramon, he wasn't there. There was a new kid. He didn't know about the type of banana I like for baking banana bread, he didn't know that I like the extra-dark cherries. He didn't know anything."

The soft *'mmm'* as confirmation he's listening while moving about the kitchen, encouraging me to continue.

"I got an audition request for a new book," I whisper, shifting my head so I can see the sharp line of his throat.

"What's this one about," he asks.

"Historical romance. You might like it, if it weren't for all the romance. Grams will though."

I can feel his chest let out a few short laughs. "Right," he says.

I have fallen, deeply, tripped foot over foot and went right into his chest, literally and figuratively, ever since that first kiss. It was supposed to be for the cameras, for paperwork, but felt like it was for my soul. But I know better. To Hudson, I am a project. Someone he consistently can save, while getting what he wants.

And all of this is a liability he is managing to avoid with precision, extracting only what we each need, except that we keep finding ourselves in situations like this where there's too much in the air that isn't logistics of a normal life and feels a lot more like lo—(DON'T think about it.) In a handful of months, the paperwork will be finalized. My visa will be secure. He will go back to his quiet without-me life, and I will go back to my apartment. Maybe this time, though, we won't be enemies. Maybe we could be the kind of friends who share coffee and talk about the time we were married.

Even though the longer this goes on, the harder it's becoming for me to imagine that. When I see him walk from the bathroom to his bedroom, towel wrapped around his waist, I imagine what it would be like stepping in to join him.

"I have something for you," he says, pulling me from my thoughts, as he pushes off from the counter and holds out his hand. I look at it, but I take it without any real pause, like it's simply the most natural thing, and he pulls me toward the door.

"I don't have shoes on," I say, as the front door opens.

"You won't need them."

We are standing in front of 7B, he has a key in his other hand, the spare he had cut when we started this arrangement. He puts it in the lock, and takes his large hand to cover my eyes. I reach for it to pull it down, so I can see what I'm walking into.

"Would you trust me, please?" It sounds annoyed, but the plea at the end is sincere. And I do trust him. Increasingly more than anyone else I know. (It's me I don't trust.)

The door swings open and the lights come on, I can tell through the cracks of his fingers. His body pushes mine into the space, each foot behind mine. Shuffling my steps forward. My back to his front as he moves us, together.

"Ready?" he asks. I don't know what has him like this, but he sounds almost giddy. I don't think I can ask. It's not the first time we've been closer. It happens more frequently now. But he's building to a surprise, and it's something that's got his blood pumping.

(He's not the only one.)

He pulls his hand back, and my eyes adjust to the freedom. I see it and I stop breathing.

My apartment has been entirely redesigned to make way for the newest addition. There, in the corner where my table used to be, is a recording booth. (A real one.)

Not large, it doesn't need to be large, but larger than the closet. It's grey-paneled, glass-windowed, prefabricated but well-made, the kind that requires research rather than just a search and a click. I know this because I have looked at them. I have had the tab open and closed a dozen times over the last year because of the price and the practicality of space.

The closet has worked well enough. (And well-enough has been the bar I've been clearing for longer than I'd like to admit.)

"I didn't build it myself, I had someone come in. So it's sturdy," he says, stepping around me to open the door. He did the research. I can tell by the model, it's not the most expensive one, it's the right one, which is a distinction that requires actually reading the specifications rather than just filtering by price to buy a flashy gift. He's thoughtful in a way I don't think anyone sees. Maybe they come to expect it from him. It's not about the gift, but the effort he puts into it. Into every single thing he does. He doesn't know how not to. (He also doesn't know what it does to me.)

And for me, that's becoming increasingly harder to separate. Because his standard setting is also the most generous man I've met, and to be on the receiving end of it is confusing at best. (And I don't think he'd see it that way.)

"I can't believe you did this, it's perfect," I say, and his smiles, large and bright, might be the thing that lights up this room.

"You have a lot of big things coming up." He's talking about the fact I am now booked out farther in advance than I ever thought possible. (And he doesn't know how much of him I have to thank for that. At least, some of the *sweatier* scenes.)

"I guess it will save you the late nights," I say. Because as I've picked up more books, my hours have broken the *'no moaning after midnight rule.'* He hasn't interrupted, though sometimes in the mornings after he groans at me as he heads off to work.

"Exactly," he says. But whatever the reason, I take the steps towards him, I outstretch my arms, about to hug him. His come up and around me, both of them, fully, not the careful half-embrace of someone calculating how much contact is appropriate, but it doesn't last long. He drops his hands from my back quickly to indicate it's done.

When I pull back his face looks smug. Actually no, not smug, just satisfied. (And I can tell the difference.)

"Go on, try it out," he says, as he then tells me about how he had someone come in to set up the microphone. *A professional, because I've heard you refer to it as 'your baby.'*

The booth is larger than the closet and it smells like new materials and possibility, which is a combination I didn't know had a smell until right now. (Never saw it on the Home Goods clearance shelf.) It also has a window, and ventilation, which means I won't die of heatstroke or claustrophobia.

I pull the door closed behind me.

The silence is immediate and total. This isn't the silence I fought to craft with foam and a neighbor that still could very much hear me, this is silence that *belongs* to me, and he gave it to me.

I look at him through the glass. (Don't be *too* obvious, Louisa!)

He's standing in my apartment, his hands loosely slipped into his pockets, and there is something almost wholesome about him, surrounded by my things, looking at me through glass. Looking at me, like that. (You see it too, right?)

He makes a small gesture with his hand. *'Go on.'*

"Can you hear me?" I say, in an entirely normal speaking voice, pointing between us.

He shakes his head. Points to his ears. Points at the booth. Gives a shoulder shrug.

I take a breath and stand here for a moment. Let the silence settle around me like something I've been waiting for without knowing I was. (As someone who is not known for being quiet.) And then, because I am a person who has spent years saying true things that belong to other people, in voices that aren't quite mine (and because the booth is soundproof and the glass between us is thick), I say the thing I have been not-saying for longer than I've known what to do with. "Okay," I say, to the silence. (Phenomenal opening, Louisa. Roma would be proud. *Not.*)

My voice sounds different in here, like a cleaner, stripped version of itself. "I don't know," I start again. Which is where everything true starts for me, in the *not* knowing. "This is the part where I'd normally caveat every thought into oblivion, add so many disclaimers, and apologize, that by the time I got to the actual point you'd have forgotten what we were talking about. I do that." I breathe a break between the thoughts. "I know, you know, I do that."

He thinks I'm testing the acoustics, getting a feel for the space, and I am.

But he also has no idea.

I take a deep breath, pulling in all the air I can through my nose, the way he taught me, except this time it isn't panic I'm trying to settle.

"I want you so badly." It's the first time I've said it out loud, and may turn out to be the last. "In ways I didn't think happened in real life, to real people. Definitely not to me." I let out a laugh, pausing, staring at his face through the glass, but it's unmoved. "I bet if you heard me, you'd laugh, say something like *'Louisa, this isn't a good idea.'* And that would do it. Because god, I want you to hear you say my name, out loud, while the thing between my legs isn't my hand, or a vibrator, but you. Sometimes I just lay there, imagining you on the other side of the apartment, and I wonder if you're thinking about me the way I am you. If the days you spend a *little* longer in the shower is because you've got your hand so tightly wrapped around your cock and you're picturing me, the way I picture you. Desperately, wantonly. Wet. Like I am now."

It's bizarre to say it all now, or as much as I will let myself. Because the thing about being truly unheard and alone in the silence that belongs to you, is that the truth stops feeling as dangerous. I wonder what it is he's imagining right now, what he thinks I'm speaking into the universe. Maybe some script pages I memorized, my favorite monologue from a movie, or my lyrics to my favorite song. And his oblivion gives me the confidence to continue.

"I just imagine what you're like. You're so intense, at everything. Every time you look at me, it's this expression you manage to contain. I've seen it soften, but that's not what I want. I want, just once, for you to let me see it. Because I know whatever is underneath, what you're controlling, has to be devastating. And I want to be devastated by it."

He's just standing there, hands in his pockets. Looking back at me like he's waiting.

He has no idea he already has me.

"You told me to come to you, well, here I am. Hiding in plain sight. Not because I want to be with anyone else, not because the arrangement has gotten to me, because it's been too long and I need a physical release. But because I want *you*." I swallow hard, as my eyes remain locked on his. "I want you... to fuck me."

The stillness in this box holds every word I just said, absorbs it into the walls the way a confessional might, and I am deeply grateful for that because I can't take any of it back and I'm not sure I would if I could. He takes a step toward the door, waiting, the way he always does. Like he has already decided and is giving me the time to catch up.

He pulls open the door when he sees me stop and reach for it.

He's right there, filling the frame the way he fills every doorway, every room, every space, every fold of my brain I have tried to keep him out of and failed at consistently. There's exactly enough room for me to step out and the door to close behind me.

Not enough room for anything else. Which is either very considerate or the cruelest thing he's ever done, and with him, I've learned, it's usually both. But I step out of the recording booth, and the door closes behind me. Keeping my secrets trapped within. (Even if he's looking at me like that.)

His eyelids look lowered, desirous in a way I have only imagined. And wonder for the splittest of seconds if the air didn't hold my secrets like I thought. "Could you hear me?"

"What did you say," he asks, but it's more of a directive than a question.

"Nothing special," I reply. Knowing how easy it would be to kiss him if I just lifted up on my toes even the smallest amount.

"Louisa," he says my name and sends a shiver down my spine in a way I'm afraid he can actually see.

"Really, it's nothing you'd care to hear," I say, and his eyes narrow ever so slightly on me.

He tuts his tongue and shakes his head. Releasing a hair that falls into his face, and he makes no movement to put back in place. "You said no lying, *remember*? With you, I want to hear *everything*."

"What is it you want me to say?" I give up, and I sound like it, my breathing is heavy, but his isn't calm either.

"I want you to tell me," he shifts his body closer, "that you want me to fuck you." His hand lands on my hip, backing me into the wall of the booth. My lips fall open as his eyes drop to my mouth, the first time he's looked away from my eyes since I stepped inside the booth.

"How would you know that?" I ask, my back arching me into him as his hand cages me in.

"If you think I don't know what it looks like for you to mouth *those* words, to me, you are sorely mistaken." His hand comes to cradle my face as the pad of his thumb runs across my lips, like it's asking them to be honest.

"You're gonna want to get a refund on the booth if you were able to hear all that."

"I'd pay more to hear the rest." His face is closer, daring me to close the distance, to admit what I said. And I want to, but the pit in my stomach prevents me.

"Won't this be a *'liability,'*" I ask, breathing life into the thing I'm most afraid to admit. Hoping my tone doesn't give me away, calling back to *his* phrase that stopped me in my tracks the first time I heard it.

"No, because you don't love me." He says it like the fact he thinks it is. "You willing to risk it?

I've risked everything else, why wouldn't I add this to the list.

"Yes." The word is strong out of my mouth, and our lips are on each other before I can question it.

Chapter Twenty-Six

WORTH THE RISK

LOUISA

I'm pinned against the recording booth as my arms wrap around his neck and my hands knot in his hair. While a million thoughts flood my head, the one that makes me laugh into his mouth, that has his eyes on mine in a way asking to be let in on the joke, "Thank god this thing is sturdy." As he has my back pressed against the prefab wall. He smiles into my kiss as his tongue curls against mine. His full lips pulling, begging, for every taste he can get.

His kiss tastes like sour candy as he reaches under my thighs and hoists me into his arms. Stepping us away from one of the greatest gifts I've been given. (The other might be what's currently happening.) He carries me to my bedroom, kicking open the door that's been left ajar for months. (In more ways than one.)

Even in his arms I can feel how hard he is, how large, and I'm desperate for him.

I was honest to the air, I didn't know this kind of wanting existed.

Our mouths are warring against each other for each pull of

the other's kiss. Trying to satisfy a craving that will be my undoing. As he breathes in my ear, I think this might just undo him, also.

He sets me on the bed, and takes a step back. An annoying, steadying step back.

"Say it again," he commands.

I sit up on my elbows, on a bed I haven't slept in since the man in front of me became my husband.

"Say what?" I ask, coyly. Knowing there are so many things I could say.

"Say it, so I can hear you." His voice is gravel at best, with every word, more and more desire slips out.

"I—" His lips are begging to be pulled into a smile as he kicks off his shoes.

"Want you." He unbuckles his belt and the button on his pants to step out of them.

"To fuck." He pulls his shirt over his head, I think I hear a button hit the hardwood, but nothing could pull his attention from me.

"*Me.*"

And with the last word he steps to me, reaching under my skirt to pull off my underwear. Not before grazing what's waiting for him between my legs. His chest is heaving and my legs twitch, betraying me completely, as his fingertips brush gently against me. He grips them from the middle, the wetness now held in the palm of his hand as he pulls them down my legs, and tosses them to the side.

"Is this how wet you get for me?" he says, and he's expecting an answer. He wants to hear me, he's made that clear.

"Yes," I say, slipping out of my skirt and ripping the bra from my body, and that makes him smile in a way I couldn't have imagined if it had been written into a script. I'm naked and exposed to him. Crawling back farther on the bed, giving him space to join me. But he's taking a moment to take it in, to see all of me, in a way he hasn't before.

"You mean to tell me," he says, stepping out of his boxer briefs, and suddenly I'm sitting even more upright for a better view. "You've been living under my roof, with a pussy like that, and you haven't said anything?"

As he says the words my whole body responds. "Maybe I did and you weren't listening," I say as he prowls on top of me.

"Louisa." His voice ripples over my skin, my name carried with it. "I have *always* been listening." I reach between us, and wrap my hand tight around him, pulsing it up and down the length of him, and I see him fighting his focus as his breath hitches.

"You're sure?" he says, guiding himself to my entrance as his lips press kisses down the column of my neck. Asking me, one more time, because this is out of the bounds of everything we agreed. We are momentarily suspended, naked and nearly pressed together. As quickly as this escalated, he's giving us the breath to decide, knowing that we could have months left of cohabitating. And how different that will be after we make this choice.

I wrap my legs around his back, locking them, locking him, as his tip is pressed against my entrance.

"I'm positive," I say. As he wraps his arm under my neck, bracing my shoulders against his forearm, and slowly, painfully fucking slowly, slides himself into me. He takes his time to let me stretch to him, to adjust to the size, the sheer thickness. And as he does, my back bows off the mattresses and presses against his chest. Tangling my arms around his neck pulling him into a deep kiss, causing me to tighten around him, and he releases a sound so uncontrolled, I can't believe it's actually from him. And then, he moves.

The pace and electricity that existed the second I stepped out of that booth picks up again. His tongue dives into my mouth as he thrusts deeper and deeper into me, each time, hitting a point so buried within me, I cry out in sheer pleasure as he does.

"That's it," he coaxes into my ear, his breath warm against my neck. "You spent months torturing me with the sound of your moans." He slams deeper into me as my nails dig into his broad shoulders. "I want to hear you now, for real." He pulls out slowly, waiting for me to reply. Grabbing my chin to face him where my head had lolled back in ecstasy. "For *me*."

He fucks me relentlessly, as he does. Like with everything between us since the beginning, it builds quickly and uncontrollably. Whimpers turn to cries, to moans of *'oh god.'* (Not that I'm religious anywhere but the bedroom, and even then, before now, I was questioning my faith.)

As I come hungrily, for him, he does, voraciously, in me.

With orgasms pulsing through both of us, our skin is sweaty and stuck together, commingled more intimately than ever imaginable. (No matter how much I imagined it.) He peels himself off me, and lays down so our shoulders remain pressed together, as we sink into my mismatched bedding.

"The husband homework was a good idea." Of all the things he thought I might say post-sex, I can tell it takes him by surprise. His head turns to mine in response, awaiting the rest of the thought. *"What kind of birth control do you and your spouse use?"* I say with a voice to mimic the severity of the form. His laugh rumbles in response.

"An IUD," he says, deep and low, as the sated grin spreads across his face.

I feel like every page I've ever narrated, every slow burn that finally combusted, every character who spent hundreds of pages pretending they weren't going to end up exactly like this, I feel it in the places that don't have names, the the ones the authors try to describe that I could only imagine existed in pages, and which I have been performing from a careful distance for longer than I knew. Simply because I didn't *know*.

I feel it, actually feel it. The *real* version. (Which is the worst-case scenario in a fake marriage.)

The one that doesn't arrive with directions on a script, that doesn't build to a chapter break and resolve itself neatly on the other side. The one that just sits in your chest like something has rearranged the location of your heart, and you won't know until you reach for it and find it somewhere else.

"It was worth the risk," I say. He kisses my temple, and pulls my body close.

"I hope so."

Chapter Twenty-Seven

HE CAME, HE LEFT

HUDSON

She's asleep next to me with no careful positioning, just like everything else, she's spread out. Now I guess we won't have to lie to Immigration about one thing. I know what it's like to share a bed with her. And even though she has made no concession to the idea that anyone else exists in this space with her, I wouldn't change a thing.

She claimed the majority of the pillows, of which there are too many. She has her one arm thrown above her head, her other, across my chest. So I've kept my breaths light, afraid too brash a movement and she'll wake up. *Though the longer I stay here, I don't know if that's true.*

Her face is the most unguarded I've ever seen it, which says something, because by nature, she's not a guarded person. The brightness she forces into every room, every conversation, the dark humor she deploys before anyone else can, all wrapped in a coat of optimism none of us deserve.

She's just here, sleeping and sated, in a bed she abandoned for the one next door, and in an apartment that— *I stop the thought before it finishes itself.*

I've been awake long enough to watch the sky shift from gray to pale gold, which means I've been lying here longer than I should have. *Long enough to know better.* I have had the conversation with myself that I always have eventually, the one that starts with *'I should tell her'* and ends somewhere I'm not ready to go.

I know what's sitting in a folder in my office, that I have been avoiding, and I know that I am not going to ruin this morning before she's even fully conscious.

I watched her mouth move for a good thirty seconds last night, behind that glass, and I couldn't hear her. The booth is soundproof. My biggest regret? I should have hit *record*. At best I got the occasional muffled, distorted sound, no clarity around what she was actually saying. But then her mouth took the shape of a sentence I have dreamed about. Not imagined. *Dreamed.*

Just behind glass, so I would never know for certain. *And she did that on purpose.*

'I want you to fuck me,' she had said. To herself. *Directly to me.*

And when she stepped out of that booth and confirmed it, there was no amount of self-control I could possess. Whatever I had managed to maintain for the duration of this so far, however many cold showers, or legal briefs and renovation plans I buried myself in to avoid lying in the dark thinking about her on the other side of the apartment. None of it was designed for that moment. *None of it would have held.*

I'm pretty sure sleeping with her has fucked everything up.

I'm certain it's fucked me up.

She doesn't look at me like anyone does. Not moved by my apartment or my salary, the dinners, or the cases I've won. It's the small things that catch her off guard. Every time I do something for her, she looks genuinely surprised, like she's still recalibrating who I am against who she decided I was. *I guess that's my fault.* I gave her every reason to decide wrong first.

And what I have to reckon with, what I've been reckoning with for longer than I'd like to admit, is that if this goes wrong, I won't be able to fix it by being more impressive. There is no achievement that covers this. And she's made it more than clear she doesn't want me swooping in to solve things. Even if that's how we got here. *Even if I can't fucking help myself.*

I've done my best to not just stare at her as she sleeps like some kind of fucking creep. But I've looked at the booth through the open door, looked out the window at the office building across the street, but I always come back to her. Looking at her instead of all of it. *Including myself.*

Her eyes open slowly, blinking as she's rising from deep sleep, and she finds me immediately, which does something to my chest I can't explain away, but not as much as the smile pressed into the pillow where her hair is wild and splayed across it.

"You're still here," she says, not accusatory. But sounds surprised, and she says just to be sure it's true.

"Where else would I be?" She adjusts herself, sitting up in bed and reaching for a shirt that's on the floor so she's not as exposed.

"I've been your neighbor long enough to know that your overnight guests don't often get breakfast. I just figured you would have gotten back to reality already, let me sleep it off a little longer." Even as she says this, putting distance between us emotionally, she leans into me.

It's not said cruelly, I don't know that she could be cruel, but it stings more than it should, no matter how honest it is.

"You're right," I say, letting out a deep sigh that I know she feels in all the ways it's expelled.

She throws her hands over her face and laughs, a little in disbelief, maybe at the idea that after months of being my wife, we have finally shared a bed. I understand why it happened, I had told her on our wedding night, if the time became too difficult, to come to me. And that's what she did. In her own way. And then she came for me. That is something I won't soon forget.

"Louisa," I begin, and her head shifts up against my shoulder so she can see me. "That was." Her cheeks flush red, and I can see the delicious contentment on her face. "It was amazing," I say. Which is true, but not even a fraction of what I mean. The world pales in comparison to what it really was to have her under me, with me, next to me, *now*. "*You* are amazing," I say, and it comes out rougher than I intended, less controlled. "I need you to know that, whatever happens, whatever we—" I stop. Her face is trying to understand something I don't, even as I say it. "I don't want you to think last night was a lapse in judgement."

She's very still as her eyebrows pinch together. "Ahh," she says, as if it's that simple.

"It was." I look at her. "It was the opposite of that, it was a conscious choice, something I've thought about before last night." Her hand is on my chest as she curls into the crook of my body. "I need you to know that before we talk about anything else."

"Okay," she says finally, a quiet agreement she is tucking somewhere careful for later. The only lapse of judgement was not being honest before it happened. But being with her, I don't think there is a single part of me, even the ones that keep me contained, that could regret it.

We stay like this, knowing there's an end to this conversation that is not the blissful morning we could suspend ourselves in. I move, adjust my body to get up, but her hand crawls up my neck to pull me into a kiss I am desperate to give her, but I can't.

"I should go," I say, and try to say it not like the fucking coward I am. "I have to get to work." *Lame excuse.*

"Can't we just stay like this a little longer?"

"That's not a good idea," I say. And her face contorts, her body sitting up now. Her eyes are more open than they've been yet.

"Right, of course," she says. "So, it's amazing, but not worth the continued risk?" She pulls her knees up to her chest, bringing the comforter with her. I get out of bed and begin to slip on my clothes. She looks at me for a long moment as I stand here more dressed than she is. But she doesn't realize just how exposed I feel. The brightness she woke up with dims, just slightly, which is worse than any biting edge. "What does it mean, Hudson?" she asks, genuinely. "To you, what did this mean?"

I open my mouth. The honest answer is there, I can feel the shape of it, but it dies there.

"It means," I say carefully, "that we agreed not to be with other people for the duration of this, and that was always going to be difficult, and I think last night was—"

"Don't," she says. Quiet. Final.

"I'm just saying it's understandable that—"

"Don't tell me what last night was a natural consequence of, like you understand anything more than your own motives." The room is very quiet, she always fills the room with noise, in the shower, at the kitchen sink, when she tells me about all the smallest parts of her day. But she lets the quiet overtake us now. So I try to claw some of it back.

"I'm not trying to diminish it," I say. "But I don't want anyone to get the wrong idea." It's me, *I am the one who could get the wrong idea*. And that's more terrifying than anything we've been up against yet.

"You've been thinking about how this ends since before you opened your eyes," she says. "I can tell. I know what it looks like when you're already writing the conclusion before even asking the question. This is your M.O., just making decisions for everyone around you."

"That's not it," I say, trying to keep my resolve, but it sounds cold.

"It's okay. I know what this is." She pulls the covers back, moving to sit on the edge of the bed, her back to me. "I've always known what this is." I'm staring at the back of her, her hair a mess from last night, the back of her head holding the sounds we screamed into the pillow.

"Look." She turns back, and there it is, the joke assembling itself, the armor she reaches for when everything else has run out. "Our first real marital fight." She gestures vaguely between us as she stands to get dressed herself. "That'll be good for the paperwork."

The smile she's forcing *almost* works. And that *almost* makes it worse. But it doesn't. And what's underneath it is something I don't have a clean argument for, something I would give a great deal to not have put there. But I did. *Because she's not wrong.*

"And given that it's our first fight? It's also the first time I'm going to kick you out." She positions her hands on her hips, a stance I know too well, but this time fueled by something much worse than neighborly hate.

"Hudson?" she says calmly.

"Yeah?"

"I'd like you to leave now." It's delivered quietly. I don't counter, which used to happen, but now happens with some regularity.

I pick up my shoes, and walk out the door.

I stand in the hallway between her apartment and mine, in the inches of air that has held the best and worst versions of us. The small man, Mr. Ambrose, sees me leaving and shuffles back into his apartment nervously. As if I'm the person you want to avoid. *Right now, might be true.*

And when I step back into 7A, I stand in the entry long enough to understand that the conversation I keep waiting for the right moment to have is running out of moments. It's how the thing that could be explained becomes a lie for no reason other than cowardice.

Before the morning becomes a pattern of something I can't walk back from without taking something from her that she didn't know she'd given.

I make coffee, sit at my desk, and pull out the folder from the drawer. I already know what's inside, and that's the problem I've been living with since the day the board approved everything I asked for and handed me the bill.

Staring at the deed to her apartment.

Chapter Twenty-Eight

ALL STEAMED UP

LOUISA

There is a pounding on the door that wakes me up immediately. I didn't bother going to bed last night, or the last three. Not the one in my apartment, and not the one I've curled into for the last months.

Besides the night we spent together, it was the first time sleeping in my own apartment since we started this whole thing. And let me tell you, I slept *horribly*. (Don't tell him.) I thought being in my own space, *alone*, would give me the chance to reset myself. To not wake up to him handing me a mug, or asking what I'm recording today. (Because he does that.)

But we were together here.

And while I knew he regretted it, I didn't realize how much. Knowing that he got out of bed that morning, to make sure I wouldn't get the wrong idea.

I stayed here to not let myself fall into this illusion of him I've made up in the folds of kindness and imagination. He couldn't let me bask in the morning light of it a little longer, because my feelings are such a liability to him—no, not feelings. Love. (Maybe just my love.)

It doesn't matter how amazing it was (*which it was.*) I know that's not a lie. But I don't understand how he can just move on. Maybe that's the point, maybe that's what he's trying to avoid by *'not wanting me to get the wrong idea,'* like I am a problem he has been quietly enduring. All the small chaos of me, tallied up behind my back into evidence that my feelings are, as suspected, too much.

I've been told that before. Just never by someone I'd started to believe might think otherwise.

So as someone is pounding on my door, I am not a woman who slept, I am a shell of a person who rehearsed her own humiliation until the sun came up. (Again.)

I pull myself off the bed and into the hallway, still in the oversized t-shirt I never changed out of, and I crack the door open. Not sure who I am expecting at 8 a.m. on a Monday morning. (I know who I'm hoping.)e left when I asked him to.

He's texted me since, the minimal logistics of our fake life, keeping it all clean, so he will be able to extract himself easily as he originally planned. Except for the one where he said, again, that we need to talk. But I can't. For the first time in my life, I'm hiding from a conversation, because I knew it was temporary, but I'm not ready to hear (again) just how temporary. So I retreated to my apartment, where I've DoorDashed every meal and spent the weekend buried in work.

At least for him, perfect timing with the recording studio, because as I moaned and screamed, he didn't show up at my door. And while I had a real memory to work with this time, I also had one for the great heartbreak third-act break-up scene.

But when I open my front door, it's not him. (Of course not.) It's a gangly, odious man, dressed in an ill-fitting suit.

"Mrs. Ellis," he says through his nose. Handing me a business card with the same seal that started this entire ruse. *United States Immigration and Customs.* "I'm hoping to speak to you and your husband, is he home?"

He is peering through the door, looking for signs of Hudson

in my apartment, of course, there are none to be found. My mouth is immediately dry and my stomach knots in a way to tell me this is a bad situation. (Like I don't already know.)

And like everything. I make it worse.

"He's in the shower, it will be a while."

Dumb! Dumb! Dumb! I might as well come clean now, this is a disaster I've backed myself into in all ways.

"I can wait," he says as he slips his narrow body through the door and takes a seat on the sofa to do just that. He makes himself comfortable, and doing so strips me of any comfort I had. (Which was already teetering after recent events.)

I shouldn't even be here right now, but we slept together, and I couldn't spend another night in the same space, not yet. Knowing that he would be just across the living room, filled with regret, just wasn't something I could deal with immediately.

I hurry into my bedroom. "Just getting dressed," I call through the door, in a voice I intend to sound casual and which sounds like someone doing an impression of casual. I pull on leggings because I refuse to face my fate without pants.

I step into the bathroom, look around like someone might be able to apparate in and save me. But I pull back the shower curtain and open my favorite (weirdest) part of the apartment. My shower window. I hang my head out and wonder if an escape is at all possible. (It's obviously not.)

I step out of the shower, but turn on the water, because I have committed to the bit and the bit requires my husband in the shower. But not before texting said (fake) husband as quickly as possible.

sos! immigration here

This will be the last crazy thing he has to deal with. Though now that I've backed myself into a corner of my own chaos, I don't know that there's really anything anyone can do. So I commit to the bit and as I'm leaving the bathroom and say to absolutely no one (but loud enough for someone to hear), *'Babe, uh, Immigration is here.'*

My reflection in the mirror is the only one that responds. (And she looks pissed.) Knowing that every minute this goes on, I'm only making it worse. (Well, there's a metaphor for ya.)

Maybe I can fill him with water, tea, *poison* (not poison), and eventually he will have to go to the bathroom, and my *husband* will still be in the world's longest shower, so he will have to leave and go somewhere else. And at that point I just run out the door and pretend this never happened. That's plausible right? (Of course not, Louisa, what is *wrong* with you.)

The only thing more fake than my already fake husband? Talking to him in an empty bathroom.

Maybe I just say *'oops I actually live next door, I just sleepwalk and get confused.'* He'd buy that, right? (Get it together.)

Before I take the steps to meet my fate, I take a long, slow inhale through my nose. The version of me watching this play out is getting steamed over by the hot, running water. But I see her doing the four counts before blowing out the breath.

I step out of the hallway where my bedroom and bathroom connect, fake laughing at something my fake husband didn't say because there is absolutely no one there.

"Can I offer you something," I ask. "Tea, how about a coffee —" The man, whose first name is Dick (appropriate), last name Ricktor (somehow also appropriate), opens his mouth like he's about to speak. "Actually I don't think I have any coffee. Tea it is!"

He had clearly been moving through my small living space. Nothing is physically out of place, but it's like I can see every step he took. As he stood in front of different parts of my life to pass judgement. (He'd probably really like my dad.)

"Nothing," he says. He isn't looking at me. He's looking at the recording booth. "What is that?"

"Recording studio. I'm a voice actor."

"Mm." He writes something down, I don't know what, and that makes me nervous because I don't know what about *'recording studio, voice actor'* requires notation, but apparently it does. "You work from home."

"Yes."

"Full time?"

"Yeah, mostly." My phone is face down on the counter and I am willing it to buzz with everything I have. Ring so I can kick him out, goddamnit. (It doesn't.) "I also, well, I *used to* work at a coffee shop, but that's on hold right now while the immigration process—" He holds his hand up to stop me as he picks up the framed photo from my bookshelf. The one of me and Theo at what must be a Christmas two years ago when he was in town, both of us in terrible sweaters with our arms around each other, squinting into the flash.

"Family?" he asks.

"My brother, he's in London."

"Your parents?" Something tightens in my chest. Not fear exactly, but discomfort at a question that is easy to answer and hard to say. "They're in England also. They moved back a few years ago." He sets the photo down and picks up another frame. This one of Chandler and me at her art show in college, and next to it one from a gallery show last year.

"No wedding pictures," Dick (literally) says. A statement so clearly pointed, he either thinks I'm an idiot or I don't care.

"It was very intimate. No phones," I say.I start following him around my apartment as if I'm imaginary saging everything he touches.

Another knock on the door. (Fucking. Great.) Seriously, the universe is punishing me with the worst morning. This is more than bad luck. I look up to the ceiling, imagining the sky all the floors above it, hoping the clouds can hear my prayers. *I know someone else must have needed my good-luck day, but please please please for the love of everything, can I please just have the good luck for a little bit this morning? And I promise you can have me trip and fall or get stuck in an elevator, whatever you need, later.'* I say to no one but myself.

Knowing there's no one to save me this time. When I should have just been honest, or a version close to it. But no. The knock at the door is louder, *great*. This is it. The police have come to take me away. *'Sorry Louisa Evans, time to go, say hi to the queen.'* (I'm sure that's how it will go.)

I squeeze my face through the gap and there is Hudson, in a suit as his Monday-through-Friday uniform would require. But his hand presses flat against the door, ready to push it open without hesitation. He looks furious. And I'm sure I can think of a few reasons why. (And I would bet they all are my fault.)

But he still came.

Lotta good it will do considering he's *'in the shower.'*

His dark eyebrows press together in a way that looks like he could have broken down the door if I hadn't gotten here by the next knock. (He might still.)

He sees my eyes bulge as I look back to my living room, peering behind the small wall that separates the entry from the main living space and blocking Hudson's view of the government agent currently assessing my kitchen. (And I feel violated by it.)

I just shake my head ever so slightly at Hudson. "Mrs. Saraceno," I say quickly, dramatically. "It's so nice of you to stop by. I have someone here waiting to speak to Hudson, but he's in the shower... you know how he is, *so* particular about his hair. I'll have to see you later." I go to slam the door but he stops it. It feels as though he looks right through me. I use my own foot to nudge his out of the way. "You understand, *don't you*? My *husband* is in the shower," I say clearly again.

Hudson's eyes narrow on mine and he nods once. Mouthing the scold *'Don't say anything'* without letting out a sound.

And I shut the door.

I take a seat in my painted cafe chair that is really an all-purpose chair for everything from ladder to dining. And drag it across the hardwood, to sit directly across from him, as he returns to the sofa after looking around my apartment with indescribable skepticism. (It's an icky feeling. I wish I had a better word, but icky is all that comes to mind.)

"I'm curious, Mrs. Ellis, can I call you that?" he asks in a way that sounds like it's a trick question.

"Uh, that's fine." (No one calls me that, but I'm not about to tell *him* that.)

"I only ask because I noticed you haven't *officially* changed your name as part of the marriage filing," he continues as he scribbles notes condemning my future on his spiral notebook. "Any reason?" And there it is, the beginning of questions meant to trip me up. With no one to defer to.

"Yeah, I uh, hadn't decided yet," I reply. Which *is* a perfectly acceptable decision. (For everyone but me apparently.) "I want to, I *will*," I stress. Not letting the idea of a last name be the thing that has this house of cards collapse. "I mean, one third of our names are already the same, what's another one?" It (almost) makes me laugh. But nothing can kill a laugh I'm learning like the sound of Agent Dick Ricktor tapping his finger against the first page of what I know is my file.

"You're living at the address on file?" His voice screeches down my spine, making me uneasy with every word.

"Mhmm." The sound comes out of my mouth, confirmation. And I think about Hudson, and exactly how much of anything is too much to say.

"It seems I've made a mistake, Mrs. Ellis. This is 7B. It seems I've knocked on the wrong door." He closes the folder and crosses his legs, hitting the voice memo on his phone as I watch the sound waves pick up his dramatic breathing. "Good thing you were *here*," he emphasizes.

"Well, you see..." I start, but don't know how to end that sentence. I should have just said that I was here recording, that Hudson was with Grams, I should have said anything but the lie that is going to single-handedly unravel this. And then what, will it have been worth it?

Anything even close to the truth would have been better, but

I'm not a good liar. I can act behind a curtain, faceless I can become someone else, but *lying* in a situation like *this*? I am too much of a people pleaser to be able to come up with a good lie on the spot. And was too frantic to realize I didn't need to. But people do thoughtless things when they are afraid. And this man in his brown suit and power trip, he terrifies me.

The sounds of the shower coming from the bathroom behind me are louder now and they become a backdrop to his voice calling to me. "Sweetheart, can you grab me a towel?"

"Excuse me," I toss quickly to the awkward, towering man, who stood as soon as he heard Hudson's voice, like a sign of respect now that my *husband* showed up. (Asshole.)

I run to grab a towel from the side closet and I knock on the bathroom door.

A strong, wet hand reaches out and wraps around my wrist, yanking me inside. He's dressed, which is the first thing I register, and soaked, which is the second, his shirt clinging to the shape of him cruelly by the wet fabric, and his hair is dark with water as his jaw is tense and set. My eyes follow the trail of his muscles shaping the fabric, and as I get to his pants, they *also* are clinging to, *well*, the rest of him, like a second skin.

"Louisa," he hisses my name in a whisper as water drips down his face. It's only now I'm struck with the reality of what just happened. Behind him, the most inconvenient, voyeuristic window to ever exist is wide open.

"Did you... oh my god!!" I snap in a whisper-scream of my own. Realization washes over me. "You climbed in the window?!" I'm yelling as loud as I can in the sharpest whisper my body can expel. "YOU COULD HAVE DIED!!" (Okay, now it's a little less of a whisper and I don't care.)

Dangerous beyond belief from someone I didn't think could be dangerous. (Except for maybe once.)

His wet hands grip my arms and back me into the wall. Pressing his body against mine, our faces so close, dripping with water and fury. The droplets cling to his eyelashes as I stare deep into the amber circles around his irises.

"What was I supposed to do," he asks as he lowers himself, making himself eye level, so he can speak the question directly in my mouth, even though I don't think he's expecting an answer.

"I'm sorry, I panicked, I didn't know what to do," I say, and the panic in my voice is definitely still here, trembling.

"Jesus, I'm not mad you texted." He stands back to his full height. "I'm mad you were in this situation alone, even for a minute. It's reckless." He turns and looks in the mirror, running his hands through dark, wet hair, but I tug his arm and force him to face me.

"You have the audacity to say *I'm* reckless? *YOU* are the one that just scaled a building seven stories in the air!" The steam is all around us, radiating off our bodies as we stare at each other with the same condemnation for different reasons.

"I'd do a lot worse if I had to" is all he says. Taking steps back towards me, his hand by my face caging me in. My breathing is heavy, my eyes are heavy, and the wetness I'm feeling is not only clinging to my skin from the steam, but inconvenient given the guest just outside. It's not my fault the person standing in front of me radiates sex by default. Dripping wet, is just unfucking fair. Even if I am mad at him. *Especially* when I am mad at him. "We'll talk about it later," he snaps. Steadying himself. "Tell me what I need to know."

"Well, he showed up, he said it was an accident, but I don't think it was, and I don't know why I lied, I should have just said I was recording, but I got confused." I'm picking up speed but not volume. No matter how hurt I was by him, he was still the only one I could call for help. And now that he's here, the words are tumbling out of my mouth. "He just came in and started taking notes, and started recording, I just didn't know what to do. He knows I'm here, and that the paperwork says we live next door, and I just shouldn't have even opened the door, but I've made it all worse...I make everything worse…" I take a pause. "And I'm supposed to change my name?! He's got questions, and I thought you said home visits were rare, I fucked it up," I say in a nervous ramble.

"Look at me," he says, his face close to mine as he lowers his eyes to my level. "This is on me. None of this is your fault, you hear me?" His eyes narrow, almost with a sense of remorse, and then he takes a step back from me. Leaving me pressed against the wall by my own paralysis of nerves. He rips the shirt off his back, dropping it to the floor. Kicks off his shoes and socks, and steps out of his pants.

Dripping wet, the only thing that prevents him being fully nude, boxer briefs that leave *nothing* to the imagination. The steam that fills this bathroom makes it feel like this all could be a hallucination, but the smell of peppermint and his cologne make it clear it's not.

"Louisa, the towel." It's a sharp whisper, and I look down. The towel is clutched to my chest like it can hide me from this. I extend it to him, he wraps it low around his waist. (Now is not the time to be distracted.) "I'll do the talking, okay?" he says, his tone finally softer. I nod. He turns off the shower, leans to my ear, and whispers, "And I am *not* particular about my hair."

He steps out of the bathroom first, and walks into the living room where the man is back to not-so-subtly surveying the space and making notes as he does.

Hudson clears his throat harshly, and its meaning is not missed. (Nor is he.) I am quite literally cowering behind him.

"Put that down," he says. Not mincing words. And the man does as he's told. Returning a snow globe to the shelf.

"So sorry," he says without an ounce of sincerity. "Glad you're here, we can continue."

"No, we're done here." Somehow, this half-naked, soaking-wet man is more intimidating than anyone I could have conjured up myself to save me from this nightmare. "You are going to be leaving." Agent Dick looks like he wants to say something, but Hudson continues with such force as he takes steps closer to him.

"You entered this apartment without permission, or a warrant, and are recording, which you and I *both* know is illegal without two-party consent." Each word brings Hudson closer to him, threatening in a way he means to be. He turns softly back to me. "Did you give consent, sweetheart?" he asks softly. And I just shake my head *no*. "Exactly," he says, his tone back to full strength.

"There's no reason to be defensive, this is just routine," he stresses, trying to take steps out of Hudson's path.

"There is nothing routine about you being here at 8 a.m., coercing *my wife* into complying with some bullshit check-in," he spits the words out like venom. "We have our interview scheduled. Anything gained from *this* illegal entry will not hold up in court, I'll make fucking sure of it, but not before making sure you never come within six feet of her ever again."

I've never seen anyone become so large, he fills the space as he moves through it. And despite everything that's happened, I'm in awe of him.

"Of course." His hands are in the air, conceding, as he walks back to his brief case and collects his folders, and heads to the door. As soon as the door shuts behind him, I step backwards until my back hits the wall behind me as I let out a breath that I have been *very* aware I'm holding, but was unable to release until he was gone.

Chapter Twenty-Nine

UNFRIENDLY NEIGHBORHOOD SPIDERMAN

HUDSON

What in the ever-loving fuck are the chances. The text came in as I was pulling on my jacket, the SOS ping hitting something primal, the way fire alarms are designed to. Not fear, exactly. *Something faster.* I don't have a word for what that does to a person. I just know I was moving before I even thought to text back. Instinct pulling ahead of logic before logic even had its shoes on.

We hadn't been in a good place, despite trying to get her to have a conversation, she made it clear what she needed was space.

Good fucking job, Hudson. Look what that allowed to happen.

The fact that she was standing in her apartment with a government agent and her SOS came directly to me. She set it all aside when she actually needed help. *Thank fucking god.*

She opened the door, and whatever she was trying to communicate with her eyes and overacting landed with all the subtlety of a thrown brick. She'd already made up something foolish and backed herself into a corner, and her cheeks were red and her eyes were terrified, and all I know is there isn't much I wouldn't have done to change that.

Which is exactly how I ended up on the balcony. Stood there

long enough to look down once, against the advice of every action movie I'd ever seen, and immediately understand why they say not to. I'll never do *that* again. I'd say I'll never scale the side of an apartment building seven floors up again either, but I wouldn't have imagined I'd be in this position now. So, who the fuck knows.

I gripped the railing and swung one leg over. Then the other. And I was standing on the wrong side of it, back flat against the building's exterior wall, both hands locked white-knuckled, one still clutching the railing as the other gripped the wall itself. There was nothing between me and the city except the early morning air, which is less romantic and much more fatal than it sounds.

'This is insane,' said the fully functioning part of my brain.

'She needs you,' said the rest of it.

Guess which part won? No. Fucking. Contest.

The exterior of the building has about eighteen inches of a ledge that allowed me to shuffle my feet the distance between my balcony and hers, which from the inside feels like a shared wall and from the outside feels like the Grand Canyon.

One foot planted. Then the other. Following step by step. My back scraped the wall as I had one hand still gripping my railing, one arm outstretched toward hers.

For a moment I imagined what Lucas would say in my eulogy. *'He died trying to protect the woman—'* Oh fuck it. I take what felt like the biggest breath of my life and released my hand that was clinging to my railing so the other could reach hers.

Then both hands on the railing, both feet on the narrow ledge, nose to nose with her bathroom window which was, thankfully, open, because of course she leaves it open, because she has never once in her life thought to herself perhaps I should close this massive view to the outside world.

I got one leg through the window, then my torso, and then the shower head, which I had not considered would actually be on, hit me directly in the side of the face with full pressure.

Both feet landed in the tub and I grabbed the curtain rod on pure reflex. *It held.* By the mercy of whatever contractor installed it thirty years ago and the grace of something I've only ever been skeptical about, it held.

I stood in the running shower, fully-dressed, soaked from the neck down, hair plastered flat, curtain rod still in my hands like I was holding a trophy for the worst morning of a calendar year. And somehow still, the first morning I woke up alone in my apartment after she told me to leave? Still might win.

When I cracked the door and called to her, she came running, towel in hand, and the way I wanted to wrap my hands around her. The way I almost did. But I was entirely on the back foot coming into it, no clue what she had already said.

She seemed surprised I got her, like I wouldn't have done whatever it takes, for her.

It's not fair to her, how I feel. I told her it would be a risk, she agreed to it as I laid her on her bed. And it should be clear to her it means I'll risk life and limb if I have to. But I was filled with rage when I saw the fear on her face. The steamed bathroom did nothing to hide it, none of the tension between us evaporated, it took the life of the steam that filled the room to push us closer together. And under different circumstances, she'd be bent over the sink so I could see her face as I took her from behind.

But I was not letting this man spend another second in a place that is hers. He was on the kind of power trip that believes his job title gives him license to be worse than he is. He uses it to justify every miserable thing he's ever done and why no one wants to fuck him.

When I stepped into her living room, towel low, clothes on the bathroom floor, the man was exactly what I expected. Brown suit, clipboard posture. Shit-eating grin on his face fueled by some red-pill thread.

I made it undeniably clear that there was a threat in my voice and he scampered his way pathetically out the door. Little does he know, I'm about to clear the rest of my fucking morning just for this.

I can feel Louisa behind me, barely breathing, her presence a warmth I have memorized without meaning to. I can feel the exhale she releases when the latch clicks. And I stand facing the closed door with my hands at my sides, clenched in fists a few phone calls will handle instead, and something I can't name pressing hard against my sternum.

I turn around.

She's got her back against the wall in an oversized t-shirt and leggings, feet bare, eyes enormous, but the relief on her face looks temporary. The absolute devastation of how much I want to protect that face. I take the few short steps toward her.

"You climbed..." She pauses. "The fucking..." Her voice gets louder, "BUILDING?!" she screams. She shoves me in the chest, and for all the feelings I've had in the last ten minutes, *in the last few days,* I am shocked in a way I can't explain.

"What choice did I have?" I say it back, not mincing my own words, my tone harsh and I don't care.

"I don't know but—" she screams at me. In all the time we stood face to face fueled by something a lot simpler than whatever it is between us now, she never screamed, not like this.

"But nothing!" I cut her off. "I wasn't going to leave you alone in here." I throw my arm out to the room as I scream it.

She pushes off the wall. "You can't just—" she begins, visibly flustered before starting again. "You don't get to be reckless and then stand there like it's nothing."

"What would you have me do?" My heart is racing, and her nostrils flare like I'm the only place she can direct rage. I've almost missed it, when so much that's happened has caused her fear. "You texted me. So here I am," I say, stepping closer, making her take steps back towards the wall where I lay my palm next to her face. "No matter the reasons, no matter what happened between us, you're my fucking wife. You understand? *That's* not nothing."

Our eyes are locked in a dangerous game, and it doesn't matter what happened. "So what do you want, Louisa?" The question carries more weight than it should, because it isn't really about the window at all. "What is it that you actually want from me? Because the last time you told me what you wanted, I gave it to you."

"You're right, you did. And you regretted it by the time the sun came up," she says for the first time, ready to talk about it.

"That's not what happened." And I mean it as a kindness, but she doesn't look at it that way. "I'm trying to protect you. We're so close to the end. I'm not going to let anything jeopardize that, not even this."

"That's the problem," she says quietly. "You'll do that, you try to protect me without even including me." She pauses, frustrated, trying to find the words. "And I'll let you." She looks at her hands, the ruby sitting on her finger where it has lived since I slipped it on. "You make every decision like I'm something to be managed."

"Louisa—"

"I don't need you to regret it." Her voice is very steady. "I just need to know you don't."

She's perhaps more decisive than I've ever seen her.

I should tell her now. I need to, before the omission becomes the lie.

But she has spent her entire life being handled, her father's disappointment dressed up as high standards. I'm not her father. I know the difference between protecting someone and deciding for them. *I do.* Except I'm standing here making the same calculation, and the only honest distinction I can find is that mine comes from love, which is exactly what every person who has ever failed her would probably say. Telling her the truth now will confirm what she *thinks* is true. And I don't know where that will leave us.

We've just barely survived this round. She's still breathing carefully, holding herself together by her will alone.

With the immigration interviews just over a month away, she has too much riding on this, and I can't be the thing that unravels her.

I bought her apartment and didn't tell her, which looks like every other time someone decided what was good for her without asking. She needs to be chosen, not managed. I know that. *And I'm doing it anyway.* So I tell myself it's protection. That I'm keeping it until after, until she has what she came here for. Then I'll let her go and it won't matter if she hates me again.

Which has always been the plan. *The worst plan I've ever had.*

"I don't regret it," I say finally to her. Her shoulders relax the smallest amount. "But we both know it can't happen again."

"Right, someone could get the wrong idea," she says. *Not knowing how much I already have.*

The morning light from her windows cuts flat and honest across the floor between us, but I won't look away from her face, which looks like there are too many things she wants to say, but she holds them tight to her chest.

"Come on," I offer instead, taking her hand, her eyes tracking mine. "Come home with me." I walk us both out the door.

It was an eventful morning, all before 9 a.m., which is great, because it means by ten, I'm already on the phone with Lucas. I have a perfectly good home office, it's not large, but it does the job. Though I always seemed to gravitate towards working from bed. *No wonder why.* Now, with her on the couch, turning on sitcom background noise, as she sips a cup of tea to calm herself from her morning, I'm working from the kitchen island. *Where she remains in view.*

"What happened this morning was not standard. He entered without consent, recorded without two-party agreement, approached her alone without prior arrangement," Lucas says. "We have absolute grounds to file a formal complaint and request reassignment of the officer on your case. Am I missing anything?" He pauses, giving me a chance to correct any of his understanding of what happened.

"That's it," I confirm. Lucas isn't an immigration attorney. But he's got contacts. He also just has more breadth of knowledge on these things than I do. Even when we were in law school, throwing himself into community support, where he could offer advice. His wife, Paola, is also a naturalized citizen, so he has some familiarity with the paperwork.

"How's everyone doing," he asks. I glance up from my laptop and see her curled under a blanket in the corner of the couch.

"We'll be okay," I say. *In some ways, it's true. In others, I've never believed myself less.*

"I'll make some calls," Lucas says. "New case agent by end of the week."

"Today."

"Today," he confirms. A beat hangs on the line between us, and then, "Hud, I'll handle this. I've got you, *both*." I know he means it. I know that if I go to war, I couldn't raise an army if I tried. But Lucas, they would all follow him. The irony is that if I have him, I don't need an army at all.

As he's hanging up I hear him, saying something in fractured Portuguese to Paola. Learning the language for her. And I know the only language Louisa has learned for me lately is mixed messages.

Chapter Thirty

GRAMS WANTS A GROWL

LOUISA

The morning after, I woke up in the guest room and shuffled out to find both a tea and a coffee already poured and waiting on the island as he stood in the corner of the kitchen the way he always does, drinking his own. (Out of Kermit the Mug.)

I drank both.

We didn't talk any more about what happened. Not us sleeping together, or *sleeping together*. Knowing that, like he said, it can't happen again. The surprise immigration visit reinforced every fear I've had, confirming exactly why we can't let ourselves get blinded.

He just stood there, reading something on his phone, and I sat at the counter in my pajamas and we existed in the kitchen together the way we had for months, ordinary in a way that should have felt strange after everything, and somehow didn't. That's the part that gets me. Not the fight, not the going to sleep in separate rooms in the same apartment after his hands roamed my body and I felt every breath of his in my ear as he came. The part that gets me is how easily we found our way back to ordinary.

Like we've had so much practice at pretending that it's second nature. (And isn't pretending at all.)

My feelings haven't changed. I know that. Which is how I ended up here on a Wednesday, in the sitting room of his grandmother, listening to her critique audiobook narrators on the basis of growling ability.

There are worse places to put yourself when you're trying not to be in love with your fake husband. (Don't tell him.)

We're sitting here as she's in the wingback chair by the window. I've made her a cup of tea (properly), and on the small table between us her tablet is propped against a stack of library books because we've been on an audiobook journey. I showed her how to search for the genres she likes (which are a lot higher on the smut scale than I expected) and we listen to them together each week.

It's got nothing to do with any marital arrangement, it just evolved. I started spending most Friday mornings with him and Grams, but Wednesdays, today, I slip in alone. In the beginning it was incidental, I was in the neighborhood so I'd stop in here and there. Then I started making myself be in the neighborhood and now, well, Grams is expecting me. So I've become the most reliable person possible for Grams. (Which is something I've never once been for anyone who isn't paying me.)

She is, in every way that matters, the keeper of him, and being near her is a fix of something sweet and secret. She knows the parts of him that existed before the armor was fitted and the walls went up and he decided that being undeniably brilliant was safer than being known.

"The narrator on this one," she says, tapping the cover of a gothic romance we started last week. "He is very good, but he doesn't growl." I laugh, out loud, because like I said, Grams likes smut.

"Show me the new one," she says, gesturing her hand to my phone.

"You don't want to hear me," I say. I always say this, it's not false modesty, it's just the discomfort of being listened to by someone who knows you. But with Grams it's very much a losing battle. I love strangers in earbuds. (They are my *bread* and butter.) But if there's one person in a room who can see my face while my voice plays through a speaker, that's a different exposure that I would prefer only against being flayed. (Or maybe some version of performing live.) I don't mind sitting here reading to her, but there's a difference when it's recorded. (Don't ask me.)

I'm saved, temporarily, by the sound of the door. There's a knock, but it's more to announce himself than be invited in, but he stops in his tracks when he sees me. And I sit up straight from where I am leaning over Grams, fiddling with her audiobook settings. Hudson and I look at each other across Grams's sitting room with an identical expression, like we've both been caught doing something far more scandalous than anything that involves a grandmother. (And I can think of a few things.)

"What are you doing here?" I ask him.

"Me? What are *you* doing here," he says.

"I thought Fridays are your day?"

"This isn't shared custody, I come on other days also." I can see his face trying to sort through how long this has been going on, and I think he's about to ask me, but instead he turns to Grams. "And you didn't tell me you were having secret meetings with my wife?"

"You never asked." She takes a sip of her tea.

He crosses to Grams and kisses the top of her head, and pulls the footstool from the corner without asking if it's needed, because he knows Grams's feet are better elevated by this time of day. (I should have thought of that.) He takes a seat on the small settee at the room's edge, but as they do in every room we're in, his eyes find mine.

"Were you showing her something?" Hudson asks me, but Grams responds before I can.

"She was avoiding it," Grams says. "She won't play me one of her books."

"Shame," he says, to Grams and also to me. "She's good."

"I don't think hearing muffled clips through drywall makes you an expert," I say. "And you definitely can't hear anything from the new studio."

The corner of his mouth moves, pulls into a smirk. "I know how to download an audiobook, Louisa."

Well, fuck me. (Seriously.)

———

He picks up the invitation that's been magneted to the side of the fridge since it arrived. (Which happened about two months after Alfie Sterling told me we *have to be there.*) Hudson sets it down in front of me. "A lot's happened since we agreed to go."

This is (objectively) the understatement of our marriage. (Which tells you everything.) A lot has happened since we agreed to go, in the same way that a lot happened to the Titanic after it left Southampton. Technically, it's accurate, but missing a lot of details. (Namely, that didn't end well.)

"If you don't want to go," he says, carefully, as he's been careful with me ever since he practically dragged Immigration by the collar out of my apartment. (That's at least how it felt.) "I can get us out of it."

Here's the thing about Hudson that I have learned over the better part of six months as his wife, and almost a year knowing him. When he offers you an exit, he means it completely and wants you to take it not at all. He will move mountains to give you a choice and quietly hope you don't make it, because he has already made up his mind.

"You've kept your end of the deal," I say. "I'll keep mine."

"You have, too," he says. "More than." He turns back to pour himself another coffee, he does that lately. Turns himself away from me at the exact moment a conversation could become something else. The co-op board approved the purchase for 8A over a month ago now. Meaning, he could abandon the plan now if he really wanted. Though I think he's going to wait until he breaks ground on the renovation before there's any real talk of separation. (Who am I kidding, he'll see this thing through. That's who he is. So that's who I'll be.)

"I want to," I say to the back of his head, something I find myself looking at more and more lately. And it's true. (Also not entirely about the gala.)

He turns back to look at me for a moment, then nods, handing me the cereal box to top off my bowl of milk that I overestimated. "I'll have the car arranged." His face is managed back into place. And while we have found ourselves somewhere past the original terms, the terms are still there. Holding everything in place. (By a fucking thread.)

"I do need a dress though." I spin my spoon in the cereal. "Chandler is getting ready for her gallery show so she is elbow deep in paint, and Paola is with Lucas, you know they're doing their whole volunteering thing, so I'm on my own, which is a problem because I've been putting it off for pretty much the entire time I've known about it." I look up at him, the question is in my eyes, and my ramble. "Will you come with me?"

"You don't want my help," he says. "I know nothing about dresses."

"Well then, I should warn you, as a courtesy, that unsupervised and under pressure with forty eight hours on the clock, my track record suggests I will come back with absolutely the wrong thing, and I'll have to end up wearing my wedding dress, except that's too short and it also has a pizza stain." I look up at him. "So I need a witness who isn't afraid to tell me the truth, and we both know you have never once had that problem."

It almost looks like he winces for a moment at that. Knowing how much of a lie we live.

"The pizza stain is gone. I had it dry cleaned," he says like this is information I should have had. "It's hanging in my closet." (I had wondered where it went.) He looks at me like this is a totally normal thing to have done and is prepared to defend that position. So I don't ask. (I don't know what I would do with the answer.)

"But it *is* too short."

"*Seeeee,* good thing I have you." And it sounds like more than I mean it to. Or exactly as much, I'm not sure anymore. "I do have some frame of reference," I say, clearly not letting sleeping dogs lie. "I once recorded a book where the FMC, Seraphina, goes to the Ember Court with the Prince of Ashbourne, who actually isn't a prince at all, but is a secret fire wielder, and he burns her gown off while she's standing in the middle of the dance floor. Boobs on full display."

"The Prince of Ashbourne," he says cooly, like he is well-versed in romantasy audiobooks. To be fair, this is a good one (Roma called it *'scorching'*), but something tells me this isn't his normal listening. He just forces a smile into his mug, and polishes off the coffee while I do the same to my second bowl of cereal.

"Go get dressed," he finally agrees.

"Now? Don't you have work?" I ask.

"I'll play hooky." With that, I eagerly hop off the stool and run to get dressed, because the last thing I'm going to do is give Hudson Ellis a chance to change his mind when he just (of his own accord) said the phrase *'play hooky.'*

By the time I reemerge he has changed out of the suit he was wearing and into the dangerously casual version of himself, which should be illegal, or at minimum require some kind of advance warning system. (Not that I'd listen to it, even if it did.)

"Let's go find you a dress," he says, grabbing his keys from the trinket dish by the door, like it should be that simple.

It has never, not for one second, been simple. And I know, it never will be.

Chapter Thirty-One

I CAN HANDLE A ZIPPER

HUDSON

I can say with certainty I have never been in this position before. Which one, you might be wondering? *Take your pick*. Specifically at this moment I'm talking about the husband chair they put outside dressing rooms for men like me. *Not like me, but in optics.* The ones their wives drag along shopping, even though they don't trust their opinions, they are still desperate for their attention.

It's different for us obviously. Neither of us can fully explain why, but it's why I find myself sitting here on this tufted relic positioned for supportive spouses, for spectatorship, for a man who should be bored and detached. *I should be at work*, but here I am, the ankles of my wife, *my fucking wife*, darting back and forth under the door, the shuffling of fabric and mismatched socks the only visible sign of her progress.

I am more transfixed by the dancing of her feet beneath the door than most men are when their wives are across from them at dinner.

Every few minutes, the dressing room door swings open, and she emerges a small tidal wave of energy, floating toward the carpeted platform and the tri-fold mirror. Every angle and posture as she flicks her hair is amplified in reflection to me. My jaw threatens to unhinge itself, drop to the floor while my brain is doing its best not to leak the entire contents of my skull.

This option is a soft mustard color, I couldn't tell you about the fabric except she twirls, and I watch the folds fan out around her. But no amount of *'twirl factor'* kept it from being discarded, hung back onto the rack of rejects. I don't know what rubric of judgement she's using. *I'm pretty sure it's 'vibes.'* But she sees something I don't, because each dress she puts on is more striking on her than the last.

"What about this one?" she asks. "Stunning? Gorgeous? *Fabuuulous*?" She changes her voice with each word. Sometimes I wonder if I can hear the slightest accent come through like a wink from her parentage, usually I decide it's the choice of acting that she lets out.

"Nice," I say. I'm at the point now, *I was six dresses ago,* where every word that slips from my lips is one too many. Because this one, much like all of the other ones, requires me to adjust in my seat, anxious at the thought of how flawless she looks.

"Hmm, I don't think *'nice'* is what I'm going for, I'm looking for more of a *'there's no other option, I'm completely obsessed, you look like a goddess and are going to impress everyone you meet'* kind of dress."

"Sounds like a lot of pressure for a dress."

"Or a person," Louisa says as she steps back into the dressing room and I watch the mustard-yellow fabric drop to her feet as she steps out of it.

"I'll just put you over here, sorry, no offense," she says, to the dress, as she must add it to the pile but of course would be remiss not to apologize for the rejection to the inanimate object. It's not the first time I've found her communicating with things that have never once communicated back. I spent a good fifteen minutes listening to her from the hallway as she unloaded dishes from the dishwasher with each one saying something like *'don't you look spiffy,'* and *'wait until the plates see you.'* It's a level of endearing I didn't know existed. She shows more kindness to the items in her life than many people do other people.

"I'm pretty sure this next option is actually black tie, not just formal," she says, over the dressing-room door.

"What's the difference?"

"It has to do with *structure*," she emphasizes before continuing. "The internet is merciless if you confuse formal attire for black-tie attire. I went down a rabbit hole I have not fully recovered from on the drive over."

When she emerges this time, *and it is emerging,* time slows so I can have an extra millisecond to look at her, *and I'll take what I can get.*

It looks like it's formed against her body, everything above the waist is precisely corseted, her breasts more exposed than I've seen them *since I saw them,* and as the dress releases from where it's cinched at her waist, a flower detail that feels like her, even in this structured gown, as it follows the line of her hips to the floor.

But I can't say all of that. *So all I say?*

"Blue is good."

"It's cornflower," she specifies, and I give a short nod, keeping my lips pressed together tightly. Cornflower, or whatever else it might be, pulls the tones from her skin and makes her look ethereal. She gathers the dress in her hand as her neon nails contrast the elegance of the fabric she's holding so she doesn't trip as she walks back towards the platform and mirror. I haven't let anything break my view of her, not even sure if I've blinked, *wouldn't be worth it.*

"You're staring and I can't tell if it's a good thing, or a really bad one." Louisa's eyes are on mine through the reflection of the mirror. Which is giving me the unique, *and painful,* opportunity to have a perfect view of her ass in fabric that clings to it like it's only fucking job, while her eyes find mine in the glass and hold, and it's not the dress that's going to be the problem. *It's every time she looks at me.*

"It's a good thing." *'Good'* is insufficient, just like I am. I clear my throat, she spins on her heels and hops back towards me, totally unaware of how affected I am. Memorizing every movement twists my stomach in a way I don't think I've experienced before.

"If this is your way of hinting that I should hurry up and pick one, you can just say *that*." Her usual brightness is sharper at its edges. What she doesn't realize is despite my curt replies, *and best interest,* I would sit here all fucking day.

"This is the one." And it is, we both know it is. She retreats back behind the dressing room door, I hear the huffing as the time ticks on until the door cracks only the smallest amount and her voice sneaks out even smaller.

"Hudson, can you get Lila?" As soon as we got here, Louisa got her name, her life story, and an offer from the fashion-student-slash-sales-associate, to make Louisa's gala dress next year. *Sorry, Lila, I'll be back to solo by then. Even though I'm pretty sure Louisa will have gotten an invite for life if she wants one.*

"What do you need?" I'm on my feet, the smallest tone in her voice sounds anxious, something I have found myself able to pick up on more than I am my own emotions at this point.

"I'm just a little *stuck*. She helped me zip into it, but now... well, I guess this is a good lesson to learn now rather than night of."

"I would have gotten you out of it." The words are calm as I say them, but my tone betrays me, gruff as it comes out. Her bottom lip pops open like she wasn't expecting me to say it. *Neither was I.*

With a quick glance it's clear we're the only ones here, Sales Associate Lila off attending to a different shopper, perhaps one who had a clearer sense of what they are looking for because Louisa said she wanted something *'friendly that makes a good impression'* and we've been here for over an hour. What we landed on may be *'friendly and makes a good impression'* to her, but to me, it's *'no one will shut the fuck up about how gorgeous she is while also occupying every fucking thought I have until I die'* and yes, will 'also make a good impression.' Casual, *right*?

"I'll do it." I move towards the door. She hesitates, just a blink, and steps aside, and the small space shrinks immediately as I step in. Her scent drifts towards me first, and I inhale the taste of air that wraps around her.

She is a race of my senses and I am losing more sense with each.

Her eyes widen and her bottom lip glistens like it's expecting me to pull it into my mouth as desperately as I want to pull her into my arms and slam us against the wall.

She breaks the lock our eyes have on each other, and turns to face the mirror, presenting the zipper in my view with the same casual, kind innocence she exists with in the world. I take another step closer, *towering* behind her. Our eyes reconnect through the reflection that is holding every unsaid thought between us. Maybe this time, holding memories I replay more than I should.

I place my hand on her shoulder, and can feel the short breath she inhales as I sweep the hair from her neck. Moving it out of the way. My other hand grips the small tab and drag it down, watching the teeth of the zipper separate, exposing her skin as I do. Afraid that if I move any faster, the speed would betray me. The hand resting on her shoulder follows the length of the zipper sliding down her back landing on her waist, where it waits for the zipper to fully expose her back. The dress yields to me, my knuckles grazing her spine as it does.

And the thought pulsing through me? We haven't been this close since that night.

She must be able to feel my pulse, if not hear it. And if she were to step even a fraction of an inch back, her ass would press against my erection fighting against a zipper of its own. The tiny quiver I feel from her is not a provocation but subconscious surrender, one she has no emotional control over, *one I cannot fucking touch*. No matter how much I want to.

The sides of the dress each released, she clutches the fabric to her chest, knowing if she were to let go, it would fall to the ground, exposing her breasts. There's no doubt in my mind she can feel the warmth I let out with each exhale, because out of the corner of my eye I can follow the trail of goosebumps down her spine, right to the dip of her back where a pair of underwear is sneaking out.

She steps just out of my grip and I urgently slip my hands into my pockets before they act of their own accord and take this a step too far. Like I have before.

"So," she says, sunny again, like we weren't both just sitting on the same ledge with our feet slipping into the deep end of a pool. "This gala, is there a band, are there rules, how's the food, is there *dancing*?" Her tone is back to bright in a way she pulls light from within regardless of the season. With more excitement about a silent auction and dance floor than I've ever shown about anything.

"Yes, there's music. The food is fine, for $1500 a head, it should be better. Dessert is always a disappointment. The rules, besides black tie, are to convince everyone in the room that they are there because they care, rather than because their name on the program costs less than a lawsuit. Smile big, bid generously, and don't say anything honest until you're back in the car." I take a pause, knowing how cynical I sound. But it's not untrue. "And generally there is dancing, but personally, there is not."

She's shifted the conversation in a way that has us both ignoring the fact that she is half dressed. Something my eyes realize before my brain as they drop to the column of her neck, where it leads down to cleavage and fabric she is clutching too tightly. I see her swallow, and that has a different thought flooding my head. *Both of them.* I clear my throat with a short forced cough, and turn so my back is to her. Implying the privacy she would have if I just left, *something I can't bring myself to do.*

"Guess that explains why we never had a first dance," Louisa says. I can hear the fabric shuffling as she's changing out of the *cornflower*-blue dress and putting back on her jeans.

"For the best. I only have one move anyway."

"Now I'm definitely going to *need* to see it. I'll even fight away all the other women who are clawing after you if I have to," she says and I can hear the smile spreading across her face as easily as if I could see it.

"You are my wife," I say low and careful. "That means you're the only one entitled to any of me." My mind is somewhere between hiking up her dress here and now, and putting the entire square footage of this shop between us for her own safety. Both feel equally urgent.

Neither feels possible.

I have been telling myself the same thing since the night she showed up at my door, and every version of the argument I've made to myself since then has been technically correct and completely fucking useless.

I'm doing my best. *Which at this moment, is not enough.*

She just laughs in reply, something she does naturally. It's a sound that could be bottled as a remedy for the worst long night to outshine anything dark that exists within me. *I drink it up every time I hear it.*

I feel a soft tap of her finger on my shoulder, having come up behind me, dressed and ready to go. Gown in hand. I exhale deeply, step out of her way, and guide her from this small space that will hold a moment I plan to revisit frequently.

Particularly tonight, when my earbuds are in, and her voice is the only thing playing.

Chapter Thirty-Two

FINALLY, A FIRST DANCE

HUDSON

"Bulb went out in my bathroom!" she says, dropping her garment bag on my bed and already crossing to the mirror above my sink like she's done it a hundred times, *which she hasn't.*

"I can change it," I say, crossing the bedroom to go grab a spare bulb from the hall closet.

"*I* can change it," she says, grabbing my arm to stop me. "It's not worth the fuss right now. I just need two secs."

There's barely space in here for her as she drops her makeup on the counter and it scatters and rolls into the sink. I'm standing here in my dress shirt, collar open, cufflinks on the counter. Buried under a 'lip combo' she decided on earlier after testing three alternatives, each time asking my opinion as she made a pout. *It went about as well for me as you can imagine.*

But here I stand, trying to remember how to do a task I've performed without thinking for twenty years. Instead, I can't take my eyes off of her. *It's going to be a long night.*

I pick up a cufflink, slip it through. *You can do this.* I reach for the second one, and this is where I fumble it, which I have never done, not once. The small monogrammed silver cuff hits the floor and rolls under the cabinet, I consider leaving it there and going cufflink-less like some kind of animal. *Might be worth it.*

She's already crouching down, *fucking kill me,* the robe is shifting at her shoulder, and she doesn't make an attempt to retrieve it. Her bare shoulder is exposed to me without any consideration, as she's dropped to her knees searching for the cufflink. I should bend down to help her. I should throw her on the bed. I should, *fuck,* I should just fucking tell her.

But I don't do any of that. I let myself get lost in the image of her, as her hair is softly wrapped and woven, done, but leaving tendrils loose around her face. Always slightly windblown. I realize the longer I'm near her, *she is the wind.*

Now, the bow tie. I *know* how to tie a bow tie, even if my hands seem distracted, called to a different purpose that I can't allow them to fulfill. "Want help?" she offers, and I want to say yes, just so she will be close to me.

"You know how to do a bowtie?"

"Is it… a clip on?" She bursts into laughter as she layers a coat of gloss across her lips, making them fuller than imaginable. *And trust me, I imagine it.*

"Sadly, not this time." I step next to her at the sink, folding the flaps of the tie until it looks like it's the only thing holding my head on straight. *It might be.* "The car will be here in fifteen minutes," I remind her, though she does not look fifteen minutes close to being ready. She turns her body to me, taking a hand to each side of my tie, and adjusting it just ever so slightly. Whether it was crooked or not, I don't care.

"Well, now that's taken care of," she says. "I just need my dress." She steps back into the bedroom, unzipping the garment bag, and I'm having flashbacks to walking out of the dressing room. I was so hard I could barely walk, and I am beginning to question how I'm going to get through tonight.

When we slept together, I thought maybe, *maybe* it would satisfy something. Let me have a taste of something that I'd find too sweet. That I'd know wasn't right for me. But that's not what happened.

She steps into the dress, holding the fabric to her front, the open zipper exposing her entire back, the line of her spine visible in the space between. I've been here before, I can do it again. I put my hand on her shoulder, *the same as then,* and feel the small breath she takes at the contact. The teeth close one by one as I pull the zipper and I watch the dress gather itself around her, the fabric finding the shape of her like it was made to. I do the small clasp at the top, and let my hands slide down the length of her arms from behind, she spins in my arms and looks up at me.

"What do you think?" she asks, like it's a reasonable question.

"I think," I start, wondering just how much is too much. "Everyone in that room is going to spend the night wondering who you are."

"And what will you tell them?" She reaches for a small thread and picks it off my jacket. Perfecting the picture of the flawless couple.

"The truth," I say. "That you're mine."

Her phone buzzes on the bed and breaks the gaze we'd become locked in. She spins on her bare foot and answers the FaceTime where Chandler's face fills the screen, takes one look at the dress, lets out a sound that is more air than word, and then her eyes find me over Louisa's shoulder.

"Lookin' a little dazed there, Ellis," she says. And it has Louisa turn, checking if it's true.

"Just looking at my wife." I clear my throat and look at my watch. "Louisa, car's here."

She blows her friend a kiss and does a frantic last-minute lap around the apartment, throwing some random things into her small purse, and forces the clip closed. She slips her shoes on at the door, reaching for my hand for balance as she does.

And without thought, slipping her arm into the crook of mine as we leave.

———

Stepping into the ballroom, it opens up before us, and she stops walking for just a moment at the threshold of it. I lay my hand atop hers, where it remains tucked into me anytime we're taking steps together. I reach for it, for the smallest extra contact I can manage.

This whole place looks as it has the last few years I've been here. The scale of it, the decor, the flowers banked along every surface, the band threading something elegant through the high-ceilinged air.

But there is one incredibly notable difference.

"There's so much to look at," she says, almost to herself, except any word she says, I want to hear. Her eyes are moving over everything, trying to take it all in at once, the way she always tries to take everything in at once, greedy for the experience of things, greedy for life. "I don't even know where to look."

"I do."

LOUISA

It is a sea of shimmering fabrics, flowing silks (the internet will be so mad), stiff tuxedos, and stiffer drinks. It's a mask-free masquerade, with high stakes and expectations for everyone in attendance. The air smells like the lilies that flood the centerpieces and faint desperation as everyone seems eager to suckle from the same tit of power. (And me, who wants to win as many of the auction items as possible.)

We find our seats, the large round table more glamorous than any wedding I've been to. (Looks more like a coronation.) Thankfully our place cards already have us seated with people I've met. (Even some I like.) But when Hudson sees that I'm again next to Alfie Sterling, he just subtly swaps the cards with Paola and Lucas so I'm next to my friend instead. (Alfie made some snide remark about how *party planners can't do anything anymore.*)

The gala and silent auction are positioned to donate money to something noble, meanwhile all these people dressed as penguins pretend to be noblemen. My focus is constantly pulled in every direction, being introduced to everyone from colleagues to colleague spouses. Staying superficial on the same levels of conversation. *'Bidding on anything good?'* or *'see you at the club.'* (They mean country, not dance.)

His hand slides down the line of my spine, and I'm thankful he can't feel the goosebumps that ripple over me through the fabric. He shifts his body slightly, and his position indicates he's going to say something meant for my ears only. (At least that's what I hope.)

But as with everything about us, reality steps in when Arthur, Hudson's boss, approaches with another couple in tow.

"Who are they?" I ask Hudson quickly because Arthur is approaching us in a way that makes me feel like I should know them.

"No idea," he says as his *'this a work event'* smile spreads across his face, preparing to greet them.

"They look important," I reach up to whisper into his ear. But he bends down so his lips are close, and I feel the warmth of each word as he speaks it in a low tone.

"*You* are important." Before kissing my cheek, gently in a way I wasn't expecting but I swallow down, accepting it's for show. Just as Arthur and the mystery, important couple stop in front of us.

"Hudson, you haven't met William Sterling," Arthur says, gesturing to the man to his left.

"Will," he corrects Arthur, as if it's not the first time. "This is my wife, Arden." The man takes any chance to look at her. Every introduction is clearly another chance for him to say *her* name like it's the most interesting one among us. Even though *his last name* is on many of the donations here. Hudson does the reciprocal introduction, and we all shake hands.

A waiter comes by to offer another round of champagne and

take drink orders, I step to the side as Hudson grabs one for each of us. Will just shakes his head with a *'no thanks'* and winks at his wife. I've never seen such small movements look like such full inside jokes.

Will looks a little more rugged than anyone here, not in build, but he has a layer of facial hair that looks like it's swings between scruff and beard regularly, his hair is not brushed back, but falls slightly in his face, and then of course, there's the smallest amount of ink that escaped from under his white cuff as he extended his hand to introduce himself. The woman next to him, while she is every bit as beautiful as every other person here, it's something much more than a layer of mascara. It's the way she moves with an ease that looks like there's not a version of herself she isn't at peace with. All while her floor-length gown clings to her. Somehow even in black tie, this woman looks like the most natural version of herself.

"Sterling?" I ask. "You're the other brother?" His laugh is not offended at all, but recognizes the honesty in the question.

"And who have you been talking to," Will says. "Because whatever they told you, I'd like it on record that I am delightful." He looks at Arden. "Tell her I'm delightful." The smile between them is unmatched.

"You're something," Arden says.

"She means delightful," he says, looking back at me. She shakes her head as she laughs, her cheeks pink with every word he says.

"It's great to finally meet you." Hudson says, "I've been working with your father for years now." His voice is smooth and professional as Will lets out a low, sincere laugh, his eyes flashing with a sudden, sharp mischief.

"If that's true, you certainly wouldn't be thrilled to meet me," he counters, gesturing toward himself with a half-empty glass.

"Will is the family's resident cautionary tale," Arden chimes in, her voice a melodic tease as she leans into him, almost sounding proud of whatever it is that makes him so *'cautionary.'*

"Black sheep," he says with a shrug, knocking his tuxedoed shoulder into his glamorous wife.

"I hope that doesn't mean you think *I'm* the shepherdess." She dramatically clutches fake pearls as he curls his arm around her waist. The two of them are more interested in each other than any other part of a conversation. (I can relate.)

"But I think," his eyes narrow on me, "I might not be the only black sheep in the bunch."

"What gave me away?" I ask, straightening my spine, and I can feel Hudson quietly enjoying this, curious to see how it ends.

"Because you look like you have no interest in who sees you here," he says, like it's the most obvious answer. "Which means everyone sees you," Arden finishes easily, like it isn't my idea of a nightmare.

"And you stepped out of the way of the waiter." He takes a sip of his drink. "Everyone else in this room would have let him navigate around them without a second thought. You moved." He glances between the two of us, and I feel Hudson laugh. "Being nice to the help? Dead giveaway."

"You should see her unload a dishwasher."

"What's that supposed to mean?!" I whip my head to him, and the smile on his face morphs from *'work smile'* to genuine.

Hudson and Arden fall deep in the kind of conversation that has words like *'acquisition'* and *'portfolio'* and *'third quarter'* in it, which tells me everything I need to know about Arden Sterling, which is that she is considerably more dangerous than she looks. (And trust me, she looks dangerous.)

Will, beside me, makes casual conversation on any topic *not* that. Besides jumping in once to warn Hudson about his brothers' love of the *'chaos play'* which is why he handed over his keys of the kingdom to a CEO friend of his years ago. But Will makes it clear he has heard the word *'corporation'* one too many times tonight (and in his life) and has forcibly made his peace with it.

"They could be at that for a while," he says. And looking at them, it looks like they could. In some ways, I wonder if this is the kind of woman Hudson should have ended up with. Someone who holds her own in a way I never could. She's taller than I am, glamorous in a way I don't think I'd know how to be. I mean, who can have such a perfect red lip? Every time I try, the lipstick bleeds and I look like the joker.

"Does it bother you?" I ask Will.

"No," he says as he leans against the chair at his back, like he's happily settled in for as long as it takes. "How could it? Look at her go." But it's looking at him that's impressive. The way he's just in awe of his wife having a conversation he's not even a part of, like her just existing near him is enough.

It wraps up, and despite the conversation that had Hudson's attention and sincerity for longer than any other he's been pulled into tonight, his hand didn't leave my back the entire time.

"What do you say, one more dance, and then we head back and order a pizza?" Will says as he puts their drinks on the table and grabs her hands, ready to pull her away.

"Hope to see you again," Hudson says.

"Me too!" (And I actually mean it.)

"So long as it's not at another one of these, sounds great," Will says with a laugh as Arden jabs him in the arm.

"Don't listen to him, he just wants to get back, order room service, and relieve the babysitter who has probably been put through three *Mamma Mias* at this point."

"*Absolutely* I do." And with that he drags her (eagerly) to the dance floor.

For the first time meeting new people, I didn't ask any follow-up questions, the way they had a conversation was like we were already included, knowing who and what they were talking about, and I'm not ready to shatter that illusion. I just wanted to stand in the generous warmth of their love for a little longer, rather than whatever sunshine I craft, whatever I pull from the depths of myself to brighten the spaces I think are too painful to exist in without it.

"How about it." Hudson's voice is smooth as I feel the question breathed into the crook of my neck. "Dance with me."

"I thought you didn't dance."

"Not usually, but I have a good reason," he says.

"What's that?" I ask.

"You." He says it without hesitation. Just as simply as he gently extends his hand and I slip mine into his grip with an almost breathless *'okay.'* Trying not to feel more than I already do.

We take steps in tandem towards the dance floor and it's painful how real this life has begun to feel. How much every movement of his feels aware of me in a way far more than some agreement. It's a bizarre reality that isn't reality at all. The way people look at him is unreal, and me next to him becomes the consolation prize. I can pretend that this is just another appearance as husband and wife, but with each step towards the polished floor, the original reasons behind the decisions we made begin to dissolve.

We move through the crowd and step onto the dance floor, where he leans close to my ear, his breath warm against it as our cheeks brush.

"No laughing at my one dance move," he says. I can feel my cheeks rounding with a smile he seems to pull from me as my heart pulses in my chest. Banging to get out. I wonder if he can see it, hear it. The way he seems to be able to see everything about me.

"I can't promise anything." His hand carries mine to his neck and slides down my bare arm as he wraps us together in his hold, landing in the curve of my back. His long fingers splayed across, feeling like the only thing that could keep me upright. As his other hand extends, offering a place for me to rest mine, enveloping my fingers with a delicacy you wouldn't expect him to hold.

Our bodies move together slowly in pace with the music, my steps naturally following his. If this is his one move, it's the only one he needs. The band transitions to another song as our bodies remain pressed together, and the slow build of music guides my feet as much as he does. The air in my lungs feels like him, it's full, and terrifying in a way that tells me when all this is over, when this is all over, I won't have anything left to breathe.

His lips are on my ear, not speaking more than each breath. Each inhale I take is that of his cologne, and I hope it clings to my skin in ways I can dream about, long after the gown is gone, and the divorce is done. I hope it lingers as more than a memory.

As the music plays, the song takes shape in a more recognizable way, an arrangement of "From Now On" and I know this was him. He knows me in ways I never thought anyone would, because no one tried. They accepted the daisy petals I gave them, and when they were done, or it felt like too much, when it took me time to feel something for them in a way that could build intimacy, they had moved on. I've always been too much in how I love people. Too freely for anyone to understand, and too fearfully for myself to trust it could be different.

But I never thought it could be *this* man. Even if somewhere I imagined it would be, it wasn't real for him. But his fake feels more real than anything.

"Our first dance." His tone is muted and gentle, it's wrapped by the music, and tightens my chest.

I can hear the music, the words in my head, as we move small and softly. The irony is that there is nothing soft or small about this man. The rest of the room falls away as his arm carries my weight, keeping my feet light against the dance floor. I hear him humming along, whispering the words to a song I'm certain he didn't know before I showed up at his door in hysterics. Since then, he has taken every opportunity to play it, the movie, the songs, it becoming the soundtrack to this fake love of ours.

I lay my head on his chest, feeling the rise and fall of it with each breath. And that's why I can feel the sharp one he takes in.

"Louisa," he begins. "We need to talk." I'm not sure which words will come out next, but I'm standing on the precipice of too much to contain anymore.

Rather than look him in the eyes and search for whatever

truth could be there, fear takes hold, and is louder than any other voice in my head. "I need to go to the bathroom," I say hurriedly, my voice feeling fractured. Cutting him off from the end of the sentence.

I drop his hand, leaving him there on the dance floor as the song (our song) concludes. My pace picks up, and I have a sneaking suspicion that he is just a stride behind me. I retreat to the bathroom, pushing the large door open, and I'll let myself hide in here just long enough to shake this feeling. The one that I know will be the reason my life goes up in flames, like everything else.

Chapter Thirty-Three

IF IT FEELS REAL

LOUISA

I'm looking at my reflection, trying to see where Louisa ends and Mrs. Hudson Ellis begins, and the scariest thought is, I can't tell anymore. He can, it's no doubt what he wants to talk about.

The door opens behind me, and she steps in dripping with a sense of beauty that inspires those around her, and you can tell it's because of who she is, not just what she looks like.

"Hoping for someone else?" Arden asks as she pulls a red lipstick from her small clutch. I just shake my head, but that's a lie, and this stranger knows it as much as I do. "Well, I'm just here for a touch up, I don't even know why I bother anymore, lord knows it always ends up on his collar before dessert." She laughs to herself as she applies the cherry red across her smile, which seems to have faded, and by the sound of it, her husband is likely doing a similar cleanup in a men's room not far. "But, if perhaps you *were* thinking someone else was going to follow you in here, you should know he's just outside." She cuts me a far-too-knowing look from the corner of her eye. "Seems like a rule follower, that one."

"Usually," I say. Knowing that yes, he does, except one exam-ple. (Or whatever you call a fake marriage for papers.)

Arden stands here, leaning against the sink with a grace and sincerity that feels entirely incomparable, just naturally glowing in a way I think people here would pay to emulate, as she hops up on the sink and watches me intently, her eyebrows raised high on her forehead as she pulls her perfectly red lips into a smirk.

I sink deeper into myself, and the tears that have been holding back, too afraid to admit what they mean, because in the recesses of my mind, in my dreams, in all the moments I have in a day, I know what it means. I just haven't told anyone else.

"I love him," I say to this practical stranger, whose smile lights up the space as she uses the pad of her thumb to wipe a tear from my cheek that I didn't know had actually fallen. "But it's just, none of it is real," I say with my voice shakier than I would have hoped. "He and I, we're too different. But then he went and did *that*. He played our song, or as close to an *'our song'* as we have. And I love him, but love isn't enough, not when he doesn't... I know he doesn't."

She exhales a knowing breath, not questioning the logistics of what I said or why, just offering me something far more profound. "Love is a lot of things, but above all else, it's action." She doesn't tell me it will be fine, that *'love is enough,'* but instead tells me what is, before she continues, "Let me tell you something about men." Her voice is stable and grounded. "Men like Hudson, *men like Will,* their lives are formed by transactions, money, power, legacy, whatever it is. For some, this hardens them in ways that are impenetrable, that requires therapy and patience to get through. But every now and then," she releases a breath, maybe from memory, "Someone gets through anyway, because they were too busy loving them." Her eyes find mine, and it's comforting in a way. "That they didn't know they were supposed to find it impen-etrable in the first place."

"But what if," I begin. "I *am* a transaction, this whole marriage it's an arrangement, a deal, that's all it is."

"Marriage is the ultimate transaction, don't believe anyone who tells you it isn't," she says, looking at me skeptically. "But loving someone, the way you love each other, that's not a deal, that's a promise."

"He doesn't feel that way about me," I say softly.

"I've seen the way men look from all sides. With possession and greed, the look of lust which is fleeting, of complacency, and of the heartbreak from which you think you'll never heal. So trust me, I know what love looks like, I see it every morning, like I bet you do. Even in the worst moments of frustration that life throws at you, loving someone doesn't dissolve with the convenience of an easy life. *That* man, the one who is standing outside the women's bathroom like it's his job to hold up the wall? He loves you."

"But what if we've been playing pretend for so long that we can't tell the difference anymore?"

"If it feels real to you, then it's not pretend, is it? Everyone deserves a happily ever after, but sometimes you have to be brave enough to fight for it."

She hops down from the sink, with her dress bunched in her hand, landing perfectly on her heels. Checking her backside for any water spots (flawless, of course), her face is one of relief when she realizes she's still in perfect form. Running her finger at the corner of her mouth to make sure her red pout is contained to her full lips. As she leaves, her body is halfway out the door, I see her say something, to someone just outside, before popping her head back in to nod toward the shoulder that is leaning outside the doorframe.

The most inspiring place is a woman's bathroom. I don't think a sense of friendship like it exists anywhere else in the world.

HUDSON

I've been keeping a secret from her. More than one. I don't know which to start with, so of course that means I've told her neither. I can't lie to her, and this now is crossing into the boundaries of a lie. I can tell myself it's to protect her, but the longer all this goes on, the more of a lie it becomes. Because it might only be to protect myself.

As I held her pressed against my body, all I could imagine is how quickly this all falls apart when she finds out. I held her closer than any narrative required, I could feel her pulse as her hand laid in mine, she's so close I could smell the vanilla and citrus scent of her. We are in the final stretch of this, and I know that means that as the doomsday divorce clock ticks closer to midnight, we will sign a new contract that lets her walk away from this, leaving me drowning in my own misery.

I want to be selfish, I want to tell her how I feel in a way that doesn't let her question if this is real. I want in my arms, in bed, in my life, in a way more permanent than anything we agreed to.

But there are *two* lies.

The first is the most dangerous. I love her in a way that is unrecoverable, I didn't think loving someone felt like this. Like a fever you don't want to break. Hot and flushed and living in fragments of a dream state. I watched my parents treat love like a chore, a performance of convenience that left everyone involved hollowed out. I never wanted to put a partner through that. I never wanted to be the reason someone's light went out. And she is pure light. Loving me would suffocate it.

But then there's the second secret. The one that makes the first more than a lie, it makes it a betrayal.

As I watched her walk off the dance floor, I followed her to the large bathroom door. I just stood there. Like a fucking creep loitering outside the women's restroom. Watching Arden walk towards me with an uncomfortably knowing smile. "She in there?" she asked. The hollow ache in my chest told me the truth I've been trying to talk myself out of. If I let her walk out of this marriage thinking it was all a game for gain, I'll be the one living a lie for the rest of my life.

"You know it's weird to hang out outside a women's bathroom," Louisa says as she exits, and it settles something in me. The banter that seems to be the foundation of our relationship still exists, even in black tie and the black hole my heart is trying to claw its way out of.

"Well, it's also rude to leave your dance partner mid-dance," I reply as I hold out my arm, and she slips hers through.

But nothing else can happen between us, not until she knows the full truth. Not until all the cards are out on the table, and I don't mean how I feel. The elephant in the room she doesn't even know is there, and the longer I am silent, the worse it becomes, the elephant becomes something more akin to Godzilla tearing apart a city. I have to tell her what I did, why I did it, but the timing never felt right. Always like it would ruin a moment too near perfect. It will be another rescue she didn't ask for. But what were the options?

"You did warn me you only had one move." Her voice is full of warmth I don't deserve from her, but I crave in a way that is unnatural.

"You mind if we skip dessert and go home?" I ask. She just pops open her small beaded purse to show off an individual bag of Nerds Clusters. "We can have dessert on the way home," she says, and my chest tightens with her use of the word *'home.'*

"You don't want to see who won the silent auction?"

"No, I've got everything I need."

Almost.

Chapter Thirty-Four

SHE IS HOME

LOUISA

The night must have gone well. Hudson bid on a handful of things, so did I (using his name and wallet of course), so he may have won more than he's expecting. I always thought I was the performer in this relationship, but he does to a degree I couldn't have imagined. Work Hudson is different from the At Home Hudson I've shared a space with. Different from my Fake Husband. None of them the Angry Neighbor I created as a character. He is bold and compelling in every conversation. Charming in a way that captivates people, and in most conversations, I just tried my best to keep up. But he kept me tucked into his side the entire time.

Walking out of the gala now towards the car is almost comical. People pay attention to him, and it's not just height or sculptural symmetry of his face, criminal jawline, or unfair thick dark eyelashes that hide depth in his eyes that I have become painfully aware of. (I also had to put falsies on to compete with.) But his ability to maneuver around a crowd and somehow get heads to turn. It's not dramatic or loud, but people always turn to look at him. *Women* always turn to look at him. A second glance to pocket for later, to think to themselves, *do I know him, is he famous, or is he just that good looking*? (It's the last one.) I'm just a bonus in the line of sight, the accessory that's free with their purchase. But I can almost feel what they are thinking. *'If he's willing to go home with her, I may still have a chance.'* Wedding ring be damned. That's not as self-deprecating as it sounds. I know how I look, I'm pretty but am the kind of pretty where whoever I'm dating also compliments my personality. Sometimes I think I look a little too Jane Austen and a little less Instagram. If you want me to star in a period piece? I'm your gal. (Except for the center of attention thing.) Stunning, but specific to a time period that doesn't always have the same mass appeal. A little too narrow in some places, a little juvenile in others, because while I've been called everything from cute and sexy, to endearing and enchanting, people have to have a preference for me. But him? He's the universal blood donor of men. Compatible for everyone. And there's something about being with someone who makes everyone look, that makes it very hard for me to look away. (Not like I was before.)

I feel his hand wrap around my waist as we take our steps, reaching the car that has pulled up in front, the same one that dropped us off. We're paced surprisingly in sync regardless of the difference in length of stride, and it's because he seems to have slowed his to match mine.

The driver comes around to get the door, but Hudson waves him off as he reaches for it himself, outstretched to the door handle preparing to open it, showing me more courtesy in this fake relationship than any man has shown me in my years of dating.

"Do you think we were convincing?" I finally ask, trying not to sound pathetic at all. The idea of him releasing me from his hold and tucking me into the car would end this moment, that has me reaching out for a bit of validation. Even though we spent the night acting for his colleagues, getting in the car and going home means we will slip out of these public masks of marital bliss, and back into the ones made for self-preservation and selfishness.

This is my problem, not his. Quintessential me. When a man shows me consistent kindness, I think it might be something, because I've never been one to just have that insta-love-at-first-sight kind of experience. It's the commitment that eventually knocks on my heart to let me know it's okay. (Even though after all that's happened, I don't know that it *is*. No matter how well we pretend.) When I speak, I feel his fingertips grip ever so slightly into where they are on my waist, as if my voice caught him off guard. His face turns to me, clearly distracted as I pull his focus to me instead of whatever else was occupying his mind. Where my mind has been running back to him since I felt him pressed against me in the dressing room.

He uses the curve of my waist, where his hand is currently seated, to turn me gently until my back is against the car door. His eyes are dark and weighted as they look down towards me, a gaze so strong he could be pouring it down my throat. (And I wish he was.)

"You are perfect," he says. His voice isn't the one that fights me in the doorway, it's not the crafted attorney *schmoozing* everyone around him. This person is who I have felt, in the early hours of the morning, between the pages of scripts and between my legs. The man whose face is wanton and hungry, looking at me the way so many people look at him.

His hand leaves the door handle. And moves it to cup the back of my head, his fingers tangling in my hair, as his thumb moves slowly across the height of my cheek. I look around, but there's no need for him to keep up this act to this degree.

"I don't think there's anyone watching, you can stop pretending," I say. Breaking silence that's given the air around us too much room to whisper in my ear. To fill it with the idea that this man could want me in any way beyond the natural physical response he had when I looked at him and told him I wanted him. I'm not an idiot (usually.) Men don't turn down women in a situation like that, especially one like him. I know that it was a temporary thing. (Like the rest of this.)

There's a sound that comes from his throat as he begins to speak that lassos itself around my ribcage and pulls me closer to him, into his.

"There's nothing pretend about the way I want you," he says plainly. Lowering his mouth to my ear, his breath is warm and drips down my neck as he hovers above my actual skin. My back is pressed against the car door as my breath increases in speed. Feeling the weight of him against me as his hand is broad against my lower back. It pulls my lower half against his as my back bows off the car door despite the fact his lips have not landed anywhere on my skin, *yet*. A very hopeful, desperate *yet*. (Because god do I want him to.) "I'm done pretending."

"Then are you going to kiss me?" I ask, as my own hand finds itself pressed against his chest, the fabric of his shirt under the tips of my fingers crisp and soft in the same contrary way I've learned he is.

There's so little space between us, yet the question has him pull back just the smallest distance, just enough to look at me more clearly. But he exhales so deeply I can feel it in my sternum and a desperation in my core *for him.*

"Would you like that?" he asks as his other hand comes up to find my face. Our bodies don't seem to care about any warnings we might have. My fingers lose their grip on my small beaded purse, it falls to the ground in the same way my grip is slipping from any self-control I have. Our attention pulled by the fallen bag, landing on the cement curb, he smoothly drops to his knee to retrieve it in a way without ever breaking his gaze from me. Standing with an achingly painful and slow return to full height, his fingers graze the bare skin of my ankle up my leg as he does. The fabric of my dress rises as it drapes across his arm as he reaches my thigh, as the wetness gathers between my legs in pleading anticipation. Our bodies are pressed closer than even a moment before as he places my small vintage purse on the roof of the car, something else in mind for the use of his hands.

The lights from above reflect the grains of amber in his eyes that feel especially visible when he is on fire. I give him the most infinitesimally small nod of agreement, because no matter how small, how invisible, he sees everything about me.

And that's all it takes.

He kisses me deeply as my back bows into him, my hands gripping his shirt to pull him closer to me in greed. All the composure we practiced, the near misses that I know he felt, 'the lapses in judgement,' the moments I imagined, tossed away under our feet as his lips move against mine with hunger and passion I've imagined ineffectively.

Even from my own memory.

This is so much more.

There's a shift in him that I can only feel with his tongue curling in my mouth, the knots he holds himself tied into are unfurling with the deepening of each kiss. Our breaths are arriving at the same erratic pace as we fulfill every earlier moment we've pulled ourselves back from the brink of.

I can feel all of him against me, and know that he would have the same intimate indication of interest if he reached between my legs. (So I squeeze them closer together.) And like everything, he notices. His lips pull back with caution, but his forehead drops to mine as he looks at me through thick lashes, behind pupils so close that despite the darkness and depth of color, I can somehow see my reflection, like it's the only thing he can see as well.

We've lost ourselves and any regard for this public display. But from all the novels I've read, I know one thing for certain, there is absolutely nothing better than an against-the-car-door kiss.

He takes a step back with his hand being the only thing keeping me upright, pulling me forward from the car. I can hear the exhale of unresolved desire as he pulls open the door, offers me his hand as I step inside the large black SUV. His jacket is still draped across my shoulders as I sink into the seat, he pulls the seatbelt across my chest, giving him reason to stay close to me. Placing a delicate kiss on my lips as it clicks into place. One I lean into in the seconds before it's gone. But he just places my purse in my lap, and shuts the door.

I look up at the rearview mirror and see the eyes of the driver, and we share an all-too-telling glance as Hudson walks to the other door and takes the seat next to me.

"Sorry for keeping you waiting, Raul," I say.

"I'm not," Hudson replies. His jacket around my shoulders, his hand stretching across my thigh, he wrapped me in something that smells like him, and I don't know if the smell of this moment will ever leave me. (Worse is that I know I don't want it to.)

The rest of the drive is silent as we pull up to The Richmond. It maybe would be easier if I could click back into my hatred of him, maybe that would keep my feelings at bay. He gets out first and comes around to my door, opens it, because he always opens it, because even in fake marriage he exceeds the real thing. (Which really has made me question the types of people I've dated.)

I hand him back his jacket as I step out and he takes it without comment. Maybe if I remove myself from the cloak of him, I'll be able to shake this feeling that has overtaken every cell in my body. (Nope, that doesn't do it.)

We walk side by side, not touching, my hand not in his for the performance of it right now. We step into the elevator, backs against the same wall, watching the doors close. The inches between us doing what our shared wall never quite managed, making the space between us feel enormous. But after the first time, he has been the one to constantly draw the lines and never cross them. I thought he might, when I was standing in this exact dress, but even then in the privacy of a dressing room, he exercised caution. Stepping back from me like he always does. And for once, I'm pissed, because this version of hot-and-cold husband is making me insane, so I snap. (For real this time.)

"I don't get it," I say sharply. "*YOU* said this can't happen." I know that whatever possessed him was something he explicitly told me wasn't an option.

"I know," he says as he runs his fingers through his hair, somewhat strained.

"*But you* said it would be a liability."

"Louisa, trust me. I fucking know." His voice is rough, agitated, but clearly more with himself than with me. Not even moving his gaze a fraction of an inch from the elevator doors, even if it's my reflection he's staring at.

"Then, why do you do it!?" I push, not sure if there's an answer I want.

"Because for once in my life, I can't control myself." He says it with a level of self-hatred.

"I, I don't understand," I say. "What changed?"

"Nothing." It's said through a defeated huff. "That's the problem."

"You're lying," I say through gritted teeth, before unlocking my jaw to let the rest of it out. "Because right now you're standing there looking like you're about to condemn yourself for even touching me. But I *want* you to." The sound trails off but he hears it, I can tell as his body adjusts to the words, consenting to a part of him he's trying to hold back.

This is the longest seven floors I've ever experienced, and yet, I'm tempted to stop the elevator all the same. (I won't.)

"There are things we need to talk about, before this goes any further. Things I need to tell you that could change your mind."

"Hudson," I say his name, and his eyes move to mine. "Nothing about you will change my mind."

From the corner of my eye I can see his chest heaving in a desperate attempt to keep something in. But we are trapped in this space together as the elevator carries us and all our baggage up the seven floors. His eyes narrow with thought, working through the risks of inching closer.

I turn to face him, and he responds as if there's not an option but to look directly at me. As my lips fall open to speak, the words that jump from his are the last I hear before we crash together.

"Fuck it," he growls out.

My arms are around his neck and I'm in his. My dress hiking up around my waist as my legs lock around his back and *my* back hits the wall of the elevator. We are ravenous for each other like we each had a taste of something we've craved and been in search of ever since. (Which is true, at least for me.)

The elevator dings at our floor and he pushes us off the wall, not releasing me from his grip as I drag my tongue up the column of his neck and he groans in a way I only thought existed between the pages of the novels I narrate. He makes it down the hallway with me in his arms and to the front door in fewer steps than I imagined possible. I'm held against him, wrapped my limbs around him, as his one arm holds me up, the other reaching in his pocket for keys, when we hear someone clearing their voice from behind.

I peer over his shoulder to find our neighbor, Mr. Ambrose. I just bury my face in the crook of Hudson's neck, hiding from embarrassment. "Sorry for the, um, disruption," he putters out. "I was just coming to leave this under your door." He hands an envelope to Hudson, who accepts graciously, as if I'm not perched in his arms. "Co-op business."

"Perfect timing," he says to the small man. "Now if you don't mind, I have *business* to attend to with my wife." The meaning can't be missed, and certainly isn't as Mr. Ambrose scurries off back to his door. "Bye, Mr. Ambrose, I'll stop by this—" I begin to say down the hall, through giggles as Hudson's lips suck against my collarbone, and he pushes the apartment door open.

It's like having cold water thrown on both of us, a grounding reminder of what we are even doing all this for. Though being in trouble with a co-op board is far less of a gamble than being full-blown deported. (Though Mrs. Saraceno is pretty scary.) Yet, the second we step inside I slide down the front of his body, feeling every inch of him as I do.

I kick the heels off my feet, losing meaningful inches. He wordlessly sets the letter down on the entry table and slips his finger into the knot on his bow tie. Loosening it without ever breaking eye contact with me. Unbuttoning the collar of his shirt, slipping off his jacket, and dropping it on the floor near my shoes. I continue to take steps backward into the main room, twisting my arms behind my back, reaching for the zipper of my dress. The smile that forms on his face is unlike I've ever seen before, one that rewrites the rest of the night. It's wicked and full, revived from a moment it was robbed of previously.

He takes steps and captures me around the waist. His lips moving against mine as his hand reaches around and drags the zipper down to the base of my back as he works his hands across my bare skin. It falls to my feet as soon as I allow it, and his eyes crawl across my breasts with gratitude, and he scoops me in his arms faster than I can react. My fingers make quick work at undoing the rest of the buttons on his shirt, pressing kisses to his neck with each one undone.

He takes long strides that land us in his bedroom as he places me on his perfectly made bed, and I lean up on my elbows in nothing but my underwear as he peels his shirt back, rips the undershirt over his head, not wanting to break his stare from where it is on me. In doing so, leaving his upper body bare. With each of our torsos naked to the other, imagining the moment they become pressed together again, this time raw skin and sweat. I've never seen him like this. Breathing for the sole purpose of me at this moment. The tightness of his chest, the hardness of, well, the rest of him, and if this is pretending, I never want to return to reality.

He moves to undo his belt, and something overtakes me, I sit up, reaching for it myself. Making quick work to undo it, pulling down his pants, and freeing the length of him at what can only be described as mouth-level. And it's too serendipitous to pass up.

I can feel the way he's looking at me, even though I'm looking at the hard thickness of him, wrapping both of my hands around it. What escapes him is uncontrolled, and sounds like it wants to be my name formed into a gasp for breath.

I sink from the edge of the bed to my knees in front of him. Sitting at his feet, looking up at him, finally seeing the devilish way he's looking at me, has the moisture between my legs pooling and my mouth watering.

With a hand braced against his thigh, and the other around the base of his cock, the pacing of his chest is begging me without words, and I'm eager to have him in my mouth. Pulling the tip in between my lips, wet and tightly. His hand comes down quickly over mine on top of his bare thigh, keeping us pressed together as I begin to move my mouth, taking in more and more of his shaft.

He's thick and fills my mouth beyond capacity, no matter how deeply I take him. He groans darkly with each pull of my lips as they drag the length and my hand moves against him. My hair has fallen in my face, but I feel his fingers pull it away, tangling deep into the waves and pulling them on top of my head. Clearing my line of sight, and more importantly for him, giving him a view of me. I can feel each twitch of him, each micromovement from gaze to stance, directive in a way I want more of him. His eyes are unbreakable on mine, on what's happening.

"You are fucking *perfect*," he says, surprisingly gentle through hard breaths as he moves a hand to cradle my jaw and brush the tears collecting in my eyes from the depth I continue to pull him into the back of my throat. His breathing is picking up. "Louisa," he putters out. "I won't last." I can see him losing control, but even that won't have him break his stare from mine. "You're good, you're doing so good." And with that, something unlocks in me, a moan from my core that seems to rattle him o deeply that he reaches to pull my head back, fingers tight in my hair to save me the mouthful of him. But instead I grip my fingers into his bare ass and pull him as deeply into my throat as possible. As I do, he releases every ounce of himself into my mouth. Legs trembling as he does. But not letting a blink or orgasm prevent him from seeing my face.

I pull my mouth off him, and freeze. I don't know what came over me, but as I sit here at his feet, mouth full of cum, he reaches for his undershirt from the floor. Smiling and holding it beneath my chin as he squeezes my cheeks, forcing the spit into the t-shirt, as he uses the clean side of it to wipe anything remaining from my face. Mascara, sweat, cum from my lips. All mingled together into this previously flawlessly white shirt, he tosses to the side of the bed.

He kicks off his shoes and removes his pants, and his hands find mine and pull me to my feet. Leaning to kiss me with a softness and invitation for more. His fingers are spread broadly across my back, pressing my front deepening into him. My nipples are hard but buried somewhere in his chest I hope they never emerge from, not if it means I feel his breath the way I do.

I twine my arms around his neck, and in one fell swoop he palms my ass and spins us both around to land me flat on my back atop his bed. He sits back on his knees, taking me in surrounded by the clean, simple bedding, as I look up at him wrapped in the dark of this room that was not preparing itself for this moment.

His body is rock hard, and like I have from the beginning, I wonder why the fuck a corporate attorney needs to look like this. (Besides for the goodness of humanity.) His hair is entirely disheveled now, and I know I look the same. Though, I'm not usually described as *cheveled*.

He loops his fingers into the bands of my underwear (which given the dress I was wearing really barely constitute as underwear at all), and he slips them down my legs. Dropping them to the side of the bed with all the other decisions we've made tonight.

We are both here so much more naturally than I've been able to experience before. His hand rings around my ankle and slides it up my calf, lifting my leg gently, opening me up to him, as he places it on his shoulder. Palming my breast, he drags his hand down the channel of my breasts, past my belly button, and uses his middle finger to split my lips that are wet and waiting for him. (And he knows it.)

He dips his fingers inside of me as he uses his thumb to apply pressure and draw circles around what feels like every nerve ending in my body clustered into a single point. My back bows from the bed, but he pushes me deep back into the comforter. Sinking himself down to where I lose his gaze between my legs. His dark hair, wet with sweat, his forehead glistening as he presses kisses to my inner thigh and he curls his fingers deep within me. He brings my other leg across his shoulder and moves his mouth to me. Sucking as he pumps his fingers deeper, and deeper, in a rhythm that feels practiced and perfected, but just for me.

My hands are grasping for something to hold on to, digging deeply into the covers around me, but the only thing I want to feel is him. The taste of him is still on my tongue, and he's repaying the favor as he slides a third finger inside of me, and I know, from memory, it's to prepare for the thickness of him. I knot my fingers in his thick hair, and while I have watched his heavy eyes monitor every breath I take, I press his mouth deeper into me. Knowing that I'm on the edge of an orgasm I don't want to let go of, and he would never ask me to.

Picking up speed, our bodies follow each other in a way of familiarity they learned from tension we exchanged long before right now. The flashes of his face between my legs, devouring me, mixing with the frames of him standing in my doorway, sweat dripping and anger across his face. And that's what does it, pushing me into the deepest orgasm I've ever experienced. That has my legs go limp around his neck, and I know he feels me tightening around his fingers. The feeling of warmth overtaking my entire body, and despite being incredibly sated, as he was, with my hand still knotted in his hair, I yank him by the handful I have, hard, up towards me.

"Careful," he says as he smiles into my kiss. "I'm particular about my hair." I just pull him closer, desperately, the joy in this, the laughter between us, never what I could have imagined being with him was like, even after the first time. Our faces barely break apart as I reach hungrily for his cock, needy for it to replace the feeling of his fingers.

Sitting back, as if back in the starting position, with his bird's-eye view of me sprawled across his bed, imprinting this image into his brain the way I am my heart. Grabbing my hips and aligning us, he pulls me up from where I lay frozen and lost in the comforter. My body feels near limp, but in his arms as he pulls me against his chest, I wrap my arm around his neck, and feel him large at my entrance. I slowly sink down, and feel the immediate painful pleasure stretching and filling me with him. With each slow rise, I take him deeper. Our bodies are joined, pulling apart only to slicken his cock to take more of him in with each rise. Until I finally land all the way, and have him so deep and seated within me, I can't immediately move. He holds my face, his mouth dangerously close to mine, as his eyes drop to the space between us to see where we are joined. And the face he makes when he looks up and reclaims mine is something I've only read about. A level of desire I don't think I've heard described outside of fantasy.

"Look at you," he says, as he drags his thumb across my swollen lip. "You're such a good girl. *My* good girl."

And I am undone. I feel myself begin to tighten around him just at the sound of his voice. I begin to ride him ferociously, greedy for another orgasm, knowing now how much he wants me to have it. His lips move across the length of my neck as we rhythmically pull pleasure from one another. Every argument we've had channelled in the aggressive way we need each other, fighting for a level of personal rapture.

He can feel the moment I'm on the edge, and lays me flat on my back as he pushes deeper than I thought possible. Hair falling in my face, his tongue dives into my mouth and he drives himself home, deep within my core.

I yell out in a way that he catches with a smile against my lips. And I know he has met me in orgasmic bliss when the sputtered *"fuuck"* falls from his lips for no one but me to hear.

"Good thing your neighbor isn't home," I say, my breathing still shallow, the feeling of his body atop mine a pressure I will crave.

"She is, right here." His voice is layered, full of the risk that he wanted to avoid. But one he clearly has set aside to worry about another time.

Chapter Thirty-Five

A FORTNOTE

LOUISA

Two weeks is not a long time. In the grand scheme of a life, a fortnight is a rounding error, a footnote. *A fortnote.* (*Get it?*) The kind of time that disappears into the seam between seasons without anyone noticing it went.

But I have noticed every single minute of it.

I know this because I have been paying attention in a way I have never paid attention to anything. The sound of his coffee cup set down when he sets it against the marble, the way he reads the newspaper on his phone, the way we get swallowed by the bedding that felt like frosting to him before, but now are clouds we live in. And every morning, the way he says my name, first thing, before either of us has said anything else, or his voice has anything to give, like it's just the only word his mouth can comprehend to reach for. While my mouth constantly reaches for him.

Two weeks of this. Two weeks of waking up tangled in him, two weeks of not a single performance except those I do in the booth. (The same booth we tested the *'soundproofness'* when he found me recording, and I explained how I could use a little inspiration.) It's a reality I didn't think we would live in, my husband, whose arms find me in the dark, while my face finds his neck.

I thought I knew happiness, I thought I had enough of it, even when I didn't. I was always able to find the pool of joy that people needed from me. But he refills it. He had been, in ways I wasn't ready to accept. And I know, because I have a certainty, a permanence I've never felt. When something is honest, not just true.

And I honestly never want this to end.

Chandler already has a margarita in hand when I arrive and the bowl of chips in front of her is half full.

"You look disgusting," she says when I sit down, as she waves over Paul (not Matteo) for another margarita.

"Why thanks, how kind." I know she doesn't mean it, so clearly dripping in jest, because she doesn't actually have a cruel bone in her body.

"You're actually glowing, I thought that was only when people got pregnant," she says.

"I'm not," I say. "Just good ol' marital bliss."

"Well, marital bliss seems to have hit you months later, because you're oozing glow."

"Ew," I say. "Truly, the grossest way you could have said that."

"No, I could have said you're oozing his—"

Paul steps up to the table to top off the chips and salsa, dropping off my margarita.

I wrap both hands around the glass and look at her as she licks the salt from the rim of her own. "I'm so in love with him, Chan," I say. The words come out like they've been waiting so long they've lost some of their volume. "I'm disgustingly in love with my husband."

Chandler stares at me for three full seconds and laughs, her whole body responds. It's like she's just heard the punchline of a joke she was waiting for. "Lou," she says. "Babe. We know."

"You don't though, none of it was real. Not in the beginning," I say. Realizing we've lasted this long. Realizing that now, it's real, there's nothing I need to hide behind because he will stand with me in it. "We both got something out of it, but, now, it's all different now."

She's looking me over with such skepticism. More than she had when I originally told her we were getting married.

"No" is all she says. The corner of her mouth pulls up to match her quirked brow. "I don't buy it."

"You don't buy what? That it was an arrangement?"

"I don't buy that it was ever *just* an arrangement," she says, setting her glass down. "I buy that you both *told* yourselves that. I buy that it was a very convenient story for two people who were absolutely feral about each other and needed a reason to be in the same room." She tilts her head. "But an arrangement? No. I was there at that wedding, Lou. He stood there and watched you walk toward him like you were the only thing worth looking at, so don't tell me that was a performance."

"We had to make it convincing—"

"I'm glad you finally convinced yourselves." I open my mouth, but she just pushes the bowl of chips towards me. "He doesn't even come in anymore," Chandler says, trying to soften the blow but still provide reinforcement to her point. "You know that, right? You must. He ordered the same drink, sat at the same table four days a week for the entire time you worked there, and then the second you weren't behind that counter, he stopped coming entirely. Toby is devastated for the data set." She laughs. "But that's a man who only wanted the coffee because you were the one making it."

The margarita glass is cold in my hands and I let myself have it, this one moment of being completely, humiliatingly, happily in love.

I'm still warm from the tequila when I turn the corner toward home. The walk takes longer than it should, but that never bothers me because I am a 'stop to smell the roses' kind of person.

And when you're happy, really happy, the world tends to smile back in the small ways you can only see if you're looking for them.

I pick up cherries at the fruit stand, although Ramon still isn't back, and the new kid does make me pay. The florist is arranging a vase in the window, deep-colored dahlias and I wonder about the brides who handed me an Altoid and pushed the door to meet my fate. I can see The Richmond from here, large and on the corner, and therefore the only reason any of this happened at all. I think about that sometimes. (A lot lately.) The unrepeatable chain of coincidence that put me in this building, on this floor, on the other side of his wall.

It's enough to make a person believe in something. The collection of small moments we miss in life that all are willing to carry us to a happily ever after we imagined but didn't trust.

Chapter Thirty-Six

BANANA BREAD BARRISTER

LOUISA

The bananas that I've had on hospice have finally crossed over to the side of brown and spotty that is perfect for banana bread. I love banana bread for that reason. It's the reminder that things sometimes have to get worse before they become what they were always supposed to be.

"What are you baking?" He comes up behind me and wraps his arms around my waist, tighter than the *'Cheesy Briesy Blueti-ful, Cheddar Girl'* apron I have on. A squeeze that pulls me off my feet momentarily as he presses his lips against the curve of my neck, before setting me back down.

"Banana bread."

He spins me to face him, and his face is fresh with sleep and it feels like something few have seen. His hand comes up to cup my cheek as his thumb drags across my lips, still swollen from all the nights before. I rise on my toes to reach him, and he cradles my head with a morning-filled kiss, like it was a natural thing to have done in the first place.

"Coffee or tea this morning?" he asks, as he pulls down two random mugs.

"Hmm..." I muse.

"While you decide," he says as he reaches past me. He drags a finger along the inside of the bowl and sucks it into his mouth. It's offensive in all the ways you'd imagine it to be. I can't look away and he knows it.

The smile that broadens starts in his eyes before his mouth catches up with it, the subtle amber always seems to wave at me before the darkness swallows it whole.

I'm pretty sure my jaw hangs open, and he knows that, too.

"That's—" I start.

"That's very good." Reaching for another dip, I swat his hand away before he can get it.

"Don't put your hands in the batter!"

"Fine," he says. Stepping closer to me he reaches for my wrist, wraps his hand around mine, shaping it so only my index finger remains extended. He dips my finger into the batter, and it's like it all happens in slow motion. He draws my hand out, and sucks the batter off my finger with a decadence that far exceeds the chocolate chunks in the mixing bowl. My entire body tightens at the idea of him, at how much closer I want him.

"I said," I breathe (*heavily*), "no hands in the batter."

"No, you said not to put *my* hands in the batter." His face has a wickedness to it that I've only dreamed about. "So I borrowed yours." I yank my arm from him, and wipe it on the apron.

"You can't lawyer your way out of this," I snap.

"For your banana bread?" he says. "Watch me." I turn back to the tins, pouring the batter. Trying to concentrate very hard on the pouring. (Failing.)

"Then I'll make it more often," I say. To the tins, to the batter, to me in the future buying bananas in varying degrees of decay so I can always have one waiting. "Since you like it."

"I love it." And I want to imagine he's not looking at the banana bread.

My arms twine around his neck and our lips crash with the taste of sweet batter on his tongue. His hands untying the apron at my waist and pulling it over my neck. Leaving just the large sleep shirt between us. He slides his hand under the hem as his mouth takes mine, voraciously, and I can feel the rise and fall of his chest as his hand palms my breast.

"You don't know how much I— *fuckkk.*" His sentence falls off as I reach my hand under the band of his briefs and wrap my fingers tightly around him. He's thick and hard, everything I remember from hours ago. His knees almost buckle, but he straightens himself. Pulling me closer, my thigh held in his palm, pinned to his side, as he lifts me away from the counter. Carrying me the short distance to my bedroom.

It's not like the night after the gala, where we violently crashed into each other. Now, we're desperate for each other but with less to prove. I know because he lays me in the bed we've shared, the bed he made for me, surrounded by pillows, and takes a moment to appreciate how far we've come. (And how much we're about to.)

I scoot back on my elbows so I'm against the cream, tufted headboard, and he crawls to me, stripped naked, the look on his face says he wants to devour me. The way our bodies crave each other is unnatural, even if it's the most animalistic thing in the world. But somehow, they always have.

He pulls my underwear from my body, the middle soaked through, as he drags a long finger up the split of me to collect the wetness himself. For the second time, I see him suck his finger into his mouth, and the smile that follows is devilish in every way.

He reaches to pull the shirt over my head but I beat him to it.

"Eager." His voice is thick, like the rest of him. He drags another finger through my core. "I can take my time," he says. "I've been so patient, Louisa." As his long finger teases my core. The slightest touch from him sets me on fire, and the way he says my name, now, ripples across my skin. "Can you?"

He lies next to me and gathers my hands into one of his. Taking my underwear and wrapping my wrists together, binding them, and pinning them above my head. All without breaking our stare. They're begging for him, giving him the consent he needs, and he watches it, watches me, like there's nothing more important than this moment.

I let out a whimper as he slides a finger inside me. His hand holding my arms above us, pressing them deep into the pile of pillows. His body is pressed against mine, and I can feel the hardness of him, begging, pulsing, to be had. But he's exercising control as his fingers pulse within me. Curling against the deepest parts that have me crying out, for him.

Crying out his *name.*

My body writhes from the bed, eager for the stretch of him,close to pushing me over the edge, as he drags his length out slowly. "Do you know how hard it was for me to have you just across the hall?" His voice is worn, and the heat of his breath sinks deep into my skin. "To hear you calling out names of people from pages of fiction, and for me, to be jealous of someone that could never touch you."

"I was thinking of you," I say, it escapes me, desperate for him to know. "I've been thinking of you, every time." He releases my hands from where they've been pinned and I loop them around his neck, pulling his face to me. "Every time I read a character," I say into his mouth. "And every time I laid right here and imagined you were inside of me."

We move, together, relentlessly charging towards a cliff neither of us are prepared for, but I'm ready to dive head first.

Chapter Thirty-Seven

DON'T TRUST THE MAILBOXES

LOUISA

I head downstairs, I've been meaning to check in on Oscar, but it looks like he must have swapped shifts, so I just hand the coffee I brought for him off to his replacement. I make my way to the mailbox because I have been very good about the mail lately. (Aren't you proud of me?) It is a real point of personal growth. It's also part of the larger deal with Hudson that now that the paperwork for immigration is all but stamped with an approval, I don't have anything else to be scared of. So I check the mail once a week, which feels like a reasonable amount.

Mrs. Saraceno is in the mailroom when I enter, standing at the long row of small metallic doors. I won't say she's waiting for me, but she might actually give me a reason to start avoiding the mail again. One Pomeranian tucked into the crook of her arm with its rhinestone collar hanging from its neck, while the other two fight it out in their parked stroller.

"Louisa," she says as adjusts the Pomeranian. "I'm so glad I've caught you." (Caught is exactly how I feel.)

"Morning!" I say leaning in for a hug, as I narrowly avoid the biter in her arm.

"I've been meaning to ask. Do you have any idea when your husband plans to start demolition?" I'm already reaching into my mailbox, pulling out the modest, well-managed stack. (I know, I'm impressed too.)

"Erm—I think he said next month, or maybe the one after?" The inflection of the question mainly because I don't exactly remember. He originally told me when this all started, but I don't think he's mentioned it since.

"Remind him to re-file the proper paperwork. Just because it's lateral, doesn't mean it's not critical structural work to address, and we haven't seen the updated plans."

"Huh?" I say as I gather the mail in my hands, even pulling out some of the circulars and coupons that I don't need, dropping them into the recycling bin by the mailboxes.

"The connecting renovation for 7B. I know he thinks it should be simple, but it takes just as much detail," she says as if this is information I had. She just keeps speaking like it's a conversation I've been a part of. Suddenly leaving me grasping at straws I can't completely remember. Did we talk about it? Did I miss it?

"I'm sorry," I say, trying to understand exactly what she's asking. Because what seemed like a surface-level question clearly has a lot more underneath that I am unprepared for. "I'm confused." My eyes must be glazed over, because the woman in front of me is going hazy as my heart begins to speed up.

Did he *say* 7B?

No. *He fucking didn't.*

"I assumed you'd discussed the timeline, since the approval, but given how busy you both are, it seems not." She gives the small satisfied nod of someone whose co-op board has done its due diligence, even if me, as a person, has not. (Clearly.) "It'll be a lovely space when it's finished." A pause. "Ambitious. Then again, he has always known exactly what he wanted, and would do anything to get it," she says, without any awareness of what it's doing to the person she's saying it to. Or if she does, she doesn't care.

"Yes," I agree, just resigned to what's happened. "He knows how to get what he wants."

When I get upstairs, the letter from the co-op board is exactly where he's left it. How fucking stupid could I be. I was there, when Mr. Ambrose handed it to him, and he just set it aside. Obviously I thought it was because we were in the middle of something. We were, at the *beginning* of something. (Little did I know.) It never occurred to me to open it, why would it? I trusted him with the paperwork, I trusted him with everything.

I take the letter and head to the one place I never venture. Walking down the hall to his office. The door opens without resistance, which it feels like it shouldn't, like there should be some kind of acknowledgment from the universe that I am crossing a threshold I never have before, and he never wanted me to cross. (I wonder why.) But the door just opens, into a room that is exactly what I should have expected and somehow still stops me.

It's smaller than I imagined, which is strange, because everything about Hudson feels large. But the room itself is just a desk and a chair with a narrow bookshelf, it doesn't even look like he works here, always instead at the counter in the kitchen. But maybe this is exactly who he is. Stripped of all the excess. (And I, I am the excess.)

The only thing on his dark wood desk is a single legal pad and a pen set parallel to its edge. Everything about it is like everything else in his life before I showed up, organized to the point of severity, to the point of loneliness, somewhere so carefully contained that there is no room in it for anything accidental. (Again, me.)

I take a seat at his desk, the letter from the co-op board confirming the wire of funds and purchase of 7B. But this is just the tip of the iceberg. And I open his top drawer, pulling out all the papers, flipping through them, and chucking them on the otherwise clean desk. I pull open another drawer, this one with hanging folders. (And seriously, what kind of person in this day and age is using hanging folders as a storage system?) I take them out, one by one. His mortgage for this apartment. Grams' financials, anything to do with her power of attorney, and then, there it is. The Louisa file.

Don't get me wrong, I knew there were Louisa files. We had to compile them to prepare for Immigration.

FUCK! Immigration. I check the time on my phone, seeing how long I have before I have to sit there and be questioned on all the things to do with my *husband.* Right now, I don't know anything about him.

In the Louisa file, our marriage paperwork, the copy of the license, the official certificate, the immigration forms in careful order, the ones originally approved, the ones he made copies of in case he needs them today.

And behind that, divorce papers.

I don't need to read them, it's clear what they are, but what jumps out above all else? His signature at the bottom of the page, neat and certain, the same signature that's on our marriage license in the folder directly in front of it.

I look at the blank line where my signature goes, the only thing he didn't have control over. If he did, I'm sure it would already be signed.

He's handled everything, he just couldn't do this without me.

Of course. There's no reality here except the one I pretended existed. Because there's a difference between something feeling real and being real. And you aren't the one who gets to decide.

I can feel the tears at the back of my throat, I can feel it behind my eyes and in my chest. A place that was once hollow, somewhere he filled slowly, is now drained of anything. Suddenly empty again.

There's a stack of letters held together with a binder clip. All from different co-op interactions, going back months. The first letter is the board approval for the acquisition of 7B in conjunction with existing ownership of 7A. I open the next one, a notification of permit approval. The third is a preliminary timeline from the contractor.

I sit here, in his chair, with the letters arranged in front of me, laid out next to divorce papers, and I let myself understand what I'm looking at. But the story is pretty clear. It was always right here. He told, that first night. Anything more than this, it's a liability. I understand now. Because falling in love with him, the way I have, that makes extracting himself from all this so much harder. When he made it clear what he was in this for. I was just the only person dumb enough to think it could be more.

It's overwhelming me in a way that makes me short of breath. So I take an inhale, and begin to count—no, fuck that. Fuck him, and his fucking breathing techniques and his manipulative bullshit.

He bought my apartment, and he's had months to tell me. It was always part of the plan. He told me the cover story, never the truth. And to him, that's perfectly fine. But to me, he's a goddamned liar.

He needed a wife to satisfy the co-op board. No, he needed his wife's apartment. And there I was, conveniently desperate, conveniently next door, conveniently willing to sign my name on anything he put in front of me because I trusted him. For no fucking reason.

The details undo me, because I cannot reconcile any of it. I feel something go very, very quiet inside me, and it isn't peaceful. It's betrayal.

I lay my head on the cool wood desk. Papers scattered around me, and just hours from now, we have our final immigration appointment, the one we have been building towards, the last piece of paperwork before everything gets filed and processed and resolved.

Except our divorce.

Chapter Thirty-Eight

THREE SILENT WORDS

LOUISA

Why am I here? *Not in the existential sense,* though that question has also been rattling around in the emptiness of my skull where up until two hours ago he occupied every single thought in a very different way. I'm staring at the wall of a federal immigration office in a blazer I borrowed from Chandler because it felt like the kind of appointment that required a blazer and I don't own one. I paired it with embroidered jeans so at least I can feel somewhat like myself when they confirm what I already know, that I am not good enough to have a life here.

All while my *husband* plans one without me.

My eyes feel like they've been turned inside out, and no amount of chocolate digestives or even Hugh Jackman could improve it. Whose fault is that? Mine. Obviously. (It's always mine.) I let myself fall in love with the wrong person and then stood in the wreckage surprised, even though, for as much as he lied about my apartment, he told me the truth. Love, loving him, a risk and liability. Well, I took the risk, and now I am most certainly liable for whatever happens next.

He played the longest game of chess I've ever watched anyone play, and I walked right into every square of it because I wanted to, because I was too busy learning bridge with his grandmother. I was so desperate to believe that someone finally saw me clearly and chose me anyway. But he didn't choose me. He chose chasing some success to claw back affection from people who never showed him when he was younger. Another notch in his belt that he can show off to prove *'look, I don't need you, Mom and Dad.'*

Should have known. The man who believes not telling someone something isn't the same as lying.

Well, I didn't tell him how I felt either.

So I suppose we are both, in our own specific ways, very honest people.

This waiting room was designed to communicate that comfort was not a consideration in its construction. They want you to be uncomfortable, but surprise, I don't need a plastic chair for that. I give up my seat for a woman who is pregnant and carrying a toddler on her hip, and stand near the wall instead, which is where I am when the door opens and he walks in. Because for once, I'm early.

I spot him as he scans the room with the focus he brings to every space he enters, already three steps ahead of wherever he is. He looks prepared (of course he does) without visible anxiety, (good for him) and something about that, about how composed he looks when I have spent the last two hours coming apart, makes my chest tighten in a way I have to actively breathe through.

Then he finds me and something in his face opens. It does that now, or it started to, this small involuntary unlocking that I have spent two weeks believing meant something, and maybe it does, maybe it means exactly what I thought it meant and to him, that just doesn't change anything, which is somehow worse.

He looks at me more carefully, trying to read me, his eyes move over my face the way they do when he's collecting information. A slight narrowing, and a stillness that means he's waiting for me to speak, because I always do. But not now, when I am barely holding it together. I wasn't even going to come, I seriously considered if it was worth it.

But if he gets what he wants out of this, then so do I.

"What's wrong," he finally asks.

"You tell me," I say through gritted teeth, trying not to cry.

"Louisa." He uses my name to coax something out of me. Frustration, cooperation, affection, friendship, an orgasm, love... and for the first time, hearing it doesn't cause my stomach to fill with butterflies.

"Hudson." I say his name back to him in the same severity he used mine, and I watch as he registers the difference.

"I can't fix it if you don't tell me what happened." He steps close to me, we're having a conversation with nothing but whispers and stares.

"I don't need you to fix everything," I snap under my breath. "But then again, it really only matters how it works out for you, right?"

"What?" His face contorts, genuinely looking confused.

"If you wanted my apartment, you should have just been honest. You didn't have to lie. I would have left, it would have been easier than staying married to you," I say, harsher than I mean it. But here we are. At a crossroads I could have never predicted.

"You know," he says, and I'm not sure if it's relief on his face.

"I do, and I'm glad," I reply, the kindness stripped from my voice. Replaced by a gross combination of anger and heartbreak. "You must have thought I was so stupid, all this time." His face searches mine for meaning he can't find.

"Please," he says, looking around. "This is the last step, let's get through it and I'll explain," he says.

"Why," I spit out. "You got everything you wanted, the apartment you can add to the list of accomplishments, you can fulfill whatever boyhood dream you think it might. But it won't, because you chase *things* instead of happiness. You know the difference and choose to have people look at you and be impressed, but you'll end up alone. You'll think it's by choice but it's not. It's every decision you made where you thought someone else being impressed by you would be as fulfilling as being proud of yourself. Well, it's not. I know because I've spent my life being unimpressive to people who love me, while strangers fall in love with me. And ya know what I learned, it doesn't fucking matter." I take a breath, my tone is filled with disgust.

"You said you were good at mergers and acquisitions. I just didn't think I was what was being acquired. So I'm glad we can stop pretending. But mostly, I'm glad you got to fulfill the fantasy and fuck me, before you completely fucked me over." The words land between us like something dropped from a great height, and I feel them hit him, one after another. I watch it move through his jaw, tightening his shoulders, he absorbs the blow. And I feel sick and righteous, completely gutted in equal measure. "At least *that* part was real."

"Lou," he says, a nickname he's never used, trying it now in desperation.

"I'll be moving out today, of both apartments," I say.

"That's not—"

"Hudson Ellis?" A woman in a lanyard is standing at the door to the interview corridor with a clipboard, looking between us. "We're ready for you."

He doesn't go immediately when they call his name the first time.

He looks at me instead. The waiting room continues around us, forms and fluorescent light and the quiet machinery of other people's lives, and he steps closer, close enough that this is only for me, his voice low, and I hate that my heart responds.

"I know you're angry, I know you think you hate me," he says. "I know you think you know what it all means." His eyes are on mine with intensity. "But you don't, so I need you to listen to me, just for a second, before I go in there." A breath. "They were going to sell it, Louisa. To someone *else*." His hand runs the length of my arm as he speaks.

"You did all of this," I say, and my voice is very quiet, "for a fucking apartment. And now you have it."

"No." The word comes out rough and immediate, stripped of everything careful. He takes one step toward me and his eyes are dark and completely unguarded. "For fuck's sake." His jaw tightens. "I did all of this *for you.*"

"Mr. Ellis." The woman with the lanyard again, losing patience. He doesn't look at her. He looks at me for one more second, and it looks like he's hoping for something, waiting for anything, and I don't know how to give him it right now. When I don't move, something reshapes his face, and it breaks my heart as much as I would imagine it breaks his. If he had one.

"And what about the divorce papers," I ask.

"Again, I did this, *for you,*" he says quietly. Then he turns and walks through the door, to play the most doting husband. But not before he turns back and mouths the three words to me that I'd understand in silence.

Chapter Thirty-Nine

ASK ME ANYTHING

HUDSON

We didn't have time to have the conversation we need to, and this isn't the place to have it. So before I disappeared behind this door, I did the only thing I had time to do. I just let the words form on my lips, clearly, making sure she could see them if she was looking.

I spent months hiding the reality of it from her, it was not a good strategy. I'm aware of that now. *I knew it at the time.*

"This should be fairly straightforward," the agent says, typing something for the record. "Everything appears to be in order." She says it with reassurance. But I have enough awareness that just because something is right doesn't mean it works out. I have seen airtight cases fall apart on technicalities. I have watched the correct outcome fail to materialize more times than I can count. Being right, in my experience, is the beginning of the argument, not the end of it. And this is the one argument I cannot afford to lose, because for once, I'm not here to win something for myself. *No matter what she thinks.*

"Are you ready to get started?" She lowers her glasses from her head, and faces the computer screen. Prepared to run through a list of questions that decide whether or not my marriage, *my wife,* passes the test.

Well, I am really fucking good at tests.

I nod.

"How long have you and your wife been living together?"

"Almost a year," I say.

"And you were neighbors before the marriage."

"Yes."

"What was that like?"

The honest answer is the only answer I have left. "We wasted a lot of time," I say. "We hated each other, we were at war." I pause, to think about the nights my feet would carry me to her door. When it was always my hidden heart pulling the strings. "Mutually, enthusiastically, I told myself it was irritating. It was easier than the alternative."

"Which was?"

"Admitting that the reason I ended my relationships, the reason I positioned myself in ways she would have to interact with me, was because she was the only thing I could hear, out of an entire city, not because she was loud." I pause. "Because she became the only part of my day worth hearing."

The agent clicks to another screen, typing something in. It's funny how someone's life can be reduced to this. That proving she's loved by someone whose love is worth as little as mine, is somehow the final step between belonging somewhere and being removed from it. That love, the most unquantifiable thing that exists, gets filed and rubber-stamped by a stranger.

"Can you describe a typical morning in your home, with your wife?"

"I'd be glad to, because when I'm out of here, I need to make sure that every morning I have after this one is just like it." I laugh to myself as the words come out, knowing how true it is. But I strengthen my voice, because there's no better use of it than right now. "Which is to say, I have absolutely no fucking idea what it'll be." She looks away from her screen, and turns to me, curious about what I'll have to say.

"She wakes up before she's ready," I start. "Every morning with an alarm that she argues with." I can see the case agent more interested with everything I say. "She doesn't eat breakfast, but she stands in front of the cabinet to decide if it should be coffee or tea, which she doesn't know until she reaches for a mug. And when she does choose a mug, she apologizes to the ones left behind. All this time, she's about half dressed, *if I'm lucky*." I hear the agent let out a soft chuckle that feels counter to the job she's trying to do. "Which means I have to fight myself to go to work, because you wouldn't want to leave her either." I take a breath, and watch the agent as she assesses the situation. This is only half of it, Louisa still has to sit in the chair and do the same thing.

"I'm sure your system flagged the dates," I say, going off script from the simple question I was asked. But with Louisa, there's never a simple answer, and I would never want there to be. "The timeline and sequence of events that a computer looks at and finds convenient, or suspicious, it finds whatever it's been programmed to find." I take another breath as I prepare myself. "But a timeline can't tell you what I know. And I know *everything*."

I lean forward on the desk.

"You want to know her brand of tampons, no problem. You want to know how much she feeds the sourdough starter or its name, I'll tell you. You want to know what her yawn sounds like when she's fighting sleep versus rising from it, *because they are different*, completely different, and I know, because both stop my heart." I let the room be quiet for a moment. "I know that she turns her phone off when she's waiting for news about something, otherwise she'll check it every minute. That's not hyperbole. Literally. Every. Minute. I know she misses the idea of a home she didn't have, so she satisfies homesickness with a kind of *terrible* cookie. I know she counts to four when she's trying not to fall apart, and I know she does that, because I taught her, on the scariest night of her life, when she showed up at my door and trusted me before she had any reason to." My jaw tightens. "I know which side of the bed she'll migrate to by two in the morning. I know there is not a person she comes in contact with whose life she won't ask about, and she'll leave with more information about a stranger than your file could possibly have on her. Just excited to know them. And she means it. Every fucking question." I look at the agent directly. "I am sitting in this chair because the love of my life happened to be born somewhere else. That's it. That's the whole story. The life she made, the one she chose, the life we have, is here, and I'm not going to let that go." My pulse is thumping, and it's the pace in which I deliver everything I need to say. "I have loved her longer than any paperwork can prove and I will love her long after I walk out of this office." A beat passes, short and shallow. "So go ahead, ask me anything."

LOUISA

He grabs my hand as we pass each other in the doorway, it's brief, his fingers wrapping around the inside of my wrist where my pulse is, which feels intentional even if it isn't (it probably is), and I look up and his mouth opens, ready to say something.

"I'm sorry, you cannot communicate until both interviews are complete." The agent's voice is absolute as she steps between us. I yank my hand back, and his face when I do it will be the only thing I think about for the next thirty minutes.

"Mrs. Ellis," the agent says, gesturing toward the door.

As I step past him into the room I hear it, so quiet it barely qualifies as sound, just the shape of the word formed close to my ear. "I'm sorry."

I don't turn around, I just walk through the door and I carry it in with me, that whispered *sorry* sitting in the center of my chest like a stone I don't know the weight of yet, ready to sink down through my stomach. Sorry for what? Sorry for the apartment, for the lie. Sorry for the last two weeks. Or sorry for something else, something larger, the *'I love you'* he mouthed across the room before he went in, three words I saw clearly. The risk he said I'd have to be willing to accept. I accepted it. It's that I'm the liability *he didn't.*

And right now, in the most important performance of my life, I have no script, no character to hide behind. It's just me, Louisa James Evans *Ellis.*

Maybe it's time to leave the performance for the recording booth.

She starts with the practical questions, the golf-ball-sized hail of specifics. Rug colors, thermostat settings, which side of the bed. Things I know from living in his space, from learning the geography of him from proximity alone. I answer everything and from some blessing from the universe, my voice stays level. (Good job, just like that, just keep doing that.)

"And how long have you and your husband been living together?"

"I moved in officially when we got married. We were neighbors before, so the transition wasn't—" I pause thinking about it more honestly than I should be. "It felt natural," I say. "More natural than it should have, you know, given where we started."

"And where was that?" she prompts, typing notes as I go. Like she can just shorthand my life away.

"Hating each other," I say. She looks up at me at that, giving me space to continue. Maybe hoping I hang myself by saying too much. I can hear Hudson in my ear, telling me to just say enough, and nothing more. *Well, sorry, Hudson.* If you haven't noticed by now, I *am* more. I might as well be myself if this is about to go up in smoke.

"We fucking hated each other." I say it, and her eyes give way to the smile she's not allowed to have while on the clock. "We shared a wall and spent months making each other miserable. Lobbing insults at each other, even the occasional official building complaint." I look down at my hands, always hoping they will hold an answer they never do. Using my thumb to spin the ruby, twirling it on my ring finger where I can't imagine the absence of it now. "We were good at it, too good at it, which looking back really should have been a sign."

"A sign of what?" she asks.

"That we didn't hate each other, not at all." I look up. "And I don't know that we ever really could."

She makes a note, and I feel the dread of what's coming, the way you can feel weather changing before it arrives.

"Mrs. Ellis," she says. "Can you tell me about your husband?" I can do this, I've prepared this, I know every minute detail about his habits, his history, even now, his body.

"He went to Columbia Law, he works in mergers and acquisitions at—"

"Not his resume," she clarifies. "Who he really is." (Maybe I can't do this.) The answer if it was asked three minutes ago, compared to three weeks ago, versus three months ago. Every one would be different.

"He's a private person," I say, and hear immediately how inadequate it is, how catastrophically insufficient for what I actually know about him, and something about the gap between those two things, between 'private person' and the full impossible truth of him, between what I just said and what I actually know, is so enormous and so absurd that I huff a laugh. Which becomes another, eventually has me throwing my head back in the United States Immigration office, completely cackling while my life in this country hangs in the balance.

"I'm sorry," I manage, gasping. "I'm so sorry, I—" Another wave of it, helpless, the kind of laughter that has tears behind it but hasn't decided if they're needed yet. "You want to know how well I know a man who made himself virtually unknowable, that's —" I press my hand to my mouth. "And the most ridiculous part is... I do...I know him!" I say. It comes out through the last of it, the laughter going quiet at the edges, leaving something more honest underneath. "Better than I've known anyone, better than myself, that's the thing. I know exactly who he is." I pause to take a breath. "Because he showed me, he is someone who loves people with everything he has, he just makes it so—" I stop, the anger from earlier is still there, but tastes different on my tongue. "He's the most impossible person to love in return, because he makes it that way, not because it's who he is, it's who he thinks he needs to be." The room is very quiet. "All the while waking up every day and loving me in a way no one ever has."

She's watching me with more intention, hanging on every word that has not even remotely answered the question in a way that allows her to check the box.

"I'm sorry, this is very unprofessional, but you have to see how this is funny." I hold my face in my hands. "I narrate audiobooks," I say. "I'm sure that's somewhere on your screen, *Louisa Evans, insufficient career for exemplary status,* isn't that right?" She gives a single nod. "But I voice romance novels, mostly. I can breathe life into an entire love story, beginning to end, listeners drown in every word of it, in the highs and lows of the most passionate, torrid love affairs. The greatest love stories you can ever imagine, *I* speak them into existence." (Okay, also some insane.) But I'm building strength, my voice getting bolder as I continue. "And right now I cannot find a single word for the most honest love I have ever felt in my life, even when I am so mad at him." A breath that comes out ragged. "Which is funny... Or maybe it will be... Later." (Assuming it's not the reason they stamp a big fat '*rejected*' across my name.)

"You can relax, Mrs. Ellis, this is all just a formality now," she says finally. And my face must contort into the '*huh*' that is on the tip of my tongue.

"What do you mean?"

"I already spoke with your husband at length." She looks at me steadily. "Whatever happened today before you walked in here, it doesn't matter. Not to the United States government. That man left this room and there was not a single person on this floor who didn't know exactly what they'd just heard."

The understanding of what she says washes over me. How is it that everyone around us, people we've never met, and those that know us best, seem to be able to say the one thing we haven't been able to. Not out loud.

"You'll receive written confirmation in four to six weeks," the agent says, clicking closed the files on her desktop. "But your application has been approved." She pauses, and shifts her glasses back to the top of head as I sit here frozen. "Congratulations, Louisa."

I stand from the chair, stunned in silence for more reasons than I know what to do with. On the list of confusing, this one takes the cake. Everyone around us has been reading the same story, we just kept insisting we were in a different one. We were so committed to it, so convinced we were performing something for everyone else's benefit, as a means to an end, that we missed the only real thing right in front of us.

We weren't pretending to be in love. We were pretending we weren't.

And we were the only ones fooled.

Chapter Forty

<hr>

LOUISA

I'm not surprised he's waiting when I step out of the office. He's not pacing or checking his phone. He's just standing against the wall of the building with his hands in his pockets and his eyes on the door, like he has been there long enough to have made peace with however long it was going to take, while also ready to charge in the second he needs to.

I see him and I stop walking. He clocks it, but it's not for the reason he thinks. It doesn't wash it all away, but the anger I was holding on to when I stepped inside that room, it's not the same now. Knowing no matter what the truth is, I got what I came here for, and in that, I also got him. No matter how long it lasts.

He pushes himself off the wall, and I don't run (I'm not a runner) but I walk toward him with momentum, and like everything, he sees that too. Stepping with the decision made somewhere between the agent's desk and the exit.

"They approved it," I say, and I can see the relief wash over his face. No matter how confident you are, you truly never know. I read enough horror stories online. "And they did, because of whatever you said in there." His lips press together in a way to contain what he might say, instead just nodding in acceptance.

Something shifts in his jaw and he takes his hands out of his pockets. "I've spent a lot of my life being the person who fixes things. Who makes himself the solution because it's the only way he knows how to stay close to something without admitting why he really wants to." He looks at me steadily. "But that's not what any of this has been, not for a long time."

He reaches for my left hand with his, and it's as if the rings see their partner on the other and have us intertwine our fingers and fates without our permission.

"I was going to tell you," he starts again. "But I was afraid that you would look at me exactly how you did. Like I had some motive, like I'm your father trying to fix a problem I don't think you're capable of on your own, when that was never it. And I became a coward, afraid of letting any remaining minute of our time together sour."

The look on his face is doing just as much work as the words coming out of his mouth, the most unguarded I've seen him.

"They approved the purchase and renovation of 8A, that was true. In exchange, *your* apartment was going to be put up for sale, since you no longer needed it. I couldn't let that happen, so I bought it instead. For you."

"So now you've been married to me for *nothing*?" His terms for this agreement were so he could buy that apartment for himself, not be my landlord. And now, it feels like a wash. I get (almost) everything I've wanted, and he's just left with... me?

"It's not been nothing, not for me. You see, the reason I couldn't let it happen—" He stops. "I couldn't let you leave, not if it wasn't your choice."

"But you signed the divorce papers."

"Because the longer we spent together, I knew I wouldn't be able to when the time came." He looks resigned, willing to accept whatever comes next. Whether it's a shove to the chest, a knee to the groin, or a kiss. But I just give him honesty.

"You were supposed to be the one thing I couldn't mess up," I say. "Because you already hated me, so there was nothing to lose." Saying it now feels like a bastardization of the truth, as he's laying himself bare in a way I've never imagined. "But then you stopped hating me and I had everything to lose and I—" I stop, grasping for straws of my emotions. "I looked at those letters and I chose the worst possible explanation because it was safer than any alternative."

"Louisa—" he says with certainty that comforts me. "This is on me, all of it." His voice is rough at the edges. "I kept waiting for the right moment and what I actually did was run out of time."

This isn't the place I thought we would have it out finally. Surrounded by people going about their lives having no idea about anything going on around them.

"Letting you *pretend* to get to know me," Hudson says, taking steps closer to me, bringing our bodies inches apart so I have to look up and see the sincerity on his face as he speaks. "That was real." His hand curls up my neck, holding here, maybe the only thing keeping my head upright now.

"It was all real. And if you come home with me, *I can prove it.*"

―――

We get back to the apartment, *his*, not mine. Though I guess, both are technically his. It's as I left it, quiet in the ways I've come to expect, familiar in the ways I never did.

He takes my hand, I allow it, and we walk through the entry hall, into the main rooms, cut across the living room, walk down the hallway past his office, where all the papers of our lives are thrown about, but he ignores the open door and the mess.

"Did you ever notice anything about your bedroom?" We take steps down the hall as we walk closer to his. The question isn't the one I thought he'd start with. But alright, here we go...

"It's beautiful, it doesn't look like you," I begin with the most obvious.

"Ouch," he says, with feigned offense. But I roll my eyes in response. Because, it matter of factly doesn't, and that was the point.

"Okay, fine, but how about your bathroom," he prompts again. Opening the door to *his* bathroom. A normal-enough looking one, in the hallway accessible for either his bedroom or office.

"Well, it doesn't have a shower window like my apartment, but it's got a great tub," I say, not sure where we're going with this.

"Sure, and the counter space, that's pretty good, right?"

"Yeah," I say, skeptical.

"My bathroom has terrible counter space," he says, as if this is a totally normal conversation. As he pulls me a few more steps down the hall to his bedroom door. Opening that and stepping us both inside.

"What about this room, what do you notice?"

"Hudson, I don't get it, you have great, *boring* taste. My room is so much nicer, and I appreciate it, but I'm not sure what dissecting your interior-decorating skills, and poor counter space, is supposed to prove."

"Hmm." He makes the sound, and it does something to me, and I know he's about to pull back a curtain on something I've missed. "Did you know I bought this apartment and moved in four years ago?"

"Yeah, I saw the paperwork," I say with sarcasm, having spent the morning elbow-deep in paperwork that hurt my feelings.

"I moved into *this* room, *last* year." He says it like it's supposed to mean something to. "This is a nice room," he continues. Deadpan, but leading to a point.

"Sure," I agree.

"It's a decent-enough size." He takes steps, walking the length of it. "Would be better if it had an ensuite," he says. "Your room, now *that's* got a great ensuite. And what would you say, maybe twenty percent bigger than this one?"

My eyes narrow, following him around the room, until he comes to stand in front of me again. "Why would I do that? Why would I move to this room, Louisa?"

I bring my hand to my mouth with the realization as he continues.

"I've slept in here, pretty much since you moved in, because the first night I heard you, it became all I wanted, and not hearing your voice, no matter how distorted through drywall, was an unbearable silence." I look around the room with new eyes, taking in what I somehow never registered before. It's not a small room by any objective measure, but it is undeniably the smaller of the two. The light is different in here, less generous, the bathroom is in the hallway. It doesn't make sense, except for the fact that it does. For Hudson, of course it does.

"You slept in here, and then intentionally tormented me for *months*, just so we would have a reason to interact?"

A very small, very controlled pull at the corner of his mouth. "Sure," he says, and it's almost said through a smile he's afraid to let out too soon. "That sounds like a reasonable summary."

"I thought you hated me," I say.

"Never, not really. I hated that you made it impossible for me to be indifferent to you. I had built a life that required very little of me emotionally. I avoided loving someone in any way that they could really know me, feeling like that was the ultimate liability." He laughs at the word now. "And then you moved in next door and I couldn't find the end of what I wanted from you. It kept getting larger and larger, this thing I had to feed within myself. I kept thinking if I argued with you enough I'd get there. At some point, you'd stop being interesting to me, I'd stop thinking about you in every voice, in every silence, in every waking fucking moment, imagining you."

"Did it work?"

"Spectacularly not." He drags his hands through his hair. "I hated not having you, I hated knowing that you loved people so freely, except me. I hated myself, but you? I've loved, I *love* you." His voice cracks. And it's a sound I could imagine in the greatest of love proclamations, and I've heard a few of them. This? Him? He puts them all to shame.

"When it finally seemed like we were in a place I could tell you, the full truth, I fucked it up. Because I was too afraid to lose you. So I bought your apartment *for you*. I signed divorce papers *for you*. If you wanted, I knew it would be worse than any of the others. You'd be leaving, knowing me completely. And while I've spent my life avoiding letting anyone close enough to do that? I told myself that if the time we had was all we would get, then so be it. That's got to be enough."

"What if that's not what I want?" I ask. He goes very still, a man I've never seen nervous appears so now.

"What do you want, Louisa?" And there it is, my name attached to the question underneath every thing we've ever asked each other, finally out loud, with nowhere to hide. He's rationing each breath, waiting for my reply.

"You," I say. "Just you. And I think." I pause. "No, I know, that's all I've ever wanted."

He doesn't wait, he crosses the room and I'm in his arms, my legs wrapped around his back, and his mouth fills mine with every desperate plea, every midnight knock on my door, everything we've withheld from each other in fear. His tongue parts my lips as I taste the peppermint of his kiss. My fingers tangle in his hair as he lands us flat, high on the mattress. My head cradled by pillows, my body crushed by the delicious weight of him.

I'm frantically unbuttoning his shirt as he growls my name into my ear, kissing his way down my neck with desperation, apology, and promise. I feel him hard pressed against me. Our kiss isn't soft, our mouths are warring to take from each other what we haven't allowed ourselves this freely. We're starved, unrestrained.

I'm kicking my shoes off while he strips himself of his clothes, standing hard in a pair of black boxer briefs that remain as the only thing containing him. The taste of him, a memory on my tongue, the feeling of him, surges to the front of my brain and between my legs as I unbutton my jeans, the awkward shimmy out them spreads a delicious smile across his face. Where he steps forward and grabs me by the ankle. Yanking me toward him, wrapping his fingers around the waist of my jeans, pulling them and my underwear down.

When my legs are free from the denim, he steps out of his own underwear as I reach for him, calling out his name. He wraps his arm under my back and slams himself hard and fast. Unlike anything imaginable, my back arches off the bed and he pulls my chest against his, so our breathing can remain frantic but in sync. I cry out, him thrusting so deeply into me I can barely keep my head up, so I sink my teeth into his shoulder, but he grabs me by the jaw and steals my mouth for his.

My head lolls back into the pillows as his hand cups my face and he runs his thumb across my bottom lip. Gathering its moisture as I suck it into my mouth. He groans as he thrusts harder, faster. As his hand moves to cradle the base of my skull.

"Eyes open, sweetheart," he says, coated in desire. I try to blink my eyes open, he comes into view as his dark hair falls in his face, and beads of sweat trickle down his chest.

I can feel my eyelids heavy, all my energy focused at my core where I feel everything all at once. He pulls out quickly, and the walls of me are desperate to keep him in, but I'm empty, painfully empty without the overwhelming thickness of him. And my eyes burst open, as does my mouth, ready to say something.

"You can have your eyes on me, or you can have your eyes on me fucking you," he says in a voice so deep it rolls through my body completely. "But I'm done pretending. It's time for you to see what you *really* do to me."

I reach down to grab him, but he just shakes his head with a deep, throaty laugh.

"Nuh uh, not until you tell me you understand," he says as he slips a middle finger inside of me, soaking wet and desperate for the rest of him, and his thumb applies pressure, making small circles, teasing me, keeping me on the edge.

"I understand," I pant out. And the dark smile that broadens his face is something I want no one but me to ever see again. He removes his hand as he thrusts hard and fast, and this time my eyes don't break from his.

The small amber ring around his pupil appears to move, like a dancing flame fighting from being swallowed up by the blackest hole. I have no control over the sounds that escape me, and he devours every. Single. One.

This is charged by every fight we ever had, tearing into each other when we should have been tearing each other apart. We're making up for it now. Despite the last weeks we spent tangled together, *this* is the most honest we've ever been.

I'm close, we're both on the edge of something more terrifying than the orgasms fighting to break free through our bodies, and the pace of this is us racing to get there.

"Lou," he groans out through a ragged breath. I throw my legs tightly around his back, locking him in me, doing all I can to keep my eyes open. He's still moving, deeper and deeper within me, and I can't contain it anymore. When my legs clinch tightly and he pulls me close to his chest, his hand holds my face as I breathe the ragged, short, shared breaths between us. I come wildly, as does he, and I dig my nails into his back, leaving the claw marks that would be carved into his skin if anyone dared to try and drag me away.

Hudson's sweat-slicked body collapses on mine, with his forearm slipped under my head. We're pressed together when he rolls us, one combined being, so he's on his back and I'm flush against his chest, nestling into his neck while he's still inside of me. The aftershocks of my orgasm tightening around him, and I feel him twitch in response.

He brushes the sweat-clustered hair from my forehead and replaces it with a soft, gentle kiss.

"I love you." It's said with all the air in his lungs.

"I love you, too," I say, and I hear him sigh in relief. "Lucky for you, we're already married."

Chapter Forty-One

SCRAMBLED PLANS

HUDSON

I left Louisa in my bed. She tangled herself in the sheets, one leg twisted around the comforter, the other twisted around me. It almost defies reality how much room she can take up in a bed, where I became part of the mattress, and she melted into me. *It was the best sleep of my life.* Even though more than once I woke up like my body needed to confirm she didn't retreat.

Once it started, once we threw down the gauntlet of our feelings, she was in my arms and I was in her faster than makes any sense. It was more than just *want*, it was the most insatiable need.

I'm standing at the stove, preparing the only thing I know how to make. *I can make a chicken breast also, but that's not breakfast.* I have everything laid out, the eggs set aside, the cream, the butter, even chives I ran out to get this morning. Knowing she wouldn't wake up before the sun. She is the sun, and even at night when she rests, she's never not burning. I could never own the light. I just want to be the thing she casts down on. I'll be Icarus and fly as close as possible. I don't care that the reference is used to describe ego, my ego is the last thing I care about now. She is the sun I'll orbit around any way I can, so long as she agrees. And at night, the darkness is just the countdown until she burns me alive all over again.

She's light on her feet, but I know when she enters the room, even when my back is to her.

"Hungry?" I say without turning around.

"Depends, I recall you saying you weren't known for much in the kitchen," she teases, and I can hear the faintest end of a yawn in her voice, and my heart, finally free from the emotional chastity belt, skips a beat.

I turn to face her as she's leaning against the kitchen island. The large marble structure dividing the living room serving as the thing that's keeping her upright. The heavy sound of sleep softens my chest and hardens my cock all at once. She looks wrecked in the most unimaginable way, the way I left her last night in a layer of sweat and her hair a mess that tells the exact story of where we were just hours ago.

It didn't matter that we had been tearing each other's clothes off since the gala, *which reminds me I have to claim all the things she 'won' for us.* But what finally happened yesterday. Being loudly in love with her, and knowing, as she does, that she feels it in return. I'll never recover, and I have no interest in trying.

She's dressed in nothing more than a t-shirt, *god* how this drove me wild for months, and now here she is, unabashedly half-dressed, this time knowing full well what it does to me.

I abandon the egg station, because my focus is singular, and the way she's looking at me through thick eyelashes and desire means hers is too.

Two steps across the hardwood floor landing me right against her. Caging her in between my arms as she looks up at me, her cheeks bloom the flawless pink, that I know from the image I seared into my brain matches her nipples, and tells me she's got the same thought I do.

I lean and drag my lips down her neck, stamping kisses deeply to be remembered long after my skin leaves hers. "Ready to see what else I'm known for in the kitchen?" I ask, the words spoken directly into her skin, as she holds herself up against the counter. Knees weakening at the thought. She throws her arms around my neck and kisses me with more passion, no, *more love,* than any man deserves. *Especially me.* I'm hard in a way I only can be for her.

"Show me," she says with a smile against my lips.

I drop my hands to her waist and spin her quickly so her ass is pressed against my cock, and bend her forward against the counter.

She snaps her head around, and over her shoulder, the grin that spreads across her face as she adjusts her hips ever so slightly, moving her ass against me, tauntingly. Tossing her hair back and forth, an invitation for my hand to wrap around it.

I pull down my pants, freeing myself as I run my hand under the large shirt and up her back, following her spin like the only road on a map home.

Her ass exposed to me completely.

"So this was your plan all along?" She does a cute little shrug.

"Maybeeee." The word is slow and soft, something we both know our bodies are not.

She kisses me over her shoulder, her lips are wet, as I know she is. I cloak her with my body, pressing us together into the cold counter. Slipping my arm under her ribs to protect her just a bit from the inevitability of what we both feel. "Hudson, please," she whimpers, knowing the waiting is causing her the same desperation I have.

I force my foot between her stance and kick her legs apart as she lets out a breath she's going to need. Reaching between her legs, she's soaked, and sensitive as I begin to play with the wetness gathered, dipping my fingers in like a forbidden fucking pool, and she tightens around me as I do. I slowly retract them, grabbing her face to pull her mouth closer to mine, dragging the wetness from her across her lips before I take her mouth with mine, the taste on our lips as I curl my tongue deep into her mouth and slide into her, painfully slowly from behind.

The shirt has ridden up, exposing her back to me, I pull it off her body and toss it to the floor, so we are both here, bare in the bright kitchen of our home.

I push deeper and deeper into her, and her eyes remain locked on mine. "What a good girl, taking all of me," I say between breaths. And she does, she has every fucking part of me. "*My perfect girl.*" She cries out in reply. My hand is knotted in her hair and she looks over her shoulder at me, her eyes every bit as open as mine. Because how could I ever look away from that face. With every thrust, she meets me, throwing herself into me, our bodies won't let this be halfway. I pick up speed, thrusting deeper into her, so hard as she is bent forward over the marble, gasping, moaning for me as I do. And it's a sound I never want to end.

I heard her crying out for months of fake orgasms through the wall between us and the ones I put up, and this? It's unimaginable, no amount of listening to her through drywall or headphones could have prepared me for what it would be like with her wrapped around my cock, crying out for more. Completely unburdened by all the things we could say.

As I thrust, her body moves. I wrap my arm around her waist to pull her tight against me, her toes barely brushing against the floor, and I tangle my free hand back in her hair. Her arms are splayed out in front of her, tits pressed into the marble in a way I hope they leave a sweaty print for me to gawk at when this is done. She reaches out, stretches her whole body forward, and her fingertips brush the papers that were left here last night. I can see the movement of her bright blue nails clawing towards them, until she gets them in her grip and swipes them all off the counter into a whirlwind of our mistakes that she refuses to share space with as our bodies push and pull desire between them.

"I...I'm... Hudson, *fuck...*" She's panting my name as I move within her.

"Come on, sweetheart." My voice is unrecognizable, a gruff that only appears for her. "I want to feel you come for me." My hand slides down the curve of her back and the round of her ass as she slams it back into me in sync, filling my palm, my fingers dig hard into the plump skin. "It's my turn, let me take all you've got."

That does it, whimpering between breaths as I unleash myself, she tightens around me, violently coming, crying out my name as she does, and I am in shambles with her.

Chapter Forty-Two

LOUISA

I pick up the shirt that had been scattered on the floor, and he's wearing very little else. It should feel strange, how insanely entwined we can become, fueled by fire and the kind of love people write (and narrate) stories about. The everydayness of it now, the post-sex sweetness, the normalcy of us standing in the same kitchen that usually smells like lemon dish soap but now just smells like us. (Sexy us, but us.) It feels instead like something clicking into a place it was always meant to occupy. We took puzzle pieces and forced them into different spots. The hatred we believed we were supposed to have for each other. That didn't fit. The pretend spouses. That didn't complete the picture. But this honest, raw version of vulnerable love, it's like it was the last open piece in the middle of a complete puzzle and we just refused to see it. Holding it in our hands, knowing the shape would fit perfectly, but too afraid of what happens when the puzzle is complete.

Do we move on to the next?

No, because no matter how satisfying the metaphor, it's not really a fucking puzzle at all.

It's our life. *It's my life.* That doesn't change if the box is shaken, or because of how long we spent forcing the wrong pieces, if we started with building the frame, or some random spot in the middle. It was always going to look like this.

For me, it was always going to be him.

"We still have a lot to figure out," Hudson says, calmly. I'm sitting with my legs swinging from the counter as he cracks some eggs into a pot. Doing the *other* thing he's known for in the kitchen. (Second best, surely.)

"I know," I reply, the words commingled with a sigh. As much as last night (and this morning) felt like we had escaped the reality of what could be looming, we didn't. And we all know Hudson loves the logistics of a problem. I'm just waiting for him to pull out a binder.

"Which means, I'm going to need the ring back." He says it with a sense of seriousness as he moves the scrambled eggs to the back burner and faces me.

"Excuse me?" I say, incredulous. I hop down on my feet, hands on my hips, leaning onto my toes to be closer to his height as he takes a step forward. His hand extended for me to return it.

"Come on, hand it over." He's so casual about it, like this isn't the biggest betrayal of them all. Sure, maybe most people don't jump from fake marriage to real one, but this is ridiculous. Surely he doesn't think we're starting at zero, not after everything that's happened.

"Ya know," I say, my voice is already getting loud. "Just when I think you might *actually* be a decent—" I'm pulling the ruby off my ring finger, my eyes narrowing with annoyance. "You, Hudson James Ellis, are without a doubt, the most infuriating man—" I continue.

He presses his lips together, forcing them flat from the smile he wants to let loose as I berate him.

"Go on, do your worst." The words are slow and punctuated as I drop the ring into his hand.

"You would be the man who tells a woman he loves her, that he's been *dreaming* about her, only to run away from it now. Well you know what, I'm not going to let you. You want the ring back, fine. But you are being a coward and I—" He's inching closer with every word.

He drops to his knee.

And I drop the end of the sentence in favor of a question that's answered in the way he's looking at me.

"What are you doing?"

"You deserved a wedding because you're a romantic. But you never got the proposal you deserve, not the one that says I'm in love with you. And it's time I fix that."

He's kneeled in front of me, with the ruby held up between us, looking up at me through his dark lashes, the irises of his eyes blooming and catching the light as the sun brightens the space, casting our shadows across the hardwood. An amorphous shape unidentifiable as two people. Maybe, now, *just one.*

"Letting you in was the most frightening thing I've done, and you're right, I am a coward. I didn't even do it bravely, I did it *badly*, through argument and pretense." His eyes hold mine, and it holds me in place, I would never let myself look away. "It was the only way I knew how," he says. "It was me letting you learn who I am without the pressure of asking you to love me back, not knowing you ever would. Even though I was falling in love with you the entire time. Every word that got through, every wall of mine you penetrated." He pauses. "*You* got through. Pretending to hate you, becoming impossible when loving you, is the most real thing I've ever known."

My eyes well with tears, the thinking about this version of myself I didn't believe existed. One who could love like this, and be loved in return, in honesty, and in hatred. The ugliest parts already seen and loved, not in spite, but because of.

"I want to be with you, not because of paperwork, or some deal we made, not because you feel you don't have a choice, but because you do. I love you, and that's not a choice for me, that's the only thing I know anymore. That you moved in next door and

I have been catastrophically, irreversibly in love with you every second since."

We each take a breath, knowing what's coming next.

"Louisa James Evans *Ellis*," he begins. The emphasis on the last name we already share on social media matches the smile stretching across his face as he says it. "Will you marry me?" I see him take a slow inhale, waiting for me to say something in response. But first, I have one more question.

"For real?"

"For *ever*."

Happiness blushes across my face as I nod in response, knowing a few tears have decided to celebrate with us. He slips the ring *back* on my finger that had become as empty as I had without it.

"What do you think, should we kiss?" I ask.

"Now is the perfect time."

As I lean down into his kiss, his arms come around me, standing from where he was kneeled and brings me back up to his full height with him. Wrapping my legs around his back, he holds me high against his chest as our kiss deepens into every real thing we've never said. Knowing we have the rest of our lives to say them now.

Chapter Forty-Three

EVERYONE DESERVES A HAPPILY EVER AFTER

some months later

LOUISA

"Hudson, I can't find my dress," I say, sliding across the hardwood in my socks like I'm trying to stick a landing, or Risky-Business Tom Cruisin' it. I'm checking the time every minute with the energy of someone who has been ready for hours, even though I'm clearly not dressed, which he doesn't seem to mind at all. "They'll be here any second!"

"It's hanging in our closet," he says, watching me blur my way through the apartment from somewhere in the kitchen, where *he* is already completely dressed. (Of course he is.)

'Our closet.' It's been a year of that. Granted, about ten months of it we weren't actually sharing the same bedroom, but now, now it really *is* ours, our kitchen, our dining table that has stopped being empty and for show, our sofa with the throw pillows he has stopped pretending to find inconvenient, our mismatched mugs in a cabinet that he gave up on organization sometime around month four. Our life, in one continuous, unre-

markable, and miraculous space, which is what happens when you take down enough walls.

Literally and otherwise. (Even if there's one more remaining.)

I find the dress exactly where he said it would be (of course), dry-cleaned and hanging in its garment bag, and I put it on because, yes it's our anniversary, and it would be a shame to only wear it once. I was not going to let her fate be sealed into the back of another closet.

It fits as it did before, but this time, I don't bother with shoes, knowing we are staying within these walls. The same ones that we fell in love in.

When I come out of the bedroom (our *real* primary, not the guest room he slept in for a year), his eyes drip down my skin as his teeth make no attempt to hide behind his full lips. Releasing the most natural smile, all before his eyes darken ever so slightly, and I know there's an entirely different meaning to his grin.

"Even better than the first time."

"Well, this time, I'm less nervous," I say. He comes up and snakes his arm around my back, kissing his way down the column of my neck.

"Oh yeah?" he asks between the time his lips leave my skin and returns. "Nothing to lose this time." He says it as he reaches my ear.

"So much more," I say as I pull his lips to mine. Swallowing down the groans that come from deep within him.

"We never did get a wedding night," he says into my mouth.

There's a knock at the door, and he drops his forehead to mine. "Leave them outside. Party's canceled. Pretend we aren't here."

I shove him in the chest, and as I slide my way to the front door, he catches up with me in a large step. Capturing me as I laugh and fight my way to get to our guests. But he doesn't let go, instead making answering the door a two-person job.

Paola and Lucas arrive first because Lucas comes from the same school of thought as Hudson, which means you're early or you're late. And Paola has never arrived anywhere empty-handed, which is great for me, because today it's my favorite custard tarts to use in lieu of a first-anniversary wedding cake. They also are on Grams-pick-up duty, she walks in, arm-in-arm with Lucas. I give them all a big hug. In many ways, Lucas is the one behind all of this. He set it all in motion. (Well, him, a cup of Throat Coat tea, tentacle smut, and US Immigration.)

Toby arrives alone, pockets his phone with genuine effort, but it's appreciated, and immediately falls into conversation with Lucas. I can't help but watch from across the room. It's always interesting to see the overlap of two people without anything in common, just because they try. Because when you look for it, you can always find *something*.

When the final knock arrives, Hudson is already pouring champagne as everyone is taking seats on the sofa and chairs. Chandler stands in the doorway, but it's the large shape behind her that immediately unfolds the smile across my face in genuine surprise. She steps out of the way, so cooly, and there is Theo. He catches me the way he always has, as I leap into his arms for a bear hug that has only been a memory for too long. With a laugh that I've only heard through FaceTime, and hair that smells like a long, transatlantic flight.

"What are you doing here?!" I ask, as my eyes well with tears.

"I missed your first wedding," he says when he puts me down. "I wasn't going to miss your second." He looks me up and down. And in all the ways, I've only ever looked up to him. "Even if it is in your living room and to the same bloke."

"The *only* bloke," I say.

"Oh, the Brit's back," Hudson says as he comes up behind me, teasing me for the parroted word choice. He reaches out a hand to Theo, but it turns into a hug.

Chandler moves past Theo into the apartment, and I watch my brother's eyes follow her helplessly.

"Don't waste your time pretending," Hudson says to him as

he claps him on the shoulder. Encouraging him to come in. "It'll only cost you in the long run."

"Speaking from experience?" Theo asks, perhaps more in jest, but Hudson doesn't restrain the answer.

"You have no idea."

When it's finally time, Hudson takes my hand in the middle of the room. One that is not void of color, but was just waiting for me to bring it to life. (At least that's what Hudson says.)

There's no officiant this time, we aren't really getting married. (I think Lucas might actually be relieved.) There are no pre-scripted vows. (I'm relieved.) And no walk down the aisle, except the steps we took together to get here.

We have a real first kiss this time. It's unhurried with his hand cradling my jaw like it's something precious. And the way he kisses me tells me he believes it is.

And when our small non-ceremony is over, we all move to the dining room, where dinner is catered just like it was the first night. The pizza arrives and we all sit around the table, this collection of people that only make sense because of us. Three conversations going five ways, with laughter threaded through each of them, all pulling from the same pie. Hudson tops off the champagne glasses, because is there anything better with pizza? Even if Chandler opts out because she is more focused on the garlic bread. (Fair.)

I sit in my wedding dress with my bare feet tucked under me and pizza in my hand, Hudson's hand on my knee. We fought so hard not to love each other, thinking the alternative was easier, better. But I've narrated enough books to know that it's all about the happily ever after.

The epilogues with children (if that's what they want) and the unguarded, unjudgemental love. And I spent too long hoping everyone had that, but myself.

I think about every version of this apartment. The wall that held all of it.

The one that's still standing. (Though, not for long.)

After we came down from the ravenous few days post-immigration, he tried to hand over the deed, officially. We laid in bed, and as my face pressed against his chest, he told me exactly what happened in that co-op board showdown.

There's no life I see here without him anymore. That's why, when we stood in the kitchen, and he re-proposed marriage, with the same ring I've had on my hand for months, it was less a question so much as an inevitability.

And with every wall I tore down for him? There is one more we would need to do together.

The space that kept us apart, or maybe brought us together, was never part of his plan. But plans change. And now, we have brand-new ones (already co-op approved) that turn our individual spaces into our single home. Why? Because it's the one we chose, and the life we built together exists in these walls.

Our guests have gone, congratulating us, *again,* on our nuptials. And while there are many ways we plan to celebrate, there's one that we need to do first.

The tarps have been pulled back, and the plaster exposed, the whole history of it right there, every argument, every midnight doorway, every muffled laugh, every held breath, and every word that got through.

He holds out a sledgehammer as we stand in the guest room staring at it.

"Don't you know how to tell time?" I ask, teasingly. "Our neighbors are going to be furious."

"Good," he says. But as I reach for the large sledgehammer, he pulls it back. "Nuh-uh." He holds out his other hand, a pair of workman's goggles and boots to protect my bare feet. "First, safety. Then, swing."

"They don't really go with this dress," I say as I slip my feet into them.

"Then I'll take it off as soon as you're done." His lips pull into a devious smile, and there's not a time I've seen it that it doesn't quicken my pulse.

"You ready for this?" I ask as I get a grip on the handle and he (smartly) steps to the side.

"Completely," he says. "For the rest of my life." And I know how true it is.

I swing. Is it a good swing? Not exactly. But I definitely hit the wall and made a hole, which totally counts for something. The plaster gives and dust rises. Okay, it was more of a symbolic swing. Knowing that the contractor and crew come tomorrow to take the whole thing down.

He takes the sledgehammer out of my hands and kisses me in the wreckage, in the dust, with the small open-space light that's trying to break through.

This, I think, is the *real version*. All it took was one fake marriage to my grumpy neighbor to remind me that everyone deserves a happily ever after. Even if you have to knock down a few walls to get there.

Epilogue

Dear Reader,

I don't usually write epilogues. This is an exception.

If you are happy with the story, don't turn the page.

Yours in prose and protest,
Diana Elliot Graham

The phone rings and startles them both awake. Louisa's small pregnant swell of a belly is the first thing Hudson reaches for in pure panic. Knowing what he would need to protect most in case of an emergency.

But Louisa is fine, he can tell by the look on her face, just confused. Disoriented as she sits up yawning, rubbing the sleep from her eyes as he reaches for his phone before it hits a third ring.

He answers the call from Lucas. Returning the 3 a.m. favor he once did for him. The one Hudson owes his life for.

"What's on fire?" he asks, as his friend did, being awoken from what he can assume was only the same blissful sleep next to his *real* wife at the time. Though the quick glance back to Louisa reminds him how real this all is.

But Lucas doesn't speak. What claws its way through the phone is gasping sobs on the other end of the line. Fractured in a way that doesn't sound like his friend at all. The pit that forms in Hudson's stomach speaks to something far worse than he could have imagined.

"Paola?" he asks, as she struggles for words. Her native Portuguese comes through rather than English in her state. He hops out of bed, knowing whatever it is that resulted in this call will require shoes and pants. Louisa follows suit, not waiting for any direction. "Paola, I'm getting dressed, I'm coming to you."

Finally her voice comes through, two words that were unimaginable before they were spoken.

"He's dead."

Everything bottoms out. Hudson stops moving, frozen except for a hand that begins to shake. "What are you talking about," he asks. The strain on his voice matches hers as Louisa moves to stand in Hudson's chest. He wraps an arm around her, needing her as close as can be. She just looks up at him, waiting for him to explain, watching the terror on his face.

"ICE, they killed him."

<h1 style="text-align:center">Author's Note</h1>

There's a reason I don't write epilogues, but this felt like a meaningful exception. It should be the mirror we should all stare into, and hold up for others.

And if you didn't read it, then I bet you're thinking to yourself, "Thank god she finally wrote a classic rom-com."

Wrong.

If you read this novel and found yourself rooting for Louisa and Hudson, but have been silent or in agreement with the actions of this administration as it relates to millions of people living in the United States, I beg you to ask yourself why.

Is it that in romance, the ends always justify the means? Do we deem anything in the name of love as acceptable? Does that only count for *romantic* love, and not that of a mother bringing her child across a border?

Or is that only in the conditions of a novel where the main characters are implied to be white and heterosexuals that we believe contribute to society in a way we might interact with. With skin colors and careers we are conditioned to believe are valuable or respectable. Or because we have been desensitized, *deliberately and systematically,* to injustice so much so that we just ignore it as it doesn't come for us.

This is not in any way an accurate depiction of immigration practices, they had resources and finances to handle anything they needed. It's also fiction.

Do you know another term for marriage of convenience?

Immigration fraud.

These two were completely, without a doubt, committing fraud.

But whether that fraud is someone marrying their broody neighbor to avoid deportation, or someone not complying with an unlawful ICE traffic stop, neither of these situations should result in loss of life. But today, one of them does.

In this novel, there was more than one instance of a background encounter that should have had you (and Louisa) question what in the ever-loving fuck is going on? Why is the Turkish street artist gone, did she leave by choice? What happened to Ramon the man selling fruit? Why was that silver sedan outside the laundromat left empty, did the owner really go back inside? What about Mateo the waiter, did he get a new job? Was Oscar the doorman just out sick or was he gone?

There are people in the background of our lives, but that does not mean they are not people with full lives, families, and dreams that brought them here. Many of which arrived on journeys much more harrowing than I've ever had to even comprehend outside a novel.

Lou's need to stay in this country is treated as something that makes her worthy of love. Even though in *this* case, she's entirely at fault, and choosing a life in this country simply because she wants to, because it's her home.

It's granted to her by a brooding, desirable male lead. But why does her need feel more legitimate than that of millions of immigrants who contribute every day to our economy and, more importantly, to our communities? Why is her desire deemed enough to justify belonging, while others are dismissed as expendable? She's not escaping a war-torn region, she's not being persecuted, she just likes the life she has made for herself. And that, too, is enough.

She can even shop at the specialty grocery store without any fear. It isn't being raided, despite having a big ol' Union Jack flag in the window. When so many people in this country are hiding their accents, hiding their cultures, because we have stopped being *the golden door,* the words etched into the Statue of Liberty hold no truth under this administration.

This book should make you uncomfortable, *but it probably didn't.*

It should make you angry, and not because you just wanted them to admit how they feel. Instead, it probably made you kick your feet as they fell in love.

This book doesn't conclude with the words 'The End' because while Louisa's story works out and is tied up in the happily ever after bow that we yearn for, for millions of people in this country, this is far from over.

Mothers, fathers, grandparents, and children are being torn apart. Families are detained, deported without due process, and terrorized for just existing. All the while, we toast with a few 'margs' or celebrate with a 'Taco Tuesday' in restaurants built on cultures we criminalize.

That is not fiction.

That is happening now.

Right outside our doors.

I won't mince words. ICE is massively funded, heavily armed, and empowered to destroy lives with impunity. It is operating as no less than a domestic terrorist organization.

This is not about safety, it is about control. It is about which humans are acceptable by an administration that does not value human life, and which are treated as threats. An administration, *and a system,* that prioritizes enforcement over humanity, and in the process has stripped this country of decency.

Because the truth is simple: Immigration makes this country great. Not by birthright, but by choice.

Louisa's immigration and preference to stay in the United States was just that, *preference*. She was not seeking asylum, she didn't take a harrowing journey to provide her children more opportunity. She wanted to stay in a country that she was comfortable in. And it works out, she gets a happily ever after. Millions of people living in America do not get that luxury.

This was not the book I was planning on publishing next. The Banks & Ollie story is sitting in draft and may sit there for some time. This book came to life quickly as Minneapolis was under siege. I watched from the comfort of my bed as the citizens were fighting for so much more than just themselves.

There's a reason I don't name the city that Lou and Hudson live in. That's because as we learned from what happened in Minneapolis, a city that's 135th in the national ranking of undocumented immigrants, it can happen anywhere. And will continue to unless we do something to change that.

I am the daughter of an immigrant, but I've never really thought about it that way. Someone who came to the United States, overstayed a visa, and eventually received a green card through marriage. And yet, I never feared for my parent's safety, nor my own. I get to have two passports, no one ever asks for my proof of citizenship. I've never worried about deportation or detention. Not because the law was kinder, but because their skin and accent were never labeled enemies of the state.

That is the difference. And it is one we cannot afford to pretend doesn't exist.

Immigrants are not criminals, the president is.

Immigrants pay taxes, billionaires don't.

Diversity makes us stronger, as individuals and as a country.

Remember that when it's time to vote.

<h1 style="text-align:center">Acknowledgments</h1>

If you're still reading, you made it through the epilogue, made it through the author's note, so it's most fitting I thank *you* for that first. And if this book (or really the author's note) managed to help you see things in a different light, or shift your perspective, thank you for trusting me with that as well.

Isabella, my editor and the resident DEG Scholar, thank you for riddling a Google Doc with corrections and commentary. One improves my writing, the other always improves my day.

Val, Marissa, McKenna, Cassie, Amber, Sarah, thanks for the messages and memos where you validated the doubts I had about this trope-filled rom-com.

Devon, thank you for answering all of my "as a voice actor, would she..." questions.

To every reader who didn't believe me when I said rom-com, thank you for your cautious optimism and interest in reading this book knowing it's a departure from what I've given you and you loved in the past.

To my Framily, there is not a thing I do in this life that you don't show up for and cheer so loud I can't hear the doubt in my own head. And you do it in custom merch. I hope you enjoyed seeing parts of yourselves in this from a matcha order, to night-light, to a couple of brides in a public bathroom. You and the people you love are the reason a book like this is so important.

To my Rom-~~Traum~~-*Com* Mom, I'm glad you laughed through this one, can't promise the same for the next one, but I'm glad I could prove to you that I *can* write a funny book.

To my husband, Sam. Thank you for supporting me in all the

ways you do, and making everything I want to do something you want to do.

The most important acknowledgement and the true dedication of this novel is for all those unlawfully detained, assaulted, separated from loved ones, lost in the bureaucratic systems, harmed in silence, or killed loudly in the street. We owe you more than acknowledgements, we owe you justice. Because even if we had a long way to go, there was a time we stood up and pledged *'with liberty and justice for all.'*

I'm sorry we let that be forgotten.

d.e.g

About the Author

Diana Elliot Graham is proof that you don't need to be an author to be an author.

First and foremost, she is an avid reader who never read a book she regretted. She calls herself the accidental author because she wrote her debut novel, *When We Were*, with some spare time and a "just keep writing" mentality. And a lot of encouragement (*bullying*) from friends and family.

She is known for a non-traditional happily ever after and an emotional twist. A small corner of the internet (like ten emotional book girlies) have dubbed her the "Queen of Rom-Traum." A title she adores, though she more often feels like the court jester.

Since the publication of *When We Were* in 2022, she has released *Six Morning Kisses*, the sequel prequel, and has numerous other projects, ideas, rambling notes in her phone that are in varying degrees of semi-finished that may or may not ever see the light of day.

Now, here she is, writing this bio as imposter syndrome ripples through her entire body, still shocked that anyone cares enough about her writing to stumble on this blurb that has been uncomfortably written in third person. So I'm just going to stop. Follow me on social media for updates on future projects. Or don't.

www.ingramcontent.com/pod-product-compliance
Lightning Source LLC
Chambersburg PA
CBHW021334150726
47989CB00005B/1982